Atlantis Reborn

A Novel
by

Larry Rhodes

WORKBOOK PRESS LLC
187 E Warm Springs Rd,
Suite B285, Las Vegas, NV 89119, USA

Website: https://workbookpress.com/
Hotline: 1-888-818-4856
Email: admin@workbookpress.com

Ordering Information:

Quantity sales. Special discounts are available on quantity purchases by corporations, associations, and others. For details, contact the publisher at the address above.

Library of Congress Control Number:

ISBN-13:   978-1-960752-90-1 (Paperback Version)
                978-1-960752-91-8 (Digital Version)

REV. DATE: 05/09/2023

Chapter 1

Peyton Anderson left New York City in the midst of a week-long sub-zero cold front. She knew winter and summer are reversed south of the equator, but she was still not prepared for the heat of a mid-December day in Manaus Brazil that enveloped her as she stepped off the plane. It was 3 PM and near the hottest part of the day and she had to stop on the tarmac and take a deep breath. When she entered the terminal, she was also surprised that the object of her visit was waiting for her.

In her 20 years of reporting for *Hydrocarbon World* she met everyone from executives to drilling rig rough necks. It had taken months to finally set up a meeting with Allied Exploration and Production's top project manager and after all this time, he was meeting her plane!

It was awkward because Peyton and Stuart Hawkins were old friends. She had met him on his first project just after he graduated with a Masters in Chemical Engineering. Now, 15 years later she was a senior staff writer for the magazine, and he was a top project manager for one of the largest independent oil and gas companies in the world. She had a long list of questions for him. Unfortunately, Stuart would only be available for the day as he had to return to his current project located deep in the Brazilian Amazon rain forest.

Peyton could be found in the gym when she wasn't writing or visiting oil and gas professionals. Slender, with dark eyes and curly dark hair, she looked a lot younger than forty years. Stuart couldn't help but notice her bright flowery blouse and tight dress slacks. She was pleased when she offered him her hand and he hugged her.

"You're looking great, Peyton."

"Thanks, you're looking fit too."

"Lots of early morning jogs. Let's have a drink."

He led her to the nearest bar in the terminal and she was relieved that the terminal was cool and the drink he offered was cold. She started a digital voice recorder and began her prepared questions when Stuart interrupted her. "I'm sorry, Peyton, some things have changed, and we had to move up the trip back to the project, so I don't have much time."

Peyton was obviously disappointed, but Stuart surprised her. "Why don't you go with me to the drill site? We have several female engineers and environmental safety staff there and I'm sure they have room in their quarters for one more. That would give us a lot more time for your questions, and you could see the latest technology we're testing."

When the shock wore off, she really wanted to go, as this was a once in a lifetime opportunity for an industry reporter, but she knew it was a bad idea. Stuart guessed she was struggling to say yes and encouraged her. "We have really frequent flights back and forth. You'd only have to be there a few days."

Her carry-on luggage was sitting next to her and she couldn't find an excuse to say no - that Stuart would believe. "Okay, when do you need to leave?"

He grinned. "In about three hours. You can stay here in the terminal or go back to Allied's field office with me and wait, but we'll be leaving from a private terminal here."

She breathed a little easier. That would give her time to make some important phone calls.

"I'll wait here if that's okay."

"It's fine. I'll call you when we are on our way to the airport."

She stood up and he hugged her again and hurried off to make last minute preparations.

When he was out of sight, she pulled out her cell phone out and desperately tried to reach her local contact.

Soon after Stuart returned to Allied's field office in Manaus he received an email from Steve Freeman, the President of Allied, confirming his promotion from Senior Project Manager to Manager of Projects. This seemingly subtle change in titles would now place him in charge of all of Allied's construction projects around the world. Stuart earned his well-deserved promotion in many harsh and inhospitable locations around the world. His current assignment in Brazil was no exception.

His current project, a drilling site located deep in the heart of the Amazon rainforest, was 50 miles north of the city of Canutama and accessible only by helicopter. In the last few years, Brazil had adopted a tough environmental stand on oil and gas exploration and especially the construction of drilling and production wells and their associated storage and operation facilities. All equipment had to be ferried in by helicopter and removed when a well was depleted and removed from operation. On-shore exploration and development costs were beginning to compete with the enormous cost of deep-water offshore platforms.

It had taken Stuart, a native New Englander, several months to adjust to the seemingly perpetual heat and humidity of

Manaus, located only three degrees north of the equator. Even though the population neared two million, Manaus continued to maintain its third world atmosphere... and charm. Stuart made many friends among the foreign nationals working for various oil and gas companies and soon felt at home in a small community of international exploration professionals on the outskirts of the city. His previous project in Canada's Northern Territory, only two years in the past, now seemed a distant memory.

Allied's tiny field office, only15 kilometers from the Eduardo Gomes airport in Manaus, sweltered in the late December heat wave. Somehow, the small air conditioner always seemed to fail during a heat wave. The tiny window fan in his office provided little relief as he pulled a tissue from a tissue box on his desk and wiped his forehead. Even his assistant Eva, a Manaus native, seemed to be suffering from the heat as she handed him a paper cup of water.

At six feet four inches with blond hair, blue eyes, and an athlete's build, the forty-year-old Stuart exuded a sense of power and authority. He certainly had the respect of the small staff of Brazilians in the field office, as well as the drilling site. Had he given less than his all-encompassing effort to the project, he might even have noticed his strikingly beautiful assistant who greeted him daily with several international newspapers, a pile of inter-company documents, contracts from contractors and vendors and a strong cup of Brazilian coffee. Eva's father had been an English geologist for an international oil company and had met and married her mother while on assignment in Manaus. The combination had produced three daughters, each one easily capable of winning an international beauty pageant. Eva's dark hair and eyes contrasted sharply with the pale complexion she had inherited from her father. Her beautiful face, friendly easygoing manner and slender figure had attracted many native men who had tried to win her affection only to lose out to an image she held subconsciously in the back of her mind of someone like her tall American boss.

Paolo Gonzales, Stuart's lead helicopter pilot and cultural liaison to the native labor force and local government, finished reading the email and thumped him on the back. "Hell of a deal! I'll guess you'll be leaving soon, eh, Stuart?" Paolo had worked for half a dozen project managers for Allied over the years and would truly miss Stuart. Unlike some of his predecessors, Stuart led by example. It was, undoubtedly, the positive feedback on Stuart by senior management, his peers and subordinates that had won him the latest promotion. Stuart had even inspired the stocky Paolo to lose some weight by joining him in early morning jogs around his community.

"You know I can't go until they find a replacement."

Paolo glanced at his watch. "We'd better be going, boss, or we'll be flying at night."

Stuart nodded and began to pack a briefcase with project information as Paolo radioed his flight crew at the airport to finalize preparations for the transport helicopter's 500-kilometer (300 mile) trip back to the Canutama site.

At Allied's private terminal, Stuart helped Peyton on-board and handed her carry-on bag to her. Peyton was sitting in a "jump seat" behind the pilot's chair and didn't have a lot of room, but she wasn't thinking about her flight accommodations when she buckled her seat belt.

The massive dual-rotor transport helicopter lumbered into the air, packed to the maximum allowable weight limit with drilling rig parts, gourmet food and other amenities provided by Allied to all of its remote locations to make their remote and often inhospitable locations more bearable. Christmas was only a few weeks away and a few small, wrapped presents from Eva to her girlfriends at the drilling site had even found their way under Stuart's seat in the cockpit. As the huge helicopter lifted slowly into the air, Stuart commented to Paolo that they seemed to be carrying more cargo than normal. Stuart made the trip so often his mind soon drifted off to the possible consequences of his promotion and the fact he could be relocated to Allied's international headquarters in Dallas, Texas. He had visited the office several times but never seriously considered he may one day be working there.

Peyton and Stuart took the opportunity to catch up on each other's career and she even snuck in a few questions from her long list.

As the setting sun dipped below the horizon, Paolo's eyes strained to pick out familiar landmarks in the seemingly endless rainforest below. Less experienced pilots would have relied solely on their onboard instrumentation and GPS to maintain their flight plan, but there had been some GPS equipment issues in the past and Paolo knew even a small navigational error could leave them searching for the project site in the dark. His own flight skills were honed by six years of flying all sorts of aircraft in the Brazilian military and almost a dozen years' service flying small survey planes and helicopters for Allied.

Despite all of his training, he was totally unprepared for a surface-to-air missile attack. He saw a flash in the jungle ahead and the telltale red glow of the rocket's tail as it raced in his direction. Instinct and years of military training forced his hands and feet to jerk the helicopter's controls in a desperate attempt at evasion. He didn't even hear the curse that burst from his lips and reverberated in the cabin.

Stuart's attention snapped back to the cockpit when he heard Paolo shout a curse and shove the craft's joystick hard to the right. The fully loaded helicopter strained under its own weight as it veered sharply to the right. Stuart almost jumped out of his chair as a small missile roared past the cockpit, barely missing the front rotor.

"What the hell?"

Peyton cursed under her breath as she knew she should have done more than left a harsh voicemail with her contact. Repeated calls to his cell phone had gone unanswered. Now, she was in the same danger as Stuart and Paolo.

Paolo was too busy fighting to regain control to answer Stuart. Despite his efforts, the helicopter continued to veer and roll to the right. The drilling parts cargo had been lashed down but not tightly enough for a panic maneuver, and it shifted sharply to the right. Peyton's overnight bag jumped from her feet and flew around the cabin hitting Paolo and Stuart, but somehow missing her. Paolo lost control and the helicopter began to spiral down to the jungle below. In a few seconds the blades began chopping away at the taller trees and brush and abruptly stopped, spinning the body of the helicopter around. Something hit Stuart in the head and he blacked out. Peyton couldn't avoid a metal emergency kit box that came loose and hit her on the head.

Consciousness returned slowly and it took Peyton a

few moments to remember what had happened. She felt something warm and wet on her forehead and she knew she was bleeding. She pulled her shirt out from her pants and wiped her eyes with her shirttails. It was almost dark, but she could see Paolo slumped over the controls of the downed helicopter, and Stuart leaning against his door, also unconscious. She unbuckled her seat belt and shook Stuart, but he didn't respond. She sighed with relief when she leaned near him and heard him breathing. She pulled on him until he was back in his seat. She put a finger on Paolo's neck and was relieved when she felt a pulse. She pulled him back to his seat and sat wondering what to do.

Power was out in the helicopter and darkness was quickly settling in as Peyton leaned forward and tried the radio but it, like the rest of the helicopter, was powerless. Stuart's door was stuck but after some effort, she finally managed to get it open. The enormous helicopter had landed on a large clump of trees and was resting precariously on the top of several. The rhythmical cacophony of birds and insects was soon mixed with the cries of several small animals and Peyton was not eager to venture out into the evening darkness with a horrendous headache and partially blurred vision. She located the emergency survival kit on the back wall of the cockpit and found a flashlight, a flare gun, a pistol, and a rifle. She stuffed the pistol into her waistband, found the emergency medical kit on the floor in front of Stuart and wrapped a bandage around her forehead.

She knew Allied would send search crews out in the morning. Memory of the missile attack kept her awake and watchful. Where in the hell was he? Would he get there before the Allied search crew? Should she stay in the helicopter or find a better place to hide from the Allied team? What if Stuart woke up? These and a dozen other questions kept rolling around in her brain, until she finally settled into a more comfortable position and hoped he would get there soon. Her hand rested on the pistol's handle, hoping she wouldn't need it.

A quiet panic spread among the office workers and drilling site crew when the helicopter failed to arrive as scheduled and repeated attempts to contact them by radio failed. Bob Tenderlake, the project engineer at the drilling site, immediately began to arrange search teams employing all of Allied's available aircraft and even a few loaned by friends working for other exploration companies. Eva worked tirelessly to make financial and logistical arrangements for additional aircraft and was on the first search helicopter to leave before dawn.

Peyton had just dozed off into an uneasy sleep when she was awakened by a flashlight shining in her eyes. She tried to shield her eyes against the glare when a gruff voice snarled at her.

"What in the hell are you doing here?"

"You idiot! When you didn't answer your phone, I left you a voicemail that Stuart invited me to the drilling site, and I asked you to wait until his next visit."

"My cell doesn't work here, and I didn't get your damn voicemail, obviously. The nearest cell tower is a hundred and fifty kilometers from here!"

"Then, why aren't you using the satellite phone I sent you?"

He seemed embarrassed. "Some locals stole everything from my camp while I was fishing."

Peyton shook her head in disbelief. "Are you out of your mind, Maller? A rocket?   How is that supposed to look like a helicopter accident?"

"I wasn't aiming to blow it up, only bring it down, and then have some fun with Stuart before I made the crash look like an accident."

"Why didn't you put the gel I sent you in the fuel system? That would make the engines stall and then you could have your fun – and make it look like an accident."

"What gel?"

"It was in the same package as the satellite phone and the information on Stuart and Allied's operations here."

"It wasn't in the package. It must have been taken out at customs. It doesn't matter, anyway. Go to my boat and wait for me. It shouldn't take too long to take care of this."

"How am I supposed to find your damn boat in the dark?"

"It's not too far from here. The pilot always files the same flight plan, and this is the closest place in the flight path that I can get by boat." He handed her his cell phone. "I set the homing function on the GPS so I could find it. Just get going before they wake up."

"I thought there were problems with GPS equipment here. And how will you find the boat when you're done, if I have your GPS?"

"I know this area pretty well. I can find it in the daylight. Now give me that rifle behind you and get going."

She handed the rifle to Maller and tossed her carry-on bag

out the door. He watched her climb out Stuart's door and heard her climbing down the tree.

As Peyton followed the GPS signal through the forest, she wished she had never gotten involved in this nightmare. She had a severe gambling problem and made an even bigger mistake by borrowing money from a loan shark to pay off the gambling debt. The loan shark became tired of waiting for the money and gave her a deadline. She was desperate for a solution when she received an unexpected call and the person on the other end offered her more money than she could earn in the rest of her career. It seemed the only way out even it if meant her old friend would become the target of an apparent revenge plot. She didn't want him hurt but she was more afraid of becoming a story on the nightly news. She hurried her pace when the growling and screeching noises of animals looking for their breakfast kept getting louder. She checked to make sure she still had the pistol, and it was gone! It must have come out when she climbed down the tree. She almost panicked. She couldn't go back and look for it. She just hoped Maller's boat wasn't too far, and his GPS wasn't sending her to the wrong place. She stopped when she heard a strange noise behind her. She couldn't see anything, but dropped her carry-on and started running through the forest as fast as she could.

Maller waited a few minutes, flashed his light on Stuart's eyes and shook him.

"Wake up, Hawkins!"

Stuart woke with a throbbing headache and rubbed his forehead trying to regain his senses. The flashlight left his eyes and began roaming the cabin. Stuart's eyes slowly adjusted and saw a huge burly man dressed in camouflage clothing, standing near him holding an automatic rifle. His cap was pulled down tightly obscuring his face. The rifle from the helicopter's emergency survival kit was slung over his shoulder.

Who was this intruder and why was he holding an automatic rifle on Stuart and the still unconscious Paolo? He glanced back and saw Peyton's empty seat. What happened to her? This guy was obviously not part of a rescue party. From his tone, Stuart guessed he had been the source of the missile attack. "Who are you? What do you want?"

"My name's not important. All you need to know is someone wants you dead enough to hire me to kill you."

"What?" Despite the unreal circumstances, Stuart couldn't believe someone would want to kill him. Stuart made friends easily and rarely encountered people he could not at least tolerate. "Who are you?"

"I was a professional hunter, back when you could take a few stupid rich people on a big game safari. When that dried up, I decided to venture into other areas. You can call me Sam or any name you like. I've hunted big game animals all over the world, but I've never hunted a human before, so I took the offer... only I'm changing the plans a little. Since my little missile missed the mark and you guys survived, I'm going to let you try and get away. Who knows? You might even make it." He chuckled softly. "But I'm pretty good at what I do, so your odds aren't very good. Why... hell... I'll even give you an hour head start."

Stuart struggled to his feet, his head pounding from the crash. He was coming to his senses now. "Where is Peyton

Anderson?”

"Who?" He flashed his light on the nametag on Paolo's uniform. "There's no one here but you…and Paolo."

"She's a magazine reporter, traveling with us."

"You must have been dreaming, Hawkins."

Stuart's head was pounding when he looked down at Paolo, who was still unconscious.

"What about Paolo?"

Sam flashed his light on Paolo and then at Stuart's feet. "I don't care about him. The company will probably have several search parties here in a few hours. They can take care of him." He paused to look out at the pre-dawn sky that was beginning to hint at the coming daylight. "You better get going. You'll be an easy target in the daylight."

Sam backed out Paolo's door and Stuart heard him climbing down one of the trees to the ground. He wracked his brain trying to remember if the rifle was the only weapon on board, but he couldn't remember anything else. The emergency supply pack was near his feet. He tossed it out the door. It sailed to the ground, and he heard the big man laugh loudly. "You missed me."

Stuart surveyed the crash site for the first time. The weight of the helicopter had crushed the four trees it had landed on, and they were less than a dozen feet from the ground. He saw Sam waiting below him, his flashlight playing on the emergency pack that had popped open when it landed on the ground.

"Not much in there to help you," he taunted Stuart.

The first few rays of morning light were beginning to pierce the jungle canopy as Stuart slowly climbed down through the broken branches and landed roughly on the ground. He walked over and stuffed as many of the emergency supplies into the pack as he could and closed it. When he stood up, Sam tossed him a small pistol while holding the automatic rifle on him.

"There's one bullet in there. You might need it if you encounter something out there worse than me. Just remember the safety's on."

Stuart stuffed the pistol into his waistband. "Why are you doing this?"

"You mean giving you a chance?"

"No. I mean why are you trying to kill me?"

"I told you... I've never hunted a human... it may be tougher than some of the big animals I've hunted."

Stuart picked up the emergency pack. "What if I said I would give you double or triple whatever they offered you to help us instead?"

"Money's not the issue. I don't need the money. It's the challenge."

Stuart took a deep breath and let it out. "What if I offered you ten times what they offered you... to help me find them?"

It was light now, and Sam turned his flashlight off and stuffed it into a pocket on the side of his pants. He stood staring at Stuart a moment before he answered.

"No. There wouldn't be any sport in that. But that's enough

talking." Sam looked at the sky. "It's getting light. You better get going if you want to have a chance." He looked at his watch. "You could get pretty far in an hour if you hustle."

Maybe Stuart had been dreaming, but he had to ask once more. "What about the reporter, Peyton Anderson?"

Sam shook his head. "Cut the crap, Hawkins, and get going. You have 59 minutes now."

Stuart glanced up at the helicopter and then pushed off into the brush walking quickly but carefully to avoid tripping over vines and stepping into pools of water. He glanced at his watch... almost 6:00 AM; he would have to hurry.

Stuart had hunted all his life. As a teenager he practically lived in the forest during deer season, but he never anticipated he would someday be on the other end of the hunt. At first he walked, jogged and ran whenever possible, certain he could outdistance his hunter until he realized he might never be found by the search parties Allied was certainly organizing when they didn't return to the drilling site. He paused to consider his options. Perhaps he should try to circle back to the helicopter? The rescue teams would find the helicopter and if he could signal them, they could help defend him against Sam. But a smart hunter like Sam would soon figure out his plan and cut him off before he could return. No, he would have to find a way to take Sam out.

He opened the emergency pack and examined its contents. It wasn't exactly what he would have assembled for an emergency but there were a few useful items. He stuffed a Swiss army knife in his pocket. A tool like that could be useful. It seemed strange, but there was even a sewing kit in the pack. He smiled when he opened the kit and found an array of needles and threads. He breathed a sigh of relief when he found a small ball of twine in the pack.

He cleaned a tree branch and quickly fashioned a crude bow and arrow with the branch and the twine, and an arrow from another stick and a needle and downed a bird unfortunate enough to be sitting in a tree near him. He plucked a few feathers from the bird, examining them as he picked up the pace, conditioned by his early morning jogs. He had just finished his first feathered arrow when his flight through the forest abruptly ended at a small tributary of the Amazon. Although it was not very wide, the water was pitch black and flowing very rapidly. Stuart knew certain tributaries contained the fierce and deadly piranha. He shuddered at the thought of swimming this unknown barrier. There wouldn't be time to build a craft that would keep his body out of the water. Maybe he could swing across on a vine? He laughed at the thought of it until he saw several clumps of reeds lining the riverbank. Maybe he wouldn't need to cross the inky water.

Sam moved through the rainforest with the ease of a large cat, silently with a deadly intent. He had never hunted a human before but the information on Stuart, provided by his temporary employer, hinted he would be hunting a worthy opponent. Sam left the small caliber rifle from the helicopter and his own automatic rifle under some brush near the downed helicopter. It would be more of a challenge if he relied on his favorite 45mm revolver to finish the job.

At the start of his hunt for Stuart, Sam had laughed at the trail of footprints and broken branches Stuart had left in his wake. It was almost like following a bulldozer through the forest. Perhaps he had overestimated his foe. His mind drifted to a vacation he planned with the money he would earn from this little adventure and almost lost his concentration. His boot was resting against a tiny cord stretched across a natural path in the forest. He bent down examining it. *Clever.* Maybe Stuart was a worthy opponent. Sam pulled a large knife from a sheath in his belt and cut a small branch of a nearby tree. He tossed it into the trail ahead and a large circular band of vines grabbed the stick and flung it into the air. He stopped smiling... that could have been his leg. He would have to be even more vigilant than he thought.

Barely a thousand yards down the trail he stopped again when a hunter's instinct warned him against going forward. He cut another sapling and cleaned it of bark and leaves. He pushed it ahead of him on the floor of the forest scattering hordes of small insects and crawling bugs of every description. Unfortunately, the stick didn't prevent him from falling into a ten-foot deep man-trap. He quickly grabbed some vines and somehow avoided falling on the sharp stakes planted at the bottom of the pit, only injuring his ankle. He managed to climb out on the small vines that were now dangling into the black pit. He took out a small first aid kit and managed to get a rough bandage around his ankle.

Sam stood staring at the pit. Stuart didn't have time to dig this. A chill ran down his back as a name floated into his consciousness. Paumaris! He pressed forward with the realization some very unfriendly natives could find him first. The trail suddenly ended at a small river tributary barely thirty feet across. Had Stuart crossed the swiftly flowing water or was he skirting it by following its banks?

From his perch high in the trees above the river, Stuart watched Sam looking for footprints or other indications of his whereabouts.

Sam was bent over slightly and searching intently for tail-tell signs of Stuart's path when he suddenly felt a sting in his neck. He swatted at the pesky insect and felt something large in his hand. He stood staring at the dart until his eyes started to blur and he felt dizzy. The sky was starting to spin when his face hit the ground and he lost consciousness.

Stuart watched with a growing apprehension as six jungle natives quietly gathered around the fallen hunter. They were clothed only in a montage of paints that made them extremely difficult to see in the forest. They could easily find him as well and he would be as powerless against them as Sam was at the moment. What should he do? He said a prayer and put the piece of reed to his mouth and blew as hard as he could. His own makeshift dart hit one of the natives on the head. The native jumped and grabbed his head, screaming in pain and startling the others. A few seconds later a second dart found the head of another native who also grabbed his head and screamed. Panic set in as the natives abandoned their intentions with Sam and fled.

Stuart waited until he was sure they were gone and slowly began climbing down. He chuckled to himself as he jumped the last few feet from the bottom of the large tree to the ground. He walked over to Sam and removed all the weapons he could find. What should he do with him? Sam moaned, rolled over and opened his eyes to find Stuart standing over him with his 45 pointed at him.

"Well, now. A few things have changed. It's time for twenty questions."

Sam sat up with a horrendous headache and rubbed his neck. "What the hell was in that dart?"

"That wasn't mine. You were about to become dinner for a little group of locals, but I managed to scare them off with a few darts of my own."

Stuart kept the gun aimed at him. Even in this state, he could be dangerous. "Since I just saved your butt, I think you owe me some answers. Who wants me dead?"

Sam struggled to his feet and stood unevenly trying to regain his balance. "I won't tell you."

"You will if you want to get out of here alive."

Sam laughed. "Unlike me, you still have a few principles. You won't shoot an unarmed person."

"Maybe not, but I wouldn't mind leaving an unarmed man out here without any clothes for that little group of locals to find again."

Sam knew Stuart would do precisely that. The pain in his neck was getting worse. There might have been a slow acting poison in the dart, and he needed to get back to his boat where he had several types of antidotes. He stared at Stuart. He had proven his match and even saved his life. What did he care about the dark-haired stranger that had given him information and large cash advance to kill Stuart? This wasn't his feud, and he could die if he didn't get his antidote medicine soon.

"All right. I'll tell you everything if you'll help me get back to my boat. I think there may have been a mixture of poisons in the dart, and I have some medicine that could act as an antidote." Even as he finished speaking, he felt his knees weaken and he felt another chill.

Stuart was suspicious. "How do I know you'll tell me the truth if I help you?"

"You just saved my life... and what the hell, whatever that guy's beef is with you doesn't really concern me."

Stuart thought Sam looked sick. He was sweating profusely and kept wiping his face with his shirt sleeve. He could have been poisoned. "All right. If you'll tell me what I want to know, I'll help you."

Sam indicated the way and started off with Stuart following behind, gun still ready.

Sam was struggling to walk as they neared the crash site. Stuart put one of Sam's arms around his neck to help him along. He touched Sam's forehead and felt his fever. He wondered if Paolo was all right as the helicopter came into view, still perched atop the trees. And where in the hell was Peyton? He hadn't seen any sign of her since he left the helicopter. Above the familiar sounds of the forest, he thought he heard a low rumbling noise. The sound grew progressively louder until an Allied helicopter was hovering above the wreck. There was no room to land, and several rescuers were lowered on stretchers to the forest floor and ran toward them. Sam's knees collapsed and he fell against Stuart. Stuart lowered him to the ground as Eva threw her arms around him in joy. The others were as equally happy at finding him alive. Paolo was immediately put on a stretcher and lifted into the waiting helicopter.

Stuart quickly explained everything, and the rescue team put Sam on a stretcher and raised him to another helicopter now hovering overhead. The team immediately started looking for Peyton. Stuart laughed, as Eva wouldn't let go of him as they were lifted on another stretcher to the same rescue helicopter where Sam was being examined.

Two paramedics injected Sam with several antidotes against the known poisons commonly used by the natives. Sam slowly opened his eyes and saw Stuart sitting near him.

"Why did you help me?"

"Because you needed it."

Sam looked away, ashamed. He knew everyone on the helicopter knew what happened by now. His fever was subsiding but the pain in his neck was almost unbearable. "I owe you some information."

"Wait until we get back to Manaus."

"There's still a good chance I won't make it. I feel like shit."

One of the paramedics leaned over him. "You need to rest. We've given you every antidote known against the poisons used by the natives here."

Sam looked at Stuart. "I'm afraid they don't know all of them." He realized he couldn't feel his legs now and the low-level pain in his chest was getting worse. He motioned to Stuart and grabbed his shirt to pull him closer, but he could only murmur a few words before he passed out. "His name was... Carballo." He whispered the last few words. "Constantine Carballo."

The roar of the helicopter was deafening, and Stuart looked at Eva who was kneeling next to him. "Eva, what did he say?"

She shrugged her shoulders. "I don't know. I couldn't hear him."

Sam's eyes were closed, and Stuart sat back and watched the rainforest pass by below. He glanced over at Eva who was sitting next to him and staring out the door. The wind was whipping her hair about and Stuart found himself watching her and remembering her joy at finding him. He also remembered her exuberant hugs and kisses and, in one of those rare moments of revelation, saw her as a woman for the first time. She looked at him and smiled. He moved closer to her, and she looked at him expectantly. He leaned over and kissed her and she wrapped her arms around him.

Sam Maller passed away quietly as they embraced.

Three days later, all the rescue team had found was Peyton's carry-on bag and they were forced to abandon their search for her when a huge rainstorm doused the crash site with almost a foot of rain. Stuart hated to make the call to her magazine's office but, by now, the likelihood she had survived was very low.

Chapter 2

Jack Garrett tightened his overcoat against the cold and windy North Sea air and surveyed the sky to confirm the projected weather forecast. The sky was cloudy and overcast but there were no ominous storm clouds on the horizon. That confirmed the last bit of information he needed, and he entered the control room of the off-shore drilling platform and gave the go-ahead to the drilling crew. The crew on the 'Maximus' oil platform held their collective breaths as the drilling rig descended to the ocean floor. The entire platform seemed to tremble as the drill bit encountered a hard formation below the soft seabed. The drilling crew let out a joyous cheer and began to congratulate each other. After ten long years of preparation, Allied Exploration and Development's first drilling platform in the North Sea was finally in operation. Jack Garrett typed a quick email, imported a few pictures of the drill crew from his cell phone and sent the good news to Stuart Hawkins in Manaus, Brazil.

As the Project Engineer and Project Manager, the decision to begin was ultimately Jack's. He noted with a sigh of relief that drilling had officially begun on December 31st at 1:00PM in the afternoon, only hours before his self-imposed deadline of commencing operation before the end of the year. Jack had been somewhat surprised but pleased at the selection of Stuart as Manager of Projects. Stuart and Jack had worked on several projects together and Stuart was now Jack's boss.

Even as he watched the email uploading the pictures in his outbox, his chief communications officer, Samantha Adams, tapped him on the shoulder and informed him three visitors would be arriving within the hour and one of them was Steve

Freeman, the president of Allied. Jack fought off a sudden anxiety attack. *What the hell is going on?* Freeman couldn't be coming here because of the startup. He couldn't have known the exact time! Why, Jack didn't even know for sure until a few moments before he gave the go-ahead for drilling.

Maybe he had screwed up somewhere? This was a trial project for Allied in which he had assumed both jobs. This gave him the ability to negotiate contracts as well as execute them. He searched his brain but couldn't think of anything he had purchased that would have caught Freeman's attention. Freeman was definitely not a detail person. He wouldn't know if there were any technical problems unless Jack told him. He looked at his watch again. Maybe he should check the conference room to make sure it was halfway presentable.

As he started to leave the communications center, he said "Sam, will you get the key project guys together in the conference room for Freeman's visit? I have a few things to do before he gets here."

Samantha looked at him sheepishly. "I, uh, I forgot to tell you. Freemen indicated he wanted to see you alone."

"Alone?" Jack swallowed hard.

Samantha nodded.

"Are you sure?"

As Samantha nodded again, she saw Jack rub his forehead. Jack often did that when he was upset. Samantha looked at her watch. "They'll be here any minute."

Even as she spoke, they heard the approach of the large personnel transport helicopter. Samantha felt sorry for Jack.

She could imagine how she would feel if Freeman were coming to visit her with no warning. "I'll take them to the conference room, if you want to meet them there."

As Jack paced impatiently in the conference room, he felt a little guilty about its lavish executive chairs, dark granite table and the thick luxurious carpeting. It was the only extravagance he had allowed on the project. The team spent countless hours in discussions here and Jack wanted to make those hours a little more bearable.

His heart beat a little faster when Steve Freeman entered alone, smiling as he saw Jack. Freeman was a no-nonsense kind of guy, tough yet fair. They were long-time acquaintances.

Jack shook Freeman's hand. "Nice to see you again, Steve. Would you like some coffee?" He motioned to a coffeepot nearby.

Freeman shook his head. "How are you, Jack? I haven't had a chance to talk to you in a while."

"I'm fine, Steve. This is quite an unexpected surprise. I didn't think you'd be following our progress this closely."

"Well, this _is_ our showcase project. But actually, this meeting isn't about the progress of your project." He paused for a moment, as though thinking how to proceed.

Jack wondered what he was up to. "What's it about then, Steve?"

Obviously under some pressure, Freeman glanced at his watch and then at Jack. "Well, to begin with, I would like to introduce you to an old friend of mine." He turned, opened the door, and nodded. He backed up as Richard Spencer and another man walked in.

Spencer, in his late fifties, was a little taller than Jack. He was slender with dark hair and eyes and, with a classic touch of gray in the temples of his hair and a dark expensive suit, was very distinguished looking. Jack instantly recognized him from newspaper and magazine articles. He was a little overwhelmed at meeting one of the most powerful industrialists in the world--and a world-class philanthropist to boot--with no advance warning. Why had he come to such a remote location, on New Year's Eve?

"It's a pleasure to finally meet you, Jack." Spencer shook Jack's hand. "This is Michael Baker, security consultant for Spencer Industries."

As Jack shook Baker's hand, he only fleetingly noticed Michael Baker's dark hair and eyes and obviously muscular build an expensive suit couldn't hide. Jack tried to make these seemingly unrelated pieces of information fit together. As he turned back to Spencer, he realized he was sweating profusely.

"It's an honor to meet you, Mr. Spencer. Would you like to have a seat?"

Freeman answered for Spencer. "Actually, we'd like a quick tour of the platform before we talk about some other business."

Jack frowned. "Of course. Please, come this way."

He led them out of the conference room and through the major sections of the platform, including the Control Center, the drilling platform, the Communication Center, even the crew's quarters. As he led them around, Spencer and Baker asked numerous questions about the platform and construction progress. They were impressed with Jack's in-depth knowledge. As Project Manager and Project Engineer, Jack was as comfortable describing the return on investment of the capital costs of the project as he was with the metallurgy and type of drilling bits they would be using to drill the production wells. Jack easily switched from the economic impact of the platform on Allied's bottom line the following year to improvements in drilling equipment he would like to implement once production began.

The tour finished, Jack poured Spencer and himself a cup of coffee and then sat down next to Spencer. Baker and Freeman declined anything to drink and sat on the opposite side of the table.

"We really appreciate the tour, Jack, but now we'd like to get to the business at hand." Spencer's face gave no indication of why they had arrived without advanced notice.

"What exactly is the business at hand, Mr. Spencer? I'm sure you didn't come here to tour an off-shore oil platform under construction."

Spencer glanced at Freeman before answering. "You're exactly right. The reason I'm here is a few months ago I asked the heads of several exploration companies for the name of the best marine engineer they knew. Your name kept coming up."

Jack's heart skipped a beat, but he managed a weak smile. "That's quite a compliment, Mr. Spencer."

"Yes, well, I decided to ask my old friend Steve here for a favor. Being Allied's majority stockholder allows me a few privileges, you know."

Freeman studied his hands, avoiding Jack's questioning look.

"Jack, I'd like you to oversee a project of mine for the next few years."

Jack was stunned. He looked at Freeman but there was no expression on his face. "What! But I've got at least six more months here! And I have two more projects scheduled that won't be over for at least three more years!"

"Steve and I discussed that. I told him I would supply replacement engineers for those projects at no cost to him and if your leaving this project caused any delay, I would reimburse the company for the lost production. And I will make sure Allied won't suffer financially because of this."

Freeman's face was still expressionless. Jack was numb, but curious. "What sort of project is it, Mr. Spencer?"

Spencer looked at Freeman and then at Jack. "I'm sorry, but I'm afraid you'll have to agree without knowing what the project is about - for security reasons."

Freeman looked at Spencer. "Richard, could I speak to Jack alone for a few minutes?"

"Certainly. Michael and I would like to visit the Communications Center to make some phone calls, wouldn't we, Michael?"

Michael Baker hadn't been paying much attention up to this point. He'd been sizing up Jack's ability to pull off an enormous project. He was also thinking he could be working for Jack soon. "Yes, Mr. Spencer. Of course."

Spencer and Baker stood up and walked out of the Conference Room, closing the door behind them.

"I can't tell you what this is all about, Jack, just that it's big. You have to believe me when I say this is the opportunity of a lifetime for you."

Jack laughed. "Every time I've ever heard that, I've usually ended up on the short end of the stick."

Freeman leaned forward, as if to emphasize the degree of urgency of what he was about to say. "Richard Spencer is one of the richest and most influential men alive today and he's asking you to do a favor for him. I guarantee, when this is over, you can write your own ticket." He looked away for a moment and then looked at Jack. "I hate to lose you, Jack, even for a few years, but I can't say no to him." He gave Jack a fragile smile. "I have a career, too, you know."

Jack appreciated the seriousness of the situation, but he was concerned for his own future. "This isn't quite fair, you know, asking me to commit to a project without even knowing what it's about."

Freeman shifted in his chair. "I know. This is one time you will have to trust me. Believe me, I've used every argument I could think of to keep you, but he guarantees Allied won't lose any money by your leaving."

The door opened and Freeman straightened in his chair as Spencer and Baker entered.

"We got lost trying to find the Communications Center. Where is everyone?"

"Everyone but the drilling crew is in the mess hall. We're having a little celebration now drilling has finally started."

Baker sat down as Spencer poured himself a cup of coffee.

He carried it to the table and sat down next to Jack and sipped his coffee. Jack looked at Freeman, who stared back with a blank expression.

Spencer set his coffee cup down. "So, Jack, what'll it be?"

Jack mentally calculated the potential consequences of leaving his current project and accepting responsibility for a new project he didn't know anything about. As the others waited for his reply, Jack decided, under the present circumstances, he really had no choice. "It sounds like an offer I can't refuse. All right, I'll help in whatever capacity you need me."

Spencer seemed pleased and Freeman was visibly relieved. Even Baker smiled.

"Great! I need you to attend a kickoff meeting in London in two days."

Jack's eyes widened. "Two days! But we're at a critical stage in the operation of this platform and I--"

"Think of someone who can finish your project, Jack, and I'll get him. I need you in London in two days."

Jack was feeling overwhelmed. "Why so soon, Mr. Spencer? When will this project start?"

"It's already started. We need you now."

Freeman saw the worried look on Jack's face. "Don't worry about the platform. Richard's project is much more important. Stuart Hawkins can take over for you until he finds a replacement. We'll try to get whomever you recommend."

"When will I find out about the project, Mr. Spencer?"

"In London. The meeting coordinator will email you the time and place of the meeting later today. Welcome aboard, Jack."

They all stood. Spencer shook Jack's hand and waved for Baker and Freeman to leave with him. Jack shook Freeman's hand.

"Thanks, Jack. I owe you one. Please contact Hawkins and tell him I need to talk to him later today. Good luck on your new project. See you." He paused at the door and looked back at Jack. "Nice conference room." He rushed to catch up with Spencer.

Baker walked over to Jack and shook his hand. "Nice to meet you, Mister Garrett. I look forward to working with you."

Jack wondered what he meant.

After they left, Jack sat down weakly. "Damn!" he muttered as Samantha Adams suddenly slammed the door open. "Jack, transport helicopter three just went down!"

Jack jumped to his feet. "What happened?" The safety of project personnel was always Jack's first concern. He was beginning to feel a little sick.

"We don't know yet, we lost contact with them a few minutes after they left the heliport at Aberdeen."

Jack and Samantha raced toward the communications center as they continued their conversation. "How many are on board?"

"Six, including the pilot."

"Damn! Get every available ship and aircraft you can to help. I'll call the authorities and see if they have anything available as well."

Samantha suddenly grabbed Jack's arm and they stopped outside the communications center.

"What is it?"

"Freeman and his visitors started to come out here on three, but they didn't want to wait for it to be serviced, so they came on two instead."

It only took a few seconds for Samantha's comment to sink in. Freeman, Spencer and Baker could have been on that fateful trip. They stared at each other in disbelief for a brief moment, and then hurried to do their best to save the six workers who lives depended on them.

Five time zones away, Bala Subramanium finished stuffing his briefcase and turned off the lights in his high-rise office. He paused to gaze out the window at the twinkling lights of Electronics City and reflected on one of the best days of his life. In less than six years he had risen from design department manager to president of Nanosecond Devices, a high technology company headquartered in India's 'Silicon Valley' and specializing in the design and manufacture of specialty computer chips.

Nanosecond had recently been named as the fastest growing company in the vast worldwide group of over two hundred companies that comprised Spencer Industries. As a further recognition of his contribution, he had just received an email confirming his promotion to Vice President, Electronics Division - Far East Region.

He quickly dialed the cell phone of his driver and wondered briefly wondered why there was no answer, but his mind was still on the promotion. He also wondered if he would have to relocate to the corporate office in London.

Security lights in the parking lot began to push the evening darkness away as he waved goodbye to the security station personnel and walked to his luxury limousine. On any other day, he would have been more observant and noticed the old van that had surely parked by mistake in the parking space next to his. As he approached his limousine, he wondered why his driver wasn't there to meet him. He felt something brush his pants leg just as he noticed the eyesore next to his own gleaming vehicle. The tripwire triggered an enormous explosion vaporizing everything within a hundred feet of the van and limousine and blew out almost every window in the Nanosecond building.

Security personnel, who rushed to the scene, could not find any sign of Subramanium or his limousine, only a huge gaping crater where the vehicle had been.

Chapter 3

Joan Mason was delighted Jack Garrett accepted Richard Spencer's offer. Of all the potential candidates for the position, only Jack Garrett had received universal praise in the execution of projects from his management and direct reports. As she stared out her office window, she reflected back on her own career and the many changes that had occurred within the last few months.

She had joined Spencer Industries five years ago as a commodities buyer in the Purchasing Department following the completion of her university degree in Business and Management Studies. She had not progressed very rapidly because she'd had to take frequent unpaid leaves to care for her invalid mother. Eventually she had to hire a woman to take care of her. Shy by nature, Joan did not make friends easily. Caring for her invalid mother had virtually eliminated any social life.

Her mother died of pneumonia in November, leaving Joan with few friends and what appeared to be a dead-end job. She inherited a small life insurance policy and discussed the possibility of quitting work and returning to school to finish her MBA with her closest friend Susan Temple, who worked in the legal department at Spencer Industries.

Susan had heard a rumor the Spencer Foundation was going to donate a large amount of money to begin a project that would utilize a new plastic. She'd also heard a new corporation was going to be set up to build the project. She suggested Joan apply for a position in the new firm because employees in startup companies often had better prospects for advancement.

Joan wasn't certain whether she wanted to continue working when Susan suggested she send an email to Richard Spencer and volunteer to work for the new company. She had been amazed Susan would even suggest she jump over five levels of management and apply directly to Spencer for a job in the new company.

"What have you got to lose? You were thinking of leaving anyway."

Joan decided to take a chance and sent an email with her qualifications and work experience, asking she be considered if a suitable position opened up in the new company. Her heart pounded as she pressed the SEND button on the computer mail program. She had either given herself a new opportunity or had flushed her present job down the drain. Her direct supervisor would be furious when she found out, let alone her superiors.

Richard Spencer was surprised word of the new corporation had leaked out to the corporate purchasing department. As he read Joan's request, he realized how hard it must have been for her to bypass her own management. After a few moments of considering her request, he admired her for attempting it. He noted her return email address but decided to call when he saw her phone number at the end of the message.

Convinced she had committed a major blunder by sending the email, Joan considered packing her personal effects and turning in her resignation even as her office phone rang. She froze when the Caller ID displayed RICHARD SPENCER. She hesitated, took a deep breath and grabbed the receiver.

"Purchasing department. Joan Mason speaking."

"Hello, Ms. Mason, this is Richard Spencer. I just received your message. I'd like you to come in and discuss a potential opening in the new company you've somehow learned about."

Joan's heart pounded. "I'm so sorry I sent the note, Mr. Spencer. I don't know what I must have been thinking about." She was so nervous and her hands were so sweaty, she dropped the handset and it landed with a loud BANG on her desk. She gasped and picked it up. "I'm sorry. I dropped the phone, too."

Spencer laughed. "Does that mean you aren't interested in a position in the new company?"

She was so nervous she was practically breathless. "Oh,

no, Mr. Spencer. I would love to be considered for whatever position you think I would qualify for."

"Are you all right, Miss Mason?" He wondered why she sounded out of breath.

Her hands were trembling and sweating even more and she dropped the phone again but this time she managed to catch it before it hit the desk. "Yes, sir. When would you like to see me?"

Spencer looked at his watch. There was another quarterly review in an hour, but he had finished preparing for it. "Are you available now?"

"Now? As in this moment?"

"Yes. I'm on the forty-fifth floor. I'll instruct security to pass you through."

"Yes, sir, Mr. Spencer. I'll be right there."

"Fine. I'll see you in a few minutes."

As she hung up the phone, she wondered how she looked. She hadn't planned on meeting anyone important today, let alone Richard Spencer. She pulled a tissue from a tissue box on her desk to dry her hands and took her compact from her purse and looked in the mirror. Luckily it was still early and her makeup was all right. She breathed a little sigh. As luck would have it she had worn her best dress that day. As she walked quickly to the elevator, she looked at her watch. It was only eight-fifteen in the morning. She would remember this day for a long time.

Susan Temple would long remember the day as well. She was eager to hear all the details of Joan's interview with Richard

Spencer and as the lunch hour approached, she assumed her usual role of shepherd, gathering her 'lunch bunch' together and herding them to the company cafeteria. In her twenty or so years as a legal secretary with Spencer Industries, Susan rarely ventured outside its massive skyscraper in the middle of downtown London. She would like to 'go out' for lunch, but she hated the noontime crowds, the high prices and often-inclement weather.

As she hurried to stake out her favorite table, Susan's eyes were drawn to an unusual shopping bag sitting on a chair in the corner of the cafeteria. She recognized the logo on the bag as a store famous for selling naughty underwear and sexual items. She wondered briefly why anyone from her company would shop at such a disreputable place. Her friends quickly joined her, but their familiar banter couldn't get her mind off the seemingly out of place shopping bag.

Joan noticed Susan's lack of focus. "What's wrong, Susan?"

Susan's attention snapped back to her closest friend. "Oh, nothing. I was just wondering who would have shopped there."

Joan followed her gaze to the shopping bag and frowned. "Who, indeed?"

Susan's curiosity was piqued. She casually stood up and glanced around the cafeteria as she walked slowly over to the bag. Susan was outgoing in nature and seemed to know everyone, but she couldn't determine an unfamiliar face in the room. She peeked into the bag and froze. A timing device with large red numerals sat on top of a large wad of cream-colored dough. Susan had never actually seen a bomb, but the word raced through her mind. As she stared at it, she realized the minute numerals were already on zero and the second numerals were racing in that direction. She knew there was no time to run or even warn anyone around her. She closed her eyes and uttered a quick prayer.

Joan touched her arm. "What's in it, Susan?" She looked in the bag.

Susan fainted and when Joan screamed the word, the crowd in the cafeteria panicked. Joan and Susan were almost trampled in the mad dash for the exits.

Chapter 4

Bob Saltzman straightened his tie and combed his hair quickly as Walt Jacobs made a few last adjustments on his Canon HD videocamera. The assistant producer of the evening news of KUSW alerted them in Jacob's headphones. "Thirty seconds, guys." Jacobs gave a thumbs-up sign to Saltzman who picked up a microphone and cleared his throat. Jacobs pointed at him.

"Good evening. This is Bob Saltzman reporting from the twenty-third annual stockholders meeting of Future Plastics, headquartered here in Seattle. Earlier today, the senior management of Future Plastics presented their objections to an offer from their majority stockholder, Spencer Industries, to acquire the remaining forty-five percent of the company and put the matter to a vote by the stockholders. Moments ago, the results were announced, and the buyout offer was approved. Several members of the management team walked off the stage in protest as Spencer Industries representative Howard Singleton thanked the shareholders and presented the names of the new board of directors."

"In a sad note to the day's events, Tom Johnson, the Chief Financial Officer of Future Plastics suffered a massive heart attack this evening and was rushed to the Harborview Medical Center where he is in intensive care. His son attributed the heart attack to the stress of fighting the buyout of Future Plastics by Spencer Industries and the no-holds-barred public relations war waged in the press prior to the stockholder vote today."

Mark Williamson jumped up from his favorite chair, turned

the TV off, threw the remote control on the floor of his study and stomped on it. "Those SOBs!" he growled as the phone rang.

"Hello!"

"Mark, this is Bill Johnson. I just wanted to let you know my dad passed away a little while ago. He never regained consciousness after the heart attack."

Mark had been expecting the call, but it still was a shock. He sat down wearily. "I'm really sorry Billy. Your dad was a great man. I'll really miss him."

"Mark, it's all their fault. They can't get away with this! We have to make them pay somehow!"

Mark closed his eyes for a moment and took a deep breath. "Did you know they fired the senior management team today?"

Bill was too stunned to speak. When he finally did, it was a whisper. "Everyone?"

Mark felt a deeply held anger rising inside him. "Ten altogether. We heard Spencer gave the order himself!"

"What are we going to do, Mark?"

"Make him pay!" he shouted and slammed the receiver down.

A cold rain drenched Seattle as several luxury sedans silently pulled into the parking lot of an upscale restaurant as it was closing for the night. The restaurant staff hurried to their cars as nine former executives of Future Plastics slipped quietly inside. The shades were drawn, and the exterior lights extinguished. Tables were drawn together, and raincoats tossed across nearby tables as the first meeting of the Council of Nine began.

A purloined memo describing the new Spencer Industries project utilizing Future Plastic materials was distributed. After a moment of silence for Tom Johnson, and a very brief discussion, each conspirator silently laid his 'golden parachute' severance check onto a plate in the middle of the table and made a personal vow of revenge on Spencer Industries, the project... and Spencer personally.

Alan Sands, the former vice president of corporate security, handed out a 'war plan' and proposed budget for their approval.

At a small, secluded restaurant halfway around the world, the six founding members of the Party of Enlightenment discussed the failed bombing attempt on the headquarters building of Spencer Industries. The head of security for the Party, Abdul Rahim, entered with copies of the same memo obtained by the Council of Nine. Several conversations began at once.

Mohammed Skerchi, the leader of the Party, held up his hands for silence. "The security of the London headquarters building has been significantly increased. Another bombing attempt is almost impossible. This new project may be our only chance at Spencer. He is certain to visit it often."

Most of the leaders nodded in agreement, but Rahim objected.

"The coast of Mexico is far from here and we don't speak the language!"

"There will be time to learn, this project will take years," replied Skerchi.

"Security at the site will also be a problem."

Skerchi pointed at him. "You will see to the problem, personally."

Rahim started to object again, but wisely changed his mind.

Chapter 5

Jack had never stayed at such a luxurious hotel. The staff of the hotel seemed to go out their way to make him feel comfortable. They had even offered to drive him to the meeting, but he explained the email invitation had clearly indicated he would be driven to the meeting.

As he waited for a ride to the Spencer Industries building, his cell phone chimed with an email message from Stuart Hawkins, congratulating him on the start of drilling on the platform and a new project for Spencer Industries. Jack chuckled to himself. Even Hawkins didn't apparently have any details on Jack's new assignment. Jack read the rest of the email with a mixture of concern and disbelief as Hawkins described his near fatal encounter with Sam Maller. Hawkins ended the note stating that he felt this was an isolated event, but he was planning to email a warning to project managers worldwide to beef up their security. Something in the note reminded Jack of the helicopter three incident, and he wondered briefly if there was a connection. He would send an email to Stuart with the details on helicopter 3 after the project kickoff meeting.

Jack's shirt collar and pants felt tight. Over the years he'd fought a constant battle with his weight. Years on remote construction sites with nothing to do but eat when not working had really been hard on him. He was only forty-one, but he felt a lot older. He had lost weight many times with every fad diet that came along but it always came back.

As he stood by the glass entry doors, he double-checked his briefcase to be sure he had the email invitation. A moment later a long black limousine pulled up in front of the hotel and the driver hurried into the lobby. Jack stepped back to let him pass, but the driver stopped as he passed Jack. He pulled out a picture, looked at Jack and introduced himself.

"Good morning, Mr. Garrett. My name is Nigel Townsend. I'll be driving you to this morning's meeting. Can I take your briefcase?"

"No. I'd rather keep it."

"Yes, sir. Shall we go?" Townsend opened the entry door and waited for Jack, then hurried to open the limousine door. After Jack got in and he maneuvered the limousine into the morning traffic, Townsend became aware they were being followed. He made a quick survey of the traffic around them and entered an emergency code on his cell phone.

Jack was lost in thought but couldn't help noticing a black sedan pull up next to them. He stared in disbelief as the barrel of a machine gun suddenly poked out the window and was aimed directly at him. Even as he began to duck, he heard a loud crashing sound and saw the black sedan careening off the busy highway and smash into a bridge abutment. It had been rammed from the rear by a limousine identical to theirs.

Townsend seemed relieved as he glanced in the rear-view mirror.

"What the hell is going on?"

"I'm sorry, sir, but we are having some problems with gangs in this area." Townsend replied. He hated lying, but he had been coached on what to say in case something did happen.

His answer was less than satisfying, but before Jack could ask for an explanation, Townsend made a hard turn, pulling into a circular drive next to a huge skyscraper. Jack suddenly fought off another wave of anxiety over his own situation. He had been to many kickoff meetings over the years, but the uncertainty surrounding the nature of this project gnawed at him. The email from Joan Mason, the meeting coordinator, had been brief but warm, congratulating him on joining the 'team', whatever that meant.

The limousine stopped and Townsend turned to him. "We're here, Mr. Garrett."

"Oh, thanks."

Jack closed his briefcase, buttoned his coat, and put his gloves on. Townsend opened the door and Jack got out. They had stopped at a private entrance, and he couldn't help but look up at the skyscraper looming overhead. His shirt collar was a noose that tightened with each step as he walked past several guards stationed outside the building.

Spencer Industries headquarters was richly furnished, attesting to the successful acquisition of new and profitable high technology startups over the years.

A security guard immediately approached him. "Excuse me, sir. This is a private entrance for officers and executives of Spencer Industries. I'll have to see some identification."

Jack was a little surprised the guard was an American. He reached into his coat pocket and pulled out a folded letter that had been waiting for him at the hotel. There was an ID card attached with a paper clip.

"This is all I was given. The driver dropped me off at this entrance."

The guard glanced at the ID and suddenly came to attention, as though he were in the military.

"Yes, sir, Mr. Garrett. I'm sorry, sir. Please come this way." The guard gave the paper and ID back to Jack with something close to a salute.

Jack followed the guard to an elevator marked PRIVATE. The guard pressed the button. When the elevator opened, the guard turned and faced Jack. "Please watch your step, sir."

The meeting was on the 45th floor, the elevator's only stop. On the way up, Jack took his gloves off and examined the ID card again. When he had first received it, he thought it was a credit card. It had a "chip" on the front and a magnetic stripe on the back. In addition to his name and an employee number, it contained some unusual symbols and script Jack didn't recognize.

The elevator door opened to a large, well-appointed lobby. In the center was an immense desk with several people manning it, some of whom appeared to be security personnel. A small group of people sat in comfortable chairs or stood near large doors that probably led to a ballroom or a series of offices. It was an odd mix of people: businessmen, government officials, Europeans, Americans, Asians and Arabs in flowing robes. Based on his experience, they were probably aides of important people. They didn't seem to have anything to do at the moment and appeared extremely bored.

As Jack walked to the desk, one of the security personnel challenged him, "Can I help you, sir?"

Odd, another American. "I have an appointment with Mr. Spencer at nine. My name is Jack Garrett." He handed him the letter.

The guard didn't even look at the letter and to Jack's surprise, saluted him. "Yes, sir! I was instructed to take you directly to the meeting as soon as you arrived. Please follow me."

The guard turned and walked briskly to a small door next to the large ballroom-type doors. As Jack followed him, he wondered why he hadn't even noticed the door. As he approached, he realized it blended in with the dark oak wall paneling. There wasn't even a doorknob to identify it as a door.

The door opened as the guard approached and Jack followed him into the room. The guard stood aside to let Jack pass, then stepped back outside and closed the door.

Jack walked into the middle of a high-level finance meeting. Seated around a large conference table were a dozen or so executives or government officials. Jack recognized some of them from pictures in newspapers and magazines. He also recognized an old acquaintance from a project in the Middle East.

Richard Spencer stood at the head of the table. Several graphs were projected on two large screens at the opposite end of the room. "Jack, right on time. I'm glad you could make it. Gentlemen, this is Jack Garrett, the key to this project's success." Richard smiled as all faces turned to look at Jack, whose shirt collar was almost choking him. He swallowed awkwardly and walked forward. Several of the attendees stood up and walked over to greet him. Their names were lost in the daze of the moment. Some were heads of corporations, others ministers of finance. Still others were powerful financiers and industrialists. *Movers and shakers.*

After a moment, Spencer made himself heard over the buzz of conversation. "Jack, come over here, please. Gentlemen, let's resume."

As Jack sat down, he realized Spencer was talking about him.

"Gentlemen, I'm afraid I haven't been able to tell Jack what he volunteered for yet, so I would like to summarize the project for him."

As Spencer began speaking directly to him, Jack felt everyone's eyes on him.

"About a year ago Future Plastics, one of my chemical companies, developed a new transparent plastic with some unique physical properties. One of those is incredible strength. It's much stronger than any previously developed plastic."

Spencer turned off the laptop projectors and pressed a button. A few seconds later, a movie began, and the narrator praised the great works of the Spencer Foundation as images flashed across the screen of children at play, housing projects and other activities sponsored by, or benefiting from, the Foundation's philanthropic activities. When the short film ended, Spencer turned to Jack.

"The head of the Spencer Foundation suggested the new plastic be used to benefit mankind, rather than just make me money." Everyone in the room laughed except Jack. "The head of the foundation came up with the idea of utilizing the strength of the plastic to build a small domed city under the sea and dedicated to research of the world's oceans. Virtually every aspect of the oceans would be examined, and the city would serve as the focal point for man's knowledge about them. A working state-of-the-art research facility and library dedicated to the study and knowledge of oceans, if you will."

Jack was stunned. He tried to absorb exactly what Spencer meant even as Spencer looked at him for comments. When Jack didn't react, Spencer continued.

"We soon realized the cost of building such a non-profit facility would be prohibitive, so we envisioned enlarging the city and combining it with a world-class resort and conference center. After some reflection on this and a technical feasibility study, I volunteered to fund the building of the basic dome structure, if a consortium of governments and corporations could be set up to fund the construction of the resort, the city and the required research facilities."

Spencer paused to let this soak in. Jack felt a cold shiver race through his body, as though a warning of what was to come.

Spencer smiled at him. "This is where you come in, Jack. I also agreed to provide the expertise to get the dome completed."

Jack laughed. Spencer couldn't be serious. He must be setting him up for the real project. "You're joking, of course?"

Spencer laughed and the others echoed him. "I'm afraid not. I have a model here." He went over to a small table on wheels and pushed it near Jack. He pulled the cover off. In the center of the table was a clear plastic geodesic dome, about five feet in diameter and about a foot tall. Surrounding the main dome were twelve smaller domes, each connected to the main dome by a clear plastic tunnel.

Spencer allowed Jack to look for a moment. "This is a scale

model. The actual dome will be about a mile in diameter and approximately twelve hundred feet high in the center. These support structures will be about a thousand feet in diameter, and each will be dedicated to a specific area of scientific research."

Jack tried to imagine how this would be done when Spencer lifted the center dome to reveal the city underneath. The city was built on a simple grid pattern, much like city blocks in large metropolitan areas. There were four tall buildings in the center Jack guessed would be close to the roof of the dome. Buildings emanating from the center were correspondingly shorter.

"These buildings will also be built utilizing the new plastic whenever possible, with a steel and concrete core, of course."

Jack had an empty feeling in his stomach. Was he serious? "And we're going to build this on the bottom of the ocean, where pressures are in the thousands of pounds per square foot?"

"Not in the deepest parts of the ocean, certainly," Spencer replied, "but we have built several test models and subjected them to pressures comparable to five thousand feet and they show no signs of fatigue or failure. The actual depth of the city will be less than fifteen hundred feet."

Jack wasn't laughing any longer. He looked at the attendees. Most of them seemed to be studying his reaction to Spencer's summary. "You're serious, aren't you?"

Spencer turned back to the city model, as if examining it while he continued. "Jack, we are talking about a twelve- to twenty-billion-dollar project here. I've agreed to fund the cost of the basic dome, which includes the foundation and plastic, and the surrounding structures. This meeting today is to finalize the structure of a consortium to fund the buildings inside the dome, the resort facilities and the scientific equipment required for the research programs. You are here to allow the founding members of the consortium to meet you and ask any questions they may have." He looked at Jack. "Yes, we are quite serious. I anticipate my cost for the main dome and supporting structures alone to be in excess of two billion dollars."

Jack sat back in his chair. The actual effort required would be enormous. The logistics required for the construction of the Maximus platform were almost trivial by comparison.

Spencer addressed the other members. "I have furnished each of you with a copy summarizing Jack's experience and qualifications to undertake this project. If you have any questions, please feel free to ask him now. If you don't have any questions, I will assume you agree with my choice." He handed Jack a copy of his biography.

Jack scanned his biography quickly and looked at each attendee. Some were reviewing a copy of his achievements; others were looking at him and smiling. One attendee studying the resume raised his hand to get Spencer's attention.

"Yes, Mr. Yamato?"

Yamato looked at Jack "Mr. Garrett, your qualifications are quite impressive. I would like to know what you think about the feasibility of building such an enormous structure on the ocean floor."

Jack quickly regained his composure. As an engineer, he

felt much better talking about actual construction methods rather than the grand and glorious plans, something Richard Spencer obviously excelled at.

"I have built off-shore platforms in depths greater than this, but this is a radical change from any sea-based construction project I've ever seen. If the plastic is as strong as Mr. Spencer claims, then I believe we can work out the actual construction details of the city. Pouring the concrete foundations will be quite a task, of course."

Jack looked at Spencer, who seemed pleased. "What kind of time frame are we talking about, Mr. Spencer?"

Spencer replaced the dome over the buildings. "We need to be operational in three years."

Jack's jaw dropped. "Three years! I don't think we could build the city infrastructure in three years if it were on an island, let alone on the bottom of the sea!"

"Once the dome is in place and filled with air, construction on the city buildings can continue on a twenty-four-hour basis."

Jack couldn't let the statement go unchallenged. "What about the support logistics? How will we support the thousands of workers that will be required? Where would they live? How will we feed them in the middle of the ocean?"

Spencer waved the questions away. "Those issues can be resolved. We're here to finalize the commitments we need to proceed with the funding of the city structures and research facilities. Are there any additional questions for Jack?"

There were no questions. Spencer looked at his watch. "Excellent. It looks like you have quite a task ahead, Jack.

Gentlemen, let's take a short break and then continue."

As Spencer walked out of the conference room, he saw Joan Mason sitting in a waiting area near the reception desk.

"Good morning, Joan. How are you?"

"Wonderful, sir. How is the meeting progressing?"

"Fine. I just introduced Jack to the Foundation's Board of Directors. They seemed to be impressed with him."

"I can't wait to meet him, sir. I've heard so much about him."

"Well, you won't have to wait much longer. We're through with him for the moment. I'd like you to show him around."

"Yes, sir. I'll be happy to."

Joan had only known Spencer a month or so, but he was so involved in the new project she met with him almost daily. She still lunched with Susan frequently and when Susan asked how she liked her new job, Joan told her she loved it. She also bragged how nice Richard Spencer was to her and everyone around him.

Joan followed him into the conference room. Even though she had set up this meeting, she was still in awe of the attendees. She'd been certain they would send representatives and was surprised when each one confirmed their attendance.

Spencer walked up to a crowd gathered around Jack and asked them to take their seats. Joan finally saw Jack, recognizing him from a photograph in his employee folder.

Earlier she had put on her best 'innocent' look and asked Michael Baker very nicely if he had any better photographs in his security files. Baker showed her several newspaper photographs and had even managed to find an interview and picture of Jack in the Allied Exploration and Development's company newsletter.

Jack had a ruddy complexion from overseeing construction activities on the rig. His light brown hair had been bleached by the sun and was closely cropped. He looked a little thinner than he did in the photos she had shown Susan. Susan had gushed over his ruggedly handsome good looks. Joan thought Jack looked particularly handsome in his suit.

Joan was wearing a dark grey business suit and an "editorial" or business hairstyle. Jack first noticed her red lipstick, which seemed to be in contrast with her very pale skin, then her raven black hair, dark eyes, slender build, and very conservative appearance. She smiled at him, and he realized the icy feeling in his hands was gone.

Some of the attendees gathered around the model and others began to discuss the financial issues at the heart of the meeting. Spencer tapped Jack on the shoulder. "I don't think you'll want to attend the rest of this meeting. I've asked Joan to show you around and help you get settled in your new office. I think we can finish around eleven. I'll come by for you then and we can talk over lunch with the rest of the project team. I really appreciate your making it here on such short notice, Jack."

Joan seemed impatient to go, so Jack nodded to everyone and followed her out of the room. "My name is Joan Mason. It's a pleasure to meet you at last, Mr. Garrett. I've heard so much about you."

Jack shook her hand. "Are you Mr. Spencer's assistant?"

"No, Mr. Garrett. I'll be the purchasing agent for the project and your assistant while you are in London. I'll also handle all your correspondence when you are at the project site."

Jack was a little surprised. He rarely ever had an assistant to help on project-related issues.

"Would you like to see your office?"

"Yes. Certainly."

"This way, please."

As they walked down a long hallway, Jack reflected on the meeting and the magnitude of the project. *My God, what have I gotten myself into?*

Chapter 6

Joan stopped at a richly decorated oak-paneled door, unlocked it with a card key exactly like the one he had and opened it. Jack was amazed at the size of the office. The floor had a thick, rich looking carpet and the entire back wall was floor-to-ceiling windows with a fabulous view of downtown London. There was an enormous wood desk near the windows, with an executive's chair behind it. Several paintings were displayed on the walls. Jack recognized one as an original Picasso. After a moment, he realized all the paintings were originals by world-famous painters.

"This is my office?" He was incredulous.

"Yes, Mr. Garrett." Joan stood by his desk, motioning to a stack of folders on the corner. "These folders will provide a summary of the key events and decisions made so far on the project. It should bring you up to date."

Jack was still looking at some of the decorations on the walls.

"Is there anything you require at this time, Mr. Garrett?"

"Only that you call me Jack."

"Yes, sir."

"And please don't call me 'sir'."

"Yes... Jack."

He smiled and turned to her. "I hope it's all right if I call you Joan?"

As she nodded, she wondered if he had eaten. "Would you like some coffee or, perhaps, some pastries?"

Jack's stomach still had not quite recovered from the meeting. "No, thank you."

"Then, I'll be going if you don't need anything."

Jack nodded and returned to the paintings on the wall.

As Joan walked to the partly open door, she glanced back at Jack and banged her head on the door. She began to cry out but managed to keep her mouth closed. She looked back at Jack again. He was so absorbed in the paintings he hadn't noticed. She closed the door and rubbed her face as she walked down the hall.

Jack walked over to the desk, picked up the top folder, sat down and began to skim the pages inside. The first memo detailed a meeting held at Spencer Industries where the first concept of building a domed city was discussed. Other documents described testing done on several small dome models. Jack quickly became absorbed in the details and didn't notice the passage of time, or someone knocking and opening the door.

"Pretty interesting reading, isn't it?" Spencer stood next to his desk. Jack instinctively began to get up.

"You don't need to get up. I'd like to talk to you about your role in all of this." Spencer sat in a chair facing Jack's desk.

"Do you mean my responsibilities as the project engineer?"

Spencer glanced at his watch. "When I started selling the whole concept of this project, I quickly realized it couldn't be handled as a regular project, where a design team is formed, they do all the planning and purchasing and then turn it over to a project engineer to complete."

He paused, as if waiting for Jack to comment. When he didn't, he continued. "There are too many corporations, too many countries, too many influences on the project. There will just be too many people wanting to help. A project engineer would not be able to withstand the constant pressure of changes and requests to offer assistance. So, we decided to form a new corporation, with total responsibility for the construction of the city and its operation. This would also isolate the people actually involved from influences that could delay the project. Initially, the corporation will be charged with getting the city completed and fully operational. Then at some point, the corporation will be responsible for operating and maintaining the city to ensure all of the original goals are met."

Jack shifted in his chair. "What does this have to do with

me?"

"We want you to be the president of the new corporation."

Jack was stunned. "How can the president of a corporation direct the building of the city?"

"Think of it as a small entrepreneurial start-up type company where the president is involved in the day-to-day operations of the company. The only difference is the initial capitalization of this company will be in excess of a billion dollars." Spencer chuckled.

Jack tried to image how it would work.

"Just think of it, Jack! This is an engineer's dream--to be given a project to build <u>and</u> the control of the checkbook as well."

They both laughed.

"I sort of had that on the oil platform. It was an experiment."

Spencer nodded. "I know about that. You will have a lot more control of everything on this project. In fact, it may be more than you want."

Jack frowned and Spencer studied his face. "There's more. You will also have the freedom to hire the people you need to get the task done. Initially, I have selected four key people to assist you and I may ask you to let me review the resumes of the people who will work directly for you. But with time, I probably won't have an opportunity to do that. I have other projects in mind for this new plastic as well. So basically, Jack, you will carry the ball on this project."

"How will the new corporation relate to Spencer Industries?"

"That's a good question. The corporation will be publicly held. The group of companies comprising Spencer Industries will collectively own fifty-one percent and a public offering will be held to sell the remaining shares. This will provide the initial funding for the equipment and resources the corporation will need to build the city. However, as president of one of the Spencer group of companies, you automatically become a vice president of Spencer Industries."

It suddenly dawned on Jack the symbols on the ID card must have identified him as an officer of Spencer Industries, hence the office. "Are you sure you have the right person for this job?"

Spencer glanced at his watch again. "I have the <u>best</u> person for the job."

Jack blushed.

"I never look for the 'right' person for a job. I've always believed in finding the best person for each job and then giving them the freedom to do it. Sometimes this costs me a lot of money, but it's always paid off in the long run, as you can see." He gestured around the office and then stood up. "We have an executive dining room on this floor. I think they're probably ready for us. I'd like to introduce you to the rest of the team."

Jack looked at his watch. Could it be 12:15 already? Had all this happened in a few short hours? He stood up, strangely calm now. Maybe this would work. At least he would still be in a hands-on role in the project. Titles didn't matter much anyway.

"I'd like to meet them, too, Mr. Spencer."

"Jack, we're going to be working together on this for quite some time. I would hope we could be on a first name basis from now on."

"That would be great, Mr. Spen--Richard."

"Before we go, I'd also like to talk to you about your salary."

Jack hadn't even thought about that. "I'd like to talk about it as well."

Spencer took a folded piece of paper out of his coat pocket and handed it to Jack. "With all the other things going on, I guess I forgot to give this to you."

Jack opened the paper. It was a letter of employment with Spencer Industries. There was no mention of a temporary assignment from Allied. As he scanned the document, his eyes got wider. Jack had been working for American companies for most of his career. This time his salary was stated in pounds but Jack didn't need a calculator to figure the difference.

Spencer saw his expression and laughed. "I took your present salary at Allied and added a zero. However, I should warn you half of your salary is dependent upon meeting certain goals in the first few years."

Jack sat back down, stunned.

"I think the compensation is in line with the responsibilities of the job. Of course, when you're at the job site, the corporation will take care of all of your expenses. Our expectations are just as high, Jack. I know you won't let us down."

Jack stared at the letter. "It doesn't say anything about returning to Allied."

"I don't think Steve Freeman will be too surprised. After all, you're his equal now in the group."

Jack stood up and stared at him, trying to absorb it all.

"Let's go eat, Jack. I'm hungry." Spencer turned to leave. He stopped to look at Jack as he opened the door. "I have a few urgent phone calls to make, but I'll meet you there in ten minutes. Joan can show you the way." He turned and walked out.

Jack stood there for a moment. "Damn," he whispered as he went to find Joan's office.

Chapter 7

As the sun peeked over the horizon, Tom Stern shivered against the cold of an early morning New England chill. He stomped his feet and breathed on his hands to bring some life back into his slender frame. He looked at his watch. It was almost 7:30 and his graveyard shift would be over in half an hour. The heater in his guard shack had chosen the first really cold fall morning of the year to fail and he had spent a pretty miserable night. He almost wished he were stationed at the contractor's gate instead of the visitor's entrance. At least he might have had a few old friends to chat with. He was wondering why they even kept the visitor's gate open on the night shift when a luxury sedan turned off the state highway and pulled slowly up to the gate. The windows were so darkly tinted Stern couldn't even see the driver. There were no government or company markings on the car. *Must be vendors.*

Saturn Enterprises manufactured advanced avionics equipment for the military and most of the visitors were either officers working on specific projects or salesmen representing a select list of suppliers. He picked up his clipboard and recorded the time. As he opened the door to the guard shack, he pressed the butt of his handgun with his elbow to make sure he hadn't forgot to wear it, a bad habit resulting in his relegation to the graveyard shift. The icy morning air slapped him in the face as he walked to the sedan.

Sean Michaelson started to pull a revolver from his jacket. Brian Mulvey quickly put a hand on his arm, stopping him.

"Don't," he whispered.

They waited patiently for the guard to walk around the car, record their license plate number and make his way slowly to the driver's window. The window slid silently down, and Michaelson smiled at Stern.

"Morning," he said, trying hard to hide his thick Celtic accent.

The guard glanced in, quickly surveying the two men dressed in dark conservative suits. Mulvey stared straight ahead, avoiding his scrutiny.

"Morning, gentlemen. This is a private entrance to Saturn Enterprises. Do you have an appointment with someone?"

"Yes, we're here to see Mr. Tooley. We're here a little early, though."

Stern was frowning as he stood upright. Jacob Tooley was the head of security and almost never had visitors. "What time is your appointment?"

Michaelson pulled a letter from his suit coat pocket and handed it to Stern. It was a confirmation of a meeting later in the morning, printed on a Saturn letterhead.

Stern handed the letter and the clipboard to Michaelson. "Please sign here."

Michaelson stuffed the letter back in his coat, signed the visitor roster and handed the clipboard back to Stern.

"The visitor's lot is straight ahead. There's a reception area just inside the entrance. You can get some coffee there while you wait."

"Thank you." Michaelson pressed a button to raise the window as Stern took a few steps back and pressed the barrier button.

"Look," hissed Mulvey pointing to a granite monument nearby. Under a huge logo of a planet with a ring were the words SATURN ENTERPRISES, A MEMBER OF THE SPENCER INDUSTRIES GROUP. He gritted his teeth.

"The hell with that. Look how far the damn visitor's lot is from the building!"

The visitor's lot was almost a hundred yards from the building. But there was a smaller lot, set aside for the officers of the company, right near the entrance.

Mulvey glanced at his watch. "Go to the smaller one. Hurry, it's almost time!"

Stern watched the sedan slowly move ahead toward the visitor's lot then slow and stop. In a flash it suddenly veered and headed toward the executive lot. "What the...." In less than a heartbeat he jumped forward and pressed a button labeled SECURITY BARRIER. A large section of the entrance to the executive's lot dropped several feet and the nose of the sedan dropped into it. He saw the two men jump out and start running toward him. Before he could pull out his own gun, he saw a flash and felt a tremendous pain in his chest as he fell backwards.

Mulvey and Michaelson rushed past him as an enormous explosion rocked the ground. Stern struggled to sit up enough to see the saboteurs and managed to get off a few shots before he passed out.

Michaelson was hit the in head and died instantly. Mulvey was wounded but managed to make it to a getaway car parked down the highway. More than a dozen people near the front of the building were not so fortunate, as large sections of the floors in the front of the building collapsed and fell on them.

Michael Baker was unpacking some boxes in his new office in London and reflecting on his new position as head of security for a company being formed within the Spencer Industries Group. Mementos of twenty years of proud service in Her Majesties army were scattered throughout the office, waiting to be hung in just the right spot. He pulled out several citations and was gazing at them when the office phone rang drawing him out of his nostalgic reminiscences. He was surprised anyone even knew his new phone number yet. He was even more surprised when the caller ID displayed RICHARD SPENCER.

"Yes, Mr. Spencer?"

"Michael, I know you are probably still moving in, but we have some real problems and need your help right away."

Chapter 8

With Joan's help, Jack found the executive dining room and arrived almost the same time as Spencer. He followed Spencer into the executive dining room, an expensive restaurant maintained by the company for its executives. The room was almost empty. Five people seated at a table in the rear were having a lively discussion. Spencer headed directly for them. They all stood up as Spencer approached.

"Good afternoon! I'd like to introduce Jack Garrett, the soon-to-be-president of the Atlantis Corporation."

As Jack walked up to the table, he tried to put faces with the security background records he'd read earlier in the morning.

The three men and two-woman team all smiled at him.

Jack recognized Michael Baker as he stepped forward. "Good afternoon, Mr. Garrett. It's nice to see you again. I'll be the head of security for the corporation."

Baker was about as tall as Jack and about the same age, but he had a more powerful build and a strong handshake. Jack remembered reading in Baker's file that he had been born in England, entered the military at eighteen and made a career of it for twenty years. He was an expert on most forms of terrorism having first-hand experience dealing with terrorists. He also was a black belt in the martial arts, but Jack couldn't quite remember which one. He also recalled Baker had never married.

Essentially a walking weapon, Baker was proficient in the use of most weapons that could be carried and a world-class marksman with a handgun. After his career in the military, he joined an American company specializing in corporate security as a senior partner. The company had been hired by Spencer to improve the building's security. It had even brought in its own personnel to quickly resolve some long-standing security issues. Jack encountered the American personnel when he first entered the building.

When Baker heard about the Atlantis project, he personally asked Spencer if he could be considered for the position of head of security. Spencer was so impressed with the security improvements made to the headquarters building; he granted his request. In fact, Baker was the first person hired to work on the project. He also brought several colleagues with him from the security firm. Baker was not necessarily someone Jack would pick as a friend, but he was someone he'd like to have on his side when problems arose.

Jack shook his hand. "Nice to see you again."

Howard Singleton was standing behind Baker and moved forward to introduce himself. He was born in Brazil of English parents. His father was an international securities broker and his mother a financial analyst. Singleton naturally followed in their tradition and upon graduating from an Ivy League College in the U.S. became a financial officer of a small startup company. The startup company was acquired by Spencer Industries and when Spencer met Singleton, he was impressed enough to offer him a lead role in the Acquisitions Department of Spencer Industries. Recently he was named as the Financial Officer of the soon-to-be-formed Atlantis Corporation. Somewhat shy, Singleton was more at ease with financial reports than people. His file indicated he was married and had several children.

"I'm Howard Singleton, your Financial Officer, Mr. Garrett," he said, shaking Jack's hand. He'd heard quite a bit about Jack and was genuinely pleased to finally meet him.

"Nice to meet you, Howard."

Emma Dawson was almost as tall as Jack, attractive, with dark hair and contrasting blue eyes. Well dressed and poised, she possessed the ideal qualities for dealing with the news media daily. Used to holding press conferences to explain a new business deal of Spencer's or address an environmental issue, she was the daughter of one of Spencer's original partners in Spencer Industries. Unfortunately for Emma, her father sold his partnership back to Spencer in order to form another company he believed stood a better chance of making money. Emma would have been quite wealthy if her father had stayed with Spencer.

She had known Spencer all her life because her father remained his friend, even after he left Spencer Industries. When Emma graduated with a degree in Communications and Media Studies from a prestigious university in England, Spencer immediately offered her a position in the corporate public relations department. Jack knew from the security file she married right after completing her degree and then divorced a few years later. He also made a mental note that she was ten years younger than himself.

"Hello, Mr. Garrett, I'm Emma Dawson, the current head of your corporate communications department." She held out her hand. Emma had a smooth even voice and a calm demeanor, ideal for dealing with the news media.

"It's a pleasure, Ms. Dawson."

Dr. Ashley Hart was a chemist and co-inventor of the new plastic at the heart of the Atlantis project. She was recruited from Future Plastics by Spencer to serve as the technical focal point for any questions regarding the properties of the plastic. Ashley wasn't as tall as Emma, but she was slender with clear blue eyes and blonde hair and could have been mistaken for a model. She often had to overcome that stereotype and was sensitive to any remarks about her looks that suggested she wasn't a brilliant chemist. She stepped forward to shake Jack's hand. "Hello, Mr. Garrett. Ashley Hart. I think I'll be a technical focal point for the dome application of the new plastic."

Jack had been impressed when he read her bio. "Nice to meet you Dr. Hart. I'm sure your expertise will come in handy once construction starts."

He was also distracted by her good looks and especially her expressive blue eyes.

The last member of the team, Bill Howell, was an American, slender and sandy-haired, he was several inches taller than Jack. Bill's background was in many ways similar to Jack's. His father owned a small construction company in West Texas and specialized in apartment construction. Bill grew up in the business and his father put him in charge of a new apartment complex the summer prior to college. He managed to finish college with a degree in construction technology.

Unlike Jack, he never worked on a marine project but spent over twenty years building employee compounds and new cities in the Middle East as new refineries and chemical plants were built. Bill was married and divorced during the years he spent in the Middle East. He was a little 'off-center' and although he was known as a prankster, he never did anything to harm anyone. He was hired to relieve Jack of the day-to-day details of the construction of the domed city. This would leave Jack free to provide an overview and keep the project on track.

Dressed in a business suit and dress boots, he held an expensive cowboy hat in one hand as he shook Jack's with the other. "Hello, Mr. Garrett. I'm Bill Howell. I think I'm the construction foreman for the project but I'm not sure."

Jack was immediately at ease with Bill. He worked with people like Bill all his life. "It's nice to meet you, Bill."

Even though it was an awkward moment, Jack wanted to put them at ease. "Please, be seated, everyone. You're probably as hungry as I am."

A waitress brought menus and they all ordered.

Spencer waited until he had their attention. "I know you all must have a million questions about the new corporation we're forming, but I thought it would be a good idea if you understood how the consortium, now known as the Atlantis Foundation, operates and how it relates to the Atlantis Corporation. The Foundation is the entry point into the research to be conducted in Atlantis. Corporations, or countries, may join by paying an entry commitment, which makes them an equity partner in the whole venture. The commitment also entitles them to have access to all the research conducted by the Foundation in Atlantis and to unlimited access to an electronic library we are building to catalogue virtually all of man's knowledge about the oceans."

Emma glanced up from her tablet notes. "Is the commitment always the same?"

"No. There's a sliding scale of commitments to ensure a small country with limited resources has the same access to the research as a larger country with greater resources. The entry commitment for a corporation seeking access to this research depends on whether it becomes a sponsor or not. We examined the funding of the last three Olympic Games and learned quite a lot. We hope in the future, the city can be self-sustaining with the use of corporate sponsors."

Howard was always seeking new revenue sources to help finance the project. "What about sponsor advertising in the city?"

"We'll try to keep it to a minimum. If a sponsor wants to use the Atlantis logo in their advertising we will allow it, as long as it's in good taste."

Baker wondered how many sponsors they would need to make the project viable. "What would a typical entry commitment be?"

"Since most of the commitments so far are in dollars, I'll be referring to amounts in dollars. For a country it would range from about five to fifteen million. For a corporation, ten to twenty-five million, depending on whether they were a sponsor or not. What's the latest total so far, Howard?"

"We have over three hundred commitments so far for the city, totaling approximately six billion dollars."

The team members looked at each other.

Bill was used to working on large projects, but the amount surprised him. "Six <u>billion</u>, Howard?"

"Yes, almost enough to complete Phase Two, or most of the buildings in the center of the dome. As you know, the Spencer Foundation is donating the dome materials and Mr. Spencer is donating the labor required to construct the domes in Phase One."

"Which leaves us with another four billion dollars or so to raise to complete the city." Spencer watched Jack absorb this additional information.

That's almost twelve billion. "Richard, you mentioned a figure like twelve to twenty billion in the finance meeting."

"Yes. An estimate of the total project cost, including the cost of the research equipment and the support facilities, like a new dock at Cancun, supply ships and submarines to transport the scientists, guests and visitors to and from the dome to Cancun."

"Submarines?"

"One of several ways we plan to get people to and from the dome."

Bill had been given a new hardhat with the new company's logo. "Where'd the name Atlantis come from?"

Spencer shrugged. "The head of the Spencer Foundation suggested it."

Ashley looked up from her notes. "How does the Atlantis Corporation fit in?"

"The Atlantis Corporation is licensed by the Foundation to build the dome and later on, to operate and maintain it."

Spencer was looking at Jack as he gestured to the team members. "This is the Atlantis Corporation at the moment, Jack. If there's anything you would like to know about the Atlantis project, these people are your first source of information at this point."

Jack thought for a moment. "I don't think I have any security, or public relations questions just yet, but I have a few logistics issues I'd like to discuss." Jack took a notepad out of his coat pocket. "I made a list." The others looked at each other as Jack scanned his notes. "Let me go through them quickly so you can be thinking about them. You've spent quite some time with the design team, Richard, so I hope they've thought of these things."

Like everyone else at the table, Richard had a blank expression.

"How was the site south of Cozumel, Mexico, determined?" Jack was intently reading his notes. "How will we light the city? How will we power it? Future Plastics will begin delivering several thousand large pieces that make up the main dome and the surrounding domes, in less than twelve months. Where will they be stored? How will we bring the concrete to the site and pour the foundations on the sea floor? Where will the construction workers live while the city is being built? How will we air condition the city? How will visitors get to the site from the nearest airports in Cancun or Cozumel?"

"Jack!" Richard interrupted.

Jack looked up at Richard and then at the rest. He could tell they didn't have a clue about these issues.

"I can answer the first question, but I don't think any of us knows the answers to the rest on your list. We need those questions answered, along with scores of others. In fact, that's why you're here."

"But these are fundamental questions that must be answered before anything can be done!"

"I agree with you. We all agree. You have the authority to decide those issues. I don't know what's possible, let alone the best option for those items."

This was going to be even harder than it seemed when he first heard about it. He had assumed the basic logistics of building the dome and city had been considered, if not finalized, by the design team. It turned out the design team had only worked out the design of the dome itself, not the city or the project as a whole. Jack wondered how he could do this by himself.

Spencer put a folder on the table in front of Jack.

"What's this?" Jack opened the folder and scanned the contents.

"A database printout of all the research laboratories of the companies that make up Spencer Industries. You'll also find the name and phone number of the key contact at each one and the areas of expertise offered by each facility. I'm sure there's someone in there capable of answering almost any question you may have. Joan Mason has already been in touch with each of the key contacts about this project. She's told them they should expect to hear from you."

Jack laughed. "These people are located all over the world! How can I expect to get in touch with them?"

"You won't have to. Joan will set up any meeting or conference or video conference you need." Spencer hesitated. "Jack, all of these people are waiting to help you, even eager to be involved in this project. The people at this table are here to help you, too. I hope you don't feel you're being asked to do this all by yourself. As the team leader, you only need to identify the task and delegate it to someone. Remember, we have the best people on this project."

Jack relaxed. Richard was right. He would have all the help he needed. But where should he start? "All right." He took a cell phone out of his coat pocket and pressed some keys. "Joan, could you come to the executive dining room now? Thanks." He looked up at Richard as he put his phone away. "You said you could answer one of these questions."

Spencer thought a moment. "Why Cozumel? This was one of the first questions the Atlantis Foundation addressed: Where should you locate a resort city and <u>the</u> premier oceanographic research facility in the world? The obvious question was near the greatest source of fish and marine life forms. We looked at many possibilities and decided it should be near a reef. We looked at the top five reefs in the world and ultimately settled on the Palancar Reef near Cozumel. We would have loved to locate it near the Great Barrier Reef of Australia, but the logistics weren't favorable. Virtually all of the technology and materials for the project would come from North America or Europe. Shipping everything to the Great Barrier Reef would have added an enormous expense to the already astronomical price for the project. The delivery times would also be unacceptable for a fast-track project."

Jack agreed. He'd built several offshore platforms in the Gulf of Mexico and found transportation and supply operations there to be excellent. "That sounds reasonable. I just wish someone had answers to the rest of the questions." He looked at his notepad.

"Someone will soon--you!" Spencer was serious. "There is one other issue I have to discuss with all of you."

They all sat waiting while he paused as if thinking how to continue.

"I must tell each of you there is some personal risk in working for Spencer Industries in general and this project in particular. The Spencer Foundation has supported numerous peace efforts, family planning, environmental conservation efforts, global climate change studies and other issues at odds with various groups around the world. This has made us the target for some extremist groups that view these efforts as obstacles to their goals and desires."

Spencer looked at Baker as he continued. "A few months ago, an unknown group planted a bomb in this building and, by some miracle, it malfunctioned. It could have killed a great number of people. We immediately brought in a world-renowned security company to prevent it from happening again. Mr. Baker worked for the company until he volunteered to head up security for the Atlantis Corporation."

Baker was stone-faced as Spencer continued.

"We think the employees of the Atlantis Corporation and the project itself could become the target of these extremist groups. I just wanted you to know that this corporation, and Mr. Baker, will do whatever is necessary to see no harm comes to any of you."

The team members sat in stunned silence, each reflecting on Spencer's revelation. The food arrived and Spencer looked at his watch. "Oh, I have another meeting to run to. I'm sorry I have to leave. I'd like to know the answers to those questions as well."

Joan Mason walked to the table as Spencer got up to leave. "You asked for me, Mr. Garrett?"

"Yes. If you have a minute, I'd like to discuss a few things and perhaps set up a planning meeting."

"Yes, of course."

Spencer motioned her to his chair and quietly left.

As she sat down the waiter placed Spencer's order in front of her. "Oh, I didn't order that!" She looked longingly at a large lobster on the plate.

"Go ahead, Joan," Emma urged. "Richard won't be back for hours."

They all began eating, except for Emma, who cleared her throat. "Jack, eventually I'll be the spokesperson for the Atlantis project."

Jack looked at her but didn't say anything.

"So, I would like to act as spokesperson for this group. We're all here because of our association with Richard. Either we volunteered or were asked to join the project."

Jack laughed loudly. "Sorry. Please continue."

"We know there are a lot of unanswered questions about the project, and you seem to have a pretty extensive list yourself. And, uh, we know you have a lot on your mind. I--we--were wondering if we could talk to you about our salaries and benefits."

Everyone's gaze shifted from Emma to Jack.

"Spencer didn't say anything to you about that?"

They each shook their heads as he looked at them.

"Well, then that's an issue all right." Jack looked at Howard. "Howard, did Richard mention anything to you about this?"

Howard, who was eating, shook his head.

"I guess this will be my first decision. I would like to offer each of you a plan similar to the one he offered to me. It's based on a bonus plan tied to performance. Initially, half of your total salary will be dependent on the success of the project... and your performance."

They looked at each other, dumbfounded.

"That sounds like a great deal for an executive, but I'd have a hard time receiving only half of my current salary, with the expectation of the rest."

"I'm sorry, Emma, I should have been more specific. You all will initially maintain your current salary as your base pay. When you're at the site, the company will also pay for all of your expenses, of course."

It took a few moments for his words to settle in.

"Mr. Garrett?" Howard looked a little upset.

"Yes?"

"Did you just commit the Atlantis Corporation to an amount equal to twice their present salaries?"

"You're real fast with numbers, Howard."

Everyone smiled but Howard.

"I should also tell you about promotions and advancements."

They couldn't have been more attentive.

"Richard just said the Atlantis Corporation <u>is</u> sitting at this table. That's not very many people right now. In a few years there could be several hundred or several thousand employees. We'll utilize contractors at first whenever possible, while keeping a few key people as heads of various departments. We'll start out calling you 'Directors' at first. You'll be on probation for two years. If you perform well, after that time you will be promoted to vice presidents of the Corporation."

They looked at each other in stunned silence.

Jack laughed. "I wouldn't worry about it right now. I know you're here because Richard thought you were the best person for the job. I have no reason to think otherwise. I should also tell you I will make sure the bonus potential for a vice president is four times base pay."

"Four times! Does that mean the total could be five times our current base pay?"

"You're pretty fast, too, Emma."

Bill leaped to his feet. "I don't know about the rest of you, but I feel motivated! When can we start!"

They all laughed except Howard.

Joan raised her hand a little as Bill sat back down.

"Yes, Joan?"

"Does this incentive plan apply to the support staff as well?"

Jack shook his head. "No, only to the key staff. We'll have a different plan for the professional staff, support staff and hourly employees."

Joan looked down, obviously disappointed. The others at the table were embarrassed at Joan obviously being left out of a highly desirable incentive plan.

Jack waited only a moment. "I have a different plan in mind for you, Joan."

She looked up at him.

"I know you're about one-half of the way through your MBA. If you will commit to finishing it in the next two years, I'll hold the Director of Purchasing position open for you, with the opportunity to become Vice President of Purchasing later. And the company will pay all of your educational expenses, of course."

Joan was too surprised to react for a few seconds. "Yes!" she shouted, then jumped up, ran around the table and hugged Jack. The others laughed and she gasped and stepped back from him. "Oh! I'm so sorry, Mr. Garrett. I forgot myself for a moment."

Jack laughed. "Forget it. I take it the answer is yes then? You may have to take some night classes."

"I don't care! It's a wonderful opportunity, Mr. Garrett. Thank you!"

"Please call me Jack."

"Yes, sir, Jack." She hurried back to her chair.

"What about a benefit plan?" Baker had his own list of concerns.

"Howard, is there any reason they can't have the same benefits as Spencer Industries employees until we can set up a formal plan?"

Howard shook his head. "Probably not, but I think we should look at the current benefit plans of similar new startups in the group of companies. We have access to the information."

"Sounds like a great idea, Howard. Can you have a draft of a recommendation on a total benefits plan in three months?"

Howard gulped. "Yes, sir," he said and began making notes in an electronic tablet.

"Joan, later this afternoon I'll give you a list of contacts at several laboratories in the group. I'd like to set up a meeting with them here in London to discuss some urgent technical issues."

"Yes, sir--err, Jack."

"Michael, we'll be hiring some new employees soon. I'd like to go over your procedures for security background checks."

"Any time you're ready, Jack."

"Emma, I'd like to go over a press release announcing the formation of the Atlantis Corporation soon."

"I'm already working on one. I'll email a draft to you later today."

Jack nodded. "I'd also like a draft of a media promotional plan for Atlantis in about a month."

Emma nodded and made some quick notes in her tablet.

"Ashley, I'd like to talk to you later today about the best way to connect the plastic dome pieces to the concrete foundations."

"Yes, Mr. Garrett. Just give me a call when you're ready to discuss it."

"Please   call   me   Jack."
"Yes…Jack." She smiled at the thought of calling the president of the company by his first name.

"Bill, I'd like to go over some ideas I have for the actual construction of the dome soon."

"Anytime, boss."

Jack smiled. "You're all going to need help soon. I suggest you begin mapping out your personnel needs for the immediate future and email them to me. I'll meet with Richard to identify the office space we'll need. We may have to move to a new location if this building can't accommodate us."

He looked at Joan. "Can you find out how much space is available in this building?"

"Yes, Jack." She scribbled furiously in her tablet.

"Also, I saw a scale model of Atlantis in this morning's meeting. Would you bring it to my office when they're done with it?"

"Yes, Jack."

"The next three years will be interesting," Jack's remark was addressed to no one in particular.

Chapter 9

Joan worked with building management to move some people's offices around to allow the offices of the new members of the Atlantis Corporation to be together on the 30th floor. After lunch, with Joan's help, Jack found Ashley Hart's new office to discuss the connection of dome pieces to the foundation. Jack actually found it difficult to concentrate on the subject matter when Ashley stared at him with her light blue eyes. It helped when she looked away to show him some Computer Aided Design (CAD) drawings of the connection of the bottom row pieces to the foundation. At least he could look at her without losing his train of thought. He noticed her name on the bottom corner of the drawings.

"These drawings are exactly what I'm looking for. Did you draw them?"

"Yes, I'm pretty good with several CAD programs. I've worked on some other applications for the plastic as well as the dome. You can keep those; I can make more if I need them."

"That's great. Sometimes I'd like to know about the other applications."

"Sure, Jack, anytime. There isn't a lot for me to do here yet and I'm kind of bored."

Her perfume was getting to him, and he needed to leave.

"Okay, thanks for the information. I may be back soon with some more questions."

Ashley just smiled as Jack hurried out of her office. She

already knew he was physically attracted to her, and she wondered if she could use that to her advantage. She was only "on loan" from Future Plastics to help the Atlantis Corporation in the design and actual construction of the dome. She probably would only be involved for a year or so. Spencer had mentioned something like a Chief Technology Officer role for her, but she doubted her ability to contribute beyond issues with the plastic. And Jack was kind of handsome, and he wasn't wearing a ring. She wondered if she could get a copy of his background from Baker. Maybe if she asked Baker nicely…

When Jack returned to his office later that afternoon, the model was near his desk. He walked over and uncovered it to study it in more detail. A report labeled CONFIDENTIAL was lying on the corner of the table. It was the final report of the design team from Future Plastics. He opened it and began reading. There were extensive drawings of the plastic pieces making up the dome structure, but he couldn't find anything on the interior of the city. The design team had worked exclusively on the domes and the foundations.

Jack laughed as the buildings in the model looked as though they had been assembled from a child's play set. They would have to be a lot more precise. He wondered how they had even estimated the overall cost of the project from this model and the final report. A large skyscraper could cost a hundred million dollars or more and there were a lot of them in the model. He began counting them and quit when he passed one hundred.

A quick calculation indicated the buildings in the city could easily cost more than twelve billion dollars. What would Spencer say if he were told that? What if the commitments were far short of what was actually required? What would happen to the Atlantis Foundation? He had been spoiled working on large projects in the oil and gas industry. He was used to volumes of drawings describing everything in exacting detail. Usually, the project had been estimated and the money approved before he began to work on it.

He sat back and rubbed his forehead. Bill Howell had worked on buildings for years. Maybe the two of them would find a way to get an accurate estimate. He would rather Richard know up front if there was a financing issue or not. One of the buttons on his office phone was marked JOAN. He pressed it.

"Yes, Mr. Garrett--err, Jack?"

"Would you find Bill Howell and ask him to come here when he can?"

"Yes, Jack."

He laughed at the computer on his desk. It was several years old and probably only useful for email. He turned it on anyway. After it booted up, he was amazed to find over 200 email messages waiting. He wondered how many people even knew he was going to be the president of a new corporation; so far there hadn't even been a press release.

He noted almost all of the messages were from Joan. He had been copied on virtually everything she had received or sent since moving into her present position. He opened the first message. It was a note Spencer had sent to all CEOs in the group describing the new plastic, its properties, and his plans to use it to build a domed city on the coast of Mexico that would become the premier center for oceanographic research. Jack began reading all the messages. He found a lot more detailed information about the entire project in these messages than in the folders Joan had given him.

Bill Howell looked in and knocked on the doorframe. Jack didn't believe in closing his office door unless there was a good reason.

"You wanted to see me, Jack?"

"Yes, Bill. Come in and have a seat."

Bill sat down and waited for Jack to finish reading the message he was on. After a moment he pulled his chair over by the model city and examined it.

Jack finished the note. "How much do you know about this project, Bill?"

"Not too much. I'm probably here because I've built a lot of buildings under some pretty tough conditions. I have to say though; I have some doubts about the whole thing."

"So do I. Look at the city carefully."

Bill stared at it for a minute then laughed. "Looks like they used alphabet blocks for the buildings."

"How about a wild guess on the cost to build this many buildings?"

Bill leaned over and started counting until Jack saved him the trouble. "One hundred and ninety-six." Bill was wondering why Jack had asked. Didn't they have an estimate already? He stared at the model and guessed the average height to be fifty floors or so, times two hundred or so, "Somewhere between ten and fifteen billion dollars, but that's a really rough guess. Shipping costs will play a big role in the final cost. It's going in near Cancun, isn't it?"

Jack nodded. Bill had basically confirmed Jack's belief the estimate Spencer had thrown about was very low. He began to wonder about the feasibility of the project. "What can we do to minimize costs?"

Bill looked at the model again. "Well, for starters, plan to build all of them alike, except for the height, obviously. Then design and build them in identical sections wherever the labor costs are the lowest. Finally, ship them in sections for final assembly in the field. We've done this for numerous housing projects all over the world. I don't recall anyone building skyscrapers that way, but the principle should be the same."

"Are you familiar with any CAD, uh…Computer Aided Design programs?"

"Not really. You want me to do this?"

"I know someone who can help us do it."

"Sounds good to me."

In a few days, Bill and Jack developed a feasible construction plan for a number of identical 'modules', each 200 feet wide, 200 feet long and about 12 feet high. A completely assembled module would be a single floor of a skyscraper. A quick calculation of the completed modules indicated they would be far too heavy for conventional construction cranes. Bill came up with the idea of fabricating small pieces that could be further assembled into sections on the deck of a large cargo ship anchored over the city site. The module sections would then be assembled on a roller system and cranes would roll them over the side and lower them onto the foundation. The modules would then be stacked and bolted together in various heights to maximize the space within the dome. The small framework pieces of the modules would be fabricated in a new port to be built in Cancun and then shipped to the site on cargo vessels.

Jack asked Ashley to help with the design of the basic city structure. They laid out a simple grid pattern, with streets running north/south and east/west between the buildings. The streets would be 100 feet wide to avoid a crowded look. With her help, they developed a three-dimensional model of the domed city. This was then linked to a video projection system and they were able to 'walk' through the model and view it from any angle. It was tough for Jack and Bill to concentrate as they had to look over her shoulder while she built the 3D CAD model.

Spencer wanted concourses built over city streets to connect the four center buildings together at the 20th floor, envisioning a shopping mall and entertainment center on those floors. With the CAD model they were even able to see what the view from the concourses would look like. Out of curiosity, they added concourses on several higher floors and examined the view. Too many concourses ruined the view in the downtown area. Jack was relieved when they finally finished the CAD model. He invited Ashley and Bill to have a drink in a nearby restaurant but Ashley had a prior commitment. Once the drinks arrived, Bill and Jack sort of stared at each other for a minute, then started laughing.

Bill never minced words. "My god, it's hard to work near her."

Jack laughed. "I know what you mean."

A few days later, when Spencer knocked on Jack's doorframe, he found Jack and Bill staring intently at a spreadsheet on Jack's new laptop computer.

"I heard a rumor our preliminary estimate for the city portion of the project was a little low."

Jack didn't want to be the bearer of bad news, but it was better to let him know the truth before the project got too far along. "If we build it the way most buildings are built, the cost of the buildings alone would be more than fifteen billion dollars, maybe even twenty billion."

"Damn! Are you sure?"

Bill glanced up from the computer screen. "As sure as we can be without requesting quotations for material, labor and transportation costs. Based on past experience, even that number might be low."

Spencer sat down slowly on a chair in front of Jack's desk. "You said you based that estimate on building them the normal way. Have you come up with an alternative?"

"We have some ideas. We've put together a little animation, if you'd care to see it."

"Of course."

Spencer stood behind Jack as he typed in a few commands. Ashely had developed a computer simulation that showed the framework pieces being fabricated, shipped to the site, further assembled on the deck of a large cargo vessel and then lowered by crane to the ocean floor. The modules were then stacked like blocks to produce a building of the correct height.

"And this will save money?"

"Yes, because all the buildings are identical, except for the height." Bill pointed to a section on the screen. "The bottom of a module will slide into the top of the one below it. After the dome is complete and we can work inside, we'll weld the modules together. It'll then be easy to put the floor grids in and pour the floors."

"What would the cost be with this system?"

"We think it has the potential to save thirty percent. That's what we're working on now. We're almost done. If you have a few minutes, we can tell you."

"Yes, please finish. This is important. I may need to get the Board of Directors together if the cost is prohibitive." Spencer walked back to the chair and sat down as Bill and Jack finished inputting cost data into the spreadsheet for each building. They looked at each other as the final value was being calculated. They stared at the number for a moment without saying anything.

Spencer saw they weren't entering any more data. "Well, what is it? Do you have the final number?"

"Yes."

"Well, what is it?"

Jack hesitated. "Between eleven and twelve billion dollars."

Richard was surprisingly upbeat. "That's a whole lot better!"

"Do you mean eleven billion <u>is</u> possible?"

"I don't know, but I do know that fifteen or twenty billion isn't."

"I need to talk to you about the city's layout."

Jack went to a table near his desk, picked up a large printout of the layout of the city and unfolded it on his desk in front of Richard and Bill.

"I was thinking about the long-term living environment in Atlantis. Permanent residents will need some amenities, like parks and places for recreation. There isn't room for recreational areas with all these buildings, so I replaced some of them with four parks, one on each quadrant, as you can see."

Jack pointed to the layout drawing and Spencer studied it. "That's a wonderful idea. I don't know why we didn't think of that before. What would the parks cost?"

"They wouldn't cost anything. In fact, we'd save a lot of money not building in these sections. The cost of trees and other greenery are insignificant."

Spencer was excited that the desirable amenities reduced the cost of the project. "How much would we save?"

Jack picked up a calculator and pressed a few buttons. "About ten percent, or a little more than a billion dollars."

"Does it lower the cost of building the city to ten billion dollars?"

Jack nodded. "It should, to a little less than ten."

"This is outstanding! I know I can sell this! We may have to split Phase Three into two phases, with the last of the buildings built a few years later, but that would certainly be acceptable."

Spencer paused as if trying to remember something.

"Oh, yes. What about the building foundations? Any progress?"

"Yes, Dr. Hart helped us finalize the bottom row connection to the foundation."

"Excellent. I'm glad we could borrow her from Future for a while."

Jack and Bill were glad too for the daylong meetings that sometimes ended in a nearby pub for dinner. Future plastics had suggested assembling one of the smaller domes first for use as a workspace to construct a section of the main dome. The dome would then be flooded and moved to construct the remaining sections. The report also recommended the construction dome have a submarine docking station to transport the construction crews back and forth. The final report on the construction of the dome had left the remaining details to the project team.

"Yes." Jack unrolled a large drawing of a deck of a supertanker, laying it on top of the plot plan for Atlantis. "We'll need a large surface area to assemble the building modules at the site, so we plan to use an oil supertanker instead of a cargo ship to transport the concrete components to the site. We'll convert a part of the supertanker to quarters for the construction crew that will live on board in the beginning. Also, concrete made with seawater has some undesirable characteristics, so we'll install a desalination plant on board. That will also provide fresh water for the construction crew. We'll mix the concrete on the tanker and pump it down to the construction dome."

"How will you handle the heavy construction equipment needed to dig the foundations?"

"We've asked Future Plastics to construct a large container that will be mounted inside the construction dome. We'll move the equipment inside before we move the dome to the next area. They felt certain it would work."

"What about the submarines for the construction crews?"

"We've already placed orders for the first two, the *Sea Horse* and the *Sea Urchin*. When construction is finished, they'll ferry the visitors and guests to and from the new port and the city."

"What about the buoyancy problem with the construction dome?"

Bill answered for Jack, "We'll put multi-ton weights on the top to hold it down and then remove a few until it just floats. We should be able to move it to the next section with the engines of the supertanker."

Spencer was beaming. "Well done, you two."

He shook their hands and walked out humming.

"Looks like we did some good."

Jack laughed. "We may have just saved our jobs."

Chapter 10

Howard Singleton walked up a flight of stairs and settled onto the end of a long wooden bench on an open-air suburban platform as he waited for the next subway train. Alan Sands and Bill Johnson watched as he placed his briefcase on the floor next to him, put an e-cigarette in his mouth and began to peruse the morning edition of the Times.

Alan Sands sensed Bill was nervous. "Bill, don't do this. You still have a clean record. He isn't worth it."

"My dad's dead because of them and Singleton's the worst of all. I know what I'm doing."

Sands shook his head and walked down the stairs to his car to wait for Johnson.

Johnson knew Singleton's daily ritual by heart and walked slowly over to stand next to his bench. He casually placed an identical briefcase on the floor next to Singleton's. Three scraggly youths bounded up the stairs to the platform as Johnson took out a cell phone.

Even though the platform was crowded with early morning commuters, several businessmen in suits and tourists with cameras slowly made an effort to move away from what most would guess to be gang members. One by one, the youths wandered over and stood in front of Singleton. One took out a pack of cigarettes, fumbled for a lighter in his pockets and turned to Singleton.

"Mate... got a light?"

Singleton looked up at the three hooligans in front of him and felt his heart racing in the eminent fear of being robbed. The platform was crowded but there were no security personnel in sight. While Singleton's attention was diverted, Johnson pretended to sneeze and blow his nose. He glanced at the youths as he casually reached down, picked up Howard's briefcase and started walking off.

Singleton shook his head and showed the youth his e-cigarette. He was totally oblivious to Johnson. The youth turned to another commuter and Howard let out a deep sigh when they turned away. Johnson paused at the top of the stairs to smirk at Singleton's predicament when the youths suddenly turned back toward Singleton. One pushed him backward while a second grabbed his wallet from his coat pocket. The third grabbed his briefcase and they ran down the stairs.

Johnson almost bolted after them but Singleton yelled and two security officers on the lower level began to chase them. Johnson cursed at the youths, the railway, Singleton and his bad luck. It had taken Alan Sands months to find an identical briefcase and the small but powerful bomb he had placed inside it. Johnson glanced at Singleton who was watching the security officers chase the thieves and laughed. If they did get away, they certainly would have an unpleasant surprise when they opened the briefcase.

As he walked quickly down the stairs, he realized he was still holding Singleton's briefcase. He wondered if there was anything useful in it. When he was out of Singleton's sight, he used a small knife to pry the locks open. Just as he was about to open it, he noticed a small scratch on one of the locks. *That looks familiar,* he thought.

A powerful explosion rocked the crowded platform and screams erupted from the commuters. Some fell off the platform but Singleton and several other commuters managed to grab onto the railing. Many more commuters were injured in a mad rush to get off the platform. As he struggled to stand, Singleton's head was hurting. He was fortunate the concrete floor of the platform had shielded him from most of the force of the explosion.

Michael Baker knocked on the frame of Jack's office door and walked quickly in. Jack was on the phone, but Baker signaled him and turned on a television. Jack hung up quickly and they watched a special broadcast on the BBC.

"A tube platform crowded with early morning commuters was almost leveled from a powerful explosion early this morning. Three died and scores were wounded..."

Baker turned the television off. "Howard was on the platform."

Jack's face turned white. "Is he all right?"

"He called from the hospital. He has a few cuts and bruises, but he'll be all right."

"Thank God!" Jack sat down heavily on a nearby chair. "Do they know who's responsible?"

"No group has claimed responsibility."

Jack stared at him for a moment. "Could Howard have been the target?"

"I don't think so. There was an aide to a Member of Parliament on the platform. It's more likely he was the target."

"I hope you're right."

Chapter 11

Michael Baker was reading his email when an urgent message came in from a former colleague in British intelligence. He scanned the note and forwarded it to Spencer and Jack.

Michael:

Informants confirm terrorist elements in AJ6, M23 and D45 are aware of new S.I. project and have targeted it for disruption. Believe the following individuals may be involved. More information when available.

Baker printed several photographs attached to the note and was studying them when Constantine Carballo, his assistant, knocked on his door.

"Come in."

Carballo peeked in. "Michael, we are waiting for you to review the latest security background checks on the construction crew."

"Oh, sorry! I have to visit the head, first. I'll meet you there." As Baker hurried off, Carballo noticed the pictures on his desk. He looked out the door and quickly sat down, read the note and forwarded a copy to himself. He picked up the pictures and thumbed through them until he came to a picture of a man with dark eyes, dark curly hair and a beard. He laughed. "This picture doesn't do you justice, Abdul," he muttered as he stuffed the picture into his pants pocket. He glanced back at the computer screen, clicked on Abdul's picture file and pressed the DELETE button. He carefully put everything back like it was and hurried out of the office to beat Michael to the review meeting.

Abdul Rahim had spent a frustrating week in Cancun trying to learn the location of the new Spencer Industries project. The only land purchase of any significance had been to The Atlantis Corporation, a new company desiring to build a shipping dock. Where could it be? Rahim had spent a considerable amount of time in bars buying drinks for laborers, businessmen and even lawyers in hopes of learning its location. He was becoming anxious as the frequent calls from Mohammed Skerchi were becoming more and more urgent, almost threatening. Unfortunately, he was the only member of the Party fluent enough in Spanish to not draw suspicion on them as they searched for the site of the new project.

He motioned to the bartender and was fishing some money out of his pocket as Ernesto Sanchez entered the bar with some friends and started bragging about a new job with The Atlantis Corporation and some crazy story about building a city on the ocean floor. Rahim thanked Allah for his good fortune. He ordered drinks for Ernesto and his friends as he congratulated him on his new job.

Chapter 12

Joan was working intently on her computer and didn't notice Jack and Bill walk in until Jack cleared his throat. Joan jumped, knocking an empty water bottle to the floor.

"Oh, I'm sorry, Joan. I didn't mean to startle you."

Joan picked up the bottle and tossed it into the trashcan. "That's all right, Jack. How can I be of assistance?"

"Bill, Howard and I are going to negotiate the final deal for the oil tanker. Bill and I are mainly interested in the technical aspects of the tanker and Howard usually focuses on the terms and conditions. I wonder if you'd like to come along to help with the overall deal from a buyer's perspective. This is your specialty, after all."

Joan was thrilled. "I'd love to. I've gone over some of the purchasing issues with Howard, but there are other areas I can help with."

Bill raised a concern. "You know, Jack, we won't be dealing with the owners directly. We'll have to work with their broker and I've dealt with them before. I think we need to give Joan a different title or they won't take her seriously. They still have a good ole boy attitude."

Jack laughed. "Perhaps you're right. Joan, get some cards printed identifying you as the Director of Purchasing. The meeting's in Dallas in two weeks."

"Right away, Jack. I really appreciate this opportunity."

"I'm sure you can help. I'll forward you an email with the

meeting information on it later today. You can make the reservations for all of us," Jack said as they left.

Joan was determined to show them what she could do. She needed the folder back from Howard on the negotiations on the tanker so far. She walked out of her office and collided with Emma, who was coming in to see her.

"Do you have a minute, Joan?"

"Of course, please sit down." She sat down at her desk.

"Do you know someone named April Turner?"

"I just made some reservations for her to fly to London and stay at the Royal Horseguards. Why do you want to know?"

"Do you know the purpose of her visit?"

"Not exactly. Jack just asked me to make the reservations."

"I had lunch with Michael Baker to get some information for his biography for a press release. We discussed a lot of things and he casually mentioned Jack has just hired someone to be in charge of all the ships and vessels the corporation will use to build Atlantis."

"Yes, I know. His name is George Atwell. He worked at Allied with Jack for a number of years. What does this have to do with April Turner?"

Emma seemed reluctant to continue. "George Atwell is from New York and Jack used to visit him there sometimes. A few years ago, George introduced him to April Turner. She's the pastor of George's family's church there. April is Jack's girlfriend."

"Girlfriend?"

"Michael didn't say 'fiancée', he said 'girlfriend'," Emma added.

Joan hoped her disappointment didn't show, but it did.

"I just wanted to let you know," Emma smiled. "I was disappointed, too."

Joan waited at Heathrow Airport for April Turner's early morning flight to arrive. It certainly wasn't her job to show April around, but Joan had volunteered. She was more than curious as she waited for the passengers to exit the security barrier. She held a sign for APRIL TURNER and after a few moments a woman younger than Joan would have guessed came over and introduced herself. April was slender, well dressed, with brown curly hair and brown eyes. She had a warm personality and Joan thought she was probably an excellent pastor.

April held out her hand. "Hello, you must be Joan Mason. My name is April Turner."

Joan shook her hand. "I'm pleased to meet you. I've been Jack's assistant for several months. I didn't know if you'd ever been to London before, so I offered to show you the sites."

"That's very nice of you, Joan."

Joan helped April collect her luggage and drove her to the Royal Horseguards Hotel. There was a note from Jack waiting for April at the check-in desk, inviting her to dinner that evening.

Joan offered to show April the usual tourist spots. "We'll be back in time for you to get ready for dinner."

April accepted and they left with the intention of getting to know each other more than seeing the sites.

They became friends during the week April was in London. Because Jack had numerous meetings, Joan spent more time with April than Jack did. She was actually sorry to see April leave and hugged her good-bye before she passed through security and boarded the plane.

The next day Ashley happened to be in Emma's office when Joan entered and Emma asked her about April's visit. Ashley listened intently as Emma and Joan speculated why April and Jack weren't married or at least engaged. Ashley just smiled as the conversation provided exactly the information she needed.

Ashley had been away from her friends and family in Seattle for almost a year and was lonely. Two weeks after April's visit, Ashely was in a day-long meeting with Jack and at the end, he suggested dinner at a pub. After they ordered, she mentioned missing her friends.

"A beautiful and smart woman like you shouldn't have any problem meeting people." Jack meant that as a compliment, but she wasn't sure how he meant it.

"Most of the men I've met here are boring and only want one thing."

"Surely there are some that aren't boring. What about Michael Baker? He was in counterintelligence in the military."

"He's okay but we don't have anything in common."

"What about Bill Howell? He's worked all over the world. I know he's a little eccentric, but he's a nice guy."

"Bill's more of a beer guy, than a wine guy."

She finished her drink and smiled at him. Jack was wondering what was next when she asked.

"What about you Jack?"

"What do you mean?"

She smiled at his surprised expression.

 "Are you seeing anyone?"

Jack blushed. "I sort of have a girlfriend. She's really nice, but we don't have a lot in common."

She leaned forward and stared at his eyes. He was unable to look away.

"Why don't we give it a try?   I won't tell anyone and it could be fun."

Jack was lost in her eyes and speechless. And now her perfume was in his consciousness. He wanted to remind her that he was her boss, at least until she went back to Future Plastics but he couldn't get it to come out of his mouth. She saw him struggling to answer and put her hand on his. "I'm not talking about a long-term relationship…"

The food arrived and Jack just stared at her, trying to figure out what to do. Ashley stood up walked around the table and kissed him on the cheek. "I'll be right back."

He watched her walk off, still dazed at what had just happened.

When Ashley returned from the bathroom, Jack was still sitting at the table staring off into space. She smiled and kissed him on the lips and sat back down. "So, Jack. What about it?"

He really wanted to, but something kept him from telling her yes. He slowly shook his head. "I'm really attracted to you, Ashley, but I have a girlfriend. Right now, it's not where either of us want it to be, but if we can work it out, it could be great."

Ashley was disappointed but not deterred.

"Want to see what you'd be missing…tonight?"

Jack laughed, but not too loudly.

Chapter 13

Negotiations with Trans-Global Marine for an oil supertanker progressed well in the beginning. Trans-Global negotiators already referred to it as the *Eye of Atlantis* as they represented the ship's owner as well as the dry-dock company that would convert the oil tanker to meet their needs. The engines were powerful, and the hull was in good shape. It could easily be reinforced to transport the components of concrete. The deck was over a thousand feet long, more than adequate for the assembly of the building modules and there was also ample room that could be converted into quarters for the construction crew.

Howard was satisfied with the basic terms and conditions of the contract, but Joan dragged the meeting into a third day over minute details on conversion schedule and delivery from the dry dock and, of course, the final price. Jack, Bill and Howard left the meeting periodically to make phone calls on other transactions that were underway. Jack was tempted to take over the negotiations but decided to give Joan one more day to finish the deal.

Bill had been right about Trans-Global's attitude. Initially they had not taken Joan seriously, until they realized they were negotiating with her instead of Jack or Howard.

Jack and Bill were in a conference call in another meeting room negotiating a price for the land needed to build the new resort near Atlantis when Bill Miller, lead negotiator for Trans-Global Marine, knocked on the door and entered.

"Mr. Garrett, Mr. Howell, we think we have finally reached an agreement. We would like you to rejoin the meeting as soon as you can."

"We'll be right there."

When Miller left, Bill remarked, "He didn't look very happy."

Joan smiled at them when they entered the room. It was apparent the other members of the Trans-Global team were not very happy either.

As they sat down, Miller addressed them. "We've been in contact with the ship's owner and the dry-dock company. Both have agreed to the fifteen-percent clause you asked for. We told them we didn't agree, but they insisted and after all, it's their ship and dry-dock facility."

Jack and Bill tried to hide their surprise. As the agent for the two companies, Trans-Global had agreed on the price based on an aggressive nine-month schedule for the dry dock conversion. If they delivered it in ten months or more, the final price would be reduced by fifteen percent. The dry-dock facility and the ship's owner would then have to determine how they would share the loss in revenue.

Joan had such a Cheshire Cat smile that Jack chuckled as he sat down next to her. "That's excellent. When can you have the papers drawn up?"

"We're working on it right now. The contract was complete, except for that clause, so it should be ready after lunch. We'd like to take you to lunch to celebrate closing the deal."

Miller sat next to Jack during lunch. He had been surprised the companies they represented had accepted the price/delivery clause Joan had insisted on. "She's a tough negotiator, Jack. I wish I had someone like her on my team."

After witnessing Trans-Global's attitude toward Joan in the beginning, this was quite a surprise to Jack. He looked across the table at Joan, who was engaged in a lively conversation with one of their vice presidents. Jack had taken some criticism when word had leaked out within Spencer Industries that Jack was holding the Director of Purchasing position for Joan. He had been right about her being the best person for the position. Maybe she should help in the negotiations for the two supply ships needed to ferry all the construction materials from the port to the new city's site.

When Joan returned to her office after the purchasing trip, she was surprised to find a letter marked CONFIDENTIAL on the top of the pile of mail waiting on her desk. It was a letter from Jack and Howard, thanking her for her help in securing timely delivery of the oil tanker. She screamed in delight at the bonus check of ten thousand pounds attached to the letter.

When she showed it Susan, she held it up to the light to see if it was real.

Chapter 14

Joan was a little surprised, less than a month later, when Jack asked her to make reservations for April Turner again. When Joan met her at the airport, April unloaded her frustrations regarding her relationship with Jack. She had even taken the unusual step of contacting Jack's first wife and asking about their marriage. April had finally come to the conclusion Jack was more interested in his current project than in maintaining a relationship. She had not been surprised to find that his first marriage had failed due to long absences. April didn't want to follow the same path as his first wife. She would try to get some kind of commitment from Jack this weekend or, reluctantly, give up on him.

Unfortunately, April picked a very stressful week for Jack. Again, she spent more time with Joan than with Jack, who attended daylong meetings with Ashley to figure out the final logistics for pouring the concrete foundations of the domes.

Joan tried to comfort her as they waited for her plane back to New York, but April surprised her. "Maybe you'll have better luck with him than his first wife or I did."

Joan was more than a little shocked. "What do you mean?"

"Someday Jack will realize he has a treasure right under his nose. I just hope you can figure out a way to get enough of his attention to be happy."

"I don't know what you're talking about. I'm not in love with him," Joan declared, a little bit too forcibly.

"I'm a people-person, Joan." April smiled. "Helping people

is my business, so here's some advice: Things worth having won't fall into your lap. You have to work for them. If you can ever honestly say you do love him, then take advantage of whatever opportunity avails itself to show him you do."

April hugged Joan good-bye. She stopped at the entrance to the security barrier and waved. Joan fought back tears as she waved back. She would miss April. She also wondered why April thought she was in love with Jack. Was it something she said?

The next day, Ashley stopped by to tell Emma that she had to return to Future Plastics. Joan happened to be in Emma's office discussing April's latest trip but Joan didn't mention April's advice to her. Ashely was shocked that April had finally broken off her relationship with Jack. Emma and Joan were shocked at Ashley's leaving and both hugged her. She said Jack had tried to change her mind, but she was determined to go.

Back in her office, she closed the door and kicked the trashcan over. One lousy day…if she had only waited one lousy day to tell Jack, he would have undoubtedly told her his relationship with April was over and Jack might have agreed to a short term, but highly satisfying relationship.

Chapter 15

At fifteen minutes before the start of the midnight shift, Ernesto Sanchez drove his pickup truck to the main gate of the new dock and port facility the Atlantis Corporation was building near Cancun. He watched the guard turn a lever on a gumball machine and hold up a white ball. He breathed a deep sigh of relief. A black ball would require a search of the truck. Luckily, most of the gumballs in the machine were white. He drove to a dark area near an enormous warehouse and stopped. He pulled a tarp off the bed and ran for a door of the warehouse. Three former executives of Future Plastics pulled black ski masks over their faces and jumped out of the truck, slung backpacks over their shoulders and ran to stand near him. Ernesto swiped his card key in a card reader and held the door open for them.

"Where's the larger crane?" demanded Alan Sands between several deep breaths as he pulled his ski mask off. The former head of security was out of shape and straining under the weight of his large backpack.

"Over there," replied Sanchez, pointing to a large hulking shape in a darkened portion of the warehouse. "But you can't do anything right now. The midnight shift starts in a few minutes and someone may come in here."

"Well, when can we start?" Sands was becoming impatient. Brian Hill and Carl Bond were shaking in fear wishing they had not agreed to this crazy idea of Sands.

"If no one comes in thirty minutes, it will be safe. I have to go and report to my foreman. Good luck." Sanchez quietly closed the door and ran for the men's locker room in the main shop building. Sands looked at his watch and motioned them behind a large crate, where they laid their backpacks on the floor with sighs of relief.

Sands fumed. Four laborers spent over two hours unloading large crates into the warehouse. Ironically, the crates were tagged with the familiar logo of Future Plastics. They finally closed the warehouse door and the 'strike team' heard a tractor trailer drive off.

"Christ," Sands hissed. "That took forever."

They picked up their backpacks and ran to a large construction crane, pulled its tarp off and started examining it. They stared in disbelief at a stainless-steel braided cable six inches in diameter.

Bond could barely lift the hook on the end of the cable. "This is the biggest damn cable I've ever seen! It must weigh a ton!"

"We'll never be able to cut this." Hill ran his fingers over the huge cable.

"We can cut it, but we need to pull out about two hundred feet so the cut won't be visible." Sands looked around and spied a forklift. "Bring the forklift over here." He jumped inside the cab of the crane and pulled on the cable release lever.

Bond maneuvered the forklift near the crane and Hill tied the end of the cable to it. The forklift complained loudly, but slowly pulled the huge cable across the floor.

Sands carefully took a portable concrete saw out of his backpack and took the regular blade off. He watched Hill start to open a small round package. "Be careful with that blade it's really sharp and--"

He was interrupted by a scream from Hill. Bond ran over and put his hand on Hill's mouth as he bent over with pain. The ends of two of Hill's fingers were missing and blood was dripping on the floor. Hill almost passed out from the pain and sudden drop in blood pressure. Bond took a knife out of his pocket, cut one of the sleeves off his shirt and wrapped it around Hill's finger and hand. "We'll get you to a hospital as soon as we're finished. Just hold on." He helped Hill sit down on the floor against the crane and very carefully finished taking a strange looking sawblade out of its packing.

"Be careful with the blade! It cost five thousand dollars." Sands voice was quiet yet forceful. "It has a special coating of industrial diamonds, tungsten carbide and cobalt crystals on it."

Bond gingerly put the blade on the saw and waited. Sands opened the door, looked around and signaled to Bond.

Bond pulled goggles over his eyes, started the saw and pressed the blade against the cable. An eerie blue glow lit the warehouse as the blade sliced through the cable. He watched fascinated, as the metal strands almost seemed to vaporize as the blade moved forward.

It went faster than Bond expected. He quickly turned the saw off. "Oh, shit!"

Sands ran back to him. "What the hell's wrong now?"

"It went through it like butter. I couldn't help it," protested Bond.

The cable had been cut almost two thirds of the way through.

"You idiot! It might break now when they lower the damn

dome, instead of when they pick it up." Sands pointed his gun at Bond, who almost fainted.

"I'm sorry. You should have done it. What difference does it make, anyway?"

"The dome's weighted when they're lowering it. If the cable broke then, it would just sink to the ocean floor. If the cable breaks when they're lifting it, it could float away from them, and they could lose it."

Bond was still cringing from the gun in his face. Sands forced himself to calm down and lowered his gun. He looked around quickly. "It's too late now to do anything about it. Let's put everything back and get the hell out of here." He jumped in the crane, fired up its massive diesel engine and started reeling in the huge cable.

The first attempt to pour a section of the main dome's foundation surpassed their expectations. When it had adequately hardened, Jack and Bill inspected it and found it to be well within the design specification. They entered the *Sea Horse* and were on the bridge of the little submarine as it undocked from the construction dome and backed up some.

The last procedure to be tested was underway as the construction equipment was driven into the waiting container. The construction crew entered the *Sea Urchin* and the construction dome was filled with water. John Darrow, captain of the *Sea Horse*, maneuvered the submarine to a point near the top of the construction dome and used its grappling hook to connect the hook of a crane on the *Eye of Atlantis* to one of the large weights from the top. The crane lifted it off and after a few more weights were removed, the larger crane on the *Eye* began to lift the dome from the sea floor. The *Eye* began to get underway, pulling the dome and crate over to the next location. They were watching the dome's relocation when it suddenly started floating near the ocean floor. Jack's radio crackled.

"Atwell to Garrett! Jack, the main support cable just snapped!"

"That's impossible!" Bill shouted. "Isn't the cable six inches thick?"

Jack nodded. He was thinking that the only thing holding the dome was the large plastic tube used to pump air down to it and a smaller tube inside air tube that served as the conduit for concrete pumped down for the foundations. The gentle current that they usually ignored was now dragging the dome away from the foundation and toward a cliff on the ocean floor. If the air tube broke, the dome would go over the cliff and down into a trench over a mile deep. The loss of the construction dome would set them back many months.

"Garrett to Atwell! Come in George!"

"Atwell here."

"Can you pull it back with the *Eye*?"

"The ship's engines probably could do it, Jack, but the transport tube is stretched to its limit. It's weakening under the strain of holding the dome. I don't think it'll last much longer."

"If the tube breaks, George, we'll lose the dome in the trench!"

"I know, Jack! We can follow the dome with the *Eye* while we try to pull it up, but I don't think the transfer tube is strong enough. It'll break if we try to lift the dome with it. Our crane was damaged when the cable broke. I don't know if we can repair it quickly enough or not."

"What if we used the other crane on the 'Eye'? We can hook it into the dome with the *Sea Horse*."

"It might work, but hurry! The transfer tube won't last very long."

Captain John Darrow looked at Jack. "I'm onto it already, Mr. Garrett."

"Can you snare it with the grappling hooks?"

Darrow flashed a searchlight on the smaller crane's hook. It was bouncing around in the ocean currents. "I don't know, but I'll try."

He maneuvered the submarine near the smaller crane's hook, and after a few attempts, he grabbed it with the *Sea Horse*'s small grappling hook.

Jack slapped him on the back. "Great job! Now let's see if we can hook it on the dome somehow."

The *Sea Horse* maneuvered near the construction dome, which had drifted closer to the trench. There wasn't any place on the dome to attach the hook.

Desperation was on Darrow's face as he turned to Jack. "What now? We'll be over the trench soon."

Bill and Jack looked at each other, each hoping the other would come up with something. Jack searched a 3D graphic of the dome on his laptop while Bill maneuvered the powerful searchlight over its surface. When the light illuminated the top, he yelled, "What about the air vent valve on the top of the dome?"

Jack slapped him on the back. "That's it! Let's go for it!"

The captain maneuvered the hook into the valve body.

"Garrett to Atwell. Try to pull the dome up with the second crane, George."

The crane began to lift the dome until the transfer tube broke and the sea currents almost flipped the dome over. The broken dome cable wrapped around the tower of the *Sea Horse* and pulled it down to the sea floor. A slow steady current dragged the sub and dome along the bottom. In a matter of minutes, the dome would be over the trench, with the submarine ensnared in its broken cable.

"George!" Jack shouted into the mike, "The dome's broken cable is wrapped around the tower of the 'Sea Horse'. We can't get free! Try to pull the dome up!"

If the smaller cable broke and they were dragged down into the trench, the submarine would be crushed as it wasn't rated for such a high pressure.

"Atwell to Garrett. The smaller crane can't lift the dome and the sub by itself, and the larger crane won't work at all from all the stress it took."

Jack fought off a panic attack. He looked at Bill. "Where's the *Sea Urchin*?"

Bill shrugged. "George would know."

"Where's the *Urchin*, George?" Jack shouted into the microphone of his radio.

"It's tied up next to the *Eye*. Do you want it? The captain, Mike Stowers, is here on the bridge with me."

"Tell him to get here as quickly as he can! Then find something heavy to put on the top of the main crane's tower and then cut it loose."

On the *Eye of Atlantis*'s bridge, Stowers and George exchanged perplexed looks. "What are you trying to do?"

"I'm hoping we can stick the crane's tower into the ocean floor and use it like an anchor to stop the dome. We need the *Urchin* to keep the tower from slipping out of the hole it'll make when it hits the ocean floor."

"Mike heard you. He's on his way."

"Hurry with the weight for the crane, George! We don't have much time!"

"We're working on it now, Jack."

Bill tapped Jack on the shoulder. "Shouldn't the *Sea Urchin* try to free us first? I mean the dome is important, but..."

"He'll have to cut the cable off with a torch. It'll take too long to get retrofitted with a cutting torch. There won't be time to stop the dome--and us--from being dragged down the trench. We have to stop the dome first and then try to get free."

The *Sea Urchin* waited as the tower was weighted and cut loose from the crane on the *Eye*. The top of the crane's tower plunged and buried itself in the sea floor. The *Sea Urchin* quickly grappled onto the other end of the tower, holding it upright so it wouldn't be dragged out of the hole it was in. As the dome and submarine dragged it, the point of the tower dug deeper into the sea floor, slowing the dome down until there was no forward motion.

Jack let out a deep sigh of relief and he had a sudden

inspiration. He grabbed the radio's mike again. "George! Lower the anchor of the *Eye* as quickly as you can!"

"It's on its way."

The anchor plunged into the seabed. Jack called the captain of the *Sea Urchin*. "Jack Garrett to Mike Stowers. Come in, Mike."

"Stowers here, Jack."

"Get a cutting torch put on the front and cut us free."

"I'm on my way."

Leaving the crane's tower stuck like a flagpole in the seabed, Stowers revved the sub's engines and surfaced. After a tense thirty minutes, he finally returned with the cutting torch attached. From the bridge of the *Sea Horse*, they could see the bottom of the *Sea Urchin* as it maneuvered above them. Stowers grabbed the cable with his grappling hook and fired up the cutting torch. Flashes from the torch lit up the bridge of the 'Sea Horse' and the inky black water around them. They heard something snap and suddenly they were free. Darrow shoved the engines into reverse and backed away.

"We're free, George!" Jack yelled into the mike.

The crew on the *Eye* cheered.

"Atwell to Garrett. Jack, one of the supply ships is here. They have a small crane that, with ours, can probably lift the dome. We'll lower the hook in a few minutes."

"Thanks, George. Garrett out."

Jack sat down and let the tension drain away. Bill wiped his face on his shirt sleeve.

"Stowers to Mr. Garrett."

Jack's radio buzzed. "Mike Stowers to Jack Garrett".

"Yes, Mike?"

"It looks like the cable on the large crane was cut almost in two. That's why it broke."

Bill, Jack and John Darrow looked at each other in disbelief.

"Say it again, Mike?"

"I have the dome's cable here in the grappling hook. I am pretty sure it was cut almost two-thirds of the way through where it broke."

Bill made a circle using both of his hands. "How can you cut a steel cable this thick?"

Jack shook his head. "I don't know, but we're going to find out."

Michael Baker began a thorough investigation.

After two months he reluctantly concluded he could find no evidence of sabotage other than the cut cable. But he also couldn't explain a faint bloodstain on the floor of the warehouse where the crane had been stored. DNA testing of the stain also failed to find a match in any criminal database.

Chapter 16

It was Thursday afternoon and Joan worked feverishly so she could leave early. The lease on her apartment had expired and she had planned to take Friday off to start moving to a new apartment.

There was a knock on the door and Jack Garrett entered. Joan stood and mentally kicked herself when she remembered the picture of Jack on her desk. She knew it was a bad idea, but Jack never visited anyone's office unless there was a problem. She had happened to be in the corporate photographer's studio picking up promotional material when she saw some photos of Jack for a press release. She had slipped one into a nearby brochure and somehow it wound up on her desk. Susan had seen it and chided her for having a crush on her boss. She denied it, of course, but she hadn't put the picture away either.

Jack smiled at her surprised expression and noticed her dark blue dress. "Joan, I need a big favor." He walked to a chair in front of her desk and sat down. She breathed a little easier and sat back down. He couldn't see the picture from there.

"I need your help preparing for Monday's mid-year review with the financiers and government officials of the Atlantis Foundation. We may have to work all weekend. You'll get compensation time, of course."

"Oh, Jack, I can't! My landlord wouldn't renew my lease and I have to move to a new apartment this weekend."

"The company will move you. Pick any moving company you

like, but I need your help to get the presentation finalized. I would really appreciate it."

The thought of the company moving her was wonderful. She hated moving.

Jack looked around her office while he waited for her answer. She had to keep him from seeing his picture on her desk so she stood up, nonchalantly walked around her desk and sat down on it in front of him. It was awkward because her dress was a little tight. He couldn't help noticing her legs, since they were right in front of him. She smiled when she saw him looking at them. When he looked up at her, he smiled back.

"It would be wonderful to have someone move me and to pack all my things, but...." She let her voice trail off and leaned back on her hands. When he wasn't looking, she put his picture face down.

"Don't you have a friend who could be there while they're doing that? I mean, you must have arranged for some friends to help you."

"Yes, but--"

"Oh, come now. Moving isn't that big of a deal. You can't have that much in an apartment. I'm sure professionals could move you in less than a day."

The desk was pretty uncomfortable. She shifted her weight from one side of her rear to the other and almost fell off the desk. Jack laughed and grabbed her hand to keep her from falling. "Careful."

"All right. I'll find someone. When will you need me to help with the presentation?"

He stood up. "Why don't you take tomorrow off and be there when they pack your things? I'll go ahead and start on the presentation. We can finish it Saturday."

"What time would you like me to be here on Saturday?" Her rear hurt so she scooted forward to stand up and bumped into him.

He laughed again.

"I'm sorry, Jack."

"That's okay. Any time after nine on Saturday is fine."

She breathed a sigh of relief as he walked out. Rubbing her rear before sitting down, she picked the picture up and stared at it. Had he seen it?

Her pulse had almost returned to normal. She picked up the phone and called the transportation department. She would let them find her a mover. She looked at his picture as she waited for the call to go through.

Corporate headquarters was nearly deserted on Saturday. Joan passed only one other non-security employee on the way to Jack's office. She felt strange wearing jeans and a sweater to work.

The door to Jack's office was open and she saw him at a small conference table, watching part of the presentation on a laptop. A projected image of the presentation filled a nearby screen. She was glad he wore jeans and a casual shirt. She knocked lightly on the doorframe and Jack waved her in.

He had been working almost non-stop on the mid-year review and was less than half finished when Joan appeared. He breathed a sigh of relief. Joan was proficient at making presentation slides, using several different graphics programs. She could take his sketches and portray exactly what he wanted.

He glanced at her. She had taken off her overcoat to reveal a tight black sweater and jeans. He had never seen her in anything but dresses or business suits. He was impressed. She was even slimmer than he would have guessed.

She walked over and stood next to him, looking through a printout of his completed overheads. Her perfume drifted into his consciousness. "I'm sure glad you're here. I'm not very good at making presentation material."

"These are pretty good."

He handed her a small stack of papers with sketches for the next slides. She went to his computer and began typing. He watched her for a moment. When he realized he was staring, he looked away.

They worked all day on the presentation, and Jack had lunch delivered, promising to take her out to dinner. When they finished the presentation, his computer finally finished shutting down just as Joan returned from a quick trip to the powder room.

Jack held her overcoat open. "Are you ready to go?"

"Ready."

He helped her and then put his own coat on. "Where would you like to eat?"

She laughed a little. "I think it would have to be some place rather casual, don't you?"

"I know just the place."

He chose a noisy pub not far from the headquarters building. Apparently, he was a regular there as everyone seemed to know him. They sat down and ordered. A soccer game was on the television behind the bar and a small but dedicated group of fans argued over each play. Another crowd was gathered around a dartboard. Joan watched the crowd and looked at the decorations.

Jack realized he was looking at her lips, wondering why she used such a bright red lipstick. Her hair was like raven feathers, a dark blue when the light shined on it a certain way and black as coal the rest of the time. Her hair was probably shoulder length, but she always had it tied up on her head. Her eyes were almost black as coals. He wondered why she usually wore such dark dresses and suits. Her makeup somehow seemed to emphasize how pale she was. He even wondered if she ever went outside in the sunshine.

He really didn't know that much about her, even though they had worked together for a year and a half. She always seemed to be in a good mood. She was efficient, punctual, and always helpful. There really wasn't much personal information in her employment file; he had looked one afternoon out of curiosity. He knew she had taken care of her mother for years and that her mother had recently died. He also knew she wasn't married. He wondered if she had a boyfriend.

"This is a pretty nice place. I've never been here before."

"The food's pretty good."

"Do you eat here a lot, Jack?"

He nodded. "I live near here. I rarely eat in my apartment.

It's too boring."

She wondered if his life could possibly be as boring as hers.

The food arrived and they began eating. There was a lot of small talk during the meal. Both enjoyed having someone to share a meal with.

When the taxi arrived in front of her apartment, Joan began to put her gloves on.

"Did you get all your stuff moved all right?"

"Yes. But I have a royal mess up there."

"I'm sorry. I guess that's my fault."

"It's okay. It would've been a mess in any case."

"Is there anything I can do to help?" he offered.

She laughed at the thought of the company president moving her furniture, but he was waiting for an answer. She suddenly remembered the old dresser that had been her mother's. It was extremely heavy, and she doubted that her girlfriends could help her move it.

"Well, maybe you could help me move my dresser. It's pretty heavy for me."

"Of course."

He paid for the taxi and they walked up four flights to her apartment. Her new apartment was very nice, with polished wooden floors and expensive draperies. It was a mess, though, with boxes everywhere and furniture placed haphazardly.

"They left it like this?"

"They finished so late; I had to spend the night in a hotel." She didn't tell him how hard it had been to find a moving company on such short notice, or the premium the company had paid.

"What do you want to move first?" He took off his overcoat.

"Jack, I couldn't ask you to do that."

"Don't be ridiculous. I can't leave it like this." He waited for her to say something.

"I guess I need help putting the bed back together." She avoided looking at him, but he didn't seem to mind.

"Do you have any tools?"

She looked around and spotted the toolbox her father had given her. "Here," she said, handing it to him.

She followed him to the bedroom, where he found the bed frame in pieces. He set it up and they put the bed back together. He moved the dresser and a few small things while she made the bed. When she finished, she found him moving some living room furniture. "Jack, that's enough. Please."

"Okay."

"Would you like a beer? I'm pretty sure they're cold now."

He nodded and she went to get him one, knowing he liked his beer cold. He was sitting on the sofa as she returned with two beers. She sat down next to him and handed him one. They smiled at each other as they drank. She looked at her watch; it was almost one in the morning.

He saw her looking at her watch and looked at his. "I probably should go." He quickly finished his beer.

As she watched him throw his beer bottle in the trashcan, she wished she had the nerve to ask him to stay, but she couldn't force it out of her mouth. What if she asked and he didn't want to? She helped him put his overcoat on and walked with him to the door.

"Uh... Jack?"

"Yes?"

"I really don't know how to thank you for helping me with the furniture."

"It's nothing. You helped me a lot today, remember?"

She looked down, avoiding his eyes.

He wondered if she were always this shy around men. It dawned on him that it was her shyness that attracted him to her in the first place. "Would you mind if I kissed you goodnight?"

She looked up and smiled. "Of course not."

As he stepped closer to kiss her, she remembered April's advice. It was now or never. She put her arms around him and kissed him hard. He was surprised at first, then pulled her against him and kissed her just as hard.

When they parted, she stepped back and smiled. It had worked for him, but he couldn't quite ask her if he could stay. He was afraid if she didn't want that, she would feel pressured to say yes because he was her boss. He could only smile back at her. She opened the door, and he walked past her to the hallway.

"Goodnight, Jack. Thanks ever so much."

He smiled back. "Thank you," he said and walked down the hall to the stairs. He looked back at her for a moment as she stood in the doorway, watching him. He wished he could stay.

Joan closed the door and leaned back against it for a moment. *So close.* She looked out a window and watched him get into a taxi. She sighed.

Chapter 17

Joan was definitely not an early riser. She struggled to make it to work by nine. She often worked late, and Jack didn't seem to mind her abnormal working hours. The night guard at the main entrance probably had a crush on her as he always insisted on walking her to the nearby London Underground entrance. He tried to draw her into conversation, but Joan was usually too tired and not particularly interested. She was grateful for the escort, and he did seem like a nice fellow, but his thick Cockney accent, frequent use of vulgar words, and small tales of the latest soccer games confused, offended, and bored her.

Susan Temple almost never worked late, but when she did, she would call Joan so they could leave together. Susan was always eager for the latest gossip or news about the Atlantis project.

Just as Joan saw Susan waiting for her in the lobby, she remembered something.

"Oh, I'm sorry Susan," she began. "There's a phone call to the states that I forgot to make. Why don't you go on without me."

"Oh, I wanted to hear all the latest. All right, meet me for lunch tomorrow."

Joan nodded and returned to the elevator as Susan walked out.

Susan closed her coat against a chilly breeze and wondered where the guards were. She started walking faster when she realized a car was following her. She started running, and ran as fast as she could, but couldn't run fast enough.

Rahim breathed a sigh of relief as a black limousine pulled into the abandoned warehouse. He stood waiting expectantly as two men got out.

"Well, where is she?"

Tas Amir and Rasala Farid looked at each other awkwardly until Farid replied sheepishly. "We tried to grab her but she ran in front of the car... by accident."

Amir shoved Farid. "Not! You were driving on the wrong side of the road!"

"Shut up, stupid." Farid yelled.

"You killed her?" Rahim shouted.

They nodded together. "What do we do now?" Amir's stomach knotted as he watched Rahim pick up a large metal rod.

Rahim was too busy pounding the metal rod onto a wooden crate to reply immediately. He stopped and looked at them. "It will be your heads the next time you fail me," he snarled.

News of Susan Temple's death in a hit and run accident had so upset Joan she had taken the day off. Even so, she couldn't evade Michael Baker who had called her several times to ask questions about her last encounter with Susan.

Michael Baker had finally shown up at her apartment with the London Police as they launched their own investigation. He was under a lot of pressure, and it was beginning to show.

When the two night security guards had been found unconscious in a lobby bathroom, it hadn't taken him, or the rest of the project team, very long to guess that Susan had been killed by mistake by someone who knew Joan's work habits. Security at the building, the project site and around the project team members was tightened even further.

Most of the security team was moving to Cancun and Constantine Carballo was packing his office when his phone rang.

"What the hell have you done?" snapped Alan Sands. "Are you out of your damn mind?"

"What are you talking about?"

"Your Middle Eastern connection just killed a legal secretary in an apparent attempt on Joan Mason, practically in front of the Spencer Building!" Sands temporarily lost control and started pounding the handset onto the convenience store payphone. He stopped when he saw several people staring at him.

Carballo jerked the handset away from his ear. "Shit!" He waited a moment. "Alan?"

"Idiot! They've just doubled the security at the dock. Do you know how hard it will be to get at them now?"

"I'm sorry, but I didn't have anything to do with this. I swear."

Sands didn't reply.

Carballo nervously wiped his forehead. "What do you want me to do?"

"Take care of them, or I'll call Michael Baker personally and tell him about you."

Rumors persisted that Baker had invented new ways to make terrorists talk. A chill ran down his spine as he thought of how Baker would make him pay.

Carballo turned his car lights out as he neared the abandoned warehouse. He turned the engine off and pulled a gun out of a shoulder holster as he got out. He stuffed the gun into his waistband as he walked quietly to the storeroom. He saw Rahim, Amir and Farid sitting at a table, arguing. "Well, you really screwed things up!" he said loudly.

Rahim stood and faced him. "It was an accident, we meant only to kidnap the woman."

"They've doubled the security at the site because of this."

Rahim shrugged.

"You're out of this from now on. Go back home and tell Skerchi we'll take it from here."

"You can't tell me what to do." Rahim replied angrily. He started to pull a gun from his pants, but Carballo was faster.

Carballo shot Rahim twice and quickly emptied the rest of his gun at Amir and Farid. He realized his heart was beating hard and he was out of breath. He started to sit down as he heard a gun being cocked behind him. He turned to face three men holding automatic rifles.

Mark Williamson lowered his rifle. "I'm glad you took care of that. We can't afford any more screw-ups like this."

"What are you doing here? Why'd you follow me?"

"We were just backing you up," Williamson replied.

The three members of the Council of Nine laughed as Carballo slumped into a chair.

Williamson rolled one of the corpses over with his foot. "Carballo?"

"What?"

"These guys had some grudge against Spencer, we have our own. What's your deal? Why are you working for the man and trying to screw him at the same time?"

Carballo took a deep breath and exhaled slowly. "When my sister was young and foolish, she joined a movement to free Cyprus from the Turks. The Spencer Foundation funded peace efforts and Michael Baker provided intelligence to the Turks. My sister was caught along with many others. She died in prison, and I vowed to get even with Spencer and Baker."

Williamson was surprised. "But--don't you work for Baker?"

"Yes. When Baker dies in Atlantis with all the others, I will take his place. This will allow me to get to Spencer. Then I will choose the time and place for him."

Williamson laughed and looked at his colleagues. "Never underestimate an ex-computer programmer."

The three former executives turned and walked slowly out of the warehouse.

Carballo looked at the three bodies on the floor and slowly stood to leave. Realization of what he had just done was beginning to dawn on him. The Party of Enlightenment would not let this go unpunished. He would have to be even more careful.

Chapter 18

Joan was in her office wrapping things up and getting ready for the weekend when Jack knocked on her door. She glanced at the picture of her parents on her desk, glad she had hidden his picture. She started to get up, but Jack motioned her to sit down.

He sat down in a chair in front of her desk. "Are you going to Richard's Christmas party?"

She laughed. "Only the CEOs of Richard's companies are invited and the last time I looked; I didn't fall into that category."

"Would you like to go? I received an invitation, but I've never been before and really don't want to go alone. I was invited last year, but I couldn't go."

Joan had heard a lot of stories about the Christmas party. She had always wanted to go but doubted she would ever be able to. Now Jack was asking her. "Oh, yes! I would love to go but..." She looked down as her voice trailed off.

"What is it?"

"The party is a very formal affair. The women there wear designer gowns and I don't have anything like that."

Jack smiled. "That's not a problem. The company will pay for your dress. It's good PR for the company."

"Are you sure, Jack? Those dresses are really expensive!"

He stood up and looked at his watch. "Would you have time to find one now? I'll accompany you, if you like."

Joan was shocked, but managed to smile, "That would be nice."

He stood back to allow her to walk out first, but she was looking at him and her foot got tangled in the leg of his chair. She ran into him so hard; she almost knocked him down. She put her hand to her mouth. "I'm sorry, Jack."

He laughed. "No harm done. Let's go."

He waited in a chair in an exclusive shop for her to come out of the fitting room. She had been right about the dresses being expensive. Price tags ranged from five hundred to several thousand pounds.

When they entered the shop, his eye was immediately drawn to a black sleeveless gown with tasteful sequins. Joan always seemed to wear black anyway so she wouldn't object to the color. He closed his eyes and opened them and looked at the tag. The price was a little more than 2700 pounds, about 4000 dollars.

He decided to show it to her, anyway. Howard Singleton would object, but it was only money. Joan loved the dress and almost ran into the fitting room to try it on. When she finally came out, Jack's jaw dropped. The dress looked like it was made for her. It had a slit up one side and the neckline plunged almost to her navel. She struggled to keep the top together as she walked over to him.

"It's a little tight in certain areas and loose in others. I'll have to have it altered a little. What do you think, Jack?"

He thought he would very much like to go to the Christmas Party with her in that dress. She stood next to him, pulling the dress up in the front a little as he stood up.

"You are gorgeous," he whispered.

Joan blushed. She never thought she would hear Jack say anything like that to her. In fact, she had never heard him say anything like that about any other woman.

"It's not too tight?"

"It's just right."

Joan was so happy she started to hug him until she remembered where they were. "Thank you," she whispered and then walked over to a mirror to admire herself.

A sales lady approached Jack. She had observed that Jack wasn't wearing a ring and neither was Joan. "Your lady looks lovely in that."

Jack started to tell her about the Christmas party, but he changed his mind. He looked at Joan and smiled. "She certainly does."

The night of the big Christmas party finally arrived. Joan was so nervous she was almost sick. She had tried the dress on twice during the day. Now she was late returning from her hair appointment and rushed to put it on. She didn't want Jack to have to wait on her. She was in such a hurry she almost broke the zipper.

She was finishing her makeup when the doorbell rang. It startled her. She took a few deep breaths and walked a bit unsteadily in her new high heels to the front door.

Jack wore a tuxedo under his overcoat. She admired how handsome he was even as he noticed how well her dress fit after alteration... and how attractive her hairdo was.

"You look lovely, Joan."

She helped him take his coat off. "You look handsome in that tuxedo."

He smiled. "Thanks, but I have a mirror, too." Jack had never thought he was handsome, although his ex-wife had told him she had been attracted to him, even before they were introduced, by his 'rugged good looks'. He had laughed.

It was pretty dark in the apartment, and he walked into the brighter light in the kitchen. "I have something I want to show you." He took a jewelry box out of his pocket. Joan gasped when she saw a large diamond necklace in it. "I rented it for the evening. Howard might not like the price of the dress, but he would have flipped over this."

"You mean those are all <u>real</u>?"

"They had better be, for the price they wanted."

He took the necklace out and she turned around as he put it on her. Her perfume crept into his brain. He followed her with his eyes as she walked to a full-length mirror in her bedroom to admire the necklace.

Joan had never seen anything like it. The diamonds sparkled even in the low light of her bedroom. Jack walked in and stood behind her, admiring her more than the necklace. She followed his eyes in the mirror and smiled. She turned around and looked into his eyes. "You didn't have to do this."

"I want the other women there to be jealous."

His cologne was subtle, but she recognized it from the night he had helped her move. She couldn't resist him any longer. She put her arms around him and kissed him. He held her tightly. When they stopped kissing, she didn't want to let go. "What time does the party start?"

"We have about an hour."

"That's a long time."

They kissed again and she felt his hands wandering all over her.

Joan gawked like a tourist as the limousine pulled into a large circular drive in front of Richard Spencer's mansion. She was reminded of several castles she had toured when she was young. She buttoned her coat and stepped out as the doorman opened her door. Jack smiled as he watched her wide-eyed expression when she looked at the house and grounds with its white dusting of snow on the trees and bushes. Jack pulled the collar of his coat tighter and took her arm as they walked toward the front door.

Joan had never met Ann, Richard's wife.

Ann had not been in very good health for the last few years and rarely came to the office. She greeted Jack and Joan warmly. She had come to know Jack rather well because Richard talked about the domed city and Jack all the time. She had never seen Richard so interested in any single project before. He made a point of inviting Jack home whenever he was in London.

Joan hit it off quickly with Ann. Like Jack, Joan was surprised at the attention she received from Ann. Richard's party list included over a hundred couples. Numerous men complimented her dress and necklace. More than a few women were obviously jealous. Joan had a great time.

After dinner, she walked through the greenhouse with Jack. It was somewhat secluded; only a few other couples were strolling there. Jack found a rare opportunity to sneak a kiss. Joan felt like a schoolgirl again, trying to sneak around and kiss a boyfriend without parents or friends seeing them.

They walked slowly back to the house. The mansion was huge and even with the large number of guests it didn't seem crowded. A band played Christmas music and a church choir sang Christmas carols. After a while they stood on a balcony in the library and looked down at other strolling couples. Joan's hand was on the balcony railing and Jack put his hand on hers. She turned to face him. He leaned forward and kissed her softly.

She put her arms around his neck. "I could get used to that."

"So could I."

They kissed deeply. Richard and Ann happened on them at that moment. They smiled at each other and walked away. When they were out of hearing range, Ann whispered, "They certainly make a lovely couple."

"They certainly do," Richard said, hoping their personal relationship wouldn't interfere with their working relationship.

The party was almost over and Jack asked Joan, "Do you have anything for a headache? I think I drank too much wine."

Joan looked in her purse and took out a small pillbox. There were several kinds of pills in the pillbox, but the only painkiller was a type she sometimes took for menstrual pain. She found a bathroom and filled a glass with water and handed it to him.

Jack didn't recognize the pill, "What is this?"

"Menstrol. It's the only pain killer I have with me."

"Menstrol?"

"For menstrual pain," she whispered in his ear.

He laughed and started to take the pill, then stopped. "I'm allergic to Naprosyn. It doesn't have any of that in it, does it?"

"I don't think so, but I'm not sure."

He stared at the pill for a moment and then took it. They had barely wished goodnight to Richard and Ann and entered the limousine when Jack passed out. She felt his pulse and thought it felt normal. She opened his eyes, relieved that the pupils were normal. Maybe he was just sleeping? She decided to take him to her apartment. Maybe he could sleep it off there.

The limousine driver helped bring Jack into her apartment and put him on her bed. She thanked him and gave him a big tip.

What now? Jack appeared to be sleeping soundly. She decided to make him more comfortable by taking off his shoes and pants. She took off his shirt and pulled the covers back, wishing he were awake.

She took off her dress and put the necklace very carefully into the jewelry box. She stared at it for a while and got ready for bed. She found the Menstrol bottle in her medicine cabinet and read the ingredients. It did have Naprosyn. She wished she had had the bottle in her purse instead of the pillbox.

"I'm sorry, Jack."

He stirred but didn't wake up as she climbed in next to him

and kissed him on the cheek. She snuggled up to him and closed her eyes.

When she woke up, Jack was still sleeping. She checked his pulse and got up to dress. She would surprise him with breakfast.

She looked in her refrigerator. She was out of everything needed for breakfast. She put on her coat and looked in on him. "I'll be right back." He stirred but didn't wake up. She walked out and headed for a nearby grocery.

Jack woke up with a splitting headache. He sat up and realized he was in Joan's apartment. He called to her but she didn't answer. He dressed and saw the jewelry box on her dresser. He stuffed it into his pocket and left.

When Joan returned, she went to the bedroom to check on Jack and was surprised to find him gone. She sat down hard on the bed. Jack was spending more and more time at the construction site and she wasn't even sure when she would see him again. Christmas would be even lonelier than usual this year, with her mother gone and Jack in Mexico.

Chapter 19

Jack struggled to finish dressing. His pants were so loose he closed his belt another notch. He couldn't even fit into those pants a few months ago. A daily exercise program in the temporary gym on the *Eye* was finally beginning to pay off. He looked at his watch. It was almost 9:00 AM. As he looked at himself in a mirror, there was a knock at the door. "Come in."

Ron Stuart, the third mate entered, hat in hand.

"Yes, Ron?"

"Captain Atwell has assembled a team in the mess room to discuss Mr. Spencer's visit and has requested your presence."

Jack finished buttoning his shirt. "Tell George I'll be there in five minutes."

"Yes, sir." Stuart turned to leave.

"Oh... Ron?" Jack straightened his collar, "What's the latest ETA for Spencer?"

"Captain Atwell would have that information, sir."

Jack smiled. "Officially, yes, but what have you heard?"

Stuart hesitated, reluctant to answer. "We heard he just arrived in Cancun. He should be here around ten."

"Fine. Thanks, Ron."

Stuart closed the door as Jack put on his shoes. After he finished dressing, he walked down a flight of stairs to the mess room. The door was closed. *That's strange*. The door was only closed when rough seas required all hatchways to be secured. He opened the door and entered to a loud crescendo of 'For He's A Jolly Good Fellow'. Most of the ship's crew was assembled, with George Atwell leading the singing.

In the middle of the room was a cake with two candles lit. Jack blushed. When the song was over, the crew gathered around to shake his hand and congratulate him.

George whistled for silence. "I know I speak for all of the crew of the 'Eye' in wishing you a happy second anniversary with the company and for the last third of the project to be as successful as the previous two-thirds have been."

Jack smiled at his old friend and drinking buddy.

"I personally hate speeches," George continued, "but I have a short one prepared for this occasion. I've had quite a few bosses in my career, but I can honestly say, I haven't had a better one than Jack Garrett."

There were a few 'Here! Here's!', and other statements of agreement.

"About eighteen months ago, Jack came to me and asked if I would be the skipper of a converted oil tanker. He wouldn't tell me what it had been converted to do, insisting that I sign on first." Everyone laughed. "I've known Jack for a long time and knew he wouldn't ask me to sign on without knowing what it was all about, unless there was a good reason. I know that you've been as amazed as I have at what has been accomplished here. And I believe it's largely due to the hands-on leadership Jack has shown. We only wish we all could be around to see it to completion."

The crew applauded. Jack held up his hands to speak. The crew quieted and he began speaking softly. "You all know this has been a team effort from the beginning. I feel lucky to have been chosen to lead the exceptional team we have managed to put together. Thank you all very much. Now, I have an announcement of my own. As you know, Richard Spencer is on his way here and should arrive within the hour. You may not know, however, that if everything continues as planned, we should be able to enter the dome today."

There was a stunned silence.

Ron Stuart stepped forward. "Are we ahead of schedule, Mr. Garrett? We thought that wouldn't happen for several more days."

"At eleven o'clock last night we attached the final research dome component and began pumping out approximately seventy-seven billion gallons of sea water at a total pump-out rate of two million gallons per second. We should be finished at ten this morning." He looked at his watch. "That's about forty-five minutes from now. We're fortunate that Mr. Spencer could work this visit into his busy schedule. We're even more fortunate that everything has remained on schedule and, hopefully, we can go inside today."

There was a buzz of conversation among the crew. George Atwell whistled for their attention again. "I think Mr. Garrett deserves a round of applause for an extraordinary job!"

Everyone applauded.

"Thanks very much. I know you're all eager to see what we've accomplished. As soon as we verify that it's safe, we'll begin assembling you in groups to have a short look around."

Ron Stuart stepped forward again. "Mr. Garrett, I know I speak for all the crew in that we know how busy the construction crew is and we appreciate your thinking of us by allowing us to be among the first to go inside."

Jack smiled. "I'm just as anxious as you, believe me."

George picked up the cake and held it in front of Jack. The word CONGRATULATIONS was emblazoned across the cake. There was also a replica of the main dome and the twelve surrounding domes. Jack blew out the two candles and everyone applauded.

"Thank you all. I really appreciate your efforts in supporting the construction crew. I know you had to ride out some pretty bad storms to allow us to finish pouring all that concrete. You're all welcome to some cake. I'd like to see Captain Atwell in the Communications Center." He motioned George to follow him.

Everyone gathered around the cake as it was cut and passed around.

As they walked to the Communications Center, George pressed Jack for more details on the upcoming visit to the dome. "Will we really be able to go in today? I know the dome's supposed to be self-supporting, but we only have the center buildings to support it."

Jack looked at his watch. "Unless all our calculations are wrong, we should."

They arrived at the Communication Center. John Williams, the Communications Officer of the 'Eye', saluted George. "We have confirmation that Mr. Spencer will arrive at oh-nine-fifty, sir."

George returned the salute. "Thanks, John."

Jack picked up a digital radio. "Jack Garrett to Bill Howell.

Are you there, Bill?"

"Howell here!"

"How's it coming along?"

"The captain of the *Sea Merchant* has just given us a visual confirmation of the level. We're pumping out the containment canal now. We should be finished by ten hundred hours."

"Even if they don't finish the canal for a while, can't you still give Spencer the guided tour?"

"Not really, George. We need to stabilize the pressure in the dome and we can't do that until we have all the water out. We're pumping in hot air as the water is pumped out."

Jack addressed Howell again. "Bill, that construction elevator had better work or you'll have a dead billionaire on your hands."

"We've checked it a dozen times, Jack. Unless all the sensors are wrong, you should have a smooth trip down."

"Please check it once more. George and I are going to be on it as well, you know."

"Aye, aye, skipper."

Jack punched a few keys on a computer keyboard. An image of the dome appeared. There were numerous green data points being updated from pressure sensors located at strategic points on the inside of the dome's walls.

George glanced at it. "Everything looks okay."

Jack touched a few buttons and one hundred pressure sensor values filled the screen. All pressure values were in the normal range. An averaged value for all the sensors indicated the pressure inside was very close to atmospheric. Any pressure reading greater or less than 0.1-inch water pressure relative to the atmosphere would cause real problems when they entered through one of the dome's loading hatches.

Jack seemed relieved. "It's holding so far."

George scanned the horizon with a pair of binoculars. "He's here, Jack."

A moment later, they heard the familiar sound of the transport helicopter as it circled overhead, preparing to land on the 'Eye's' helideck.

Jack glanced at his reflection in the window. "Showtime."

As the helicopter approached the *Eye*, Spencer, Howard Singleton, Michael Baker and Emma Dawson saw ten huge plumes of water spraying over the side of the converted oil tanker.

Spencer laughed when he saw Jack and George Atwell standing on a platform next to the ship's bridge. "Jack must have dressed up just for us." He'd heard Jack always wore short-sleeved shirts and shorts. After experiencing the heat at the airport, he realized why.

As the helicopter circled the ship, Emma smiled. "I need to get off first to get some publicity pictures for the corporate newsletter and the press."

Spencer laughed. "I must look like a child eager to get to a new playground."

"That understandable. You've put a lot of time and money in it; you have a right to be proud."

Spencer sighed. "I hope we can go in today."

Howard Singleton closed his briefcase. "I'll be glad when we can start selling timeshares and advertising. We need to get some revenue streams going."

"You know that we don't expect to break even on this for several years."

"I know, Richard, but some black ink would be nice for a change."

Baker's primary concern was for Richard's safety. "Richard, I think we should limit the entry party as much as possible until we can determine if there are any safety issues."

Spencer was thoughtful. "Perhaps you're right."

"Do you think it's a good idea for you to go in without giving us a chance to make sure it's safe?"

"All the king's horses couldn't keep me out, Michael!"

"Then I would limit it to you, Jack, Bill, George and myself. Just to be on the safe side."

"I need to be included so I can get the pictures we need for the media," Emma reminded them. "They're all after me for some."

As Spencer was about to reply, the helicopter touched down. A moment later a crewman on the *Eye* opened the door and pulled a small set of stairs to the door. Spencer allowed Emma to exit first.

Jack and George waited as Spencer stepped onto the helideck and Emma completed her photographic session before greeting him.

"Jack, great to see you!" Spencer held out his hand as he approached. Jack hugged him instead. Spencer shook George's hand. "The two of you have really worked wonders here. It's hard to believe you're only a week behind an optimistic schedule."

George took his hat off and wiped his forehead. "We've been pretty lucky with the weather. It's just been hot."

Spencer waited as Jack greeted Baker, Emma and Howard. Howard waved and headed for the mess hall. Emma left to find a restroom.

Spencer began walking toward the bridge. "What's the status, Jack? The pumps are still in operation."

"We're pumping out the canal now. We should be able to go in shortly. Let's go inside and check the status."

He led the way to the Communications Center and stopped in front of the computer displaying the dome sensors. Spencer stared intently at the computer. "The pressure's stable enough. Let's go!"

Jack keyed his radio. "Jack Garrett to Bill Howell."

"Howell here."

"How much longer on the canal?"

"Look out the window, Jack."

They walked to a window on the bridge. The pump sprays were falling off and even as they watched, the pumps shut off.

"Jack, the captain of the *Sea Merchant* has just reported a visual confirmation on the supporting domes as well."

Jack looked at George. "You heard the man! It's time to go!"

George smiled. "Roger, that."

Baker turned to Jack. "I discussed with Spencer the need to limit the number in the initial entry party until we can determine if there are any safety issues."

"Fine. The four of us, with Emma to take some pictures, is probably a good number."

Baker nodded in agreement.

The radio crackled and George thought of Bill. "What about Bill Howell?"

"We need Bill out here in case something goes wrong. He's the only one who can get us out."

Spencer, Baker and George were thinking about Jack's comment as they walked silently down a flight of stairs to the main deck of the 'Eye' where Emma waited for them. George signaled to a crane operator and a cage was lowered next to them. They got in and the operator gently lowered them onto a waiting hovercraft next to the 'Eye'. As the hovercraft moved away from the *Eye*, Jack keyed his radio.

"Jack Garrett to Bill Howell. Are you there, Bill?"

"Aye, Captain Jack," Bill replied in his best pirate voice.

"Open it; we're on our way."

"Aye, Aye!"

Spencer laughed. "Howell's a little eccentric, isn't he?"

"I think he's played a few too many video games."

The sky was clear and the sea was calm, as the hovercraft headed out into the open water. Suddenly, a huge concave plastic and metal tower rose out of the sea, seawater cascading off of it as the hovercraft neared an opening in a vertical section. Spencer was awed at the size of the loading hatches. There were four similar delivery elevators that also served as emergency escape hatches. The mechanism in the northwest quadrant building was designed for heavier materials and most of the building was a temporary storage area for equipment or materials brought into the city.

Spencer stared at the huge hatch. "I've seen sketches and pictures of the loading hatches so many times, I probably could draw one in my sleep. But seeing one actually work... it's still pretty amazing."

Jack waited with a coiled rope as the hovercraft maneuvered into position at a dock on the outside of the loading hatch. The inside of the hatch was a large quarter-circle platform that could serve as a temporary holding area for personnel needing to escape from Atlantis, with railings around the wall evacuees could hold onto if they felt the need. The battery backup system for the emergency lights inside the hatch hadn't been installed yet and it was fairly dark inside. A crewman scampered out onto the dock and Jack threw him the rope. When the hovercraft was secured, the entry team walked up a flight of stairs and through the hatch to a large entry door at the back. Emma took several pictures of Spencer and Jack together near the entry door. Spencer watched the hovercraft prepare to leave.

"Well, after all this time, we're almost there."

"Be sure you have your jackets on; it's going to be pretty cold in there." Jack pulled a digital radio out of his belt. "Garrett to Bill Howell."

"Howell here."

"Let us down gently."

"Aye, skipper."

The entry party watched as the hovercraft departed.

Jack handed a jacket to Emma, "When everything is functional, we'll be able to do everything from this panel."

Emma took a picture of Jack standing next to the panel. They felt a slight jerk as the external door of the hatch closed, sealing off the outside world. As it closed, Jack turned on a powerful quartz lamp he carried. After a few seconds, the hatch began a slow descent to the dome.

Emma started to hold onto a handrail, but jerked back when her hand touched the icy cold metal. "How far down are we going, Jack?"

"The top of the dome is about sixty feet below the surface. This platform will stop about another hundred or so feet below the top of the dome." When the hatch stopped moving, Jack cautioned, "Hold onto the railing, just in case. If the pressure is less than atmospheric, the air in here will get sucked inside. If it's greater than atmospheric, we'll feel some air come out."

He pressed a button and the main door opened. An enormous rush of cold, wet air howled through the hatch knocking most of them down. Emma screamed and grabbed her camera just as it was about to hit the floor. When the rush of air finally stopped, they got to their feet and walked to the entry door.

"Well, that was fun." George straightened his jacket as Jack's radio buzzed.

"What in the hell happened, Jack?" Bill Howell asked anxiously. "It looked like someone set off a depth charge in an old war movie out here."

The rush of air out of the dome hadn't surprised Jack. "When we come back up, someone needs to check the seal on the outside door. There was a little pressure in the dome and it came out through the hatch."

"We'll get right on it. Howell out."

"Okay, let's go." Jack's hand-held light illuminated only a small area and they walked in a single file, following him.

The dome was cold, dark, wet and eerily quiet. They walked a short distance and stopped to listen but could only hear a faint dripping of water. They continued on and stepped through a small puddle on the way to an observation deck. The steel structure of the building was just about the limit of the lighted area. They lined up along a railing at the end of the deck, straining to see anything. The light couldn't penetrate very far into the inky darkness.

Emma watched Jack examining the building's structure. "How high are we?"

"About eleven hundred feet above the foundation. It's kind of like being in a cave, isn't it?"

He listened for possible sounds of the dome leaking, but he didn't hear anything. "Stay where you are for a minute." He turned off the light.

As their eyes adjusted to the darkness, they could see a dull green glow at the top of the dome from the sunlight filtering down through sixty feet of seawater.

"Are we ready for the ride down?" Jack turned the light on, flashed it around, then pulled the radio out of his belt. "Bill, where's the elevator?"

"It's on its way up to your level. You should see it any minute now."

Even as Bill finished speaking, the freight elevator silently stopped a few feet away from them. Jack lifted a gate and they entered. "This elevator and the loading hatch are just about the only things hooked to the external power system at this point."

Spencer eagerly entered the elevator. "How long will it take to go down?"

"We have it set on slow today; about two minutes to the bottom."

There was a little bump and the elevator began a slow, smooth descent to the floor of the dome. The elevator proceeded smoothly to the bottom, arriving with only another small bump. Jack opened the gate and walked out, the others quickly following him, not wanting to be away from the light.

"Stay where you are for a moment." He turned the light off and they looked up in the dark. The green glow at the top couldn't be seen from the floor.

Emma held her hand in front of her face and couldn't even see her fingers. "Jack, what can we see now? It's too dark for pictures."

He turned the light back on. "Well, unless it floated away at the last moment, there should be a watertight enclosure at the center of the dome. If we can find it, there are some pretty powerful lights inside that will run for about thirty minutes on batteries."

"Great! Let's find it."

"This way!" Jack and George led them to the center of the downtown area. After a moment, George called out, "Here it is!"

The others hurried to join them as Jack opened a large box. He pulled a small dolly out and lifted the box onto it. Then he took out a ring of small lights and set it on a tripod that folded out from a side of the box. Cables connected the lights to a large battery pack in the box. "Don't look at these lights, directly," he warned.

As he turned the lights on, the area defined by the four towering skyscrapers became visible. There were some "Ooohs" and "Ahhhs" as the size of the dome became apparent.

"One hundred million candlepower." Jack noted proudly.

Spencer was so happy; he was almost crying. Emma began taking pictures in earnest.

"This is on wheels, so we can move it around to look at everything."

As the others gawked, Jack inspected the concrete floor. It looked pretty smooth but there were small puddles on it.

George saw Jack examining the floor. "Was it done correctly? I know it's extremely hard to pour concrete when it's so cold."

Jack nodded. "It's within spec. We checked the foundation

each time before we moved the construction dome.”

“If you two have finished examining the concrete, can we look around some? This is a pretty amazing place and I want to take more pictures.”

“Sorry Emma. Let's get going.” He walked over to the light box and pushed it out of the downtown area, the others walking along with him, impressed by the size of the building modules that had already been set in place on the dome foundation.

After a while, they stood next to the dome wall, looking up. The dome disappeared into the darkness beyond the limit of the light pack.

Emma put her hand on the wall. “It's freezing!”

Spencer shivered from a stream of cold air flowing down the dome wall. “What's the outside temperature at this level, Jack?”

“About thirty-eight or thirty-nine degrees Fahrenheit, or three to four degrees Centigrade. Pretty cold.”

Emma rubbed her arms. “This jacket doesn't keep you very warm.”

“It's the humidity that makes it feel so cold. We pumped in hot, dry air to help dry it out, but there's still quite a lot of cold water to dry out.”

Spencer, who was holding the portable quartz light, pointed it at the floor. “Aren't we standing over the containment canal?”

Jack glanced down at the decorative grate covering a canal that ran around the perimeter of the dome. “Yes.”

They all looked down and saw light below the grate they were standing on.

Emma took a picture of the canal grate. "What is that, exactly? I've heard that mentioned several times."

"Statistically, you have to plan that at least one of the dome components might fail, despite all the testing that was done. If it did, a huge quantity of seawater would rush in before we could put a replacement piece in place. The canal around the perimeter of the dome should have enough capacity to contain water leaking in until we can get the canal pump going."

Emma knelt on the protective grating, peering into the canal. "How big is the canal?"

"It's ten feet deep and ten feet wide all along the dome wall. It's not obvious because of this decorative grate over it. The grate is there for safety reasons. We also didn't want to lose that much real estate, so we'll use this area mostly for recreational purposes, probably a jogging track."

"What's the volume of the canal?"

"About forty-six million gallons or one hundred and seventy-six million liters."

"If a wall piece failed, how long would it take to fill it up?"

"That depends on where the hole is. If it's at the top, everyone will get rained on. It would take quite a long time before we had a problem. However, if it's at the bottom of the dome, the pressure is high, and seawater would quickly fill the canal. The pump can handle the failure of a bottom wall piece until we can replace it."

When the light pack began to dim, George began pushing

it toward the downtown area. "Uh-oh. I think we should start walking back to the elevator." Everyone scurried to catch up with him.

Chapter 20

The entry team ate a late lunch in the mess room and discussed their visit to the dome. When Howard Singleton appeared with his briefcase, Spencer tapped on his glass to get their attention.

"I just want to say that today was one of the most memorable days of my life. I was confident two years ago when we formed this team that we'd be able to tour the dome someday, but the task seemed almost impossible to accomplish in two years. I have to say, there were some real innovations that made this all possible and most of them are due to the presence of the team gathered at this table. I congratulate all of you.

"I did want to mention, however, that when I arrived today, the heat at the airport almost knocked me out. It was probably five degrees Celsius when I got on my plane in London and almost forty when I arrived in Cancun. Isn't there a better way of getting the visitors here than going through regular airports?"

Jack absently began scratching the stubble on his chin. "Well, a lot of them will be coming off cruise ships that will berth at our new dock and then get on one of the new small people transfer submarines we're building. There really isn't any other way to get the rest of them here, except for the airports at Cancun and Cozumel."

"Couldn't we use the plastic to build a floating airstrip so jets can land right above the dome and then use the submarines to bring them in?"

No one moved or volunteered anything.

Jack leaned forward in his chair and rubbed his forehead. "Damn. I hope this is a dream and that you really didn't say that."

"I'm serious, Jack. I'd like you to look into it."

Jack laughed. "A floating airport?"

"Only the runway."

Jack leaned back in his chair. "If a plane couldn't stop for some reason, it wouldn't run off into grass and mud at the end of the runway, it would fall into the damn ocean!" He took a deep breath and tried to calm himself.

Spencer smiled. "Well then, the design would have to prevent that, wouldn't it?"

Jack folded his arms. "Can we finish one impossible task before we begin on another?"

The other team members were trying to be invisible.

"Why can't we just look at the feasibility?"

"Well, assuming it would be technically feasible, there are aviation and cost issues. For one thing, I don't think the Mexican government would relish the idea that a simple pilot error would put a jetliner in the ocean. And the second thing is that the cost would probably be astronomical."

"But we don't know that any of those issues can't be worked out, do we? And we don't know the cost either."

Surely, Spencer was testing him. Jack let out a sigh. "No, we don't." Suddenly, he thought of a possible way to get out of it. "Let's say, for argument sake, that it's technically feasible and by some miracle the Mexican government reviewed the design and approved the project. Is there a cost you would consider unreasonable? Just for argument's sake, of course."

Spencer thought for a moment. "Yes, of course there is."

"Can you give that to me, in pounds, euros or dollars? What's the capability to land visitors a hundred meters from the dome worth to the Atlantis Foundation?"

Everyone looked at Spencer, who thought hard about it. "Not more than ten times whatever it would cost to build a runway on the coast near here."

Jack smiled. He had the out he needed. He was certain there was no way in hell a floating runway over a mile long could be built for anywhere near that price.

Spencer saw Jack smile. "What are you thinking?"

Jack pulled out his radio. "Jack Garrett to John Williams. Come in, John."

The Communications Officer answered immediately. "Williams here, Jack."

"John, I need you to call Stan Jacobs in Chicago. And patch him through when you get him. His name and phone number are on the approved consultant and contractors' list."

"What shall I tell him this is about when he asks?"

"Tell him we need his help on a project related to Atlantis in a hurry."

"I'll contact him immediately. Williams out."

Jack chuckled. "He'll probably hurt himself getting to the

next plane down here."

"Who is he, Jack?" Baker was always concerned with potential security issues.

"Probably the foremost expert in the world on international aviation issues and jurisdictions."

Jack picked up his radio again. "Jack Garrett to Bill Howell. Are you there, Bill?"

"Yes, Jack."

"I need a cost estimate on building a commercial quality runway on the coast near here. It has to be capable of landing jumbo jets. Can you do that for me?"

"What? Can you repeat that, Jack?"

Jack did.

"Are you serious?"

"Yes. Get help if you need it. Garrett out."

Spencer smiled. "See how easy that was?"

Jack closed his eyes and rubbed his forehead. "Sure. Is there anything else?"

Spencer pulled on his chin, trying to remember something else he wanted an estimate on. "Can you get a cost on a tunnel from the main dome to the mainland? I was thinking it would be nice if guests could walk to the beach for an evening stroll after dinner."

Jack closed his eyes again. When he opened them, everyone at the table was looking at him. He laughed, "How big?"

"About three meters wide and three meters tall. Built out of the new plastic, of course, to give a nice view."

"Of course," Jack replied, ever so nicely. "And what would be an unrealistic cost for this tunnel?"

"I would say not more than five million pounds."

Jack made a note in his electronic tablet. "And when would you like this estimate?"

Spencer smiled. "I would have said when you can get to it, but I think a month would be enough time, don't you?"

"Of course. Is there anything else?"

"Yes. Howard has something to say."

Singleton stood up. "About two years ago, when Jack signed on to lead this effort, Mr. Spencer offered him a bonus plan based on meeting several key targets during the construction phase. Jack insisted the key team members be given the same opportunities for accomplishing their tasks. One of those rather optimistic targets was the completion of the dome within two years, plus or minus two weeks. Since that task has been met, Mr. Spencer and I are pleased to present these checks to you in recognition of this outstanding accomplishment."

He walked around the table and handed each person an envelope with their name on it.

"Don't spend it all in one place," Spencer joked.

Surprised at the size of their checks, they all looked at Spencer, waiting for him to say something.

"What? You earned it!"

Spencer turned to Jack. "I have a meeting in London tomorrow, so I need to be going. I'd like to talk to you on the way out." They both stood. "I hope to see you all soon, when we really get going on the city and can move inside."

Jack looked at the team. "I'll be right back. I have something else I need to talk to you about."

The team stood as Spencer and Jack walked out. Emma looked at Baker. "Jesus Christ, I hope he doesn't ever give me anything like that to do."

Baker laughed. "I think Jack found a way out of actually having to do them. He'll get a price and Spencer will say 'forget it'."

"What if they <u>are</u> feasible, acceptable and not cost prohibitive?" George wondered out loud.

"Then I'll have to set up security stations on them."

The sun was setting as Spencer and Jack walked to the helideck. The pilot was just beginning his pre-flight checklist when he saw them. "Five minutes, Mr. Spencer."

Spencer looked at Jack. "I don't think we would have made it this far without you. Why don't you take a few weeks off and relax? They can get by without you for a little while. I don't want to see you burned out on this. I've lost some good executives who couldn't balance their personal life with their work."

Jack thought about that. "I might take a week off and go skiing."

"That's a great idea."

Jack looked down. "I didn't mean to sound negative back there, but we have a ton of work to do without taking on any additional projects."

Spencer smiled. "Don't worry about it. I have some crazy ideas sometimes and I need someone like you to see if the benefits justify the cost."

The pilot signaled that he was ready. Spencer held out his hand to Jack, who held it for a moment before walking off. Spencer stared after him until he disappeared through a gangway, then turned and climbed up into the helicopter.

The key officers of the Atlantis Corporation had gathered in a small conference room near the crew's quarters. Jack carried a small cardboard box and set it down on the table. He smiled. "I'm pleased to tell you that your probationary period is over, you all have demonstrated the leadership needed to get this company through its first couple of years. So, I have something for you."

He pulled out several small boxes and desk nameplates. Bill Howell was nearest so Jack handed him a nameplate and small box. "Congratulations, Bill. You are now the Vice President of Operations and Construction. If you're ever at your desk, you can put this nameplate on it. And here are some new business cards."

Jack repeated the procedure for Emma, the new Vice President of Corporate Communications. George looked at his business cards and laughed. He was the Vice President of Sea-Based Operations. Howard Singleton became Vice President and Chief Financial Officer and Michael Baker the Vice President of Corporate Security.

Jack made another announcement. "Joan Mason has completed her MBA course work and should have her degree in a few months. She officially became the Director of Purchasing today."

It was almost dark as Bill Howell sat in the cockpit of a transport helicopter going over his pre-flight checklist. He happened to look up as Emma walked out of the crew quarters and onto the deck of the *Eye*. She stood by the railing, looking at the last rays of the sun as it sank into the sea. A warm, gentle breeze blew her hair about as she unconsciously pulled it back behind her head. He watched her for a few minutes and then climbed out of the helicopter and walked over to her. "I thought you were going back to London tonight."

She turned to him. "I'm taking a few vacation days first. I've never been to Mexico before."

"It's nice."

They watched the last rays of the setting sun.

"Would you like a ride back to Cancun?"

"I'm waiting for the hovercraft to come back."

"No, I mean, I'm about ready to leave. I can give you a lift back on the helicopter."

"Oh, sure. If you don't mind."

"Not at all."

He helped her into the helicopter, then walked around and got in the pilot's seat. He picked up the pre-flight checklist.

She watched him. "Where's the pilot?"

"I can fly helicopters now."

"What? When did you qualify for that? I don't remember that in your bio. I thought you could only fly single engine planes."

"I asked Jack if I could get training on it because I travel around a lot. We could always use another helicopter pilot and it would free up one of the others if I knew how. It took about six months."

"I'm impressed," she said truthfully.

He finished the pre-flight checklist, received clearance, and took off. He circled the *Eye* and then headed for Cancun. When he looked at her, she was smiling at him.

The flight only took a few minutes. As they neared the airport, Bill decided to ask her to dinner. "If you don't have any plans, would you like to go to a restaurant tonight? I know some really good ones here."

"Okay, sure. When?"

"It's almost seven. I'll drop you off at your hotel and pick you up about eight, if that's okay."

"It's fine."

"Have you ever been to a Country and Western saloon?"

She stared at him for a minute then shook her head.

"Do you like to dance?"

"Oh, yes. I love to dance."

"That's great. Then you'll love this place!"

Chapter 21

Bill Howell put a piece of paper on Jack's desk and Jack motioned for him to sit down. "What's that?"

"The estimate on the tunnel to the beach that Spencer wants."

Jack quickly scanned it. The bottom line was about five million dollars. A design team from Future Plastics had recommended fabricating one single tunnel piece about fifteen feet long. The pieces would interlock and although about 400 would be required, the cost of fabrication would be low. They also recommended beginning the tunnel at the concourse level in the center of the dome. This would allow the tunnel to exit the dome at 200 feet above the sea floor and reduce the thickness needed to withstand the pressure. The tunnel would need to be attached to cables secured to the ocean floor every ten pieces to keep it from swaying with the currents. Despite these concerns, the design team was enthusiastic about the tunnel and even eager to start on its fabrication. There were also several drawings attached to the estimate. His attention was immediately drawn to the symbols for a level controller and a vessel.

Jack frowned. "What's the vessel for?"

Bill looked at the drawing. "I spoke with the lead designer when I got the estimate. They put it in there in case one of the tunnel connections starts to leak. The tunnel slopes down from the beach and water would run down it into the dome." He pointed to a line on the drawing. "There's a drain and grate just inside the dome to carry any water away. This drain line is connected to the collection vessel, which is connected to the canal pump. The level controller will turn the canal pump on and pump the vessel out when it's almost full."

"Why is the drain line so large?"

"They thought it would be cheaper if they used regular tunnel components rather than fabricate smaller ones."

Jack studied the drawings. "Why is there a hatch with an emergency door where the tunnel enters the dome?"

"If the tunnel broke somehow, the drain alone couldn't keep water out of the dome. The emergency door will."

Jack nodded. "Well, it looks like you have the honor, Bill."

Bill pointed to the connection where the tunnel passed through the dome wall on the drawing. "We'll have to replace four dome wall pieces at the exit point of the dome with a special tunnel interface piece somehow."

"Well, we were planning on building a small construction dome anyway for replacing leaking dome pieces. We can put a priority on getting it built, and use it here. The little dome attaches to the exterior of the main dome, you pump it out and then pull the main dome pieces out. Then you can put in the tunnel interface. Sort of like the work we did on the foundations."

Bill nodded. "I would guess about six to ten months to complete it, with all the other things we have to do."

He handed Jack a purchase order for the tunnel components, the cabling support system and supports that had to be built inside the dome to hold the tunnel up between the center concourse and the wall of the dome. Jack signed it.

"Have you heard anything on the cost of the floating landing strip?"

"Not yet. Your consultant is still working on it."

"I hope it's too damn high."

Bill laughed.

Bill was waiting as Emma arrived on a commercial flight from London. She was preparing for a press conference to update the world's media on the progress of the new city. Bill waved to her as she walked out of the security area. She smiled and waved back. Bill hugged her. "How was your trip?"

"Not as comfortable as Spencer's jet, but it was fine."

"Let's get your luggage."

They collected her luggage and Bill carried it out to his car. As they headed for her hotel, he glanced at her. "I'm sorry but I won't be able to attend the press conference tomorrow. We're in the middle of finalizing the work on the power system."

"That's all right, Bill. I'm surprised you took the time out to meet me at the airport. You didn't have to, you know."

"I know, but I wanted to ask you something." He took a deep breath and let it out. "I was wondering if you'd like to go skiing with me when you're done here."

She felt her heart beat faster. She certainly hadn't expected that. Her first impression was that it was a little too soon for that.

He saw her mull it over. "You don't have to answer now."

"I just need a little while to answer." Emma appeared relieved.

"Okay."

They didn't say much until they arrived at the hotel. A porter took her luggage and Bill got in his car and started the engine.

Why not? "Bill! Wait!"

Bill got out of the car and stood waiting for her to say something.

"I've thought about it. I'll go. You can make the reservations."

Bill grinned, walked over, and kissed her.

She smiled. "I'm not a very good skier."

"I'm probably not much better."

"Would you like to go out to dinner tomorrow night, my treat?"

"Of course."

"Call me tomorrow."

"You can count on it."

He kissed her one more time and got into the car. He was so happy; he almost got a speeding ticket on the way back to the port.

Jack entered the conference room with his laptop for the weekly status meeting and saw two new people sitting at the table.

Michael Baker, who had been trying to draw one of them into a conversation, stood up. "Jack, this is Lucia Ortiz, our new Library Director and Anna Mordid, our new Museum Director."

Lucia Ortiz was a world-renowned expert in coral reefs

and an associate professor at an Ivy League university in the United States. In addition to her obvious academic accomplishments, she was even prettier than her picture. Her biographical information indicated she had been the runner-up to Miss Mexico in the Miss World competition while still studying Library Science at a renowned university in Mexico City. With her dark eyes and hair and beautiful face, she probably could still win a beauty competition. Baker obviously hadn't missed this either.

Jack shook her hand. "It's a pleasure to meet you, Dr. Ortiz. I was quite impressed with your qualifications."

Lucia wasn't very tall, but she exuded a confidence and bearing Jack immediately attributed to her years as an associate professor and the numerous appearances she must have endured in beauty pageants. A question about her marital status even floated briefly through his consciousness.

The library she would assemble would actually contain very few books. Mostly it would consist of research material that had been gathered from all over the world, digitized and made available at numerous consoles in the library. Jack liked to refer to it as a 'virtual' library.

"Thank you, Mr. Garrett. I look forward to working with you and the other key members of the Atlantis staff."

Anna Mordid stood up and Jack moved forward to shake her hand. Anna also came highly recommended to head up the new museum Jack hoped would be recognized internationally in a few years. He would certainly support whatever technology she recommended to help achieve that. "It's a pleasure to meet you, Dr. Mordid. I've heard a lot of good things about you."

Anna Mordid was a full professor in Library Science, recruited from a major university in Lithuania. Jack hadn't expected her to have red hair and blue eyes. She was almost as tall as Emma and strikingly attractive.

"Thank you, Mr. Garrett. I have heard a lot about you also since I arrived. I also look forward to working with you and the other staff members here."

"Thank you. Please call me Jack. We're pretty informal here. I'd like to talk to both of you after this meeting for a few minutes."

Jack was in the middle of the weekly status meeting when John Williams entered, waving a piece of paper around. "We finally got it!"

Jack took the paper, glancing at a page filled with legalese and numbers. "What is this?"

"The estimate on the landing strip and the floating runway Spencer wants."

Bill stood and walked over to read it over Jack's shoulder. Jack read it quickly. He couldn't believe the Mexican government had actually approved the project! The bottom line from Future Plastics was approximately 110 million dollars.

Jack was ecstatic. He jumped to his feet. "One hundred and ten million dollars!"

Bill Howell gave Jack a high five.

George laughed. "How much was the landing strip on the coast, Bill?"

"About ten million dollars." He turned to Jack. "It looks like you have your out, Jack."

Jack stopped smiling. "Yes! This is outrageous! I'm sure Richard will be disappointed," he said in a mock-serious tone. Everyone in the room laughed. Jack handed the paper back to John. "Would you please give him the bad news?"

"Shall I email him the estimate, or call him?"

"Email it. He'll believe it if it's in black and white."

"I'll do it right now."

"You really didn't want to do that, did you?"

"George, we have enough concerns here, without planes going down in the ocean. I know the design should prevent that, but why even bother? Besides, they didn't address landing planes in high winds or stormy weather. It's just better if we use conventional airports."

George nodded. "How will Spencer take it?"

"He'll be disappointed at first, but the grand opening that's coming up should take his mind off it. Besides, he's getting his tunnel." Jack sat down. At least one weight had been taken off his shoulders. "Let's get back to the dull and routine stuff."

Bill tapped Jack on the shoulder and spoke so softly that only he could hear. "Jack?"

"Yes?"

"I'll be taking a few days off next week."

Jack was looking at the next slide and thinking about what he was going to say and not really paying attention. "Okay, Bill."

"Emma and I are going skiing."

Jack still wasn't paying attention. "That's nice, Bill. Have a good time."

Bill smiled. He certainly planned to.

When the meeting ended, Lucia and Anna remained seated, waiting for Jack to talk to them. Bill, who was standing next to Jack, heard George speaking to Anna in Russian. "I didn't know George knew Russian."

"George's grandfather left Russia when the Communists took over. He came to the States as an emigrant and settled in New York. George's parents still live there."

"My grandparents emigrated from Germany and settled in Texas," Bill commented as he gathered his papers to leave.

George finished his conversation with Anna and followed Bill out of the room. Baker remained behind, near Lucia, trying to draw her into a conversation as Jack walked over. Jack smiled at Baker's obvious fawning.

"Michael, are there any particular security issues around the library or the museum I should know about?"

Baker didn't get it. He just stared back at Jack. "Uh, no, Jack."

"Don't you have some urgent security issues to get to?"

Baker just stared. "No."

"Would you like me to give you something else to do?"

Baker suddenly got it. He stood up quickly. "No, sir. I'm on my way."

Construction on the center buildings proceeded smoothly on a 24-hour basis. The two supply ships, the *Critias* and the *Timaeus*, which were named after characters in Plato's story of Atlantis, ferried equipment to the dome on a round-the-clock basis, transferring building materials and apartment and office furnishings through the loading hatches. Materials poured in from all over the world to Atlantis' new port in Cancun. A small party was held on the day the first inhabitants moved into their apartments in the Ursa Minor building. On that same day, a support dome was completed and researchers desiring to start work on research projects began moving equipment in. Jack decided to wait for the Orion building to be furnished as he had selected an apartment on the 80th floor. He wanted to be near the control center on the 75th floor of that building.

Jack and Bill were waiting for Spencer's jet to land. Spencer was eager to see his new penthouse apartment on the 90th floor of the Ursa Minor building. Emma, Joan and Howard had also been invited to see the progress of the city. It was a warm day, but not as hot as the last time Spencer had arrived.

They watched the plane land and taxi to the security point Baker had set up for arriving visitors. Spencer walked out first and, as expected, was hugged by Jack. Bill shook his hand.

"Nice to see you again."

Emma exited right after Spencer. Jack was surprised that she walked right by him and hugged Bill. He was even more surprised when she kissed him. Bill put his arm around her and they walked toward the helicopter.

Jack's jaw dropped. "What? I didn't get one of those!"

Spencer laughed. "Don't you know?"

"Know what?"

"Emma and Bill are in a relationship."

Jack stared at them. "Emma--and Bill?"

"Stranger things have happened. Come on, I want to see my new apartment."

Joan had been standing next to Spencer and heard Jack's comment. She walked up to Jack, kissed him and started walking toward the helicopter. Spencer and Jack smiled at each other.

As they walked to the transport helicopter, Spencer looked at Howard. "The officers of the Atlantis Corporation sure are a friendly lot, aren't they?"

Chapter 22

After only five years as the news room night editor, Julie Stevens had just been promoted to Night Manager of the Chicago Times. Some of the news department personnel wondered how she had advanced so rapidly in such a short time. Shortly after she had arrived, right out of college with a journalism degree, she had become a feature writer in the business section. Her critics were probably not aware of the endless hours she spent researching her articles, or the countless trips she had taken to visit and interview important executives in the oil and gas industry.

One of her early assignments had been to interview Jack Garrett aboard an oil platform off the coast of Louisiana. The platform boasted many new industry 'firsts' and Julie had been given the assignment to write a feature story on it. She was extremely lucky when the newspaper chain that owned the Times picked up the story and carried it in all of their papers.

"A definite career enhancement," she often told her fellow reporters.

She often remembered the week spent in New Orleans working on the story with Jack, who had been married to the daughter of a wealthy attorney for a little over two years. The marriage was floundering due to his long absences working on projects all over the world. Formally separated, they were finalizing the details of the divorce.

Jack was working on the off-shore platform when Julie arrived to interview him. What started as a casual business dinner soon blossomed into a passionate affair. When she had formally finished the interview, they had one last emotional night together. Jack, in the middle of his divorce, was too emotionally drained to commit to another relationship.

Julie reluctantly returned to Chicago but she kept close tabs on Jack over the years, especially after the divorce was final. In the ten years that followed their parting, she moved quickly from reporter, to assistant editor, to night editor and finally to night manager.

She happened to be at her desk when the call came from the newspaper chain's management informing her she had been selected by the Atlantis Corporation to represent the newspaper at the gala opening of the new city of Atlantis. Her editors and reporters were furious. She was constantly reminded that she was no longer a reporter, that one of them should get the assignment.

Knowledgeable newspaper reporters had followed the development of the domed city since the very first reports came out of London describing the scope of the project. Several reporters had interviewed renowned oceanographers and their possible role in the numerous research projects that were being proposed by member companies and governments involved in the newly formed Atlantis Foundation.

Reporters at the Times had made known their desire to attend the first press conference to be held in the domed city. Julie didn't know that Jack had personally asked for her to represent the newspaper chain.

As she packed her bags for the flight to Cancun, she wondered if Jack would even remember her. Ten years can wipe out a lot of memories.

Chapter 23

Joan Mason entered the Operations Room and found Spencer, Emma and Jack seated at a planning table discussing the last minute details of the information to be presented at a press conference to be held later in the week. She handed Jack a thick folder. "These are high priority purchase orders requiring your signature. If you'll sign the ones with the yellow tags, I'll fax them immediately."

Emma turned to Spencer. "This is a copy of the press release I plan to give out before the press conference. I thought we could begin with this. It should only take five minutes or so. Then I thought we'd turn the show over to you. You can explain the organization of the consortium and how the Atlantis Corporation relates to the Atlantis Foundation. Jack should provide some details on how the dome was constructed, with a summary of where we are now and our near-term plans for completing everything. Does that sound acceptable?"

Spencer scanned the press release. "Yes, of course."

Jack signed the papers and handed the folder back to Joan.

"How many media people have arrived so far?" Jack directed the question to Emma.

"About half. They'll all be here, though. We've received confirmations from everyone."

Joan glanced around, amazed at the number of computers in the operations room. "They wouldn't miss this for the world, believe me. I still can't believe I'm here... and I've been here almost a week."

"It's a pretty amazing place," Spencer agreed. "I can't get over how fast everything goes together, once the basic construction is done."

Bill Howell had begun the habit of referring to each new building put under construction by a star constellation. The names stuck to the buildings because there was no formal naming system. Jack agreed to allow the constellation names to be used until a corporate sponsor could be found that would occupy it, then their name would be utilized. A common practice in the real estate industry.

Jack watched Joan as she wandered around the room examining the displays. "Joan, have you tried the new French Restaurant in the Orion building?"

"No. It's pretty expensive isn't it? That may not be a consideration for the three of you, but most of us still have to think about how much things cost." Joan was still paying off her mother's medical bills.

Jack laughed, "I've been on this project so long, I forget about things like that."

Jack's mention of a restaurant reminded Joan that she had been eating too much. "By the way, where's that health spa you put in? I was thinking of going there for a workout."

"On the eightieth floor of the Little Dipper."

"I can't seem to remember those stupid names. Which building is it?"

"It's the northeast building in the center. There's a map on the wall if you can't remember which one it is."

As Joan walked over to the map Spencer finished reading

the press release. "What are you going to say, Jack?"

"I have a short speech written. I'll give you a copy later today."

Emma stood up. "I have to make some phone calls. I'll see you both later."

Spencer leaned over near Jack and whispered, "Joan talked about you constantly on the flight here. I think she likes you."

He looked at Joan, who was still looking at the map. He suddenly realized how much he missed not having her around. He wondered if the dress she was wearing was new. He realized he was staring at her, happy that she wasn't looking at him.

Jack leaned over and whispered to Spencer, "Let's see." He cleared his throat. "Joan!"

She looked at him and walked back to the table. "Yes?"

"Would you like to go to the French Restaurant for dinner?"

"Uh, sure, Jack. What time?"

"Around eight. I'll meet you on the center concourse and we can walk there."

"That would be nice." Joan was extremely pleased at his offer.

"I think it's a little upscale. Did you bring an appropriate dress?"

"Yes, I have one." She looked at her watch. "I have to go. I have a videoconference with some of the Foundation members today. I'll see you both later."

Jack watched her leave. She glanced back right before closing the door and smiled.

Spencer was clearly enjoying this. "I told you so."

"I'll let you know how it turns out."

He finished dressing and looked at himself one last time in the mirror. He hadn't been out on a date since the Christmas party. His daily workouts had paid off, his black suit was even a little loose on him. He remembered it wasn't that long ago when he couldn't close the pants.

He took the elevator down to the concourse level. As he got close to the building on the other side, he saw Joan come out of the connecting door. She wore the designer dress she had worn to the Christmas party. Her hair was slightly curled and down around her shoulders and she wore a pearl necklace.

When she saw his reaction, she laughed. "Hi, Jack. You look nice." She stopped a few steps away. "Come on, I don't look that different, do I?"

He recovered his composure. "I'm sorry. I didn't mean to stare, but you look beautiful."

She blushed and he walked over and kissed her hand. He could tell she liked it. He offered his arm. "Shall we go?"

They walked back across the concourse and into the restaurant where they were seated on a balcony overlooking the downtown area. He couldn't take his eyes off of her.

She smiled at him as the waiter put menus in front of them. She picked hers up and leaned forward to whisper, "I'm not the main course, Jack."

He looked away. "I'm sorry." He picked up the menu and scanned it, occasionally sneaking a peak at her as she read her menu.

She leaned forward and whispered, "Dessert, maybe."

Jack was speechless, fortunately the waiter returned to take their order.

After dinner, Jack took her hand as they approached the open concourse. When they were in the middle, they stopped and looked at the city street twenty stories below them. Electric cars and bikes moved at a quick pace through the streets.

Atlantians really couldn't talk about the weather, since it never changed inside the dome. The temperature was controlled to within a single degree and there was never a breeze or wind. The conditioned air flowing into the city was dissipated by countless vents located at strategic points. Each building had its own circulation system to prevent air stagnation and high humidity conditions that could lead to algae and mold formation.

He turned to her, searching for something to say. "Did you find the spa?"

"Yes. It's really nice. Was that your idea?"

"I made a comment to Spencer about gaining too much weight with all the food available on the project. He suggested the spa."

"It's funny, I don't remember you being overweight."

Jack laughed. "You weren't here while we were building the dome. I had lost a lot of it by the time you came with Spencer to see the dome." He looked at his watch. It was almost 11:00

PM. He turned to face her. "Would you like me to walk you back to your apartment?"

His hand was on the railing. She put her hand over his. "It's still early."

They moved a little closer together and kissed. They remained close when their lips parted. Her perfume was working on him. "What's that perfume you're wearing?"

"It's called *More.* Do you like it?"

"It's nice. Very nice."

She smiled. "Would you like to come over for a drink?"

"Sure."

She ran her fingers down his tie and pulled on it. "Let's go."

Jack stood on the balcony of Joan's suite and looked at the city. The activity in the center contrasted sharply with the ghostly skeletons of buildings fading into absolute darkness beyond. *It'll take years to finish all this.*

Joan walked out with two drinks and handed him one. "Bourbon and Coke."

"Thanks."

They sipped their drinks and watched the traffic below. Electric cars and carts didn't make much noise, even at ground level, but there was the occasional horn toot. Joan's suite was on the 40th floor, above the point where traffic sounds could be heard. The loudest noise in her suite was the air blowing out of several vents in the room.

"It's too peaceful, Jack."

"I think I've been missing out on some of the better things in life."

She took his drink and put it down on a nearby table and moved close to him. He put his arms around her. She put her arms around his neck and kissed him. She felt his hands roaming. "I thought humans only had two hands."

He laughed.

She gazed into his eyes. "Would you like to dance?"

"That would be great."

Joan put on some slow music and Jack put his arms around her waist. She put hers around his neck and put her head against his chest. After a while they stopped dancing and she let go of him. "Would you like another drink?"

He nodded and she brought him another. He drank his quickly but she felt a little dizzy and sipped slowly on hers. She closed her eyes and took a deep breath. When she opened them, Jack was rubbing his forehead. "Are you all right, Jack?" she wasn't feeling very well herself.

"Yes, but I have a little headache, probably from drinking a little too much. Would you have any pain relievers?"

"Just a second." She walked to the bathroom and opened the medicine cabinet. The only thing she had was the pain reliever she sometimes used for menstrual cramps. As she took one out of the bottle something nagged at her. She stared at the medicine bottle in her hand, trying to remember what it was. The alcohol she had consumed pushed the thought right out of her mind and she realized Jack was waiting for a pill. She handed it to him.

"Thanks."

He picked up his Bourbon and Coke and washed the pill down with it. As they danced again, he passed out.

Jack woke up with an excruciating headache. When he opened his eyes, it took a second to realize he was in Joan's apartment and that he didn't have any clothes on. A clock on the nightstand indicated 10:00 AM. He found a note on the pillow next to him. He unfolded it:

"Dear Jack,

Last night was a dream. The dinner was excellent and you were wonderful. I am kind of confused now and need a few days to sort things out. I'm going back to London for a while. I hope to see you soon.

-- Joan."

He stared at the note for a long time, trying to figure out what she meant and, more importantly, what had happened. His head pounded. He couldn't remember anything after they had started to dance. He looked around, found his clothes and put them on quickly. He saw his picture on her dresser in the middle of a group of press photos of each team member. *That's nice.*

He reread her note and put it in his pocket.

Chapter 24

The flight to Cancun from Chicago had given Julie time to reminisce about Jack. She often wondered if he ever thought about her. When the jet parked at the gate, she lifted her small carry-on bag to her shoulder and picked up her briefcase. As she made her way through a crowd waiting for the passengers, she hoped Tim was already there. She really didn't want to go to Atlantis and see Jack by herself.

Tim Barnes had been a photographer for the Times for nearly ten years. Almost a foot taller than Julie, he had seemed almost anorexic the last time she had seen him. With his long blond hair, she once told him he looked like a free spirit from the '60s. But she liked him and thought he had a natural gift for photography.

She was relieved when she spotted Tim waiting with some other photographers. He smiled when he saw her. "Long time no see, Julie."

The other photographers shook her hand and told her how great she looked.

"How have you been, Tim?"

"Fine. I was in Chili covering the latest elections when Hugh called me and told me to report here. This is pretty exciting, isn't it? A whole new city on the ocean floor!"

Julie nodded. "I can hardly wait."

"Have you lost some weight?"

"Yes." It was always nice to hear that, even if she hadn't lost any weight recently.

"I located our transportation, it's this way."

He took her carry-on bag and started walking off and she called after him. "Tim, what about our luggage!"

"They'll take care it. I understand they'll x-ray all of it anyway. Come on, the next group will be leaving soon."

A 'greeter' stood with a small ATLANTIS sign. A small graphic on the sign outlined a city under a dome. Julie recognized several reporters and began conversations while they waited. Several photographers took pictures of the greeter, who didn't look very happy. Finally he looked at his watch and asked everyone to follow him.

They walked out to a large, air-conditioned bus and filed on board. A few minutes later they arrived at a brand-new seaport still under construction and stopped at an ultra-modern dock. The *Sea Merchant* was waiting for them sporting a tropical design and a gangplank with bright yellow plastic chain railings to make boarding easy. Photographers jockeyed for position to take photos of their reporters crossing the gangplank to the submarine.

The top half of the *Sea Merchant* had been replaced with the same hard plastic as the dome and allowed excellent viewing from each of the two long rows of comfortable chairs in the main cabin. The submarine had a crew of three and a guest capacity of fifty. The crew included a steward or stewardess to make the trip more comfortable.

Julie walked across the gangplank through an oval entry hatch and found a seat near the front. Tim sat down across from her and took her picture. An announcement about the ship getting underway was made and the outside hatch closed. The little submarine backed away from the dock and headed south along the coast at surface level. The reporters and photographers settled in for an hour's journey through a diver's paradise.

After a little while, the island of Cozumel appeared in the distance. They were apparently following a pre-determined course between the island and the coastline. The door to the cockpit in the front was closed and a reporter wondered aloud if someone was actually piloting the ship or if it were being remotely controlled by a computer.

As the submarine neared the island, it began a slow dive. A woman's recorded voice informed them they were nearing the world-famous Palancar Reef and the journey would be partially underwater to maximize viewing of the marine life.

"We are now nearing the city of New Atlantis. Please be seated," a recorded announcement urged. Immediately the submarine began a nose-dive, catching some of the reporters off balance. The warm green glow of coastal waters became darker and darker, until it was totally black. A few fish were outlined by a large spotlight on the front of the submarine. The approach to the city was made near the sea floor to maximize the contrast of the lit city with its ink-like surroundings.

Everyone gasped as the glow of the city grew in the distance. Some even tried to take pictures. As the city grew in size, details of the buildings inside began to emerge. Although the four larger support domes were brightly lit, most of the smaller research domes were dark and difficult to see.

The submarine descended to within a few feet of the ocean floor, maneuvered inside a brightly lit docking station and settled into an indentation until the top part of the submarine was at the same level as the docking station's floor.

The visitors were asked to remain seated until the docking procedure was completed. They watched a huge hatch on the docking station close and the water in the station being pumped out. A gangplank extended out to the entry hatch on the submarine. There was a loud hiss as the door opened. They watched a smaller hatch on the main dome open.

Julie walked across the gangplank with Tim to a small security area at the entrance to the dome. There a security team handed each visitor a small badge. They were told to wear it at all times and to listen for announcements in case there was an emergency. The interior of the dome was brightly lit, even though no lights were visible in the dome wall.

Each was compelled to look up at the dome as it curved up and away into the distance. Some felt the urge to walk over and touch the wall. "It's a little cool to the touch," they told the others. Each hexagonal piece of the dome appeared to glow, although the light it transmitted did not obscure the view through it. At this depth there wasn't much to see.

The visitors climbed onto an unmanned tram. A beep preceded its departure and it followed a predetermined course into the downtown portion of the dome. Several electric cars and bikes whizzed by them as they neared the downtown area. Several reporters noted the star constellation names on the center buildings. The tram stopped outside the Orion Building and the guests walked briskly into the building's ultra-modern lobby. Signs near the elevators directed them to a buffet waiting for them on the top floor.

As the doors opened, they scurried to the observation deck

to look out over the city. Everyone looked up to see the top of the dome, which was less than 100 feet away. Several visitors thought they saw clouds in the upper portion of the dome.

Eventually, they found the media room, where a banquet table was set up with fruits and cold cuts. Emma Dawson greeted them at the door. Each received a personalized package of information in his or her own language advising them which hotel they had reservations in, along with directions on how to get there.

The bright, clean-looking interior hallways of the Orion building caught Julie's attention. She quickly realized the walls and ceiling were made of a white, opaque plastic. Light entered each floor at observation points and was funneled down the hallways by the plastic providing a warm even glow. Julie found her hotel room and removed a security access card from her information packet. As she turned it over to look at the directions, she heard the lock click and the door silently slid open. A cool rush of air blew past her as she entered. As the door closed silently behind her, a plastic coating on the ceiling began to glow until the room was bathed in a soft white glow.

Her room was a large, comfortable suite. She walked past her luggage sitting on a sofa and went into the bedroom. At first glance there didn't seem to be anything out of the ordinary--several pieces of oak furniture and a king size bed with what appeared to be a silk bedspread. She sat down on the bed and ran her hand over the bedcover. It was so soft and smooth she picked up the corner of the bedspread and examined it. After a moment, she realized it was woven from hair-thin plastic fibers.

As she continued to look around, she realized that the furniture she first thought was oak was actually made of plastic. She laughed as she opened the door to the balcony. Her room was on the 60th floor, well above any traffic noise from the streets below. As she gazed into the distance, she realized the light in the dome was rapidly fading away. She looked at her watch and smiled. The sun must have just set.

She jumped as a chime sounded on her ID badge. She fumbled with it and a moment later heard Tim's voice. "Hi, Julie. A few of us are getting together for dinner. Would you like to join us?"

"Tim! How are you calling me? I'm hearing you on my ID badge!"

"I just called the operator, got your number and called you from the phone in my room."

She walked into the bedroom and watched a tiny red light on the ID flash in sequence with a red light on the phone in her room. "The badge must act like a speaker for the phone. Where are you guys going for dinner?"

Chapter 25

The Range Rover rolled slowly down the beach with its lights out as Mark Williamson and Alan Sands trained their infrared binoculars on the top of the sand berm. They were trying to locate the remote power sub-station that was located at the edge of uninhabited jungle just south of Playa Del Carmen. It provided the backup power for Atlantis. With the increased security implemented since Susan Temple's death there was a good chance the remote power station would be guarded. This sortie was too risky to involve the other team members.

"There it is," whispered Sands pointing. A small security light at the station flickered on and off as Williamson revved the Range Rover's engine a little and started climbing the steep sand embankment.

"Are you nuts? You'll never make it up that hill!" snapped Sands.

"I had one of these babies in the mountains, watch this," replied Williamson.

The Range Rover almost flew over the top of the berm and bounced a few times before he killed the engine.

"See!"

Sands had been holding onto two handles tightly. He let out a breath and began studying the station through his binoculars. "I don't see anyone, let's go." They picked up several duffel bags and headed for the power station.

Three men in casual clothes walked past a hotel security officer, carrying several large bags. They entered the elevator and stopped at the sixth floor. They silently moved down the hall and stopped in front of room 614, laid their bags on the floor and took out a formidable array of weaponry. Mahmood Katcher and Hussein Ghoshar stood to the sides of the door as Mohammed Skerchi knocked on the door. He screwed a silencer onto a pistol as he backed up and waited.

Carl Bond looked up from his poker hand. "They can't be back already, can they?"

The others shook their heads. Bond opened the door, was pushed backward and fell to the floor as two men rushed past him. A third man put a gun in his face.

"Where is Carballo?" shouted Skerchi as he pointed his gun at the three men seated at a small table. They looked at each other in amazement and fear, put their hands up and slowly stood.

"We don't know," replied Brian Hill nervously.

Skerchi shot Hill in the head and turned to the others. "That was the wrong answer. Where is he?"

Tony Roberts and Sean Daniels were shaking in fear. "Honestly, we don't know. Alan Sands is the only one who has ever seen him. Sands would know, but we don't," replied Daniels, his voice quivering from fear. He had never seen anyone killed before.

Skerchi pointed his gun down at Bond. "Where is Sands?"

Bond closed his eyes. "He's trying to set a bomb at a station that supplies power to Atlantis."

Skerchi reached down, grabbed Bond by his shirt and jerked him to his feet. "You will take us there!" Katcher walked past

Bond and pulled him into the hallway, holding a gun at his head.

Ghoshar motioned to Roberts and Daniels. "What about these two, Mohammed? They have seen our faces."

Skerchi stood at the door looking at them for a moment. "You know what must be done." He closed the door and walked quickly to join the others at the elevator.

Sands and Williamson stood next to the Range Rover and drank a quick beer to celebrate a successful mission. They heard the sound of an off-road vehicle approaching along the beach. Williamson instinctively tossed his beer bottle away. "Guards?" Sands grabbed his binoculars and trained them on the beach. Moonlight reflected off the hood of the vehicle as it drew near.

"No, but there are four of them. Get your rifle."

They picked up two high-powered rifles and a box of ammunition, took up positions on the top of the berm and waited. Williamson was squinting through the binoculars when he suddenly gasped.

"What is it?"

"Someone in the back just got shot!"

"Well, we know they're not the authorities, so it's them or us." Sands attached a high powered scope to his rifle and took the safety off.

Chapter 26

The reporter pool invited to the grand opening consisted of fifty reporters and fifty photographers/cameramen from newspapers, TV networks and radio networks around the world. There were 100 seats in the pressroom, but most of the photographers and cameramen stood in strategic locations near the podium in order to film the speakers.

Julie was seated at the end of a row of reporters. Tim was near the back entry door, waiting for Richard Spencer and Jack Garrett. Reporters had obtained a press release an hour before and copies were currently being faxed all over the world. Julie tried not to yawn as Emma spoke of all the great accomplishments of the Atlantis Foundation and Corporation. She was waiting to see Jack, wondering how much he had changed. She had checked her makeup twice in the ladies room before the press conference began.

Emma's speech was almost over when Richard Spencer entered and photographers quickly began taking pictures. When Jack walked in behind him, only photographers who had actually looked at the pre-meeting material recognized him as president of the Atlantis Corporation. Julie strained to see if Tim had taken Jack's picture. She was relieved to see he was taking a lot of pictures.

She realized she was sweating, even though the large room was not hot and there were only 100 people in it. "He may not even recognize me," she had told Tim shortly before the conference started. The publisher, as well as the management of the Times had urged her to seek an exclusive because they knew Jack and Julie had been friends before.

"He may not even be interested in that," she had told them. Their expectations were high for something unique or interesting that they could beat all the other papers with. Julie felt the pressure.

She could barely see Jack after he sat down. She thought about standing up, but Emma had been explicit in explaining the rules: They would be civil or it would not continue. No questions shouted out; reporters would hold up their hands to ask a question.

Finally, Richard Spencer began to speak. Julie scribbled in her notebook as he spoke about the beginnings of the consortium, how the current Atlantis Foundation functioned and finally about the Atlantis Corporation.

Then Jack took the podium, describing how the dome and city were constructed. She turned on a digital voice recorder and wrote furiously, glancing up every now and then to make sure Tim was taking pictures.

When Jack had followed Spencer into the pressroom, he was taken aback by the crowd of photographers and cameramen pressing forward to take pictures. It took a moment before his eyes recovered from the camera flashes. He strained to find Julie in the crowd, but he couldn't see her. He sat down next to Spencer and they waited for Emma to finish. Michael Baker stood beside Spencer.

While Spencer spoke, Jack began a systematic scan of the reporters, looking for Julie. He finally found her at the end of a row on the opposite side of the room. Her hair was lighter than he remembered and she was a little thinner. She really hadn't changed that much. *Just a little older*, he thought.

Memories of their time in New Orleans rushed back and he felt a strange aching sensation he hadn't felt since high school. Random thoughts of them walking together along the river, eating in restaurants, kissing--it all came back to him.

He saw that she wrote furiously as Spencer talked. He almost missed his cue as Spencer finished his speech. Jack hated speeches. He remembered a drama teacher in college once told him to pick out someone in a crowd and give the speech to them. This would take away the pressure of seeing so many faces looking at you. He directed his speech to Julie.

There wasn't anything particularly interesting in his speech, a speech an engineer would give to an audience of engineers. There were many facts and some interesting tales about the construction of the dome. Reporters not particularly interested in such a technical speech picked up on Jack's singular focus to someone in particular and tried to figure out who it was. All the media would carry the same basic story, amazing as it was, but a human-interest story--now that was much more appealing.

A few times Julie saw Jack looking in her direction, but she missed the fact he was giving the speech to her. When he finished, even as the applause began, a few reporters had narrowed the possibility down to a few people, including Julie.

Emma fielded or directed numerous questions to Jack or Spencer. When she asked for one last question, she chose Julie's.

"A question for Mr. Garrett. Mr. Spencer spoke of a lot of applications for this new plastic. Will the Atlantis Corporation be involved in those and will you personally oversee the construction effort on one of those projects?"

Reporters in the know had their target. They sensed the conference was almost over and slowly began walking to Julie.

Jack had not even considered any other projects not related to Atlantis. Spencer had never been specific about them, or asked that he lead the effort. He walked to the podium and answered Julie directly. "I'm totally committed to completing this city as soon as possible. If an opportunity becomes available after that, I'll consider it. There's still a lot to do here, however."

Emma thanked everyone with a reminder that a tour of the city would begin at 3:00 PM in the pressroom. Some reporters signaled their photographers and suddenly Julie became the object of their attention. Surprised they were taking pictures of her; she gathered her things and hurried out the main door.

Several reporters waited outside the pressroom and surrounded Julie pounding her with questions. "Miss Stevens, why would Mr. Garrett direct his speech to you? Do you have an exclusive arrangement with him?"

"I don't know what you're talking about!" she replied.

Tim approached her. "Julie, Jack Garrett has asked to see you in the press room."

That started another round of questioning and picture taking. Tim had to help her fight the crowd to get back to the pressroom.

Chapter 27

Jack watched with some curiosity as Julie re-entered the pressroom with her photographer and a crowd of other photographers. Michael Baker and another security guard stopped everyone but Julie and her photographer from entering.

Julie smiled. Maybe she would get an exclusive interview after all.

Jack admired her figure. He hugged her. "I'm so glad you could make it. Let's go out the back door. We have a lot of catching up to do."

She wanted to kiss him, but Tim was behind her with the head of Security. "Tim, why don't you go to lunch? I'll meet you here at three for the tour."

Obviously disappointed, Tim would have liked a special tour as well. "Okay. I'll see you then."

Jack took Julie's hand and led her down to the Control Center. There were four operator stations, but only one operator was in the Control Center and he was reading a manual.

As soon as Jack closed the door, she turned to face him. He kissed her. "I must have been crazy to leave you that night. I can't tell you how many times I wanted to kick myself for doing that."

"I let you, remember? You were still married."

"Only on paper." He stood back and looked at her. "You look great, Julie. You've hardly changed."

Her blue eyes twinkled. "You must be exercising. You look thinner now."

"Your eyes are even bluer than I remember."

They laughed and started kissing.

"We have a lot of catching up to do. But first, I'd like you to meet everyone. They are in the VIP lounge."

Julie felt her heart start to beat a little faster. Maybe she would get an exclusive after all.

"I'd love to."

Jack led Julie down a hallway to a door marked PRIVATE. He opened the door for her and she entered the executive dining room. There were only a dozen or so tables but the décor was befitting the entertainment of heads of state and other designated VIPs. Spencer waited at a table with Emma Dawson and Bill Howell. The men stood up as Julie approached.

Jack introduced her. "Everyone, I would like you to meet an old friend of mine, Julie Stevens. Julie is the night editor for the news desk for the Chicago Times."

Spencer was the first to shake her hand. "Nice to meet you, Miss Stevens."

Julie was still in awe of meeting Richard Spencer, having seen literally hundreds of news stories about him over the course of her career. She had even attended a few press conferences where he introduced new business alliances or exclusive arrangements with governments. She could easily imagine a picture gallery of Spencer standing next to heads of government. She worried that her handshake would show how nervous she was. "It's a pleasure to meet you, Mr. Spencer."

"And this is Emma Dawson, Vice President of Corporate Communications," Jack continued.

Emma was smiling as she shook her hand. "We met at the media social." Emma looked at Julie. "You must be a very good reporter, Miss Stevens. Your name was the only one Jack gave me when I asked for suggestions."

Jack was signaling her to not say that, but she couldn't help it. Spencer enjoyed watching Jack squirm a little.

Julie looked at Jack and he smiled uncomfortably. He tried to change the subject by introducing her to Bill Howell.

Bill shook her hand. "Pleased to meet you, ma'am."

Julie's mind raced back to an interview she once had with an oilman in West Texas. Julie smiled at Bill. "West Texas. Amarillo?"

"How did you know that, ma'am?"

"I'm a good reporter." Julie replied, looking at Emma, who smiled back at her.

"Shall we sit down?" The waiter was waiting with menus as they settled in.

Emma waited until Jack looked up from his menu. "Are you going to join us on the tour this afternoon, Jack? You have a rather unique point of view and probably could answer questions Bill and I wouldn't have a clue about." She meant that as a compliment. No one had a greater grasp of the whole picture or the intricate knowledge of the parts and systems that made up Atlantis.

"I wasn't planning on it, but I just might." He was looking at Julie, who enjoyed being the object of Jack's attention. It wasn't lost on the others at the table either.

Jack asked Spencer to explain the origins of Atlantis to Julie. While he was doing that, Jack had the opportunity to study her in every detail. Fond memories came flooding back. He glanced at Emma. She was listening to Richard but she had her hand on Bill's and Bill was looking at her instead of Spencer.

He probably feels about Emma the way I feel about Julie. He made up his mind he wasn't going to let her slip away from him again. How could he let her know how he felt without scaring her off? What if she wasn't ready for a serious relationship? She might even have a boyfriend. He had asked a friend who had a friend that worked at the Times if Julie was married. The word back was that she had never married. They didn't know if she had a boyfriend but they had never seen her with one at the paper.

He would have to be careful.

When they had finished lunch, Emma and Bill got up to leave. Jack asked Emma if she would show Julie the Communications Center because it was not part of the planned tour later in the afternoon. Spencer sensed Jack wanted to talk to him alone so he made no effort to leave.

After Julie and the others left, Jack confided his intentions to Richard. "I can't let her get away again."

Spencer sat back in his chair. "Why are you telling me this? What do you want me to do?"

"I would like to offer her a job here."

"You don't have to ask me about that. I told you a long time ago that you were free to hire whomever you felt you need. I have often wondered how you were able to accomplish as much as you have with so few people.

Jack imitated Richard's voice. "I always get the best."

Spencer laughed.

"Seriously, Richard, what about Emma? Will she return to Spencer Industries?"

He realized why Jack was asking him about Emma. "You want to offer Julie the public relations position?"

"That would be my first choice. I have other ideas if that doesn't work out."

"I really don't know what Emma wants to do. A year ago I would have assumed she wanted to return to London. Now that she's developing a relationship with Bill, I'm not sure what she'll do, or even where she might want to live."

"In that case, let me tell you about some ideas I have for expanding the multi-use facilities we have here."

Spencer smiled.

Jack went to the communications center and found Julie talking to the communications officer about transmitting a story back to the Times. Jack tapped her on the shoulder. She had been concentrating so intently on the details of the story, she jumped when he touched her.

"Sorry. I'd like to talk to you about something." He motioned for her to follow him.

She excused herself from the others and followed him to his office. She was impressed with the tasteful decor. On the walls were numerous pictures of oil platforms, refineries, seaports and other projects he had worked on over the years. Jack watched as she walked along, examining the pictures. She recognized the platform in Louisiana where she first met Jack. She looked at him. "Belle Chase Number Two!"

He smiled at her.

She continued walking around the room. There was a large model of an oil platform in the corner of the room a little taller than her. She spent a moment looking at the incredibly detailed model. "This looks new."

"That's the Maximus platform in the North Sea. I was working on it when Richard made me an offer I couldn't refuse."

She laughed and looked around a little more.

"Please sit down." He felt his heart beat a little faster, something it seemed to do whenever she was near.

Julie sat in a large chair in front of his desk. He sat on the desk in front of her and cleared his throat. She settled comfortably into the overstuffed chair waiting for him to say something.

"How's your job at the Times?"

"It's fine. I was just promoted to Night Manager. I've put in a lot of time there."

"I know." He didn't look at her. "Has it been rewarding?"

"I guess so. It takes a long time to move up in the newspaper business. You almost have to wait until someone retires or dies at their desk."

Jack laughed. "Have you ever wondered if changing fields would help you progress faster?"

She frowned. "Jack, get to the point."

"Okay. How would you like to come to work for the Atlantis Corporation?"

"Doing what?"

"As the Entertainment Director."

She laughed so hard she almost fell out of her chair. "Entertainment Director? Are you out of your mind? I'm a reporter, for Christ's sake!" She stopped laughing when she saw he was serious. "Err... I didn't mean that there's anything wrong with being an entertainment director, but I don't think I'd be a suitable candidate for the job."

"It pays well."

She wasn't laughing now. Her salary increases over the last five years had averaged five percent and that was above the industry average.

"How well?"

Jack smiled. He knew he had her complete attention. "Spencer and I have discussed turning Atlantis into a five star resort to generate enough revenue and cash flow that would allow us to finish Phase Four a few years earlier than planned." He paused. "You would have to live here, of course."

She stared at him. The nature of the job was beginning to sink in. Not only would she have to leave her job at the Times, she would have to say good-bye to all of her friends. On the other hand, she would be happy to leave her apartment and noisy neighbors. Crime was getting worse in her neighborhood....

"It may be the reporter in me asking, Jack, but I think there's something you aren't telling me."

"You're right. I hoped I could find out if you had any commitments in Chicago that would keep you from working here."

"Was that offer for real?" She was a little miffed. "Why don't you just ask me what you want to know?"

"It is real." He sighed. He might as well go for it. "Are you in a relationship now, Julie?"

That was direct enough for her. Realizing where he was going with this, wanting him to say it, she smiled. "Why do you want to know?"

"Because I was hoping we had a chance to start where we left off."

She stared at him for a second, then stood up and put her arms around his neck and kissed him. He pulled her against him. When their lips parted, she ran her fingers through his hair. "Why didn't you just ask?"

They looked deeply into each other's eyes.

"I love you, Jack."

"Enough to marry me?"

Her heart skipped a beat but recovered quickly. She gazed into his eyes. "I would have married you ten years ago.

Nothing's changed."

"I must have been the world's biggest idiot then." He leaned her back against the chair, forcing her to sit down. He knelt down in front of her. "You want it on one knee or two?"

"Jack, don't be silly."

"Will you marry me?"

"Of course I will."

"How would you like to be the first woman to be married in Atlantis in ten thousand years?"

He must be referring to Plato's Atlantis. "Sounds like quite a news story."

"One you can send back to the Times if you want."

They hugged. She tried hard not to cry but she couldn't help it.

He closed his eyes. Her perfume was intoxicating. He could barely wait until later, when he would have her to himself again after all those years. When he opened his eyes, she was looking at him with a sly grin on her face.

"What are we going to do for the rest of the day?"

He laughed and looked at his watch. "The tour starts in thirty minutes."

She picked up her handbag and pulled out a tissue to dry her eyes. "Where is the nearest bathroom? My makeup needs fixing."

"Right behind you."

Just as she was about to close the door to the bathroom, he called to her. "Julie?"

"Yes?"

"I really <u>do</u> need an Entertainment Director."

She laughed. "We can talk about it over dinner."

Chapter 28

The tour began precisely at three in the press conference room and proceeded to the Control Center twenty floors below it. The Control Center was the highlight of the tour for many reporters. Divided into four operational sections, a dozen computers and printers sat atop curved tables that formed a circle in each section. Several large computer displays were centered above each circle so operators could see all of them without entering the other operator's circles.

Jack swiped his cardkey and entered a code on the push-button keypad of an electronic lock on a door in the back of the room and led them into the 'rack' room, cautioning them to not touch anything. Ten long rows of cabinets were full of electronic gear and wired to a myriad of sensors located all over the dome. Computers converted the sensors' signals and controlled thousands of individual pieces of equipment, including the emergency shutdown equipment. Five full-time programmers constantly worked at modifying or enhancing the computer code.

The tour resumed with a visit to Atlantis' library. Jack described how a supercomputer located in Cancun assisted in the analysis of data from scientific research already underway in the surrounding domes.

The museum caused quite a stir with its thousands of sea creatures and fossils on display, many borrowed from private collections, national museums and universities from around the world. Only a few were gathered from the nearby reefs.

A part of the tour was conducted on the 20th floor where the four central buildings were connected with wide pedestrian concourses over the roadway below. Numerous movie theaters, art galleries, jewelry stores, expensive boutiques and fine restaurants were already open. Reporters began to refer to the shopping area as the 'Rodeo' Concourse.

As they passed a European restaurant just recently opened, the lights went out in Atlantis and a few screams were heard. "Stay where you are!" Jack shouted. In a few seconds emergency lights came on and the crowd quieted down. He spoke softly to Bill. "What the hell is going on?" Even as he spoke, the lights came back on and his radio buzzed.

"Control Center to Mr. Garrett."

Jack keyed his radio. "What happened, Jim?"

"Mr. Baker would like to see you here as soon as possible."

"I'll be right there."

Jack pulled Bill aside. "Bill, finish the tour for me and try to reassure them. Tell them it was a glitch and nothing to worry about."

Bill nodded.

Jack whispered to Julie "I have to find out what happened."

"Can I tag along?"

He started to object, but considered her new role in the operation of Atlantis and changed his mind. He nodded to her and they started walking quickly to the Orion building's elevator.

Bill turned to the group. "Shall we continue? Spencer's tunnel is just ahead."

The tunnel was connected to the same large lobby of the Ursa Minor building as the concourses to the other center buildings. They stopped and looked into the tunnel. Lights built into the roof of each tunnel segment throughout the mile-long tunnel glistened like a sparkling necklace that disappeared in the distance.

"Richard Spencer originally conceived this tunnel as a means for Atlantians to be able to take an evening stroll on the beach. As a result of the easy access the tunnel affords, many new beach recreational facilities have been planned and are currently in the design phase. The inside of the tunnel," Bill explained, "is approximately ten feet wide and ten feet high and is made up of over four hundred identical pieces, each about fifteen feet long. A special non-slip coating has been applied to the floor of the tunnel because the plastic becomes very slippery when wet."

The tour continued on to the research domes.

Chapter 29

Baker looked up from a console as Jack and Julie entered. "We have a problem."

"What the hell happened, Michael?"

"We were temporarily hooked to the backup system while we were making some minor adjustments on the OTEC system. The backup power system was knocked off-line and it took a few seconds to switch back. I just got a call from Abrams at the power station. Come and look."

Baker walked over to a large screen TV and punched a few buttons. Tom Abrams was Bill Howell's construction foreman. He was waiting for them as the picture came into view.

"Jack, we have some bad news. The power substation near Playa Del Carmen was knocked out a little while ago. The power plant manager claims it was lightning and I think he may be right, but we need you to look at this, Michael."

Baker moved into Abrams's view. "I'm leaving now. I'll be there in thirty minutes." He looked at Jack. "You know what this means."

"Yes. I'll shut off everything that isn't critical and keep it under wraps."

A worried look crept onto Julie's face. "What's going on, Jack?"

"A minor problem." He sat down at a computer and began typing.

Julie watched as he brought up pictures of various electrical and mechanical systems and turned them off. When he was finished, he motioned for her to sit down.

"Atlantis is powered by an Ocean Thermal Energy Conversion system or OTEC for short. It relies on the difference in water temperature between the surface and the ocean floor to heat and cool ammonia. Warm water at the surface is used to vaporize liquid ammonia, which turns a turbine that produces power."

"The expanded gas is pumped to a heat exchanger on the bottom, where cold water is used to condense it back to a liquid. The process is repeated over and over to produce electrical power. We have what's called a hybrid system that also provides fresh water and powers another system that electrically separates water into hydrogen and oxygen. We store the hydrogen in a catalyst bed during the day, when we're producing more power than we can use. During the night, we heat the catalyst to drive off the hydrogen, which is burned to power a turbine that produces energy. We use the oxygen produced to help control the oxygen concentration in the air re-circulation systems in the buildings. We have an emergency backup link to a Mexican power plant in case something fails or we have to shut the system down for maintenance."

"And the backup system was damaged?"

He nodded. "The actual power line is buried. The only exposed part is a transformer sub-station near the coast. Baker has been on me to bury it to reduce the potential for sabotage or vandalism. You can't tell anyone about this," he cautioned. "It would cause unnecessary worry. Besides, we can run on the OTEC system for a very long time. We're currently running at less than five percent of its full capacity right now."

"I promise. I'll let you read everything before I send it on."

Spencer's voice came over a loudspeaker. "Hey, what's going on over there? Why did you stop the elevator?"

Jack picked up a microphone. "Richard, we're having a problem with the backup power system so we shut down the non-essential systems. We didn't shut down the elevators, though."

"Well, I'm in the Ursa Minor building and the elevator just stopped!"

Jack scanned the computer displays. That system was active, according to the computer. "It's supposed to be on, Richard."

"Well, it's not!"

"We'll look into it immediately," Jack promised, puzzled.

He picked up the current operations roster and looked for the programmer on duty. He picked up his radio. "Jack Garrett to Steve Smith. Come in, Steve." There was no reply. He looked for the first programmer call-out name. "Jack Garrett to Robert Jones."

"Jones here, Mr. Garrett."

"We need someone to trace out the wiring to the shutdown systems. Something must be crossed."

"No possible way on that, Mr. Garrett! We just finished verifying them last week."

"We're having a Level Three drill and the tertiary systems

are turned off. The elevators in Ursa Minor are off as well."

"That's just not possible!"

"Then go tell Richard Spencer. He's stuck in the damn elevator!" Jack shouted into the radio.

"Uh-oh. I'll be right there. Jones out."

Julie watched the monitors as Jones blasted through the door. He ran to an auxiliary console in the back of the room and pounded the keyboard, totally oblivious of Jack and Julie. Jack walked over and watched him. Julie followed.

Jones was down in the computer code of the shutdown system, reading the ladder logic of a Programmable Logic Controller, the brains of the elevator system in the Ursa Minor building. Jack knew some code, but Jones's fingers flew over the keyboard, the code scrolling up at a fast rate.

"Why are you looking at code, instead of the wiring?"

Jones didn't even look at him. "I checked all that stuff three days ago, Mr. Garrett. No way it's the wiring!" Suddenly he stopped and stared at the code. "Dammit!" he yelled.

"What is it, Robert?"

"Someone's changed the code! The addresses for the elevators have been replaced with support dome submarine docking area addresses. Someone's had access to this computer, or one of the two backup computers!"

"Someone with security clearance!" Jack gritted his teeth.

Julie had seen Jack mad only once, glad at that moment that she wasn't the object of his anger.

Jack tore his radio out. "Garrett to Baker! Come in Michael!" he yelled.

"Baker to Garrett. Jack, we're here at the transformer station. Turn the satellite link on. We want to show you something. Baker out."

Jack turned to Jones. "How long to fix it?"

Jones was expressionless. "I've already fixed it. Mr. Spencer should be on his way."

"How long to check everything?"

"Everything?" Jones was wide-eyed. "All of the code?"

"Get whatever help you need. Get people off vacation, do whatever it takes! We have to be sure we're not in for something a whole lot worse than this."

Jones looked at his watch. "Twenty-four hours--if we bring everyone in to help."

"Do it! I'll give everyone a bonus."

Julie walked over the projection TV and the black box next to it. She punched the ON button and Baker's face came into view. He was surprised to see her. "Where's Jack?"

"He'll be here in a minute."

When Jack was in view, Baker took hold of the satellite uplink camera and pulled it closer to a huge transformer. "Jack, look at this!" There were black streaks on everything and a large piece of the transformer was missing, almost as though something had bitten it off. "That's deliberate, Jack, no doubt about it."

Abrams walked into view. "Jack, I've seen damage like this done by lightning before. I would have to agree with the plant officials. Or at least I would say it was <u>possibly</u> caused by lightning."

Baker turned to Abrams. "That's bloody crap and you know it, Abrams!"

"Mr. Garrett, Plant operations personnel showed me pictures of similar damage caused by lightning."

"Okay! Okay! How long to fix it?"

"We have a replacement on the way in a cargo plane. It should be here in ten to twelve hours. I would say no more than twenty-four hours to have it all back to normal--"

"What are we going to do to prevent this from happening again?" Baker interrupted. "Even if it was lightning, which it wasn't, we can't take the chance of it being knocked out so easily again."

Jack thought for a moment. "All right... lightening or sabotage, we can't let this happen again. I'll authorize Tom to start on it immediately."

Tom was not happy. "It's almost a hundred degrees out here, Mr. Garrett! Do you know how hard it will be to bury the damn thing here--in the middle of nowhere?"

"Get whatever help you need." Jack glanced around the Control Room. All the operators were too busy to pay any attention to them. "Tom, would you excuse us for a moment? I'd like to speak with Baker privately."

Abrams disappeared and a moment later Baker came into view. "What's going on?"

"We've just discovered a breach in security."

"That can't be true!" Baker croaked.

"When I shut down all the tertiary systems, all the elevators in the buildings with escape hatches were shut down. The one in the Ursa Minor building even stopped in-between floors."

"It can't! The elevators aren't even tied into that system!" Baker felt faint but not from the heat.

"Spencer was in it and he wasn't very damn happy when he called the Control Center. The programmer, Jones, found coding changes."

"If it's a coding change, isn't this just a programmer's error, and not a security breach?"

"All software changes are logged in a history file. The changes were made in one of the backup computers in the rack room."

"But all the programmers have access to them!"

"We looked at the time and date the changes were made and the cardkey entry files. Only two persons were in the rack room at that time, Stan Smith and someone who used one of your temporary security passes."

Jack could almost see the veins in Baker's neck bulging out as he continued. "It had to be someone with the know-how to do it, as well as access to the computer. Stan Smith is missing and we're looking for him."

Baker shook his head. The number of security people with this type of access was very limited. There was only one other man who had the skills to get into the complicated code structure and substitute wrong but actual addresses. "Constantine Carballo!" he yelled.

"Your second in command?"

Baker was furious. He kicked something out of view. "I'll kill the bastard!"

"Take care of this as quietly as you can," Jack cautioned. "There may be others."

"Others?"

"Remember that note you received that indicated three different groups may try to sabotage the project just to make headlines?"

Michael frowned. "Yes."

Jack spoke in low tones and Baker had to strain to hear him. "What if all three are here and they don't know about each other?"

Baker was taken aback. "No! They can't be!"

"This morning you wouldn't have believed that one of your men could do something like this."

Michael was thoughtful. "I'll try to wrap this up as quickly as I can and be there in a flash. I'm sorry it turned out to be one of my men. I would have put my life in their hands, I was that sure of them."

"I'm sure you were. Let's just hope we can find all of the bad guys before they can do any real harm. I'll see you in a little while."

Jack turned the videoconference system off and looked at

Julie. "I'm sorry you had to see all this."

Julie put her arms around his neck. "I wouldn't have missed it. It's just a shame I can't put it out as an exclusive."

Jack pulled her against him. "Now, where were we?"

"Jack, if you don't mind, I would like to rejoin the tour group. I do need to file a story, remember."

"All right. I'll meet you for dinner."

She kissed him and walked out, stopping briefly to throw him a kiss before she closed the door.

Jack laughed as he went to check on the programmer's progress.

Chapter 30

Later, after the media tour was over, Richard Spencer stopped his electric cart when he saw Jack returning from the jogging track. "Did Julie accept the entertainment director's job?"

"We're going to talk about that over dinner. She did accept my offer of marriage."

Spencer's surprise showed. "Congratulations! I really mean that, Jack. She seems like a really nice woman. I'm happy for you."

"Thanks. I'm working on balancing my personal life with work."

They both laughed.

"Do you want a ride back?"

"No, thanks. It's such a lovely evening, I think I'll walk."

"All evenings are lovely here. Will I see you at dinner?"

"Probably not, I have a date."

Richard laughed and drove off.

Jack keyed his radio. He had one more task for the evening. "Garrett to control."

"Yes, sir," the night operator answered.

"Give me the phone number of the new jewelry shop in Ursa Minor."

It was almost sunset and Julio Perez and Juan Sanchez had just come on duty. They were standing guard at the tunnel entrance when they heard a loud crashing sound up on the coast road. They wondered what had happened when a man appeared, running over a nearby sand berm and down to the beach toward them. Immediately two men appeared, chasing the first one and Julio and Juan heard them cursing and swearing at the first man. They were faster and caught up with the man almost in front of Julio and Juan and started a no-holds barred fistfight. From their yelling it appeared they have been involved in an auto accident caused by the first man. Julio and Juan walked over to watch.

Mark Williamson and Alan Sands climbed over a sand dune and ran as quickly as they could toward the entrance of the land tunnel to Atlantis. When they were sure the guards were watching the fight, they slipped quietly into the tunnel carrying two large duffel bags.

"That was too easy." Sands commented.

"Those actors deserve a bonus."

They laughed.

"How long until the meeting?"

"About two hours. Then the fun really begins." Sands couldn't help laughing out loud.

Jack finished tying his necktie and looked at himself in the mirror. "Betrothed," he smiled as he closed the door of his apartment and walked to the elevator. The ride from the 80th to the 20th floor came to rest with a slight jerk. Jack made a mental note to check that system in the morning.

He walked out onto the concourse and waited for Julie. As he looked at his watch, she touched his arm from behind. He turned and took a quick breath. She shimmered in a black sleeveless dress. Her blond hair was down around her shoulders and she wore her 'evening' makeup. Jack's jaw dropped. Julie never had been overweight, but in the last year she had been exercising routinely and had successfully dropped a whole dress size.

She smiled as she watched his eyes examining her. "Do you like my dress? It's an original. I bought it for the big gala ball this weekend."

Jack was still staring and didn't answer.

"Jack!" Julie snapped her fingers in front of his face.

"You look lovely," he finally replied.

She blushed. "Thanks. You look nice, too." Jack couldn't take his eyes off her. "I'm hungry too, Jack."

They were seated on the balcony by the railing and had an excellent view of the city below. The waiter brought them menus, opened a bottle of wine and filled their glasses before he left. They touched their glasses together.

"Can we talk about the director of entertainment job, Jack? I am curious what you have in mind, now that I'll be living here."

Jack's heart skipped a beat. It looked like a done deal. He felt the jewelry box in his coat pocket. "You can't tell anyone this, but the funding for Phase Four is still uncertain. The Foundation has the money to complete Phase Three now, but that will leave about twenty percent of the planned buildings unfunded. We think there's room here to accommodate all the researchers, their families, occasional visitors and dignitaries, some time-share vacationers... and a lot of tourists."

"Tourists?"

"Yes. We've already started construction of new recreational facilities on the beach. We've modified the new dock we built on the coast to accommodate cruise ships. Atlantis will be a stop on their itinerary. We think we can get approval to build a casino in one of the support domes because we probably won't need all four for storage. We wouldn't touch the eight research domes, of course."

"A casino?" Julie was shocked. "You'd mix a casino in with the premier oceanic research facility in the world?"

"Why not? Researchers are people, too. They need occasional recreation. We're also thinking about expanding the planned amenities on the coast. The Foundation owns a pretty big chunk of the beach and the land behind it. This is in addition to the corporations that might want to hold conferences here, of course. And there are the parties we'll hold for visiting heads of state. There are also facilities to be built for the resident's and researcher's children--churches, schools, day care facilities and so on."

"That doesn't sound like entertainment."

Jack thought for a moment. "You're right. Maybe a better title would be Director of Facilities Operations."

"It sounds like a lot of responsibility. You said it pays well?"

Jack studied her expression. "With a bonus plan, it could be twice what you are earning now."

She took in a deep breath. "Twice?"

He nodded.

"And you would really offer this to a newspaper editor?"

"It takes quite a bit of organizing to get a paper out each day, doesn't it?"

"Well, yes, but--"

"How about it, Julie? It's yours if you want it."

"Are you offering me this because you love me?"

Jack smiled again. "No. It's because I think you are the best person for the job."

"The Atlantis Corporation is a public company. Wouldn't a stockholder question your wife having such a prominent role in the corporation?"

"Of course they could. You'll be on probation for the first two years, just like everyone else. You'll have to prove to everyone that I made the best choice." He smiled. "I know you can do it. By the way, Directors become Vice Presidents once they finish their probationary period. Then the bonus potential becomes four times your base pay."

She stared at him for a few seconds. "Does that mean the chance for five times my current salary?"

"Yes, it does."

I'll never get two offers like this in one day again. She put her hands on his. "I'll do it."

As they left the restaurant, Julie looked at her watch. It was only 10 PM. Jack probably wanted to go to his apartment for the night's recreation, but she was feeling the effect of too much food. She remembered Spencer's tunnel. "Jack? Can we go for a walk on the beach? I really need to walk off that meal."

"The beach is a long walk from here. It takes over an hour just to walk there and back," he protested.

"Please? I've never been to a beach in Mexico before. Wouldn't you like to take a romantic walk along the beach in the moonlight?"

When he didn't answer immediately, she said, "There will still be plenty of time for <u>that</u> later."

He laughed. "All right. Let's go."

They joined a group of strollers entering the tunnel.

Two security guards stood at the land side entrance to the tunnel. As they neared the end of a small platform, Julie took off her shoes and walked down a set of stairs to the beach. Jack watched her for a moment and took off his socks and shoes and rolled up his pants. A warm breeze blew and the sky was full of stars. The moon was up and provided a little light as they held hands and walked along the beach.

"It's magnificent!" she said, running her feet through the sand.

"Imagine this a year from now, with swimming pools, a golf course, tennis courts and a dance floor."

She turned and kissed him. He kissed her back but she broke away laughing and ran to the water.

"Can't catch me!" she said, running down the beach.

Jack ran after her. As he got near, she kicked water on him. She laughed at his reaction as she put her arms around his neck. "I'm sorry."

"No you're not."

"You're right." She was laughing as she let go of him, kicked water at him again and ran away.

When he caught her he kissed her hard. "Have you ever made love on the beach?"

"I paid almost a thousand dollars for this dress. If you think I'm going to take it off here, you're out of your mind!" she said teasingly.

He remembered the jewelry box. "I have something for you."

"I said I'm not going to take this dress off here." She put her arms around his neck and whispered in his ear, "You'll have to wait until we get back."

He managed to take the jewelry box out. It was so dark he held it up to her face so she could see it. Her eyes got big. "What is that?"

"Open it."

When she opened the box, moonlight sparkled on the diamond inside. "Jack!" She was so surprised she dropped it. "Oops!"

They felt around in the dark until she found it. He put the ring on her finger. "I had to guess at the size."

She kissed him until he had to take a breath. "Thank you. I think it's time to go back."

Jack opened the door to his apartment and Julie walked in. It wasn't what she expected at all. She'd been in a few bachelors' apartments where she was afraid to sit down. Jack's was spotless. There was very little actual furniture but what was there was expensive and tasteful.

When Jack went into the kitchen, she looked at some rather unusual paintings on the wall. She recognized one as an original Picasso. A huge balcony ran the whole length of a wall. She looked around and headed for the bathroom. She closed the door and looked at the ring in the light. It wasn't a huge stone, she guessed about one and a half carats, but she knew enough about diamonds, and Jack, to know it was perfect.

When she came out, Jack was on the balcony looking out at the city, two drinks on a nearby table. She picked them up and handed him one. They touched the glasses and drank.

Julie looked at the street eighty floors below. It was almost midnight; there was very little traffic. A few soft sounds were audible in the distance.

Jack saw her looking at the diamond on her finger. "That was the biggest they had here that didn't have any defects."

I knew it! She thought. "It's wonderful Jack."

"I'll get a bigger one when we go to Cancun."

"I don't need anything bigger."

Julie took the glass from his hand and put both glasses down on the table. She put her arms around him and kissed him. The intensity of his touch increased until she had to take a breath. "Why don't we go inside?"

She led him to the bedroom. She remembered he could be pretty intense at times. She needed to remind him that slow was better for her. He put his arms around her. She ran her fingers through his hair. "Don't eat me up."

He laughed. He hadn't heard that since New Orleans, but he knew what she meant.

"Jack?" she said between kisses.

"Yes?"

"We have all night. I haven't done this in a long time."

"I don't think I have either."

She wondered what he meant as she closed her eyes and he began kissing her neck and shoulders.

Chapter 31

Julie's head was on Jack's chest, her fingers twisting his chest hair. "I like listening to your heartbeat."

"Is it back to normal yet?"

They both laughed.

The air conditioning vent moved the vertical blinds back and forth as Jack stroked her hair, almost asleep. He thought he heard a muffled sound in the distance. He might have been dreaming.

"Jack, I swear I felt the earth move and we weren't even doing it."

Jack bolted from the bed and grabbed his clothes off the floor.

Julie had never seen anyone dress that fast. She sat up. "Hey, I was only kidding, Jack. What was that, thunder? Where are you going?"

"It's bad, whatever it was." He put his socks on, kissed her good-bye and ran for the door carrying his shoes.

"Be careful, Jack, please!" Julie shouted as the door slammed behind him. She looked at the clock on the nightstand; it was a little after three. She went to the closet, put on one of Jack's shirts and walked out onto the balcony. The city was very quiet, with only an occasional car on the street below her. Her heart was beating faster than normal.

Jack had his radio out as he ran down the stairs. "Garrett to control. Come in!"

Mike Osborne, the night operations supervisor answered. "Control here. Where are you, Mr. Garrett?"

"I'm on my way to the Control Center. What happened? What was that noise?"

"We don't know yet. All systems are normal. We think it came from the north end. We have a team on the way there now."

"What channel are they on?"

"Channel nine, sir."

Jack switched channels on his radio.

After learning of the potential threat to the dome by terrorists, Baker divided his forces into teams of two because it was harder to surprise two people rather than one.

"Security Three to Control. We're nearing the north docking station and I--" The transmission went dead, then, "Oh, my God!"

Jack's pulse raced. "Garrett to Security Three, what have you found?" He was at the entry door to the 75th floor as the security team replied.

"There's a hole in the dome and water is coming in like a waterfall!"

Jack's stomach knotted. He pushed open the entry door, ran to the nearest elevator and pressed the button for the ground level. When the elevator finally arrived at the ground level, he ran for the north docking station.

He couldn't believe his eyes as he neared the docking station.

A section of the dome on the second row was completely gone. Seawater poured in through a hole about six feet wide and eight feet high and pounded onto the grate above the containment canal. Water had surged forward until it found a step up and then flowed back toward the canal.

Jason Edwards, a member of Baker's security team, ran over to him. "What should we do, Mr. Garrett?"

"Call Baker and tell him what happened. Then cordon off this area. Get Howell here and find the captain of the *Sea Merchant*. We need it here as well."

Edwards ran back to the others.

Jack wondered if he should call Spencer, then he thought about Julie. She didn't need to know about this. Maybe they could get it fixed before the city woke up. Did they have a spare piece for that row? The manufacturer had been slow in making spares. Spencer had put enormous pressure on them to produce the thousands of pieces required to build the main dome and the twelve support domes. Once they had delivered those, they were desperately trying to fill backorders for their other customers.

Obviously there had been an explosion of some sort. He was wondering why the entire piece was missing, instead of simply having a hole in it, as Spencer drove up in his cart. He got out and stared at the water pouring in.

"Michael called me. Will any of the pieces in the support domes replace it?"

Jack shook his head. "Not even close." He picked up his radio. "Garrett to Howell."

"Yes, sir?"

"Have you heard what happened?"

"Yes, sir."

"Are there any spare pieces for row two in storage anywhere?"

"I don't think so, Jack. We have a few spares, though. I have some people looking into it. There might be one in a warehouse at the new dock in Cancun. We checked the inventory database for the support domes here and can't find one."

Spencer stared in fascination at the huge quantity of water pouring through the opening. "Any guess on how much water is coming in, Jack? Can the canal pumps take it out?"

"Unless something else happens, water should never get out of the canal when a row one or row two piece is out. Why did the whole piece come out?"

"The plastic is very strong, much stronger than the seal. The explosive device merely pushed the piece out. I'm certain it's in good shape and probably sitting on the sea floor not far from here."

"Hopefully, the crew of the *Sea Merchant* will find it soon." Jack remarked wistfully.

Baker screeched to a stop on an electric scooter. He ran over and stood near Spencer. "What the hell happened?" He stared at the water gushing in.

"An explosive device blew that piece out."

"Jack, can the canal pump handle it?"

"Unless it gets worse than that, yes."

They watched the water pound the canal grate.

"The grate won't take that for long though." Jack's radio buzzed.

"Control Center to Mr. Garrett. Please come in."

"Garrett here."

"Uh--the canal pump won't start."

The knot in Jack's stomach got bigger. "Why not?"

"We have a team going there to check it now, Mr. Garrett."

Jack looked at Baker. "We'd better take a look at this one, Michael." They started to walk off.

"Take my cart," Spencer offered.

They drove as fast as they could to the support dome containing the canal pump, jumped out and ran to the pump. The operations team arrived just after them.

At first Jack couldn't see anything wrong as they approached the enormous pump. The motor was intact and the pump appeared to be in good shape. He rubbed his eyes. The shaft coupling that connected the pump to the motor was gone!

Baker saw the problem almost the same time as Jack. "Oh, hell!"

The operations team looked at the pump in disbelief. One of them turned to Jack. "We checked this pump yesterday on a routine maintenance schedule. It was fine, Mr. Garrett."

Baker was on the radio to the night security team. "Meet me

in the armory in ten minutes."

Jack turned to him. "What are you going to do, Michael?"

"This is sabotage. Whoever did this is still here... and we're going to find him! He could be armed so we're going to be also."

"There are a lot of innocent civilians here now. Please be careful."

"We will."

Jack heard the nearest field operator cursing. "What is it?"

"We're supposed to have two spare couplings in stock, but they're gone!"

"Gone!" Jack gritted his teeth. "How long if we have to make one?"

"We have a machine shop, but the machinist is sick."

"Well, get him out of bed if you have to!"

"He has meningitis, sir."

Jack felt a headache coming on. He rubbed his forehead. "Do what you can. We have to get this pump in operation as soon as we can."

He walked back to the main dome and looked down at the water level in the canal. It was already half full of dark swirling seawater. A chill ran down his spine. He ran the day's events over and over in his mind. What had he missed?

It was after 5:00 AM and Jack was frustrated that nothing had been accomplished. They still hadn't found the missing dome wall piece and water was spilling out of the canal. The entire spare parts inventory had been searched and a replacement shaft coupling could not be found for the canal pump. The machinist was in the machine shop trying to make another, but he was so weak he had to sit down every few minutes. The doctor was not happy. Jack ran into security teams looking for the saboteur every now and then.

Chapter 32

Michael Baker had every available security person out searching for the saboteur. He had been careful not to say 'terrorist' when describing the person or persons responsible. He was determined to find whoever had done this 'on his watch'.

It was almost six in the morning when Baker and the teams assembled in front of the Orion building, to review their efforts. His men had looked everywhere and found nothing. They had stopped everyone moving about, even early morning joggers, who had been surprised to find the whole perimeter off limits. Some had even seen the water pouring through the missing wall piece and had hurried back to their rooms. He couldn't keep this quiet much longer. He was about to address his men when they heard another distant sound like thunder. Suddenly he felt nauseous. *This is a bad dream and I'll wake up soon.*

He jumped on his scooter and headed in the direction of the noise. He didn't have to go far to see that another wall piece was missing and water was cascading in on the water already starting to pool near the dome wall. Amazingly, the missing piece was in the third row, almost twenty feet from the dome floor.

Jack drove up behind Baker and got out. They watched the problem worsen.

"This is more than the canal pump could handle even if it were working."

"If we had the missing pieces, how long would it take to put them in?"

Jack thought for a moment. "Well, we could use the small construction dome to replace a broken dome piece. One of the mini-subs could position it over a broken piece, or the hole in this case, then we pump it out, insert the new piece and seal it. We used this method to put the tunnel connection piece in. I can't remember what happened to that dome, but I think we took it apart and stored it in one of the support domes. But we could still put it together and replace the pieces in a day or so, if we have them."

"What if we don't? How long would it take to make new ones?"

"Weeks, maybe a month for them to gear back up for it."

"A month? How much higher is the downtown area than the perimeter?"

"Less than ten feet," Jack replied grimly. He couldn't help but wonder out loud, "How could they blow out a piece that high up?"

Baker shook his head as Jack's radio buzzed.

"Control to Mr. Garrett."

"Garrett here."

"We started the canal pump."

Baker sighed. "Thank God. That'll give us a little time."

"That's great, Control. What's the pump rate?"

"Uh--Mr. Garrett?"

"Yes, what is it?"

"It's showing a negative flow rate value! I didn't think that was possible."

"Negative? Are you sure?"

The field operator shouted into his mike, "Turn the damn pump off! It's flowing in reverse! We're pumping water <u>into</u> the canal!"

"Oh, crap!" came the reply from the Control Center.

Jack and Baker looked at each other and headed for the support dome housing the canal pump but they couldn't get to it for the waves of water surging from the containment canal. Jack turned the cart around and drove to the Orion building. They didn't say anything as they rode up the elevator to the Control Center. Water would inundate the downtown area in less than an hour.

As they entered the Control Center, everyone stopped and stared at them. The shift foreman walked over to them. "We've shut all the emergency doors to all the support buildings, Mister Garrett. We can't seem to stop the canal pump and we can't get to it without a wet suit. We've checked everything we can from here and we don't think it's the wiring. We think the pump's control logic has been altered."

Jack looked around the Control Center. "Where are the programmers?"

"They're all working on the backup computers. They haven't found the problem yet."

Jack looked at Baker then back at the foreman. "How many people are in the city right now?"

The operator touched an interactive computer display. "Less

than two thousand. One thousand, nine hundred and fifty-seven."

"How long would it take to evacuate them?"

"Evacuate them? Are you serious, Mr. Garrett?"

"If we can't find those missing wall pieces by seven, start the evacuation." He turned to Baker, who was staring at him in disbelief. "We're going to need all of your people to help do this in an orderly way, Michael."

"Mr. Garrett," the operator interrupted, "it would take hours to get them out the four loading hatches. Each one can only hold about a hundred people and it takes thirty minutes to load, raise, empty and lower each one."

"What if we got them all to the twentieth level and they walked out the land bridge tunnel?"

The operator hadn't thought of that since it had been taken over by the 'recreation' department. "They could get out pretty quick that way."

"Fine. At seven o'clock, if we haven't made any progress."

"Yes, Mr. Garrett!"

Baker motioned Jack to the side. "Do you really think that's necessary?"

"If we can't stop the water coming in, we have no choice."

"I'll get everyone together and tell them." Baker turned and walked out.

Jack stood for a moment lost in thought, until he thought of Julie. He wanted to run to her, but he had one more thing to do. He went to the rear portion of the Control Center, swiped his cardkey and entered a code in the electronic lock to the rack room. All five programmers were frantically trying to figure out what was wrong with the canal pump. He decided not to bother them and walked out. He was thinking of Julie as he headed for the main door when the shift supervisor called to him.

"Mr. Garrett!"

"Yes?"

"Would you look at this?" He was staring at a computer screen.

Jack walked over and scanned the OTEC system summary screen. The system was at five-percent power and on its way down. What the hell was going on? He narrowed his view to the ammonia re-circulation system. The ammonia pressure was way down and falling. The emergency vent valve was open and wouldn't respond to the touch screen command to close. Without the cooling medium, the system could not produce any electric power. Even as he watched, a red warning flashed across the screen. INADEQUATE MEDIA FOR TURBINE OPERATION. SHUTDOWN SYSTEM COMMENCING.

Jack felt a chill. He walked out the Control Center door and realized the power was about to go off in the dome. He keyed his radio. "Garrett to Howell."

"Yes, Jack?"

"What is the status of the land power connection?"

"The crew set the replacement transformer in place yesterday, but they haven't finished hooking it up. They probably aren't in to work yet, since it's six-thirty. They should be able to finish it up today, though. We have another two weeks to finish the concrete cover."

"That'll be too late."

"Say that again, Jack?"

"The OTEC system is going down! We won't have any power in Atlantis in a few minutes."

The only exception to the power supply in the main dome was the emergency lighting system and the Control Center, which ran off an Uninterruptable Power Supply. The UPS system was enormous. It was adequate to run the equipment in the Control Center for 24 hours on batteries alone. The support domes also had their own UPS emergency lighting systems. The four emergency escape hatches had large UPS systems as well.

Baker was in the street in front of the Orion building watching a dark pool of water creep up the street to the center of the downtown area. He shook his head and looked at his watch as he walked into the lobby. It was almost seven, time to start the evacuation. He pressed the elevator button just as power went out in the dome. He almost panicked but calmed down when the emergency lighting system came on. He ran to the stairwell and up the stairs to the 20th floor.

His men were already knocking on doors and telling people to go to the 20th floor and leave though the tunnel on the west side of the dome.

Jack closed the door of the Control Center behind him and walked out in the darkness to a nearby lookout area on the 75th floor. At observation points on the floors below, he saw people walking down the corridors with flashlights. There was a lot of activity on the 20th floor. He felt a sense of relief. It was ironic that Spencer had insisted on the tunnel and he had tried to derail it as a waste of money. He also felt guilty that he'd given his original Picasso to one of the security guards as he was about to leave through the tunnel. After all, many people were losing precious possessions.

After a moment of reflection, he went to the stairwell and started walking down to the 20th floor to find Julie.

Chapter 33

Michael Baker had been certain that at least a few people would panic when Garrett ordered the general evacuation. As he watched the orderly process from the observation deck on the 21st floor of the Orion building he still could not believe there hadn't been even one incident. Suddenly, he felt a gun in his back and heard a familiar voice.

"Drop your gun, Baker." Constantine Carballo whispered.

"Carballo! Where the hell have you been?"

"Never mind, just drop the gun!" Carballo's voice was rising even as he tried to control it. He had to restrain his desire to keep from pulling the trigger, but it had to look like Baker died accidentally, or his plan to get Spencer wouldn't work.

Baker dropped his gun on the floor and Carballo kicked it away.

"Let's go!" Carballo hissed.

"What the hell are you doing? Where are we going?"

"To the loading hatch on the Little Dipper building."

"You'll never get past the guys on the concourse level!"

"You're going to be my shield."

"You're out of your mind if you think I'm going to help you get out."

"You will, or I'll shoot you right here." Carballo pushed his gun harder into Baker's back. "Now move!"

They walked to the stairwell and down the flight of stairs to the 20th floor. As they exited the stairwell door, one of Baker's men happened to shine a light on them. It startled Carballo and he shot at the security guard. People nearby screamed and ran away. Baker grabbed for Carballo's gun and it went off, hitting him in the shoulder. He fell to the floor as Jack ran up.

Jack saw Baker laying on the floor and became enraged. He grabbed a gun from the nearest security guard and began firing at Carballo, who turned and ran back to the stairwell, with Jack close behind him. Carballo fired at Jack and then opened the stairwell door and ran up the stairs.

Jack started up after him and fired his last bullet just as Carballo opened the door to the 21st floor. The bullet ricocheted, hitting Carballo in the arm. He yelled and fell to the floor as the door closed behind him. He struggled to his feet and ran down the hallway as he heard the door behind him open.

Jack burst through the door and saw Carballo running away. As he started after him, he saw his gun on the floor. He scooped it up and stuffed it into his waistband as he ran. He stopped when he saw Carballo at an observation point, climbing over the railing.

"Don't do that, Constantine. If the fall doesn't kill you, you'll die in the cold water!"

"I'd rather die here than in a jail cell." Carballo looked at the dark swirling water below him and hesitated.

Jack ran forward and tried to grab him, but managed to grab only his hand. When Carballo jumped, Jack was slammed into the railing, holding onto his hand. He looked down at him. "Pull yourself up! I can't hold on!"

"No! It's over for me." Carballo twisted his hand and Jack lost his grip.

Jack watched as Carballo disappeared into the darkness below. He suddenly remembered Baker and ran for the stairwell.

As he exited the stairwell, he saw two medical technicians lifting Baker onto a stretcher. "How is he?" he demanded of one of the technicians.

"It appears to be a minor shoulder wound, but we won't know for sure until they operate on him."

Jack wasn't an expert but he guessed the bullet had probably passed through without hitting anything vital. He took a deep breath and let it out. He looked at the guards gathered around them. "Don't just stand there! Go help the people evacuate!"

They all scattered, except for one of Baker's key men.

When Jack moved into his view, Baker grabbed his arm. "What about Carballo?"

"He's dead."

Baker closed his eyes and passed out.

Jack's radio buzzed.

"Jack!"

It was Spencer. "Oh Christ," he murmured.

"We heard gunshots? What's going on?"

"The security officer we've been looking for tried to use Michael as a shield to get by the security team. He shot Michael, but he's going to be all right."

Spencer had his finger on the SEND button and involuntarily pressed it when he heard about Michael.

Jack heard Julie scream.

"Where are you, Jack?" Spencer was trying not to get upset when Julie buried her head in his shoulder.

"We're on the twentieth floor, near the land tunnel exit."

"We're on the twentieth floor of the Little Dipper" Spencer replied. "We'll be right there."

The EMTs were picking the stretcher up when Spencer and Julie arrived. She ran over to Jack and hugged him, gasping when she saw the blood on Baker's shoulder. She saw that he was unconscious. "How bad is it?"

"I think it's just a flesh wound. I don't think it hit an artery."

"What happened?"

"It's a long story. I'll tell you on the way to the medical facility."

The medics hurried up the stairs toward the medical facility on the 50th floor with Julie, Spencer and Jack behind them.

As he plunged into the icy water, the pain in Carballo's arm was lost among the pain of thousands of icy needles jabbing at his skin. For a brief instant, he wanted to let it all go but an even stronger instinct to survive grabbed him and he tried to fight his way to the surface. He realized his foot was trapped somehow. He bent over and felt a railing. He was still at an observation point! He quickly took his shoes off and swam desperately for the surface. He gasped as his head broke the surface. When he opened his eyes, he saw an emergency light shining through a railing only a few feet in front of him. He grabbed the railing and somehow managed to pull himself over it. He stood panting and shivering for a moment until a voice hissed his name.

"Carballo?" Stan Smith walked out of a shadow. "What happened?"

"Never mind. What floor are we on?"

"Twelve."

"Why are you still here?"

"Baker's men are looking for me and they are everywhere on the twentieth floor. I couldn't get past them."

"We have to get to a loading hatch. It's the only way out now." Carballo took his shirt off. "Give me your shirt."

A dark pool of water began to creep onto the twelfth floor as Smith took his shirt off. They looked at each other for a moment and ran toward the stairwell. A sharp pain in Carballo's arm made him suddenly nauseous. He took a deep breath and hurried after Smith.

Chapter 34

Julio Perez and Juan Sanchez were usually bored. They had been hired by the Atlantis Corporation as security guards, but all they had to guard so far was the entrance to a big plastic tube that ran down to Atlantis. The support facilities hadn't been completed yet, so few people even used the tunnel, except for the occasional couples that came out in the evening to stroll along the beach. They had been so bored they even built a little guard shack at the entrance with a table in front of it so they could play cards.

Julio had his feet up on the table. He looked into a donut box and picked up the last donut and munched on it. A fly buzzed his ear. He picked up a newspaper and swatted it. The sun was coming up and it would get hot soon. Luckily, his shift was almost over.

He was watching Juan wash their security truck when he heard a rumbling noise. He stood up and looked around. He couldn't see any boats or helicopters.

"Juan, did you hear that?"

Juan stopped and listened for a moment. "Hear what?"

"I thought I heard something."

Juan shook his head and continued to wipe off the truck.

The noise got louder. It almost sounded like a herd of cattle. He walked to the tunnel entrance. The noise was coming from the tunnel. Suddenly he saw a mass of people coming toward them.

He instinctively backed up. "Juan!" he yelled.

Juan looked over at the entrance to the tunnel and couldn't believe his eyes as people poured out of the tunnel. He suddenly remembered his radio. He pulled it out and found that it was off. When he turned it on, Baker's voice screamed at them, "Baker to tunnel security! Where in the hell are you guys?"

Juan gulped and replied, "Tunnel security to Baker. We're here, sir."

"Where the hell have you been? I've been calling for over an hour. We have an emergency here and are evacuating the dome. There are some buses and trucks coming to take the people to the port area. Try to keep them calm and lead them to the coast road."

Julio heard the instructions. He knew they would pay for this. Baker was not a patient man.

"Yes, sir!" Juan swallowed hard.

They gathered the people into groups until they heard a rumbling noise and saw a caravan of trucks and buses pulling off the coast road near them. Juan ran to their truck and took out a box of flares. He lit them and lighted a path up the beach to the coast road.

Juan and Julio watched in amazement as over 1900 people walked out of the tunnel to the waiting buses and trucks. Emergency personnel on the buses and trucks handed the evacuees drinks and pastries as they boarded. The evacuation was completed with little problem due to detailed emergency plans that had been adopted almost at the beginning of the project. The tunnel had turned out to be an excellent evacuation route, much better than the use of the sea-based escape hatches as originally developed.

When the last of the evacuees had left, Julio and Juan sat down near the tunnel, relieved that the ordeal was over. The next shift of security personnel arrived unaware of what had gone on. Evilio and Ramon parked next to Juan and Julio's truck and saw a few flares still burning.

"Hey, what's going on?" Evilio shouted.

"A million people just walked out of the dome and we put them on buses and trucks. I think there is some kind of big problem down there."

As the emergency room team made preparations to operate on Baker, Jack asked the attending physician if they could carry him out the tunnel and perform the operation in a hospital in Cancun.

The doctor shook his head. "We need to stop the bleeding now. We don't have any of his blood type here."

Jack watched them cut Baker's shirt off and swab the area with antiseptic. As the physician began an exploratory search for damaged arteries, Jack realized he wasn't feeling very well and walked out to talk to Spencer and Julie.

A little while later Julie saw the physician leaving the emergency room. "How is he, doctor?"

"He was lucky. There is no major internal damage. We sewed him up and he's stable now."

Julie put her head on Jack's shoulder as Spencer sat down on a chair in the waiting room and sighed with relief.

Even before Baker opened his eyes, he realized he was in the medical center. He was in lot of pain but he smiled weakly at Jack, Julie and Spencer.

"What happened to Carballo?"

He jumped into the water rather than go to jail."

"What about the evacuation?"

"Almost everyone's out. I just made the medical team leave."

"We need to get going then."

"We can't leave without triggering all the shutdown systems."

Michael sat up with a grimace. "Jack, the operators did all that before they left. There isn't anything else we can do."

"We have to turn off the canal pump, for one thing."

"In case you hadn't noticed, the power is off. The pump can't still be running."

"The pump is on a separate UPS in one of the support domes. It will run until the batteries go dead, or water gets into that dome. It's a big battery pack; the pump will run for another hour." He looked at his watch. "The Control Center UPS has more than twenty hours left."

"Jack, if the programmers can't find the problem, what can we do? It's too late for that. It's too late for Atlantis, I'm afraid."

Jack helped Baker stand up. "It ain't over till the fat lady sings."

The pain in Michael's shoulder almost caused him to black out again. Jack grabbed his arm to help steady him.

"I think she's already finished." Baker struggled to stand without help.

"Why don't the three of you leave? I'll just run up and check a few things and meet you at the end of the tunnel."

Julie shook her head. "There's no way I'm going to leave you."

"I won't do that either," Spencer added.

Baker smiled. "What the hell. I can't leave all of you. Okay, Jack. Let's do your thing in the Control Center and then let's get the hell out of here."

"Thanks, but I think you all should leave now."

Spencer shook his head. "No!"

"No possible way." Julie was adamant.

Baker walked slowly to the door. "Come on, Jack. Let's go."

Jack smiled at them and walked out the door to the observation point on the 50th level. He shined a flashlight down. The others joined him and looked down.

The water was probably at the 17th or 18th level by now. They didn't have a lot of time. He walked quickly to the stairs. Jack had to help Baker up the last few flights to the Control Center. He swiped his cardkey and punched in the code on the electronic lock and the heavy door opened with a hiss. The brightly-lit room was empty as all the operations personnel and the programmers were gone.

Jack checked a display. The canal pump was still pumping seawater into the dome. He gritted his teeth. How could

Carballo reverse the action of the pump in software and the programmers not be able to find it? The others were sitting in chairs or looking at screens, waiting for him. Julie brought some water to Baker and he sat down on a couch in the conference area of the Control Center.

Jack knew he didn't have much time. Something was nagging at him. Hadn't Robert mentioned something about just checking all the wiring? What if Carballo had reversed some of the wiring? Jack went to a file cabinet and pulled out a copy of the wiring diagrams.

"Richard, look up the loop number for the canal pump."

"Where would I find it?"

"Computer Four, Display One."

Spencer pushed a few buttons. "It's F-4 one-zero-one."

Jack traced the wiring at the back of the canal shutdown controller. He couldn't believe how easy it was. Carballo had merely switched two wires. He found a screwdriver in a drawer and put them on the correct terminals. "What's the flow now?"

"It shows zero and the loop is down. You got it, Jack!"

Baker struggled to his feet. "Now, let's get the hell out of here!"

Jack continued turning things off, until Baker pulled on his arm. "Let's go!"

Chapter 35

Constantine Carballo's apartment happened to be on the 70th floor of the Orion building. He ran from the stairwell and opened the door with his security master key. After a quick change of clothes, he ran back to the stairwell where Stan Smith waited and tossed him his shirt back. Smith watched him finish loading a handgun and stick it in his waistband.

"What's that for?"

"You never know when a gun will come in handy. Come on."

They started up the stairs when a stairwell door opened somewhere above them and they heard several people talking. Carballo whispered in Smith's ear. "Jackpot! It's Garrett and Spencer. Come on."

As Jack entered the stairwell a gunshot rang out and a bullet whizzed by his ear. As they ran back toward the control center, Julie fell on a trashcan knocking it over. They all crouched down as several more shots rang out in the dark and bullets ricocheted around them. Jack pulled Baker's gun out and fired several shots at the stairwell door and they heard someone laugh, then footsteps going down the stairs. Jack ran to the stairs but couldn't see who it was. Another gunshot made him jump back. He waited a moment and walked back to his companions.

"Whoever it is, he's probably waiting for us on the twentieth level. He knows that's the only way out down there." He went to the observation point and counted the lights of the observation points for the levels below. "It's too late anyway. The water is at least at the 30th floor and coming up fast. That means he's trapped, too. He'll probably come back here since he can't get out, except through the escape hatch."

Baker began walking quickly to the stairs. "We'd better head for the ninety-fifth floor before he gets there. He could mess up the hatch controls on the way out."

Jack looked at him. "Oh, damn! Let's go!"

Few people slept more soundly than Emma Dawson. She missed the explosions, the evacuation alarm, the security people pounding on her door, the power failure, even her battery-powered alarm clock that went off at 7:30. She sat up in bed, pulled her sleep mask off and got out of bed. She tried to turn on the lights but nothing worked. She thought it must be a construction problem.

It was hard finding her clothes in the dark until she found her purse and a small flashlight she always carried with her. She finished dressing quickly. She couldn't find her security badge and locked her door manually as she left. She noticed the emergency lights were on in the hallway, and turned her flashlight off. She pressed the elevator button but nothing happened. *That's strange,* she thought.

She walked to the stairwell and opened the door as a gunshot rang out. She jumped back as a man rushed past in the dark going down the stairs. She heard Jack's voice and yelled to him, but there was no response.

Emma began walking up the stairs when she realized the man was running up the stairs below her. She became frightened and sprinted up the stairs. He was yelling something at her as he gained on her. When he was only a flight away she yanked open the nearest stairwell door and ran inside.

She recognized the Control Center area and saw its lights on through its partially open door.

The stairwell door opened behind her. The man yelled as she ran to the Control Center, but she couldn't hear him. Her heart was beating so hard, she could only hear her own heartbeat in her ears. An overturned trashcan was preventing the Control Center door from closing. She kicked it away as she ran through, spun around and pulled on the door handle, trying to force the massive door to close faster than its huge pneumatic closer would normally allow.

Just before it closed, the man on the other side grabbed the door and tried to pull it open. He yelled something she couldn't understand and pulled even harder. He was winning the tug-of-war and would be on her in a minute!

An idea flashed through her mind and she suddenly pushed hard on the door. It flew open hitting him in the face, causing him to let go. She saw his gun lying on the floor, picked it up and pulled on the door until it closed. She began to take deep breaths to help her calm down when she heard him pound on the door and rattle it. She knew he couldn't open it without a cardkey and the code combination and started to relax. She looked at the gun in her hand, checked the chamber and found two bullets. Emma had only fired a gun on a practice range, but she was a decent shot.

She heard a clicking sound. He was trying to enter a code on the pushbutton keypad! What if he knew the code! Emma began to panic. She spotted a red emergency door release button on the wall. When the lock clicked open and he began to pull on the door, she pressed the emergency release button. The door flew open. She pointed the gun into the darkness, closed her eyes, and squeezed the trigger twice.

He screamed and she pulled the door closed.

She shook from fear and forced herself to calm down. She didn't hear him anymore and walked over to the planning table and sat down. After a moment she calmed down and began looking for a radio.

Even as he struggled to open the huge Control Center door, it flew open smacking Carballo in the face, knocking him backward. Stan Smith had been standing behind him and was hit squarely in the chest by Emma's first bullet. Her second bullet grazed Carballo's head, as he was struggling to stand up. Dazed, he managed to get up on his knees. He saw Stan Smith lying next to him and tried to pick him up to carry him to the stairs, but only succeeded in re-opening the wound in his arm. Fatigue was setting in as he watched a black pool of water leap through an observation point and race toward him. The icy water seemed to creep up his body pulling him down into it.

Mark Williamson's luck finally ran out. He finished all of his evil deeds and had just entered an elevator at the ground level when the power went out. He pounded frantically on the doors but no one heard him. He tried jumping, but couldn't reach the emergency hatch in the roof. He waited for the icy water to pick him up and lift him until he could reach the top of the elevator and open the hatch. He managed to crawl out the hatch and even managed to climb the maintenance ladder for more than fifty floors with icy water lapping at his legs. Exhaustion finally took over and the icy water picked him up again and carried him slowly to the top of the elevator shaft. He even felt a maintenance access door with his hands but just couldn't find the energy to turn the release lever before the trapped pocket of air disappeared.

Alan Sands had been luckier. He had walked out through the tunnel with the 1900 other evacuees. But, where was Williamson? They were supposed to meet at the tunnel entrance and break away from the crowd when no one was looking.

Chapter 36

They all ran up the stairs, pausing every now and then for Baker and Spencer to rest. Jack swept the walls with his flashlight until he found the nearest door. "Only five more floors, Richard. Can you make it?"

Spencer took one more deep breath. "Yes. Let's go!"

"Michael?"

"I'm okay for now. Let's go."

Julie helped Richard and Jack helped Michael climb the last few flights. Julie opened the door to the 95th level and they hurried to the loading hatch door. They all stopped at the same time. In the beam of Julie's flashlight, they saw the smashed control panel for the escape hatch dangling from the wall.

"Bloody hell!" Baker yelled. "How can they be everywhere at once? There was no alarm on this system!"

Spencer glanced at Jack. "Now what?"

Julie gave Jack his flashlight back. He slowly walked to the edge of the observation deck. The others followed him silently. He aimed his flashlight down at the black, swirling water.

The pain in Baker's shoulder had found its way to his head. He was so dizzy he had to hold onto the railing to keep from falling down. "How high is it now?"

"Probably at the seventieth level or so." Jack's voice was unusually calm.

Julie glanced down at the rising water and shivered in a

sudden anxiety attack. "At this rate, it won't be long before it's in the Control Center. Is there any way to get to another escape hatch from here?"

Jack's flashlight wasn't very powerful. They couldn't see the escape hatches on the other center buildings.

"All the connecting concourses are at the twentieth floor, the elevators are out and we can't fly."

He wasn't trying to be funny but Spencer laughed.

Julie wondered how cold the water was. "Can we swim?"

"The water's coming in from the bottom and it's close to freezing. We'd have to swim at least a hundred feet or more in unknown currents. We'd never make it."

"There must be another way out!" Desperation crept into Julie's voice.

Something Julie said triggered Jack's memory. He looked up suddenly. In the dark, the top of the dome glowed a dull green.

"Life vests and a raft!" Jack shouted.

Spencer jumped "What?"

"We need to find some life vests and some inflatable life rafts." Jack was still looking up and everyone followed his gaze.

Julie's anxiety level dropped a little. "What is it? Is there another way out?"

"There's a pressure relief valve in the top of the dome, just in case we over-pressurized it when we first pumped it out and filled it with air. A little bit too much pressure and some of the wall components would have popped out."

Julie tried but couldn't see it. "Where is it?"

"It's only six feet in diameter. You can't see it from here."

Baker strained to see it. "I'm not an engineer but isn't the water pressure outside pretty high, even at the top of the dome? Why would it be open?"

"You're absolutely right. Normally it wouldn't be, but with all the water coming in, the air above the water is being compressed and the atmospheric pressure control system is holding it open to control the pressure inside."

"What happens when the Control Center becomes flooded and the pressure control system fails?" Spencer hated to ask the obvious.

"The valve will close. Then the pressure in the air pocket inside will rise until it pops a wall piece out."

"What would happen to us?"

"We'd be unconscious when the end comes."

They could tell Jack wasn't kidding. They all were silent as they reflected on his comment.

Julie remembered Jack's earlier statement. "You said something about life vests and life rafts. What did you mean?"

"If we can find a life raft, we could float to the top of the dome and try to get out through the valve. If we have the kind of life vests that inflate, we could make it to the surface."

"What if the relief valve closes first?"

"We might be able to force it open by hand. It's just a butterfly valve." Jack began searching for the life vests and rafts.

Julie looked at Spencer. "Just a butterfly?"

Spencer shrugged.

Jack was already looking through storage rooms near the hatch. One was locked so he shot the lock off and shined his flashlight inside.

"Eureka!"

The others ran to the door. Hundreds of life vests were stacked neatly on shelves. Jack turned to Baker. "Why would you lock up the life vests?"

"We wouldn't have." He took the gun from Jack's hand. "Maybe he's still here."

"He's long gone, forget it." Jack flashed his light up and down the shelves. "Where in the hell are the rafts?"

"Here they are!" Baker said, struggling to drag two large rafts to the door.

Jack and Spencer grabbed them and pulled them out onto the observation deck.

Spencer was panting a little from the exertion. "How many do we need?"

"Two. One for in here and one for the surface," Jack read the instructions on the raft with the aid of the flashlight. "These will hold ten people. That's a good size."

They each put a life vest on. Jack shined his light down from the observation deck. The water was less than ten floors away and rising rapidly.

Baker tightened the straps on his vest. "The Control Center must be underwater by now. Won't the valve be closed?"

"I don't know. I don't feel the pressure increasing." Jack looked back at the storage room. Julie was trying on different jackets, Spencer was holding the flashlight on her.

Jack walked into the storage room. "This isn't a fashion show! Let's go!"

Before leaving, Jack looked for something to pry the valve open with, just in case. He picked up a sign on a pole, broke the sign off, unscrewed the tripod feet and hurried back to the others.

Baker was watching the water rise. "It's almost here."

Spencer helped Jack pick up one of the rafts, lift it over the railing and tie it on the top. Jack pulled the ripcord and it inflated instantly.

"When the level is high enough, we'll have to get in quickly." Jack watched the water rising quickly toward them. The volume of air remaining at the top of the dome began to rapidly disappear.

"Get on the railing!" Jack ordered.

The air rushing past them was beginning to roar. They climbed up on the railing as a torrent of cold water rushed onto the floor and began to lap at their legs.

Spencer teeth started chattering. "Christ, it's cold!"

"Think you could swim in that?" Jack yelled.

They all shook their heads.

"You'll have to swim to the surface but the water above the top of the dome isn't cold," he shouted.

The water lifted the raft and Jack held it against the railing as they got in. Jack got in last and untied the raft. It rose rapidly toward the top of the dome.

"Find the paddles! We need to row to the middle!" Jack yelled.

Jack and Spencer flashed their lights around until they found paddles attached to the insides of the raft. They pulled them out, screwed the pieces together and began paddling toward the center. Air rushing out of the dome generated an even louder howling.

Jack pointed to the top and they all saw a small opening. They stopped paddling when they were directly under it. It was getting closer at a very fast rate. The tops of the center buildings were now underwater.

Baker yelled to Jack, "Won't we have to get out one by one?"

Jack nodded.

"Will there be time?"

Jack shrugged. He saw a frightened look on Julie's face. He yelled to her, "Ladies first!" and then smiled.

She tried to smile back. The raft was bathed in the green light of the top of the dome. It began to swirl around, as if in a vortex.

As the raft neared the valve, the sound became deafening.

Jack motioned Julie to stand. Baker and Spencer held onto her when the raft began to spin. Suddenly, the howling stopped and the water stilled. After all the noise, the silence was eerie.

Baker grimaced at a sudden pain in his shoulder. "What happened?"

It was too quiet. Then they heard a roar in the distance.

Jack put his paddle down. "It's just a guess, but I think a dome wall piece popped out and relieved the pressure. That's why the valve closed."

Spencer wiped his forehead. "What do we do now?"

The bottom of the valve was only six feet above them. Pressure built up in their ears and their skin began to tingle. The air was beginning to become pressurized again.

Jack studied the relief valve above them. "We don't have much time."

"What do we do?"

"I may be able to reach the valve if I stand on your shoulders. I might even be able to pry it open."

Baker rubbed his shoulder. "Won't the sea above us rush in if we open it now?"

"The pressure of the water coming in the bottom is greater. Enough pressure has built up so it just may push us out."

"May?"

"An educated guess. If we don't try, it won't matter anyway."

The pressure in their ears was beginning to hurt and their

eyes watered.

Baker cupped his hands and held them out to Jack at knee level. "Let's do it. I don't want to wait for the end here."

Jack stepped into his hands and Spencer and Baker lifted him until he was standing on Spencer's shoulder and Michael's uninjured shoulder.

"Hand me the rod."

Julie handed him the rod he had taken from the storage room and then pointed the light at the opening. Jack struck the valve controller box and the air regulator on the valve. Nothing happened. He tried to pry open the flat plastic plate in the middle of the valve but it wouldn't budge. "It's stuck!"

The pressure in their ears was excruciating. Jack struck the valve controller box with the rod again and suddenly the valve opened. Warm water rushed in one side of the valve, knocking Jack into the raft as air rushed out the other side of the valve. The air rushed out in surges as water cascaded on them.

The raft began to rise as the air in the dome burped out.

Jack helped Julie stand up. When the bottom of the opening was near, she held her arms up to guide her through the opening in the valve. The raft rose until it blocked the opening. Jack picked her up until she was almost through. Warm water flowing down from the valve began to push the remaining air out the other side of the valve. They all took one last breath as the last of the air surged out of the dome.

The water lifted Julie through the relief valve as she pulled on the inflation valve of the life vest. She rose rapidly to the surface.

Baker helped Spencer through the opening as he pulled on the vest's inflation valve. Spencer was carried to the surface and gasped for air when he broke through. Baker followed him out.

Jack pushed the second raft through ahead of him and pulled on his vest's inflation valve. Jack and Baker surfaced almost at the same time and saw Julie holding Spencer's head above the water.

"I think he passed out!" she yelled.

Jack pulled the ripcord on the raft and it inflated with a load roar. He swam to Spencer and Julie. Julie climbed into the raft while Jack held Spencer's head above water. Baker got in and together they all pulled and pushed Spencer into the raft. Baker and Julie helped Jack climb in.

Jack examined Spencer. "I think he's okay." He found the first aid kit strapped to the raft and waved smelling salts under Spencer's nose.

Spencer coughed and opened his eyes. When he saw Jack leaning over him, he frowned. "This can't be heaven."

They all laughed.

Jack watched as the last bubbles from the dome burst to the surface and the sea became still. It was a beautiful day, with a slight breeze and a few clouds in the sky. They all closed their eyes to rest. After a while Spencer looked at Jack, "I hate to sound like a broken record, but what now?"

Jack opened his eyes. "What do you mean?"

"What about Atlantis?"

"What about it?"

"Well, do we say to hell with it and go home, or do we clean it out and start over?"

All eyes were on Jack. He looked at each of them. They were a mess. "I don't know."

"Well," Spencer began, "I can say that, for me, today was a near religious experience. I've never been this close to death." He sighed. "I have some mixed feelings. I'd hate to lose all this effort, not to mention the money, but I couldn't get it back without you, Jack. If you say forget it, I will."

Jack didn't answer. He looked at Baker.

"I'm here for you either way, boss."

When he looked at Julie, she was smiling at him. She gave him a thumbs up. "I still want to be the first woman married in Atlantis."

Jack took a deep breath and sighed. "I have an excruciating headache."

Julie crawled to him and got up on her knees. She began rubbing the temples of his forehead with her fingers. "I've heard this helps."

They looked at each other for a moment and she bent down and kissed him. She rubbed his forehead again and then screamed.

Jack bolted upright. "What is it?"

Julie pointed to a body floating in the water.

Jack and Spencer pulled the oars out and began rowing.

Baker leaned over and pulled the body closer and rolled it over.

Spencer laid his paddle down. "Who is it?"

"Steve Smith, the computer programmer we've been looking for. Looks like he's paid for his sins."

Julie put her hands over her eyes. Baker motioned for Jack to look closer at the body. When Jack moved closer, Baker pointed to a bullet hole in Smith's chest. Jack and Michael looked at each other wondering who the killer was.

"Look, the transport helicopter," Spencer yelled, pointing to a speck in the sky.

The helicopter circled overhead and they saw Bill Howell by an open door in the side with a bullhorn. "Ahoy, Atlantians! I have something for you." He tossed a small package that landed in the water next to the raft, spraying Baker and Spencer. Baker shook his fist at Bill and fished the package out of the water. He opened it and rummaged through it. "Food and supplies."

He took the food out and tossed a cellular phone to Jack. The helicopter backed away and headed for the coast.

"Where the hell are they going?" Baker slapped the top of the watertight container in frustration.

Jack turned the phone on and punched in a number. "Howell?" He pressed the speaker button so they could all hear. "Where are you going, Bill?"

"The *Critias* is two minutes away. I didn't think you wanted to be picked up with a sling. The *Critias* has better gear to pick you up and the *Timaeus* is on its way."

"Bill?"

"Yes, Jack?"

"Is everyone accounted for?"

"There are only four not accounted for."

"Who are they?"

"Constantine, as you know. Hugh Bagly, Steve Smith and--" he paused as if he couldn't say the name. "--Emma Dawson."

"Oh, no!" Julie cried.

Spencer slumped down in the raft as Baker looked away.

Julie hugged Jack. "I'm so sorry."

Jack felt sick. He wasn't sure whether it was all the seawater he had swallowed or the news about Emma. He felt a wave of nausea and rolled over to put his face over the side. As he did, the radio in his belt fell off and landed on Julie's shoe. It crackled.

"Is anyone there?" Emma's voice came though loudly.

They all jumped.

Jack grabbed the radio. "Emma! Where the devil are you?"

"In the Control Center."

"What? Say it again!" Jack yelled.

"I'm in the bloody Control Center and the doors won't open. What do I do?"

Chapter 37

Jack tried to be calm. "Emma, the city is full of water. The Control Center must have sealed itself off somehow. We'll try to figure out how to get you out. Try to stay calm. I'll get back to you in a minute."

"Okay, Jack, but hurry! There are a lot of creaking noises in here, like something's about to give way."

"Emma?"

"Yes."

"Is there any water in there?"

"No."

"Are the systems still on?"

"I don't know. The computer screens are still on."

"That's good. Just sit tight and don't touch anything. I'll be back in a minute."

"Okay, Jack."

Spencer shook his head. "It's not possible! The city is full of water!"

"The seals on the control center doors must have held." Jack punched keys on the phone. They heard a number ring.

"Howell."

"Emma's alive in the control center!" Jack cried into the microphone.

"What! That can't be! How can we get her out?" Bill was so excited he forgot the usual salutations.

All in the raft looked at Jack. "It looks like we have a reason to breathe some life back into Atlantis. Bill, where's the *Eye*? Do we still have the pumps?"

"We sold the *Eye*, remember? She's in dry dock. I think they are converting her to a floating casino or something."

"Where are the pipeline pumps?"

Bill was afraid to reply. They all waited. "They're in the dome. I mean, one of the support domes."

Jack sat down. "Damn! Which one?"

"Support Four, Jack."

Support Four storage dome was the largest. It also had its own submarine docking station. Jack immediately thought of the *Sea Merchant*. Maybe he could get inside.

"Are they hooked up, Bill?"

"The first five are hooked to the canal pumpout line. I always thought the canal pump was too small."

"Why didn't you tell anyone? The operators didn't even know about that."

"I wanted to correct the drawings first, and there's a big backlog waiting to be updated."

Jack laughed. "We could pump a million gallons a second out of the canal and the dome if the walls didn't have holes in them. Okay, Bill, the *Critias* is here. I'll get back to you."

"Roger, Jack."

The *Critias* pulled alongside of them, with the *Timaeus* nearby. The two sister supply ships weren't very big compared to the *Eye*, but when viewed from a life raft, they were huge.

The crew lowered a platform next to the raft and they were quickly evacuated. Several crewmen were waiting with towels and blankets when the platform touched the deck. Jack sprinted to the bridge, Baker right behind. Spencer and Julie went below deck to find some dry clothes.

Raphael Tartella, the captain, saluted Jack as he entered.

"Where's the *Sea Merchant*, Raphael?"

"We thought you might need her. She's five minutes from here, sir."

Jack keyed the radio again. "Emma, can you hear me?"

"Thank goodness, I thought you forgot about me."

"No chance of that. I need you to check something for me on one of the computers."

"Which one? There are dozens of computers in here."

"Each computer has a number on it. Its monitor has a large number on the top in the front. Can you find number six?"

"Yes. I'm in front of it."

"What's the status of support dome number four?"

There was a pause before she replied. "The emergency hatches are locked and it's fully operational."

Jack and Baker smiled at each other.

"Does that mean the pumps are all right?"

Jack nodded. "It means we have a chance to pump out the dome."

"How can we do that with those missing wall pieces? That's why it filled up in the first place."

"If we can find them, we can use the *Sea Merchant* and *Sea Horse* to put them back in place. Raphael, what's the status of the *Clieto* and the *Poseidon*?" These were the next submarines of the *Sea Merchant* class to be delivered from the manufacturer.

"I saw the *Clieto* in port today, sir. I don't know the status of the *Poseidon*. Oh, by the way, Mr. Garrett, the *Sea Horse* is in dry dock for routine maintenance and the crew and captain are on shore leave."

Jack pressed a button on his phone. "Bill, is there anyone in port who can operate the *Clieto*? We need it here to search for the missing wall sections."

"I don't know but I'll find out, Jack."

"Also, what's the status of the land power system?"

"We've replaced the transformer but we haven't finished the concrete cover."

"Is it ready to re-connect?"

"The foreman says it is, but he checked the line going to the city and it's shorted somewhere inside the dome. We can't connect it until that's fixed."

"Okay. Get back to me on a pilot for the *Clieto*."

"Roger. Howell out."

Baker looked up from a wiring diagram. "Doesn't power come into Support Dome One?"

"Yes."

Richard and Julie entered the bridge and stood near them, listening. She handed Jack a cup of coffee.

"Then, shouldn't we try and find the power problem in Support One first?"

Jack shook his head. "The submarine docking station on Support One isn't operational yet. I've been thinking about how we can pump the water out. The pumps are on the bottom of the sea. Where can we pump the water to? The pressure is too great, even for those pumps and the canal pump's outlet line to the shore is only a few feet in diameter."

"Can we run a line to the surface?"

"It would have to be pretty big. We don't have anything like that around here."

"There's no other way to the surface?"

Spencer was drinking a cup of coffee. Seeing Spencer jogged Jack's memory. "Richard, maybe we can find another use for that damn tunnel you wanted."

Spencer stared at him with a blank expression.

Jack pressed his radio button. "Emma!"

"Yes?"

"Can you find computer eleven?"

"Yes, I see it."

"Press F-one."

"Okay."

"Are you looking at Display One?"

"Yes."

"See if you can operate emergency door S-four-three. It's a touch screen, so all you have to do is touch the button image on the screen."

"There's an error message: NOT ENOUGH POWER TO OPERATE CONTROLLER."

"Damn!" Jack muttered. "Okay, Emma. Stand by."

"We need power," Jack was looking at Baker.

"Any chance of getting the OTEC system back in operation?"

"The saboteurs bled the ammonia out into the ocean, remember?"

"Can we re-charge it?"

"I don't think we have any ammonia. We were supposed to store some in Support Four, eventually."

"Maybe it came in already," Spencer suggested.

Jack flipped through some drawings, then keyed his radio. "Emma?"

"Yes?"

"Can you find computer five?"

After a moment, she answered, "I have it."

"Press F-one and tell me the level in T-seven-zero-one."

"It has thirty thousand gallons in it and it looks almost full, Jack. What is that, anyway?"

"Ammonia. Stand by."

Jack was surprised. "Thirty thousand gallons! That's more than enough to recharge the whole damn thing--if we can close the external vent valve and pump it to the system."

"Can we pump it by hand?" Spencer volunteered.

"No." Jack thought a moment. "But submarines have bilge pumps! The *Clieto* would have a brand new one. But…can it pump liquid ammonia?" he wondered out loud. He keyed his digital phone.

"Howell."

"Bill, what about a pilot for the *Clieto*?"

"We found him. He arrived with the submarine."

"Great! Get him to bring it out here ASAP."

"Roger. Uh--Jack?"

"Yes?"

"How's Emma?"

"She's fine so far."

"Thanks."

Jack's radio crackled. "Jack, there's a little water on the floor here!" Emma cried.

"Okay. We're working on getting you out as fast as we can."

Julie touched Jack on the shoulder. "How far down is the Control Center?"

"Over three hundred feet."

Julie grimaced.

The ship's radio buzzed. "*Sea Merchant* to *Critias*."

Captain Tartella answered. "*Critias* here. What is it, John?"

"Tell Mr. Garrett we found one of the wall pieces."

Jack walked over to the ship's radio mike. "What kind of shape is it in, John?"

"It looks fine, Mr. Garrett."

"Can you put it back in?"

"I can't tell which one it is. Row two and row three pieces look almost alike out here."

"Row two is taller than row three," Jack replied. "There's no pressure difference now, you can try it in either row. It'll fit or it won't."

"Yes, I heard that Mr. Garrett. I've lassoed it and secured it to the front and am maneuvering it to the hole in row two. I'll let you know what I find. *Sea Merchant* out."

An officer on the *Critias* approached Captain Tartella. "Sir, Mr. Howell has landed on the helideck."

"Thank you, Mr. Johnson."

A moment later, Bill entered the bridge. "I couldn't stay away.

I want to help and get her out, Jack."

"We all want to help, Bill." Spencer replied.

Jack scanned the horizon with binoculars. "Where is the *Clieto*, Captain?"

"Twenty minutes from here, sir."

Jack thought for a moment, then looked at Bill. "See if you can find some hoses with quick-connects on board this ship and meet me on the deck in fifteen minutes.

"I'm on my way."

Spencer watched Bill leave. "What are you going to do, Jack?"

"I'm going to suck the seawater out of the OTEC system and try to pump ammonia into it."

Jack and Baker were waiting on the deck of the *Critias* as Bill arrived carrying several large hoses. Jack took one off his shoulder.

As soon as the *Clieto* surfaced next to the *Critias*, the three men entered a personnel transfer platform. Jack signaled to the crane operator who picked them up and set them on the back of the *Clieto*. They exited carefully and entered the submarine. The new captain and a crewman of the *Clieto* came aft to greet them.

"Hi. I'm Walt Stewart, Mr. Garrett." He shook Jack's hand.

Howell and Baker walked in and introduced themselves.

"Can you take her down now, Captain?"

"Yes, sir."

"Let's go. I'll show you where we're going."

The submarine circled around the dome and settled next to Support Dome Four. The lights in the little dome were still running on the UPS backup system. Under Jack's direction, the captain moved the ship forward until it settled into the docking position. The docking station hatch slowly slid shut. The water level in the station was partially pumped out but stopped when the level was still above the hatch on the submarine.

"Ran out of power, probably," Jack commented.

Stewart shut off most of the submarine's power. "What do we do now?"

"Open the hatch."

"But the seawater in the docking station will come in," the captain protested.

"Yes, it will."

The captain reluctantly opened the hatch and several hundred gallons of icy seawater poured into the tiny submarine, lapping at his feet.

"Ick!"

Jack walked quickly to the deck of the submarine. The gangplank had not extended so he jumped to the floor of the docking station. The water was knee deep and icy cold. He twisted the locking mechanism on the dome hatch and the door swung inward. Air rushed into the docking station as water poured into the dome. He called to Bill and Michael, "Bring the hoses."

Stewart watched the water level drop to the floor of the docking station, and then signaled to his crewman to pump the water out of the submarine. When that was done, he blew the bilge into the docking station. He watched the crewman connect the transfer hose to the inlet of the bilge pump, and waited for Jack's signal.

Everything appeared normal to Jack, but Baker had never been in one of the support domes before and he was busy looking around. Bill dragged the hoses out of the submarine. Crates of equipment were piled almost to the ceiling of the support dome and Jack had to search for the ammonia storage section.

Bill hooked the hoses together and dragged the end to Jack, who hooked them into the ammonia storage system. Bill then ran back to the submarine. "Start the bilge pump!" he yelled to the captain.

"Yes, sir," came the reply.

Jack held onto the hose and felt it get colder as the liquid ammonia was pumped into the bilge tank on the *Clieto*.

Baker stood next to him. "According to Stewart, it will only hold two thousand gallons."

"That may be enough to get the OTEC system going."

"That's it!" yelled the captain to Baker who relayed the message to Jack.

"Okay." Jack closed the valve on the ammonia storage tank and shut off the valve at the end of the hose. He twisted the hose connection and it popped off. Baker and Bill pulled the hoses back to the submarine. They got in and Jack secured the support dome hatch. When he had secured the submarine door, he called to the captain, "We're ready!"

"Yes, sir."

The captain initiated a radio signal to the outside hatch on the docking station and it grudgingly opened, drawing the last of the power out of the support dome's UPS system. The emergency lighting flickered off as the captain backed the submarine out of the docking station. He maneuvered it around the main dome to Support Dome One while Bill shut off and disconnected the outlet line of the bilge tank going to the external exhaust port of the sub. Working together, Bill and the crewman disconnected the outlet of the bilge pump from the bilge tank and connected the pump inlet to the external bilge exhaust port on the submarine. That would allow the pump to suck seawater from the OTEC system into the main cabin of the sub.

Jack maneuvered a spotlight on the front of the sub and pointed out the ammonia vent valve on the outside of Support Dome One.

Bill had rigged up an adapter and the bilge exit port on the submarine slipped inside the ammonia vent valve.

"We're connected, Mr. Garrett." The captain pressed a button opening a valve on the exhaust port, and started the pump. Seawater rushed into the submarine as the little bilge pump sucked seawater out of the ammonia tank of the OTEC system and into the submarine. The level of water in the sub rose rapidly, then finally stopped.

"That's twenty thousand gallons, in case you're curious, Captain."

The captain wasn't happy to have that much seawater in his brand new ship. "Yes, sir," was all he could manage.

Bill connected the pump between the bilge tank and the exhaust port and turned it on. Ammonia in the bilge tank began to enter the OTEC system. When the pump went dry, Bill quickly shut it off. Stewart backed the sub away from the OTEC vent port and deftly manipulated a mechanical arm on the front of the sub to twist an emergency shutoff valve on the OTEC's vent port. As soon as Bill connected the bilge pump to its normal configuration, the captain pressed a button again and the seawater in the submarine began to be pumped into the bilge tank. When the tank was full, the captain blew the bilge tank. "I don't have enough air to pump all of this out," he told Jack.

"We only need to get to the surface, Walt."

"Roger." Stewart repeated the bilge operation until he ran out of pressurized air. He then revved up the engine and the submarine started forward. The nose slowly pointed up and a few minutes later they were on the surface. He positioned the submarine next to the *Critias* and the crane operator lowered the platform to the back of the submarine.

When they were in the bridge again, Julie handed each a cup of hot coffee. Jack picked up his radio. "Emma?"

"Yes, Jack?"

"How are you doing?"

"There's about six inches of water in here and it's damn cold."

"What about the computers?"

"I put them all on the tables. They're okay, so far."

"That's great, Emma! We've partially recharged the OTEC system and should have some power soon."

"Hurry!" she urged.

"Emma, find computer nine, press F-one-two-five and tell me what the display says."

After a moment she reported back. "It says the OTEC system has restarted and is at five percent power."

Baker and Bill slapped Jack on the back and shook hands with each other.

"Emma, see if you can operate S-four-three again on Computer eleven, display one."

There was a brief pause. "It's working. I can open and close it."

Bill looked the most relieved.

Jack had a flash of inspiration. "Bill, where can we find the status of the *Eye*'s pumps?"

Bill thought for a moment. "The containment canal status screen."

"Emma, look at computer seven, display one. Do you see some pump symbols on the screen?"

"Yes, I see them, Jack."

"See if you can operate the pump closest to the pumpout line."

"I can start and stop it, Jack."

Jack jumped up and down he was so happy. "Yes!"

Bill tugged on Jack's sleeve. "Jack?"

"What?"

"I was just wondering where the air to fill the dome will come from when you pump it out."

Jack stared at him for a moment. "From the emergency air supply line that runs to the coast."

"But that line enters the dome at the base, doesn't it?"

"Yes, so?"

"Won't you have a vacuum at the top of the dome at first?"

Jack looked at him, dumbfounded. "Oh, hell!"

"You might be able to open a loading hatch with a radio signal from one of the submarines," Spencer suggested, "but I don't know if it will work with the Control Center knocked out. And the hydraulic systems that operate the hatches are located in the support domes, so they may still be working. The hatches could provide a direct connection to the atmosphere at the top of the dome."

Jack looked at him for a second and then understood what he meant. "What if you opened the inner hatch door and the dome hatch door while the loading hatch is open? Wouldn't you have a direct connection to the outside through the guide shafts?"

Spencer nodded. "I think so."

Baker was lost. "What are you two talking about?"

"The loading hatches are hydraulically operated and slide up and down on four large guide shafts. It's kind of risky, but if a loading hatch were in the up position and the inner door of the hatch and dome hatch door were opened, air could get into the dome through the hatch's guide shafts. The control system wouldn't normally allow both doors to be open when the hatch is up, but we could bypass the safety system with an override code."

Bill was wondering how quickly they could get to Emma. "Is there any way for a person to get in the dome while the hatch is open?"

Jack thought for a moment, then laughed. "You could open the guide shaft maintenance access door and slide down the shaft."

Spencer laughed. "You aren't serious! That's almost a free fall of two hundred feet to the bottom of the shaft. He couldn't do that."

"He could lower himself with a rope," Jack suggested.

"Where would I go when I got to the bottom?"

"It's too risky, Bill," Spencer objected.

"It may be the only way to save Emma. How about it, Jack?"

"No, Richard's right. Air will be coming into the dome at the bottom of the guide shaft. You'd probably get sucked inside."

"What other choice is there?"

Jack thought a moment. "There's another maintenance access door about half way down the shaft. It opens to the stairwell on the hundredth floor of the building."

"I'm game," Bill offered. "How about the loading hatch itself? How can we open it?"

"Couldn't the *Clieto* operate it?" Spencer wondered.

"Garrett to the *Clieto*. Come in, Walt."

"Yes, Mr. Garrett?"

"Walt, I need you to maneuver close to the northeast corner of the dome and try to operate the loading hatch with your docking console ASAP."

"Aye, sir. I'm on my way."

A few minutes passed. *"Clieto* to Mr. Garrett. The hatch responded with a confirmation signal, but I don't see--my God! What is that?"

Bill stood by the window as the loading hatch emerged. "Yes!" he yelled as he thumped Jack on the shoulder.

"We might be able to signal the inside hatch door and the building hatch door to open from the sub as well." Jack keyed his radio. "Garrett to the *Clieto*."

"Clieto here, Mr. Garrett."

Jack searched the loading hatch drawing until he found the emergency controls section. "Walt, see if you can operate the inside door of the hatch and building hatch door from your docking station console. The emergency override code is three-two-five-six-seven."

There was a pause. *"Clieto* to Mr. Garrett. The green lights came on. The doors should be open."

"Great! Thanks, Walt. Garrett to the *Sea Merchant*. John,

what's the status of that wall piece?"

John Darrow was not happy. "It doesn't seem to fit in either hole, sir."

Bill was frustrated. "Why can't they put the piece back in?"

"Either the piece has been damaged, or it's not a row two or row three component. Or there's another hole in the wall!" Jack keyed his radio. "Garrett to the *Clieto*. Are you there, Walt?"

"Yes, sir. I'm still pumping this damn water out!"

"Forget that and go look for missing pieces in the dome wall. We found a piece that won't fit in the holes we know about. It's probably near the top of the dome."

"Yes, sir. I'll be there in two minutes. *Clieto* out."

Spencer tugged on Jack's arm.

"Yes, Richard?"

"With the water pressure the same on both sides of the dome wall, theoretically, any component that wasn't sealed properly could just pop out and float to the bottom. The density of the plastic is just a little heavier than seawater."

Jack stared in disbelief.

Then the *Clieto* called. "*Clieto* to Mr. Garrett."

"Yes, Walt?"

"There's a piece missing in the top of the dome, near some kind of a vent. There's also a raft of some sort stuck in the hole."

Baker laughed. "I guess we did that."

Jack pressed the mike button. "Did you hear that, *Sea Merchant*?"

"Yes, sir. We're on our way there now."

"Garrett to the *Clieto*. Walt, can you get the raft out of the hole?"

"Probably, I'm pretty good with that mechanical grappler on the front."

"Do it as quickly as you can."

"Yes, Mr. Garrett."

A few tense minutes passed. *"Sea Merchant* to Mr. Garrett."

"Yes?"

"The *Clieto* pulled the raft out and our piece slid right in."

Everyone on the bridge cheered.

"One down and two to go!" Spencer said.

"*Clieto* to Mr. Garrett."

"Yes, Walt?"

"I think I've found another piece but it's sitting on the edge of a cliff and it may fall down into a deep ravine if we try to get it. This submarine won't be able to dive that deep."

"Garrett to *Sea Merchant* and *Clieto*. If you both approach it from the cliff side, can you push it back some so it won't fall?"

They were both willing to try. A few minutes passed. Jack kept looking at his watch.

"*Sea Merchant* to Mr. Garrett. We have it."

Jack leaned against the nearest bulkhead. "I don't think I can take much more of this."

A few more minutes passed.

"*Sea Merchant* to Mr. Garrett. It's in. It was the row two piece."

Jack went to the captain's chair and sat down. Julie walked in and handed him another cup of coffee. Jack's radio buzzed.

Emma's voice was stressed. "Jack, there's almost two feet of water in here! It will be up on the tables soon. I can't lift the computers any higher. They're all connected with too many wires."

"Hang on, Emma! We're almost there," Jack urged. He thought for a moment. "Bill, did you bring any dome plans with you?"

"A few of the early plans."

"Would they show all the emergency doors?"

"Probably. I'll get them." He hurried out and returned with a set of plans. Jack took them to a small map table in the bridge and spread them out. He keyed his radio again.

"Emma, I need you to open and close some doors for me."

"Okay, but make it fast! I'm standing on a chair. The water's almost on the tables."

Jack rattled off a series of doors to open and close. Each time Emma confirmed that they worked. Baker, Bill and Spencer stared at the floor plan, trying to figure out what Jack was doing.

After a moment, Bill had to ask, "What are you doing, Jack?"

"Connecting Support Dome Four to the land tunnel."

Bill and Baker looked at each other.

"Okay, Emma, on computer seven, turn on pump one on display one."

"It's on, Jack."

"What's the flow rate?"

"Two hundred. Is that good?"

Jack looked at Baker and Bill as he pressed his radio send key. "Two hundred thousand gallons per second is pretty good, Emma."

Evilio and Ramon had spent the morning cleaning up the mess left by the evacuees. They put out the last of the flares and cleaned up everything. It was near noon and the two guards ate their lunch. Evilio propped his feet up on the card table and read a magazine. Ramon talked to his girlfriend on a new cellular telephone given to each of the guards by Michael Baker. Evilio swatted at a fly. It was a lazy, hot, cloudless day.

The ground rumbled.

Evilio put his feet down. "What is that?"

"I don't know, maybe an earthquake!"

They both stood up and realized the noise was coming from the tunnel.

Julio stared into the dark tunnel. "What are they doing? Uh-oh!"

They both dove out of the way as a wall of water shot out of the tunnel. It picked up the guard shack and flung it through the air until the guard shack and water exploded into the sand. The shack washed back toward the beach in a thousand pieces. Evilio and Ramon could only stare in horrid fascination at the column of water rushing out of the tunnel.

"Real good, Emma. Now turn on pumps two through five."

A moment passed. "They're all on."

"What's the flow in the canal pumpout line on the top of the display?"

"One million and fifty thousand gallons per second. Is that right, Jack?"

"It's perfect, Emma."

Jack looked at Bill and Baker. "That's three times the rate water can enter through that last hole."

Julio and Juan walked a little closer to the tunnel. The column of water was pounding a huge hole in the beach, exposing some long-lost Mayan artifacts. Suddenly, the column of water burst higher and landed on an uninhabited piece of land way beyond the beach. The noise was horrendous and both men had to cup their ears against it.

Jack's radio buzzed. Tom Abrams was calling. "Mr. Garrett, we got a call from the Mexican authorities that we're pumping seawater onto the land south of Playa Del Carmen. That can't be right, can it?"

"You're damn right we are! One million gallons per second."

"Say that again, Mr. Garrett?"

"Just tell them we're having a few problems here and that we won't have to do it much longer."

They all laughed. Jack's radio buzzed again. "*Clieto* to Mr. Garrett."

"Yes, Walt?"

"We found the last wall piece. The *Sea Merchant* is putting it in now."

Jack was so happy he hugged Bill and pounded Baker on the back. He picked up the mike again. "Walt, can you get a visual for me on the level in the dome?"

"Yes, sir. It'll take a minute or so."

"Jack, the water's on the tables! The computers are getting wet!" Emma yelled.

"Hold on, Emma. We're pumping out the dome now."

There was no reply. Baker suggested, "Maybe the power went out."

"The OTEC system is on. The pumps are running. Ask Tom."

Bill's patience was just about gone. "How long will it take to pump the water out to the Control Center level?"

"At least another thirty minutes." Jack looked at his watch.

"The hovercraft will be here in twenty minutes," Captain Tartella reported.

"I can't wait any longer! I'm going in!"

Bill ran down the stairs to the deck where a crewman handed him a rope that he wrapped around his waist. He took his shoes off and dove in. Jack thought about following him, but he wasn't a good swimmer. Baker and Spencer stood at the deck railing, watching Bill swim to the hatch.

"I hope he can make it in time."

Jack was watching Bill from the bridge when Tartella pointed to a dot on the horizon. "The hovercraft is here, Mr. Garrett."

"Garrett to the *Clieto*. Walt, try and open as many of the hatches as you can. We need to take some of the suction pressure off the pumps."

"Yes, sir."

Chapter 38

Bill was exhausted when he finally swam up to the dock beside the hatch. As he climbed the stairs, a torrent of air rushed past him into the hatch. He untied his rope, grabbed onto a railing and slowly made his way to the inner hatch door. The howl of air rushing into the dome was deafening and he had to hold tightly to the railing as he made his way to a small access door in front of the inner hatch door.

He pulled up on the locking mechanism and the door swung down into the guide shaft. There was an even faster flow of air into the dome. He looked down into the pitch-black shaft and shuddered. He tied the rope onto the railing, around his waist and between his legs. He took a deep breath and began lowering himself into the guide shaft.

Jack smiled as the arriving hovercraft had to quickly dodge two loading hatches as they burst into view. Jack and a *Critias* crewman jumped on board with ropes. The pilot backed up, spun about and headed for the loading hatch. When it arrived, Jack and the crewman jumped onto the stairs, grabbed the railing and made their way slowly to the open maintenance access door.

When Jack aimed his flashlight into the shaft, he saw Bill struggling to pull open the locking lever on the inner maintenance door. When Bill looked up, Jack signaled him to twist the lever. It didn't seem logical to Bill, but he twisted it. The access door immediately flew inward, sucking Bill in with it. Jack and the crewman looked at each other, wondering if Bill were all right. The roar of air into the dome was so great it forced Jack and the crewman to return to the hatch entrance.

Jack took out his radio and waited for Bill to call.

Bill tumbled into the dark, wet stairwell and rolled down a few stairs until he could grab onto the railing and stop himself. Air rushed down the stairwell but he managed to run down the stairs by holding onto the railing. When he reached the 95th level, he opened the door and ran to the observation deck and pointed his flashlight down.

The water was about ten to twenty stories below him. He couldn't tell if it was still above the Control Center floor or not. He ran back to the stairwell and started down, then stopped suddenly when he realized he wasn't in the right building. The flow of air into the dome seemed to be slowing down a little. He could stand without holding onto the railing.

He grabbed his radio. "Howell to Garrett."

"Bill, are you all right?"

"I'm fine, but why didn't we open the hatch on the Control Center building?"

"The controls on that one were destroyed by the saboteurs. We can't open it."

Bill was standing in front of the Safety Equipment Room filled with life preservers. He searched frantically for a raft without success.

"I found the life preservers, but there are no rafts. Maybe I could swim?"

"The water's too cold and the currents are too swift. You'd never make it."

"Then how am I supposed to get over there?"

"I hate to tell you this, but we had the same problem trying to get out. I have a long rope with me. Maybe you can use it to get over there."

"Swing on a rope? I don't think I can do that."

"That's the only chance Emma has, Bill. Come to the access door on the shaft and I'll lower a long rope to you."

Bill charged up the stairs to the inner maintenance access door. Jack was standing at the upper door holding a long coiled rope tied to another rope. He lowered it to Bill, who then ran back down the stairs to the railing on the 95th floor's platform looking for a place to tie the rope. The only place was the railing. He tied it and let the rope down. The bottom of the rope was almost in the water. He started to climb down and then thought better of it when he realized there was a lookout point on each level below him.

He ran down the stairs until he found water and then ran back up one level. He saw that he was on the 78th floor. He opened the stair door, ran to the observation point and grabbed the rope. How could he swing over there?

He looked around and realized he was on the corner of the building. He made a slipknot and stepped in the loop, tightening it around the seat of his pants. He looped the end of the rope around his waist and between his legs and stepped off the railing. The rope stretched a little and he dropped down a floor. He pushed away from the building and managed to get around the corner. He pushed back along the wall until he couldn't stretch the rope anymore and then let go.

Jack watched the hovercraft return with emergency medical personnel. When they arrived, Jack operated the hatch controls and the outer door closed. As the hatch began a quick descent, Jack pulled his radio out and waited for Bill to call.

Bill closed his eyes for a second as he swung across the gap between the two buildings. He didn't get close enough to grab the opposite building's railing and had to try again. He managed to back up a little farther this time and when he let go, he knew he had it. He let go of the rope with one hand and grabbed the railing, pulling himself over it. He untied himself and ran to the stairwell. He pushed the door to the 76th floor open and started down.

Water was still above the 75th floor's entry door. He dove into the icy water. For a brief instant his body stiffened and refused to swim but he somehow reached the hallway door and pulled it open. There was a pocket of air inside and he swam to the Control Center door. The water level was just above the door. He pounded on the door but there was no answer.

He panicked. How was he going to open a door that had resisted even the pressure of the sea? He wasn't sure how much longer he could swim in the cold water.

He thought he heard a muffled voice. He yelled Emma's name. Again, he thought he heard a reply. Suddenly the water in the hallway dropped and he was standing in water waist deep. He pulled his cardkey from his pants pocket and slid it in the reader, but the door didn't open. He pounded on the door again until he remembered the door had an electronic lock in addition to the security lock. What was the combination?

The water continued to fall and was now at his feet. He pulled out his radio, hoping it wasn't dead. He pressed the button and it buzzed. He was grateful they had purchased waterproof radios.

"Howell to Garrett."

"Jack here. What's going on, Bill?"

"I'm at the Control Center door but it's locked and I can't get in. What's the combination?"

"It's five-three-two-seven-one."

Bill slid his cardkey again and pushed the button sequence. The door opened with a hiss as a torrent of water rushed out into the hallway. A few seconds later the remaining water in the hallway rushed out and down the stairwell. Bill ran inside. Emma had piled some tables on top of each other and was laying on the topmost one near the ceiling. He jumped on a table and pulled her off. Her body was cold and wet. She was semi-conscious, probably in hypothermic shock.

He put her over his shoulder and carried her up the stairs to the next level. He still had to get back across the gap between the buildings. He heard someone calling his name. Jack was standing with several emergency personnel and two crewmen from the hovercraft on a lower observation point of the building he had entered. One of the crewmen inflated a raft, tied it to the railing and tossed it into the water.

Bill waved back at them and then felt Emma's pulse. It seemed a little slow and her hands were like ice. He knew he couldn't wait for them to get to him. Making a sling with the rope as he had done before, he climbed the railing with Emma.

He heard Jack's voice across the dome. "Are you out of your mind? We'll be there in twenty minutes, Bill."

He yelled back. "She won't make it that long."

He stepped off the railing and dropped more than a story this time. The pain of holding Emma almost caused him to black out. He kicked away from the building and around the side until he couldn't back up any more. Jack and the first-aid people stared in disbelief. Jack closed his eyes.

Bill pushed away from the building and started across the gap. With Emma's additional weight his head smacked into the wall next to a railing. He couldn't open his eyes for the pain. He felt one of the first-aid people grabbing him. They pulled Emma off of him and then pulled him over the railing. He blacked out as they put Emma on a stretcher and rushed toward the hatch.

Chapter 39

Bill Howell opened his eyes to the cool white walls of a hospital room. He looked around and saw Michael Baker sitting in a chair, reading a magazine. He started to sit up but an excruciating pain on the side of his head made him lay back down. He took a deep breath. The room was very quiet except for the hum of an air conditioner in the background.

"Michael."

Baker jumped noticeably at hearing his name. He stood up and walked to the side of the bed. "How are you feeling, Bill?"

"My head hurts."

"I'll bet it does. The doctor says you have a concussion. Probably from when you smacked against the wall."

"How's Emma?"

"She'll be okay. They brought her here first and stabilized her, then they flew her in Spencer's jet to a trauma hospital in Miami. I heard she's awake and doing fine. Thanks to you, buddy. I heard that was one gutsy Tarzan act you did."

Bill smiled. Baker rarely referred to him in a friendly manner but he liked it.

"Where are we?"

"In a Cancun hospital. Spencer and Jack are here also."

"What happened to them?"

"Jack tore a gash in his leg getting out through that valve. He didn't even realize it until he almost passed out from blood loss. He had surgery yesterday to fix it. He's fine."

"Yesterday! How long have I been here?"

"About forty-eight hours. The doctor says that's normal."

"What about Spencer?"

"He's here, just resting. His doctor in London insisted on it."

"How's your shoulder?"

"The doctor in the medical center did a good job. I'm fine."

Bill felt better. Maybe it was the knowledge that Emma was all right.

"By the way, Jack asked if I minded staying with you until you woke up. He wants to talk to you. Are you up to it?"

"Sure. Anytime."

"I'll be right back."

Jack was discussing the cleanup of Atlantis with Spencer when Michael entered his room.

"Howell just woke up, Jack."

"Great. I want to talk to him."

Baker handed Jack a piece of paper.

"What's this, Michael?"

"My resignation. I've tried my best but I can't seem to keep these loonies from putting the two of you in danger all of the time. I think you need to find someone who can."

Spencer was obviously disappointed but he didn't say

anything as he watched Jack's reaction.

Jack scanned the letter quickly, tore it into pieces and handed them back to Baker, who dumbly stared at the pieces in his hand.

"We'll have a security meeting when we get back there." Jack returned to his conversation with Spencer.

"Hey, I typed this myself!" Baker protested.

Jack smiled. "I know. Resignation is misspelled. Is there anything else?"

"I'm serious about this, Jack."

"I know you are, but I think the worst thing for Atlantis right now is to have a totally new security team. I know you can work this out."

"Okay, Jack, I'll stay a little longer. But if I can't stop this, you'll get my resignation again."

"Sure, Michael."

Spencer watched Baker leave. "I'd sure hate to lose him."

Jack stood up to leave. "He'll figure it out eventually. I'd better go see Howell."

Bill saw the large bandage on Jack's leg as he limped in and sat down on the bed.

"How are you doing?"

"My head hurts, but otherwise I'm fine."

"I know you're worried about Emma, so I wanted to give you the latest. I spoke with her this morning and she's fine. The first thing she did was ask about you. I told her you hadn't woken up yet."

"Is she really all right?"

Jack smiled. "She's one hundred percent functional, if that's what you mean."

Bill laughed. "Thanks."

Jack put his hand on Bill's arm. "I want you to go to Miami and be with her, Bill. I send an email to Howard Singleton this morning that I'm giving you a two-week leave of absence, paid of course."

Bill's heart beat a little faster.

"Probably no one but Howard would know or care if we took vacation or a leave anyway. So it was pretty much a formality."

"Thanks a lot, Jack."

"Also, I spoke with Richard and he okayed flying you to Miami on his jet. He won't be leaving here for a week or so anyway. So, as soon as you feel like it, and the doctor signs your discharge papers, you're on your way."

"I really don't know how to thank you."

"You don't have to; you earned it." Jack stood up. "The doctor said I could only have a few minutes, so I'd better go."

"How's your leg?"

"I messed it up getting out of that valve. They had to stitch it back up, but I'm fine now."

Bill wondered about the dome. "What about Atlantis?"

"We had it pumped out in twenty-four hours. It turns out there really wasn't that much damage, since the center buildings were the only ones occupied."

"It must be a mess."

"The OTEC system is at full capacity now and we have it on max clean water production. We're using that with some biodegradable disinfectants to wash out the buildings onto the streets. The pumps are cleaning that mess out of the canal. It's going pretty fast. We'll be done by the time you get back."

"What about the Control Center? It looked like a disaster area."

Jack smiled. "The rack room never flooded, that's why the key code worked on the entry door. Do you remember the backup Control Center that we never quite got going here in Cancun?"

Bill nodded.

"We just threw all the computers out and replaced them with the ones from here. It only took a few hours to get everything back in control." Jack smiled. "The city's humming now!"

Bill closed his eyes with relief and Jack patted his arm. "See you later, matey!"

Julie was dressed in a business suit, waiting for Jack in his room.

"How's Bill?"

"He's okay. I think the doctor will release him tomorrow. Richard okayed flying him to Miami."

"I'm sure Emma will be glad to see him." Julie smiled. "By the way, when are we going back to Atlantis?"

"Tomorrow, if the doctor signs my release. We'll have to sleep aboard one of the supply ships until we can get replacement furniture for the apartment."

Julie went to him and put her arms around his neck. "We'll just have to think of something to do until then."

They were kissing when Richard entered. He cleared his throat. "I'm glad you're both feeling better."

Julie quickly let go of Jack. "How are you, Richard?"

"I'm fine. I keep hearing nothing but good news from Atlantis. When can we get back on track with another news conference?"

"It may be a little premature, but I'm thinking it will take less than two months."

"That's excellent! I hope everything goes better then than it did last week. By the way, what are we going to do about the losses the merchants sustained when the dome flooded? We certainly don't want them to give up on us."

"I've been thinking about that. I plan to offer them free lifetime rent on their shops if they will eat this loss and rebuild. And I'll offer to help them with the logistics of getting replacement goods."

Richard nodded. "That's a very reasonable approach. I hope they buy into it."

"By the way," Julie began, "while you two have been loafing here in the hospital, I've been making progress on some new facilities for Atlantis. I'd like to discuss them with you when you have the time."

Jack and Richard looked at each other, before Richard replied. "Why not now? Let's go to the cafeteria."

Julie carried a roll of drawings as they sat down with coffee in the hospital cafeteria. She unrolled them on a table.

"I found the office that deals with land development and discussed the possibility of leaving that lake we made when we pumped out the dome. They were receptive to putting in a marina and a canal to the sea. The land is almost a worthless jungle right now and we could sell lots along the lake's edge for beach houses and private docks. The lake would become part of an even greater overall development. They almost drooled at the thought of all of the taxes they could collect."

They all laughed. Jack and Spencer looked at a sketch of the lake and marina development.

Spencer wondered about the cost of obtaining fresh water in such a remote place. "Where would we get the fresh water needed for a resort?"

"Use the desalination unit from the *Eye*. It's just sitting in a warehouse at the dock in Cancun. It has the capacity to furnish enough clean water for future phases of the development as well."

While they thought about that, she pulled out a floor plan for a new casino. "The land use office gave us the name of the officials who would have to review a proposal for a casino. I called them this morning and explained what we wanted to do in a real general way and they are willing to review a formal proposal."

"That's great, Julie," Spencer beamed.

"A land-based casino would probably be a problem, but ours will be off-shore, and even out of sight, so it has a pretty good chance of being approved." She looked at her watch. "Oh! I have a meeting with them in a few hours, so I have to go. I'll see you both later." She kissed Jack, rolled up the drawings and hurried out.

Jack looked at Spencer. "I told you I had the best person for the job."

"I never doubted it."

Chapter 40

Bill Howell wondered if Emma would be receptive to a marriage proposal. Maybe he should wait a little longer.

The doctor finally came out of her room. "You can see her now. Please don't stay any longer than is absolutely necessary."

Bill had brought flowers and candy. Emma was sitting up in bed, looking bored. When she saw him she grinned. "Bill!"

As he walked over to her, she held out her arms and they hugged for a few minutes. He handed her the flowers and she smelled them. "Thanks, Bill. I don't know how I can ever thank you enough for coming for me like that. The doctors said I probably wouldn't have made it if I had stayed there much longer."

Bill sat down on the bed next to her and kissed her. This might be the right time to ask. He reached into his pocket and pulled out a jewelry box. "Emma, we've only been dating for a short while but I feel as if I've known since the beginning, that you were the one I've been waiting for. This may not be the right time, I don't know if there ever is a right time, but--I love you and I think you feel the same about me. Would you consider marrying me?"

Emma tried not to cry but she couldn't help it when he showed her the ring. It had been a long time since someone had told her they loved her enough to marry her. She was crying so hard she couldn't say anything.

Bill found a box of tissues near the bed and handed it to her.

"Why are you crying?"

She pulled several tissues out and wiped her eyes. "I'm sorry. My first marriage was such a disaster that I thought there was something wrong with me. I thought no one would ever want to marry me again."

"I'd marry you right here, right now, if I could find a preacher."

"I will marry you, Bill," she said between sobs.

He leaned over to hug her and she put her arms around him. "Emma?"

"Yes."

"Jack told me that he and Julie are going to get married in Atlantis in a few months. I told him I was going to ask you to marry me. He asked if we'd like to make it a double wedding. I told him I'd ask you, assuming you said yes. What do you think?"

Emma thought it would make a great media story for Atlantis. "I think it's a great idea."

"How soon can you get out of here?"

"Not for a few more days." She could tell Bill was disappointed. She leaned over and whispered in his ear. "Have you ever made love in a hospital bed?"

Bill grinned.

When the phone rang, the last person Joan expected to hear from was Emma.

"Emma, how are you doing? Are you all right?"

"I'm fine, Joan. Thanks to Bill. He risked his life to save me. The doctors say I wouldn't have made it, if he hadn't tried."

"I'm so glad you're all right."

"Have you heard from Jack lately?" Emma hoped someone had told her about Jack's engagement to Julie.

"No, but I heard he's okay. He just a cut in a leg or something. Why do you ask? Did you hear something?"

"Yes... and no. I mean, nothing about their escape on the raft or anything, but I..." Emma's voice trailed off as she tried to figure out a delicate way to tell Joan about Jack and Julie.

"What are you talking about?"

Emma took a deep breath and tried to relax, but it didn't work. She would have to tell Joan straight away. The sooner she knew the better.

"Joan, do you remember that day I came to your office and asked you about April Turner?"

Joan thought for a moment. "Yes, what about it?"

"Well, that was pretty hard for me and I have something even harder to tell you now."

Joan's heart started beating a little faster. Was Emma in love with Jack? She managed a weak "What is it, Emma?"

"One of the reporters that showed up at the grand opening was an old flame of Jack's. Apparently, the flame had never really gone out, because they became engaged the night before Atlantis was sabotaged."

Joan dropped the phone and stared at Jack's picture in a

state of shock.

"Joan, are you still there? Joan? Joan!"

Joan picked up the phone. "I'm still here." She replied in a broken voice.

"I wish there had been some other way to tell you."

"Emma, I'll call you back, okay?"

"Sure, I'm not going anywhere. And, Joan?"

"Yes?"

"I'm sorry."

"I know."

Emma hung up the phone. Joan would take this very hard at first, but she would recover. It was just a matter of time. It had taken Bill's arrival and proposal to snap Emma out of her doldrums. She couldn't even begin to tell Bill how hard Joan had taken the news of Jack's engagement. Emma decided to return to London and talk to Joan as soon as she was released.

With Constantine Carballo's help, Tom Smith managed to get his son, Steve, a job as a computer programmer for Atlantis. Steve Smith shared in his father's desire for revenge at the heart attack and resulting death of Tom Johnson. Tom Smith had become enraged when he learned of his own son's death by a gunshot wound.

The elder Smith was also heartbroken to learn of the death of Jason Douglas, the former president of Future Plastics, who had managed to sneak into Atlantis disguised as a reporter. He then had swapped places and identification with Hugh Bagly, one of their operatives working as a construction foreman. During the evacuation of Atlantis, Douglas had managed to knock out one of the control panels for the emergency escape hatches. Unfortunately, he failed to get back to one of the last three working escape hatches and drowned. He was unaware of the tunnel because it had been added later.

Chapter 41

Jack and Spencer walked out of the terminal building toward Spencer's jet. When the pilot saw Spencer approach, he unlocked his window and leaned out. "We've been cleared for takeoff, Mr. Spencer."

Spencer waved to him. "I guess I'll see you at the next quarterly review in London, Jack." He held out his hand but Jack hugged him instead.

Spencer laughed. "I'll get used to that one of these days."

After Spencer boarded, Jack walked back to the terminal and watched the jet take off. It was a warm, clear day as he watched Spencer's jet climb and disappear into the horizon. A gentle breeze blew in from the sea.

Bill Howell appeared next to Jack. "Ready to go when you are, Jack."

"Are you sure you're okay to fly?"

"I haven't had a headache in days. I'm fine."

"Okay, let's go."

They walked to the waiting helicopter. Bill completed a pre-flight checklist, received clearance and they lifted off. He circled the airport and headed out to sea.

Jack was busy watching a school of porpoises playing near a reef when the drone of the helicopter changed and then stopped. They were slowing down. Jack looked at Bill, who was struggling to restart the engines.

"What's wrong?" Jack shouted.

"I don't know! We have plenty of fuel!"

Bill frantically keyed the radio. "May-Day! May-Day!" He yelled. "This is the *Spirit of Atlantis*! We're in trouble and going down about fifteen miles south of Cozumel!"

Jack looked down. The sea was getting closer. He looked up at the blades. They were turning but slowing down.

"Get ready to jump, Jack!"

Their rate of descent increased. Bill tried to get his seatbelt unfastened but it wouldn't budge. He tried loosening the belt but the retractor was stuck.

Jack couldn't release his seat belt either. In desperation, he took off his shoe and pounded on the retractor until it opened. He watched the sea rushing up at them, unaware Bill was still struggling to get his belt open. A few seconds before the chopper hit the sea, Jack jumped out.

Bill tried to brace himself as the helicopter hit the water. On impact, his head hit a bulkhead and he blacked out.

Jack went into the water feet first. When he broke the surface, he looked wildly around for Bill but didn't see him. The helicopter, still on the surface, was slowly sinking. Jack took off his pants and his other shoe and began swimming toward it.

George Atwell was on the bridge of the *Timaeus* when Bill's May-Day call came over the loudspeaker. He pressed the emergency alarm and made a general announcement of what had just happened and that they would take the lead role in the search.

He called the captains of the other ships of the Atlantis Corporation and mapped out a rescue plan.

Julie was driving down the coast highway to the new dock, reveling in the deal she had just completed for Atlantis. The lake development project had gotten a preliminary approval and she had received word from Howard Singleton that the Board of Directors had approved the necessary money to begin construction of the marina and canal.

Julie's cell phone rang.

"Julie, George Atwell."

"Hi, George. What's going on?"

"I'm afraid I have some bad news."

Julie felt a cold chill.

"We received a distress call from Bill, and Jack, on the *Spirit* a little while ago. They were having trouble and were going down. We sent everything that flies or floats out to look for them. I thought you should be the first to know."

Julie pulled off the highway at the next gravel road. She was nauseous and breathed deeply to keep from vomiting.

"Julie, are you there?"

The nauseous feeling began to subside. "Yes, George. What the hell happened?"

"I don't know. Bill didn't say what the problem was, just that they were going down. Where are you?"

"About ten minutes from the port."

"Come to the office. We're trying to get the hovercraft ready. I knew you'd want to join the rescue party."

"Thanks, George, I really appreciate it. I'll be there in a few minutes."

She was crying when she pulled back onto the highway and pushed the gas pedal to the floor. They had spent most of last weekend planning their wedding. She wasn't going to lose him again.

Jack found Bill still strapped in his seat, unconscious, blood seeping from a gash on his head. Jack tried unfastening the seat belt but it wouldn't budge. He tried to pull more of the belt out but the retractor wouldn't release. There wasn't much time left before the chopper sank. Already the water was up to Bill's knees. Jack looked around but he couldn't find anything to pry the belt loose with.

He reached under the water and pulled off one of Bill's shoes and used it to hammer on the catch. When that wouldn't open it, he hammered on the retractor. After several attempts, it finally let more of the belt out. He pulled the shoulder belt out as far as it would go and then pulled Bill's lap belt out enough to pull Bill out.

He held Bill's head above water as he pulled a life raft out of a holder and tossed it into the sea. The chopper sank as he swam toward the raft with Bill.

Jack pulled the inflation cord on the raft, pushed Bill inside when it had inflated and climbed in. He checked Bill's pulse and breathing. He seemed all right. When he realized they weren't very far from land, he pulled the oars out and started rowing.

Emma happened to be in Joan's office when the call from Mexico came in that the helicopter had gone down somewhere between the port and Atlantis. Joan had put the call on the speakerphone and they looked at each other with shocked expressions.

"Oh, my God!" Emma was thinking first of Bill and then of Jack and the need to tell Spencer.

Joan took several deep breaths to fight off a nauseous feeling.

"I have to tell Richard!" Emma started to walk to the door, then she realized how hard Joan might be taking the news of Jack. She walked back and put her hand on Joan's shoulder. When Joan stood up, Emma saw the tears in her eyes just before she hugged her.

Several port workers jumped out of the way as Julie's car careened through the port. When she got to the office, she jumped out and ran inside. The communications officer told her the hovercraft was ready. She waited for a signal from the pilot and then ran to it. A crewman helped her onboard and quickly cast off the mooring lines.

Pablo Sanchez was tired from fishing all night as he spread out his nets to dry on the beach. He had caught barely enough to cover his expenses. He sat down to drink some water when he heard a helicopter in the distance. Shading his eyes, he scanned the horizon, remembering the first time he'd seen a helicopter. It had flown over his boat and scared the hell out of him. That had been three years ago, when the Atlantis Foundation was scouting for a potential site for a research facility.

Pablo knew a lot about the Atlantis Corporation now because his brother was a heavy equipment mechanic in their new port near Cancun. His brother made a lot of money and bragged about it all the time. He had even tried to talk Pablo into applying for a day laborer's job. Pablo told him he didn't like working for someone else; he liked fishing. Since then he had become used to the helicopters and often waved to them. One crew had even thrown him a package of candy bars and other snacks.

But something was wrong with this one. It was flying low and fast. Pablo heard the engine cough and die, and saw the helicopter start to go down. He watched with amazement as it crashed into the sea. He felt he should do something, but his nets were strung out all over the boat and the beach.

As he watched the helicopter sink, a raft appeared next to it. When he saw someone start rowing to shore, he ran out into the surf and waited to help. As the raft got closer, the rower yelled something to him. He strained to hear, but he couldn't understand. "No se, Ingles!" he yelled back.

As Jack neared the beach, he spotted a fisherman watching him. "We need help!" he yelled. He repeated it again, but the man didn't respond. After a moment, he heard the man yell in Spanish.

As he neared the shore, the man grabbed the raft and saw that Bill was injured. He looked at Jack, who again asked him for help in his best, if somewhat broken, Spanish. The man nodded. Jack jumped into the water and they both pulled the raft to the beach. The fisherman pointed at the beach and Jack saw an old pickup truck parked at the top of a sand dune. He nodded.

Together they carried Bill up the sand dunes to the pickup. Once in the truck, the fisherman backed up, pulled onto the coast road and headed for Cancun.

A few minutes later, Jack began to feel faint. He looked down and saw blood oozing from a long shallow cut in his arm. When had that happened? He tried to tear his shirt to make a bandage but he didn't have the strength. He put his head back and closed his eyes.

Back at the beach, a wave washed over the raft and carried it back out to sea. The wind increased and the raft picked up speed.

Mike McKenzie, pilot of the hovercraft, saw his first mate ogling Julie, who was on the observation deck scanning the horizon with binoculars. She didn't notice that the wind blew her hair and whipped her dress up in the back. The first mate did.

"Don't get any ideas," McKenzie whispered to his first mate. "She's Garrett's fiancée."

The mate quickly looked away.

"George Atwell to *Hover One*."

"Yes, sir." McKenzie responded.

"John, let me speak to Miss Stevens."

"Yes, sir." McKenzie motioned for the mate to inform Julie.

"Miss Stevens, Admiral Atwell would like to talk to you."

As worried as Julie was, she smiled at the mate calling George, 'Admiral'. Bill Howell had started that and it somehow stuck.

She hurried inside and McKenzie handed her the mike.

"Yes, George?"

"Julie, one of the helicopters has spotted a raft down the coast. It's one of ours but there's no one in it."

A wave of nausea washed over her. "Are you sure it's ours?"

"The pilot confirmed it."

"Have you looked along the beach?"

"The only thing for miles is a fishing boat, but there's no one around it."

"Okay. Let me know if you find anything."

"Roger, Julie. Atwell out."

Julie handed the mike to McKenzie and ran outside, fighting another wave of nausea.

Pablo pulled into the emergency entrance of the hospital and rushed inside. He was so excited the emergency personnel had to calm him down. When they could understand him, they rushed out to the pickup with two stretchers and rushed Bill and Jack inside to treat their injuries. The emergency room physician thought Jack looked familiar but couldn't place him. He turned to the orderly. "Who are they?"

"We don't know. They didn't have any papers on them. A fisherman found them near the beach. He said they were in a helicopter that crashed in the sea."

"Helicopter?" The physician thought of the several oil

companies that operated off-shore platforms in the area.

"Call the police and ask them if anyone's reported a helicopter accident."

The orderly nodded and left.

The physician looked at Jack again and frowned.

It was nearly dark when McKenzie went up on the observation deck to talk to Julie. "Miss Stevens, we have to go back now. We're almost out of fuel. Maybe you can get on one of the helicopters. They'll continue the search tonight with spotlights."

Julie looked at him but didn't say anything for a moment. He was right. She was so tired she could barely stand up. "All right, Captain. Let's go."

The hovercraft turned and headed for the port. Julie sat down, fighting back tears.

Julie was in the bridge, drinking a cup of coffee, when George called.

McKenzie picked up the mike. "Yes, sir?"

"Get Miss Stevens for me."

Julie took the mike from McKenzie. "Yes, George?"

"Jack and Bill are in a hospital in Cancun. A fisherman found them and brought them there this afternoon."

Julie was so relieved, she almost passed out. "How is Jack--and Bill?"

"We don't know. The police called a few minutes ago."

"Why didn't they call sooner if they were brought in this afternoon."

"The police said they didn't have any identification on them."

"Thanks, George. I think we're only a few minutes from the port."

"I'll have a helicopter waiting to take you there."

"Thanks, George."

"I'm trying to get in touch with the hospital emergency room now. I'll let you know if I find out anything. Atwell out."

Julie sat down and leaned her head back against a windowpane. She wanted to cry but she was too tired. She looked out the window and saw the port's lights in the distance.

Chapter 42

George and Baker had rushed to the hospital when the police called asking if any of their helicopters had gone down that day. The emergency room physician would not let them see either one for several hours. While they waited, they tried to find out who had brought Jack and Bill to the hospital. An orderly told them that Pablo Sanchez had brought them in. He had given his name and telephone number to the admissions clerk.

George and Baker agreed that Pablo deserved a reward for helping Jack and Bill. They made a quick stop at the bank and drove with an interpreter to Pablo's house where they gave him a hundred thousand pesos. He hadn't expected a reward for helping someone in trouble. They had to convince him that they were grateful and that he should take it. The reward was more than Pablo earned in a good year.

Pablo used his unexpected fortune to pay off a loan he had taken out to fix his boat and to pay off some other debts. When he returned home, he excitedly told his brother what had happened.

Ernesto Sanchez couldn't believe his bad luck. He had taken a great risk putting that gel in the fuel tank the night before. The crazy American who had paid him to do it would not be happy.

Baker was waiting outside of Jack's room when Julie rushed in.

"How is he?"

"He's fine. He lost some blood, but he's going to be all right. The doctor is in there now." He looked at his watch. "He should be out pretty soon."

When the doctor walked out of the room he said, "You can go in now."

Julie hurried in. Jack was standing beside a table, trying to put his shirt on. There was a large bandage on his forearm.

"Jack!" She hugged and kissed him.

Baker waited a discrete distance away, then came over and helped him put his shirt on. "How are you feeling, Jack?"

"My arm hurts like hell and I feel a little weak. But I'm all right. How's Bill?"

"Still unconscious."

"I hope he's all right. He hit his head pretty hard on that panel."

"Let's go see him," Julie urged.

George was standing watch outside Bill's room when they arrived. "He's still unconscious."

The doctor was writing on a clipboard as he came out of the room. They gathered around and waited for him to finish.

"All his vital signs are normal. He should wake up soon. One of you can wait with him, but I don't want you making any noise."

"I'll stay with him for a while," Julie offered. She pushed open the door and walked in. The others went to a nearby waiting room.

As they sat down, Jack said, "I'm fairly certain we had plenty of fuel. I don't know why the engine stopped."

"I bet he pushed the wrong button or something. He shouldn't have been flying so soon after hitting his head like that."

"I don't think so. He seemed fine. If I didn't know better, I'd say it was sabotage."

"Sabotage? No way! We have the tightest security possible at the port. There's no way a saboteur could get to that helicopter."

"What if it was an inside job?"

"You can't be serious, Jack. You know how extensive our background checks are."

"I know. It was just a thought."

Baker crossed his arms in frustration.

As Bill returned to consciousness, the disinfectant smell told him he was in a hospital. He also knew that Julie was around because he could smell her perfume. He saw she had pulled a chair next to the bed and had nodded off.

"Hey, Julie! Can you get the nurse for me? My head is killing me."

Julie jumped awake. "Bill!" She hugged him. "I'm so glad you're all right."

The others walked in when Julie pressed the nurse's call button. Jack put his hand on Bill's arm. "How are you feeling?"

"My head is killing me."

"I'll bet. You hit that panel pretty hard." He paused. "Bill, I hate to ask this now, but is there anything you remember about the accident? Do you have any idea why we went down?"

"We had plenty of fuel. The engines just conked out for no reason."

Julie looked at them. "Hey, can't you talk about this later? He needs to rest."

Baker turned to Jack. "They should have recovered the '*Spirit*' by now and returned it to the port. We'll have a team go over it with a fine-tooth comb."

"See if they can find out why our seat belts wouldn't release, too."

Baker's eyes widened. "What?"

"I had to beat on the catches with my shoe to free them."

As Baker made a note of that, a nurse came in and shooed them all out.

Julie kissed Bill on the cheek. "We'll be back in a while."

Baker and Jack stood in the cafeteria line to get coffee and a snack. Jack turned to Baker. "I'm sorry, I didn't mean to imply that your security is lax or anything."

"I know you didn't. I guess these last six months have been pretty hard on me. I just can't figure out how they can get to you so easily."

Jack looked at him questioningly. "Why did you say 'get to you' instead of 'get to us' so easily?"

It was Baker's turn to look confused. "I said that?"

"Yes."

"I guess it appears to me that someone is trying to kill you and we get in his way sometimes. Just a gut feeling, really."

"What if you're right? Who would want to kill me?"

Baker stared back. "Who indeed?"

When they returned to their table where George and Julie were waiting, they discussed the crash.

"Michael seems to think someone is trying to kill me."

"I've been wondering that myself," Julie mused aloud.

Jack was suddenly angry. "I don't know about the rest of you, but I'm tired of feeling like I have a damn target on my back. I think I am going to offer a reward for anyone who has any information about this incident."

They all looked at each other. No one could think of a reason why he shouldn't do it.

Chapter 43

The entire port work force was gathered in a large warehouse. Jack told them, through an interpreter, about the accident and offered 500,000 pesos for information leading to the arrest of anyone committing sabotage.

Afterward, two laborers spoke with Jack's interpreter, Juan Hernandez. Baker waited for them to finish.

"These workers were on the late shift and claim to have seen someone leaving the hanger late that night," the interpreter said.

"Do they know his name?"

"Ernesto Sanchez."

Baker called John Jacobs, his assistant, and told him to search the database for an address.

"We have it, sir."

"Get the A-team together and meet me in an hour at the main gate."

Jack overheard the conversation. "You can't take a SWAT team there! This is an issue for the Mexican authorities. If someone gets hurt, we'll be in big trouble."

"Don't try and stop me, Jack. I'm not going there to hurt him. I just want to question him."

"Jack's right." Julie walked into the middle of their conversation. "We're in the middle of complex negotiations with the Mexican government over future land development projects. We can't be seen taking the law into our own hands in their jurisdiction. We have to be good corporate citizens or everything we're trying to do will go down the drain. Please don't do this."

Baker was torn between getting to the apparent saboteur and giving in to Jack and Julie's demand to stay out of it. He knew they were right, yet he couldn't take the chance of Sanchez getting away.

He keyed his radio. "Baker to Jacobs. Cancel the team for now."

"Yes, sir."

Julie and Jack looked relieved.

Baker pulled his handgun out and checked it. He looked at Jack. "I don't see anything wrong with the head of security visiting an employee, do you?"

"You can't go alone."

"Then why don't you join me? You can be my backup."

Julie objected immediately. "You can't be serious! Two officers of the corporation making a personal visit to an employee, carrying guns?"

Baker looked at Jack. "Are you up to it?"

Jack looked at Julie. She shook her head but Baker was right. If they waited for the police, Sanchez would get away. He turned to Baker. "Let's do it."

"Don't do it! Please!" Julie pleaded. She needed someone to help her talk them out of it. She saw George talking to the interpreter. "George, come over here!" she yelled.

George walked over.

"George, these two want to go get Sanchez themselves. Please tell them they're crazy. Tell them not to do it. We can't take the law into our own hands. The Mexican authorities will never stand for it. Please tell them!" she begged.

George looked at Jack and Baker. "You guys need any help?"

Baker smiled. "Thanks, but I think Jack and I can handle it."

Julie was so furious she stomped her foot. "Are you <u>all</u> crazy?"

"No," Jack said. "We just can't take the chance of this guy getting away. And I have a personal issue in this." He held up his bandaged arm.

Baker smiled at Jack. "Come on. Let's get some firepower."

In a storeroom in back of the security station Julie watched Baker unlock a large cabinet. Inside was a large array of weapons, from handguns to automatic rifles. Jack whistled in amazement.

"Take your shirt off and put this on." Baker handed Jack a bulletproof vest.

Julie watched Baker help Jack put the vest on. She decided to give it one more try. "Please don't do this. If someone gets hurt we won't be able to explain it away. This is deliberate. Jack, I don't know what I'd do if something happened to you."

"We'll be careful." Jack put his shirt on over the vest.

Baker handed him an automatic rifle. "Have you ever used one of these?"

Jack took the gun apart and put it back together quickly, surprising Baker.

"Where's the ammo?"

Baker laughed and handed Jack several clips. Jack put a clip in the gun and stuffed the rest into his pants. Baker looked at the cabinet and took out a small handgun, checked the safety, and stuffed it into his waistband.

"Have you guys written your wills yet?" Julie inquired.

It was a hot and muggy evening as Baker and Jack drove to Sanchez' house located in a rather remote and out of the way place. Ramshackle and run down, there was a new car in front that seemed out of place with the broken down wrecks and other junk in the yard. Most of the windows in the house were open. A fan turned lazily in one of them.

"This doesn't look good," Jack scanned the house through binoculars.

They parked on the street and stood behind the car. The only sounds they heard were crickets and grasshoppers in the nearby scrub brush. Jack was sweating heavily beneath his bulletproof vest.

Baker explained the plan to Jack. He would walk up to the house as though there was nothing wrong and ring the bell, his handgun concealed in his pants. Jack would stand behind the car, rifle at the ready in case anything went wrong. Jack had a pair of high-powered binoculars and would radio Baker if he saw anything suspicious. The powerful scope on the top of his rifle would allow him to hit almost anything at this range.

With the radio on in his pocket, Baker walked through the yard and up the front porch. He could hear a television but no other sounds. He knocked on the door and then quickly stood with his back to the wall, his gun drawn, ready to use if necessary.

A few seconds later he heard, "<u>Sí</u>?"

"Hello! This is Michael Baker of the Atlantis Corporation. I'd like to talk to Ernesto Sanchez for a moment," he said in a calm, even tone. Two men talked in Spanish and it soon turned into an argument. Baker was just about to break in the door when he heard a gunshot. He backed up a little. He saw Jack point his rifle and aim through the scope.

Alan Sands couldn't believe his eyes when he saw the SUV with an Atlantis logo stop in front of Sanchez' house. He looked through his binoculars and saw Michael Baker get out of the truck. *Baker? What the hell is going on?*

Ernesto ran into the back bedroom where Sands was loading an automatic rifle.

"Baker is here!"

"I know that."

"He must know about me!"

"Baker doesn't know anything. Keep your shirt on. I'll take care of him."

"I don't want to be in this anymore. I am going to tell him everything."

"You won't tell him anything!" shouted Sands pointing a revolver at him.

"I haven't hurt anyone, they won't do anything to me." Ernesto shouted back.

"How does prison sound?"

"What can they prove? At most, I'll get a year or two. Then I'll be out and have all that money I've saved to live well."

"You're not going to tell Baker anything! I won't have you screw up everything I've worked for years to accomplish!" Sands was furious.

"Don't try and stop me!"

Sanchez started to leave. He heard Sands cock his pistol, but he opened the door anyway.

Sands only needed one bullet to stop him. He looked out the window and saw the glint of Jack's rifle by the SUV. Baker must have brought his SWAT team! He looked at Sanchez' body on the floor. The thought of spending the rest of his life in a Mexican prison was too much for Sands. He looked at the pistol in his hand, put the barrel in his mouth... and pulled the trigger.

Baker waited a few moments and kicked at the door. There was another gunshot. He backed up against the wall again.

"I can't see anyone moving inside," Jack radioed. "Be careful, Michael."

The only sound Baker heard was the television. He waited a few moments then spun about, kicked the door in and jumped back against the wall. There was no response. He took a deep breath, jumped inside and hit the floor with a quick roll, his gun cocked and ready. He didn't see anyone. Slowly he got to his feet and walked carefully to the back bedroom. The door was partially open. He kicked it open and jumped aside. Nothing happened so he carefully entered.

Two bodies were on the floor. One man had been shot in the head and the other had shot himself in the mouth. Baker had seen a lot of death in his life but these were so pointless he fought the urge to throw up.

Jack walked in a moment later. "Christ, what a mess! I guess we won't be questioning either of them. Is one of them Sanchez?"

"I don't know but I'm not touching anything. Let's go put our stuff away and call the authorities."

On the way back to their SUV, Baker stopped to look in the late model car in the driveway. He saw a briefcase on the back seat. It had a sticker on it that he had seen before. He couldn't quite place it.

Chapter 44

When Baker called from the police station, Julie expected the worst. To her surprise, Baker merely asked her to come there. He hadn't seemed upset and said nothing about being arrested.

Her stomach was twisted in knots when she arrived. She was so relieved to see Jack and Baker that she hugged both of them. Jack's arm was throbbing and he sat down to rest.

"What the hell happened?"

Baker sat down next to Jack. "It looks like Sanchez was shot by the other guy. They're checking on him now. I told them I'd be happy to help with that."

"So, you're not under arrest, then?"

"No. They just brought us here for further questioning."

Jack let out a deep sigh. "They weren't happy about the whole thing. When they found we hadn't fired our guns, they were satisfied we didn't have anything to do with the deaths."

Manual Rodriguez, the detective assigned to the case walked in, carrying the briefcase from the car. He saw Julie and smiled. "You must be Julie Stevens."

She shook his hand. "It's a pleasure to meet you."

Rodriguez motioned them all to sit down. "We understand that Mr. Sanchez may have played a role in the unfortunate helicopter crash a few days ago that almost killed Mr. Howell and you, Mr. Garrett."

Jack nodded. "Yes. We're trying to find the underlying reason for that and other sabotage activities, at Atlantis."

Rodriguez put the briefcase on his desk. "We have been through this for fingerprints and other evidence. I understand it may have some significance to you?"

Jack and Baker looked in the briefcase. There were several file folders and the ordinary things found in briefcases.

"It's the only lead we have so far. Have you been able to identify the logo, Mr. Rodriguez?"

"We did a preliminary search, Mister Baker. It's not a Mexican company. We'll search the U.S. Copyright Office files on the Internet and several international databases."

Jack stared at the logo. "I've seen it somewhere." He struggled to remember where he had seen the logo. He was sure he had seen it on the side of a crate, or on an invoice. Suddenly it came to him. "Future Plastics of Seattle, Washington!"

Julie and Baker looked at each other in disbelief. Detective Rodriguez waited for more details.

"Future Plastics developed the plastic and fabricated the pieces of the dome over the city of Atlantis," Jack informed the detective.

Rodriguez made some notes.

"That explains the late model car," Jack commented.

"Maybe it's time to pay them a visit," Baker offered.

Julie stood up. "Detective Rodriguez, we really appreciate all of your help. As you know, the Atlantis Corporation prides itself on being a good neighbor and corporate citizen. We're also working on some plans for future developments that should greatly benefit the local residents. I think we would like to make a donation to the police department's favorite charity in thanks for your help."

Rodriguez stood up. "Thank you, Miss Stevens, but that really isn't necessary. We're just doing our job."

"It's just something we'd like to do."

Rodriguez smiled.

Tom Smith, former Vice President of Legal Affairs at Future Plastics, received a call from one of his lower-level field operatives that fellow conspirators, Alan Sands and Ernesto Sanchez, had been surprised by Michael Baker. Certain that he would spend the rest of his life in a Mexican prison, Sands had committed suicide. He had also killed Ernesto Sanchez to keep him from talking.

This news greatly depressed Smith. Alan Sands had been the head of security at Future Plastics and had been the brains behind the successful penetrations of Atlantis' security so far. Without Alan Sands, Smith's chances of sabotaging Atlantis were greatly diminished. The only way to get back at Richard Spencer at this point, was to kill one or more officers of the Atlantis Corporation.

Chapter 45

Atlantis was fully operational in a little less than two months. The second Grand Opening had occurred on schedule, without incident, and received favorable coverage by the World's press.

Emma had received a special commendation for her efforts by the Board of Directors. This was the time for her to cash in on her recent successes but she took a big risk in asking Spencer for the favor. She had known him all of her life and had never asked him for any favors, at least that she could remember.

She watched him walk to a window in his office and look out. "Do you know what you are asking me to do? This violates most of the ethics I have lived by for most of my life. I've never used my position to interfere in the personal life of any of my employees, ever."

Emma wished she could slink out of the office, unnoticed.

Spencer looked at her and sighed. There wasn't any point in getting angry at her. She had never asked him for anything and she wasn't asking for a favor for herself. He went to his chair and sat down.

"You realize if they ever found out about this, there'd be hell to pay?"

She nodded, not wanting to say anything. She hoped for the best but was prepared for the worst.

Spencer looked at his watch; it was 10:00 AM in New York. He picked up the phone and looked at Emma. "Are you sure about this?”

Emma forced herself to relax. “All I have to base it on is women's intuition.” Her voice was barely above a whisper.

Richard laughed. “Oh that's comforting!”

He pushed the button for his secretary. “Get me John Simon of New World Media in New York.”

Emma avoided his eyes as he continued. “What if Julie takes the offer and Jack isn't really in love with Joan?”

“I'll have to tell him it was my idea and then take the consequences, whatever happens.”

“I won't be able to help you in this.”

Emma nodded. When she finally looked at him, she could see he was quite upset.

“Jack is almost like a son to me now. I don't know what I'd do if this blew up in our faces and he quit.”

Emma wished she had the energy to run out the door but she had to see it through. She gripped the arms of the chair when Richard's phone beeped. He pressed the intercom button.

“Mr. Spencer, John Simon is on line one.”

“Thank you, Ms. Rodgers.”

They looked at each other as Spencer pushed the speaker button on the phone. “This is Richard Spencer. Are you there, John?”

“Hello, Mr. Spencer. This is quite a privilege. I haven't heard from you since Christmas. How's Ann?”

"She's fine, John. How's Susan?"

"She's great. We had our second grandchild last week."

"That's wonderful."

Emma sank lower in her chair. The loss of Richard's only child in a hunting accident had taken away the opportunity for any grandchildren. She regretted getting out of bed this day.

"John, the reason I am calling, is that I need a favor."

"Anything, Mr. Spencer. We owe you a great deal after you fended off that takeover attempt on New World last year. We really appreciate your 'White Night' offer at the last minute. We've also grown considerably from the additional capital you provided."

"I'm happy to hear that. This may sound a bit unusual, but it has to do with one of your newspapers in Chicago."

Emma closed her eyes, praying she was right.

Chapter 46

As the new Director of Business Development, Julie daydreamed even as she stared at the stack of drawings in front of her. On the job a little over three months, she was beginning to wonder if she really were the best person for the job, as Jack had insisted. Even though she had scored some big successes, she was now bogged down in the bureaucratic nightmare of getting permits for the Casino and land development projects. Her days were filled with endless meetings that didn't appear to produce any obvious or immediate benefits. This wasn't like fighting deadlines or the hustle and bustle of the newsroom. At least at the end of the day, they put out a newspaper that was read by hundreds of thousands of people in Chicago, perhaps millions on the Internet.

What she really wanted to do was cover the next earth-shattering news story in some exotic location, fighting hard to get her story in before other reporters could beat her to it.

Covering the story of the New Atlantis for the Times had reawakened her love of reporting and the need to be in the thick of news-breaking events. Julie had recently emailed her last story to the Times, an exclusive report on the building of Atlantis. She had even dared to state that she would be the first woman to be married in Atlantis in ten thousand years, using Jack's words.

She had called the Times to state her intention to resign and to begin employment with the Atlantis Corporation in the Business Development Office. She had informed the acting publisher, Bill LaRosario, of her decision. He was sorry to hear that she would be leaving but he wished her the best of luck in her new job and marriage. It hadn't seemed to bother him that she was leaving.

Her phone rang, snapping her out of her reverie. A long distance operator informed her the call was from John Simon in New York City. The only John Simon she knew was the current head of New World Media, the newspaper syndicate that owned the Times.

Julie was certain this was a hoax carried out by her former staff in Chicago. John Simon had not even visited the Times since Julie was a freshman reporter.

"Hello, Julie, this is John Simon in New York."

"I'm sorry, but I don't appreciate being made fun of, or being the object of a practical joke."

"Excuse me?"

"I'm really sure this isn't John Simon of New World Media, so you better get your laughs now. I'm about to hang up," she threatened. Maybe Bill Howell was up to his usual tricks.

"Actually, I'm afraid it is John Simon. I'd like to talk to you about the story you emailed to the Times yesterday."

"I knew it! You guys are a real riot. Look, I have to go now." She started to hang up.

"Wait! I really _am_ John Simon. I asked Bill LaRosario to send me a copy of your story when it arrived. I shared it with several members of the Board of Directors of New World Media. Like me, they were rightfully impressed at what has been accomplished by such a small team. They were also impressed with the in-depth nature of your story."

Julie decided to play along with the joke. In the end, the joke would be on them anyway.

"Yes, the city is quite amazing."

"I've been talking with other members of the board and we agree that, as much as we like the story, we'd like to change the ending."

Julie was puzzled. "I'm not sure what you mean."

"Julie, we'd like to offer you the position currently held by Tom LaRosario, as publisher of the Times. We've spoken to him and he's highly supportive of you. He thinks you'd be the ideal candidate for the job."

What a cruel hoax! The chance of her being promoted to Night Manager and then immediately up two levels to Publisher of the Times was next to impossible.

"Are you on the other end, Bill?" Julie was thinking Bill Howell had really gone too far.

"I'm sorry, Julie, there's no Bill here. This isn't a joke."

Julie was beginning to believe the phone call could be real, but she needed some proof. She wondered if there were some facts Simon could give that the 'guys' in the office would not have access to. Suddenly she knew. "If this really is John Simon, then what was the percent increase in my pay associated with my promotion to Night Manager?"

There was a pause and then Simon laughed a little. "I wouldn't know that off the top of my head, of course. We have over twelve thousand employees worldwide, Miss Stevens. But if you can hold on for a moment, I'll call Tom LaRosario and ask him."

Julie was suddenly nervous. What if this call <u>was</u> real? "Oh, sure, Mr. Simon."

"Hold on."

She heard music in the background. What if this really were John Simon? Her knees began to tremble. John Simon was a legend in the publishing world. She took a bottle of antacid pills out of her desk drawer and chewed some, hoping the phone call was a joke and, somewhere deep inside her, hoping it wasn't.

After a few minutes, Simon returned. "Miss Stevens?"

"Yes, Mr. Simon?"

"You had a twelve and a half percent increase in pay, according to LaRosario. I have to take his word, of course."

Julie swallowed the rest of the pills and took a deep breath. "Oh--I'm so sorry, Mr. Simon. I was sure this was an elaborate joke the guys in the newsroom were trying to pull on me."

"That's all right. If I were you, I probably would have thought the same thing. But now, let's get back to the original intent of this call. The board has agreed to offer you the position of Publisher if you are inclined to accept it. I know this is unexpected, but we need to know your answer no later than Friday afternoon. We have a second candidate we will make the offer to if you decline."

Julie had to take another deep breath to slow her heartbeat. "What about Mr. LaRosario?"

"He's moving to New York as the vice president of the news division of New World Media. You might be interested to know he recommended you over several people with more seniority--and a few other candidates from our other corporate newspapers."

Julie was too stunned to answer. She had been in several meetings with LaRosario and he had seemed like a nice person. He always greeted her by name and asked what she was working on. She had assumed he treated everyone this way. Now she was being asked to take his place--and she had less than two days to answer.

"Miss Stevens?"

"Yes?" she replied weakly.

"Can we expect your answer by Friday afternoon?"

"Yes, sir."

"Fine. I'm hoping you will say yes. You were clearly identified as the leading candidate. I hope this doesn't interfere in your present plans too much."

"Yes, sir--I mean no, sir."

"I have to go. Please let us know as soon as you can."

"I will, sir."

Julie looked at the bottle of antacid pills in her hand. She poured several in her mouth and chewed. Her stomach was in knots.

She decided to take a day off to think about the offer. Her biggest concern was Jack. If she took the offer, her marriage plans would leave with her. Jack was fully committed to finishing the city and had spoken of living there indefinitely, even if other projects came along. He would never leave his job to follow her to Chicago.

Julie packed her clothes and made reservations at a hotel in Cancun. She needed to think about New World Media's offer and she needed to be away from Jack to do that. She couldn't really express it, but her instincts told her there was another issue that she was avoiding.

Jack had asked her to marry him so quickly that she had agreed without thinking. After all, hadn't she prayed he would call her? Hadn't she tried to call him a hundred times, only to hang up when his phone rang? It had taken almost ten years before she stopped thinking about him every day. She had settled into a comfortable lifestyle that didn't leave much time for romance or a relationship. She missed not having her own family sometimes, but the respect she had won from her peers balanced that out.

Now it all came back to her. Jack had done everything to make up for those years. He spent every moment with her that he could and told her constantly how happy he was that she was back in his life. The only thing he hadn't done was tell her that he loved her.

Once when she asked him why he never told her he loved her, he had provided only a rather feeble, "Actions speak louder than words." That had frustrated her and she let him know it. His only response had been to kiss her until she pulled away. Knowing Jack, that would be the best she would ever get.

But there was something else. If Jack hadn't been so attentive, she would have thought she had his mind but not his heart. Something wasn't quite right. She couldn't put her finger on it so she had called her best friend and talked about the fact that Jack never told her he loved her. Her friend read her a romance test she'd found in a magazine. After dozens of questions that were really difficult for her to answer, her friend read her the results. "His heart is really with someone else and he probably doesn't even realize it."

That had really depressed Julie. Was Jack in love with someone else? Who could it be? There wasn't anyone else around when she had arrived in Atlantis. Jack liked Emma but she was in a serious relationship with Bill Howell. Michael Baker appeared to be head over heels in love with Lucia Ortiz. Anna Mordid was a possibility but she was in Cancun all the time working on the library. Jack never went there as far as she could tell.

She must be missing the obvious. She knew Jack still had some feelings for his first wife, but he had told her ten years ago that the marriage had been a mistake. No, that couldn't be it.

'The Team' as Jack called them, had been extremely nice to her ever since she arrived, but she had wondered more than once if they thought she had come back into Jack's life at the wrong time.

She must be missing something. Perhaps someone in London? After all, he traveled to London almost every month to attend meetings.

She wondered if there were other meetings she wasn't aware of and laughed. She put her suitcase down and looked around her room for the last time. Suddenly it came to her as clearly as if someone showed her a picture: Joan Mason. She'd been Jack's assistant until he promoted her to Director of Purchasing. He had taken some flak for that until Joan had proven she was more than capable of the job. When she completed her MBA with honors, her remaining critics shut up.

It was kind of ironic but Julie really liked Joan. More than anyone else, Joan had made an extra effort to help Julie move into the corporation and adjust to the city life that was developing in Atlantis. Jack would be attracted to her shy manner and the funny little things she did when she was upset or nervous.

Joan was in Cancun on business. Julie decided she would pay her a visit before she left.

Julie stood on the balcony of her hotel room, watching the sunset when her cell phone rang.

"Julie, what's going on? Why didn't you tell me you were going to Cancun for a few days? I would have joined you."

Tears welled up in her eyes. How could she tell him she had decided to accept Simon's offer? "It was sort of a last minute thing."

He sensed she was upset. "Are you all right?"

"Yes. Jack, would you meet me for dinner at Antonio's? There is something I need to talk to you about."

He didn't say anything for a moment. "Okay. What time?"

"Eight?"

"I'll be there."

"Thanks, Jack."

She hung up and went back to the balcony to catch the last rays of sunset. Telling him would be the hardest thing she would ever do.

A waiter escorted Jack to Julie's table. He thought how pretty she was as he sat down, yet he could tell something was wrong. The waiter took his drink order and left.

Julie avoided his eyes.

"What is it, Julie?" When she looked up at him, he saw that she had been crying.

"I got a call Wednesday from John Simon. He's the CEO of New World Media."

"They own the Times, don't they?"

"Yes and about a hundred other newspapers."

Jack didn't say anything. Whatever had happened to her was personal, not professional.

"He offered me the job of Publisher of the Times."

Jack knew immediately why they were in a restaurant and not at the apartment. She could have told him this over dinner in Atlantis. He waited for the other shoe to fall.

"I've decided to accept the offer."

Neither said anything for a few minutes.

"What about your job as Director of Business Development?"

"I'm not really cut out for that. I've been in the newspaper business all of my life; it's all I really know. I used to tell my friends I had ink in my veins." She laughed but stopped when she saw the hurt look on his face. "Jack, this is an opportunity of a lifetime for me. I know I would regret it for the rest of my life if I turned it down. My career is as important to me as yours is to you."

Jack's hands were cold. "I know that. I guess I already know the answer to the other obvious question." The waiter brought his drink and Jack said to him, "We need a little more time."

The waiter nodded and left.

Julie finished her drink. "I'm not the kind of person who can handle a long distance marriage. I don't think you are, either."

As much as that hurt, Jack knew she was telling the truth. He watched as she took the ring off her finger and put it on the table in front of him.

"I can't even dream of anything else that would make me give this up," she said. "I can't tell you how sorry I am."

Jack couldn't say anything, he just stared at the ring.

"I used to think about you all the time after I left New Orleans. I used to cry myself to sleep, but life went on. Sometimes I think my career was the only thing that kept me going."

Jack put his hand on hers. "We all make decisions, Julie. I lost Jane because my career was more important than her. It's hard to imagine what would have happened if we'd had children."

He looked away from her until she squeezed his hand. When he looked back at her, he tried to smile. "Why don't you try it for a while? Maybe it isn't what you think it is. I'll be here."

She shook her head. "I know you'll find someone else, Jack. I don't know that I ever will but I want you to promise that you won't do something stupid and wait for me if the right person comes along."

"How can I answer that?"

"You don't need to."

He stood up. She picked the ring up, put it in his hand and stood in front of him.

"I won't say good-bye." He dropped some money on the table for the drinks, kissed her and walked out.

As Jack stood in front of the restaurant waiting for a taxi, a little girl tugged on his pants and held out a small box of chewing gum packets for sale. He stared at her dirty face, wrinkled dress and bare feet. Somehow, his own problems didn't seem as important as before. As he fished some peso notes from his pocket he felt Julie's diamond ring. As he gave her the money, he saw her mother standing nearby holding an infant in her arms. There were grindingly poor. On an impulse he walked over to the mother and held out his hand. When she held her hand out, he dropped the diamond ring in it.

"I hope it brings you better luck than it did me," he said in his best Spanish.

The woman stared at the ring in disbelief. The taxi arrived and Jack entered it. As they were about to leave, he saw the mother biting on the ring to see if it was real. He laughed loudly.

Chapter 47

The hovercraft was docked to the floating helipad near Atlantis, waiting to take Jack to the entry hatch. When they arrived at the entry hatch, he walked up the stairs and watched the hovercraft leave. He pressed some buttons, the outer door closed and the hatch descended. When the inside door opened, he pressed the elevator button. He really didn't want to go back to his apartment right now. He decided to get drunk instead. There'd never been a better reason to get drunk.

He entered the first night club he found and went to the bar, surprised to find Joan Mason seated at a table nearby. She was dressed in a black suit and she'd had a few. He walked over to her. She was staring at the drink in her hands and didn't see him.

"What's wrong, Joan?"

She looked up at him. "My aunt died last night."

He sat down next to her and put a hand on her shoulder.

"Oh, I'm sorry. Do you need to go back to London?"

"No. We weren't that close." She looked at him sympathetically. "I'm sorry about Julie," she said without thinking.

Jack's brain fogged for a moment. "What?"

Joan suddenly looked at him like she had revealed a secret. She had. "Oh--I mean--"

The drinks had taken their toll and she didn't know how to take her foot out of her mouth. It had been a particularly bad day, but Jack's full attention was on her now.

"Joan, what did you mean when you said you were sorry about Julie?"

Joan couldn't figure a way out. She closed her eyes and decided to tell him the truth. "Julie came by and told me about the job offer at the Times."

Jack was suddenly angry. Who all had she told? Was he the last to know? He put his hands on hers. Her hands were cold and he could feel her trembling.

"When did she see you? More importantly, why did she tell you?"

Joan drunkenly hoped this would blow over. She tried to think of something to divert his attention. She knew him well enough to know that the truth was better in the long run. Besides drugs, there were only two things she knew Jack didn't tolerate, lying and stealing. Any employee guilty of any of these was out, without a second chance.

"She came by yesterday morning." She looked at his hands on hers and wished she could run out of the room.

"Why would she tell you before she told me?" He was still angry but there was no reason to take it out on Joan. He remembered their last date.

"Because women sense things that men can't even see, even when it's right in front of their eyes."

He frowned as the fog factor crept back. "What are you talking about?" What had he missed? What was right in front of his eyes that he couldn't see? The truth dawned on him so suddenly he sat back in his chair, letting go of her hands.

She smiled when she saw his expression.

He stood, uncertain what to do. She stood. He walked up to her and hugged her. Her perfume was familiar now. They didn't say anything for a moment.

"Let's go outside." He paid the bar tab and they walked the concourse between the buildings. It was late and there weren't many people out. They looked into each other's eyes for a moment and then kissed. When they pulled their lips apart, she put her head against his chest.

"Jack?"

"Yes?"

"Don't say or do anything tonight. You need some time to think about what you really want. Tomorrow's Saturday. Call me if you feel like talking, or if you just want some company."

He let go of her and she stepped back. "Thanks, Joan."

She turned to walk to her apartment.

"Joan?"

She looked back.

"You won't get away so easily next time."

She laughed as she walked into the Ursa Minor building. She pressed the elevator button and leaned against the wall. The brief encounter with Jack had taken more out of her than the news of her aunt's death.

The door opened and Richard Spencer walked out. He saw she had been crying as he stepped out. "What's wrong, Joan?"

She stepped past him into the elevator and pressed her floor's button. "Absolutely nothing, now," she said as the door closed.

Spencer frowned as he walked out on the concourse for an evening stroll. He saw Jack standing at the railing, looking at the cars below.

"I just saw Joan. She's been crying. What happened?"

"Her aunt died."

"Oh, I'm sorry to hear that. Joan's such a nice girl. I hope she gets over it." He looked around. "Where's Julie?"

"I need to talk to you about Julie."

Spencer put his hand on Jack's shoulder. "I need to talk to you about Julie too."

Jack frowned. "Why don't we go have a drink and talk?"

"Lead on."

Chapter 48

Joan ignored the doorbell the first time it rang. Who would ring her doorbell at 7:00 AM on a Saturday? The doorbell rang again. "Just a minute!" she yelled.

She put on her robe and slippers. When she opened the door, she was surprised to see Jack.

Jack looked at her fuzzy pink bathrobe with slippers to match and laughed. "Can I come in?"

Fully awake now, she tried to straighten her hair. "I'm sorry. Come in, please." She stepped aside so he could enter. "I must look like a mess. I'm sorry."

Jack had never seen her without her hair fixed just so. Now it was tossed willy-nilly around her head and shoulders. She wasn't as pale as usual, either. He kissed her.

"Joan?"

"Yes?" She snuggled closer.

"How would you like to go to Puerto Vallarta with me today?"

"Yes! Where is it?"

"On the Pacific side."

"Isn't that pretty far?"

"I borrowed Spencer's jet and pilot for the weekend. You'll need to pack a bag."

Joan's heart beat a little faster. She wondered if it were too soon after Julie left. She didn't want him on the rebound. As much as she wanted to go, she had to give him time. She put her head back on his chest. "Don't you think it's a little too soon, Jack? I mean, Julie just left."

Jack put his hand under her chin, forcing her to look into his eyes. "I had a conversation with Spencer last night that I need to tell you about, but not right now. I was up all night thinking about Julie and you. We've had a few missed opportunities that I've regretted later. I don't want to miss another one. Come with me to Puerto Vallarta. I want to spend some time with you, alone, to talk about some things."

"Things?"

"You and me--us."

She smiled. "What should I take."

"You won't need much."

She laughed.

They checked in at a luxury hotel on the marina, near the Puerto Vallarta airport. They walked out onto the balcony, taking in the bay and the city in the distance. When he insisted they go swimming in the pool, she tried to talk him out of it. She hadn't brought a swimsuit and she hadn't been swimming in a long time.

They looked through the swimsuits in a shop in the hotel and he picked out several for her to try on.

"I can't wear that!" she said when he held up a tiny bikini.

"Why not? You have a very sexy figure."

She blushed. "I just couldn't." She looked away.

He whispered in her ear. "Even if I said 'please'?"

She finally gave up and tried it on. When she walked out of the changing room, she had never seen Jack so surprised.

"Wow! It's wonderful!" he said.

She was self-conscious. Luckily, there were no other customers near them. She motioned him nearer and whispered, "What happens when it gets wet?"

He laughed. "I'll like it even better."

Jack put their things on a lounge chair by the pool. He took his shirt off and waited for her. "Come on."

She took her shirt off, sat down on the pool's edge and put her feet in the water. She looked up as Jack took her picture with his cell phone.

"Jack, don't," she pleaded when he took several more. She held her hand out in front of her.

He put the cell phone down and jumped into the pool, swam over to her and tried to pull her in.

"Jack, don't! Please! It'll get wet."

"I have lots of room on my cell's SIM card," he said after he had successfully pulled her in.

She wiped her eyes. When she saw him laughing, she splashed him. How would she be able to get out in this skimpy thing that didn't even cover her?

He swam up next to her and kissed her. She forgot about the swimsuit and wrapped her arms around him. After a while she wrapped her legs around him.

They spent the afternoon on a shopping spree. Jack insisted she buy a new dress for dinner and he bought a new suit.

At the restaurant Joan admired Jack's new suit, thinking how handsome he was as he poured her wine. They touched their glasses together and drank.

"Jack, what did Spencer tell you last night that made you stay up all night?"

Jack put his glass down. "You probably won't believe this, but I'll tell you exactly what he told me."

Joan listened to Jack's description of Emma's effort to test Julie's love of Jack with a mixture of sorrow, anger and disbelief. How could she do that to Julie? When Jack finished, he told her he loved her and didn't hold anything against Emma. They didn't say much for the rest of the meal. Jack could tell she was pretty upset.

Back in their room, Joan put her handbag on a dresser and went into the bathroom. Jack opened the mini-bar and made two drinks. He went to the balcony and put the drinks on a table. He was looking at the lights of the city in the distance when Joan joined him. As he handed her a drink, he could tell she was still thinking about Emma and Julie.

"Do you want to talk about it?"

She shook her head. "I'm okay. I know Emma didn't want to hurt you, Julie or me. The most amazing thing to me is that Richard made the call."

"I do know he wouldn't have done it, if he didn't care a great deal about you. He never does that sort of thing."

Joan knew he was right. "I just want to forget about the past, when there's so much future ahead."

Jack hugged her and remembered something. He let go and looked into her eyes.

"Joan, what happened that night we went to the French restaurant and went back to your apartment for a drink?"

She hadn't expected that. She unconsciously took a step back. "Why... do you want to know?"

"I've always wondered." He laughed. "That's the first time I've ever opened my eyes and couldn't remember what happened the night before."

She breathed a little easier. "You don't remember?"

He shook his head. "I woke up and you were gone. There was a note that said you were going back to London to think about things. I didn't even know what you meant." He laughed again. "I wasn't wearing any clothes, either, and don't remember getting undressed."

She laughed. "What do you remember?"

"I remember drinking a lot and--dancing?"

She smiled. "We danced for a while."

"After that, everything is gone."

She turned and looked at the city lights. "This might not be a good time to discuss that."

"Why not?"

"You might not like me anymore."

Jack rubbed his ear. "What! Why?"

"All right," she sighed. "You said you had a headache so I gave you one of my Menstrol pills. It was the only pain reliever I had."

"Isn't that the one for relief of menstrual problems?"

She nodded. "It has Naprosyn in it. I forgot that you are allergic to it."

Jack looked surprised. "What happened then?"

"You passed out, sort of, but your eyes were open. It was kind of strange. I managed to get you onto the bed and take your shoes off. I went to get some water and when I sat down to give it to you, you pulled me down and kissed me."

Jack was dumbfounded. "I did?"

Joan looked away for a second. "You told me you loved me and tried to take my dress off. I managed to get away and you just laid there staring at me."

"What happened then?"

She laughed. "I took advantage of you."

Jack stared at her in disbelief.

"I took my dress off and helped you take your clothes off."

"What happened, then?"

"We made love, of course."

Jack laughed loudly. Joan was a little annoyed that he would laugh at the thought of them making love.

"I'm sorry. I didn't mean to imply that the thought of us making love was funny. I'm just sorry I missed it. By the way, I know how a man can take advantage of an unconscious woman, but how can a woman take advantage of an unconscious man?"

She smiled. "I kept whispering naughty things in your ear until you were ready."

They both laughed.

"I'm myself now, Joan, and I want to tell you that there isn't any place else I'd rather be than here with you." He hugged her. "Want to show me what I missed?"

Joan woke up, stretched, and looked at the clock. It was almost nine in the morning. They hadn't slept much last night. The last thing she remembered before she fell asleep was Jack telling her he loved her. Julie had told her that Jack never told her that he loved her.

She watched Jack sleep. After a while, she quietly slipped out of bed and put on his shirt. She put a pot of coffee on and took her cup to the balcony. The air was already warm and a steady breeze blew in from the bay. She sat down on a lounge chair and closed her eyes. After a few minutes of listening to the waves pounding the beach below, she dozed off.

Jack woke up and looked around for her. He pulled on his underwear and went to the balcony, where he found her asleep in the lounge chair. He watched her for a few minutes then went inside, opened his suitcase and took out a small jewelry box. He opened it and saw the diamond ring he had bought for her. The jeweler had not liked being awakened at four in the morning to open the only jewelry store in Atlantis, but Jack's purchase of a four carat ring had turned his ire into elation.

He knelt down beside Joan's chair and slipped the ring on

her finger, surprised that his guess at her ring size was so close. Joan didn't wake up so he went inside to order room service.

"Where did this come from?" Joan said when she awoke. She held out her hand so he'd see the ring.

"That's from when I asked you to marry me last night and you said yes."

"Was I awake when you asked?"

He laughed and stood up. "I'm kidding." He put his arms around her waist and looked into her eyes. "I love you, Joan."

"I love you too, Jack."

"Will you marry me?"

She put her arms around his neck and played with his hair. "You know I will."

They sealed it with a kiss.

"I was thinking the other day, Joan, that I have a really lousy track record with women. Will you promise me to tell me if I do something wrong? I don't want to lose you."

She smiled. "The truth is difficult sometimes."

"I don't care. I don't want to come home one day and have you tell me your career is more important than us. I promise you right now that I'll never do that."

"I promise too, Jack."

On the way back to Atlantis in Richard's jet, Joan snuggled next to Jack and said, "Do you want to set a date for the wedding?"

"I'd marry you today but that wouldn't be fair to you. I'll agree to any date you want. Just figure out how long you'll need to make plans for it and then choose a date."

"What about Emma and Bill?"

"They both have been married before. I don't know what they have in mind. We can have a double wedding if you want, if they're agreeable."

"And until the wedding?"

"Move in with me. I want us to spend as much time together as we can. But if you want to stay in your apartment until then, that's fine, too."

"I like your apartment. I think there's room."

Chapter 49

On Monday Jack had gathered the key corporate officials together for a monthly review. He always held a review right before he had to travel to the quarterly review in London.

"The last topic for today concerns the potential relocation of the corporate headquarters from London to Cancun. We currently have several hundred employees here, along with about two thousand contractors. The number of contractors is decreasing because we're finishing the construction of the remaining buildings in the city itself and the last of the eight research facilities. However, there are also less than twenty full-time employees in London so I'm proposing we relocate the corporate headquarters to Cancun. I think of it as a cost-cutting initiative because office space in Cancun is much cheaper than in London. Richard Spencer agrees, by the way."

He looked at Joan and smiled. She blushed and looked away. He waited for a few minutes, but they all remained silent. "That's it, then. The London employees will be offered positions here and the company will pay all of their relocation expenses. I'll send out a letter later this week. Are there any additional issues?"

There weren't any and he adjourned the meeting.

He walked over to Joan. "I have another meeting now. I'll see you later." He squeezed her shoulder and left. Joan smiled as she watched him leave.

Most of the employees left. Emma, Joan, Lucia and Anna remained behind to talk. They all knew Joan had spent the weekend with Jack and they waited to hear all the details.

Joan began by showing them the ring.

Bill Howell and Baker walked with Jack as they left the meeting room. Bill cleared his throat. "How was the weekend with Joan?"

"It started out great and then got even better." Jack stopped and showed them a cell phone picture of Joan in the bikini by the pool.

"That's Joan?" Baker gasped, staring at the picture.

Bill shook his head in disbelief. "I wonder if Emma would wear one of those?"

"I asked her to marry me."

"You what!"

Jack finished a meeting with the Merchant's Association to discuss rental rates, problems with delivery of goods and other issues. It had been productive but tiring. He looked at his watch. It was only five o'clock. Joan was in an all-day purchasing meeting in Cancun and probably wouldn't be back until almost seven.

He decided to have a drink. He went to the same bar where he had found Joan crying after her aunt died and was surprised to find Baker sitting alone. "Can I join you, Michael?"

Baker looked up. "Sure, Jack."

Jack sat down and ordered a drink from a waitress. "Is there something wrong? You look a little down."

Baker looked at him. "I can't seem to get anywhere with Lucia. She ignores all my invitations to dinner or a movie or anything. I think she must work on that damned library twenty-four hours a day."

From his tone Jack thought Baker blamed him. "I don't have anything to do with that, you know. I can't help it if she's a workaholic. She certainly isn't paid to work twenty-four hours a day and I would rather she didn't. That's a sure path to burnout."

"I know you aren't responsible, but isn't there something you can do?"

"I can't order her to work less, or to go out with you."

"I know," Baker replied morosely.

The waitress delivered Jack's drink. "I'm certainly not an expert in this, but if she won't go out to dinner with you, why don't you bring dinner to her?"

"Yes, I could do that!"

"Bring candles and flowers, too."

"Yes! That's a great idea, Jack. Why didn't I think of that?"

"You probably would have, eventually."

"Which restaurants deliver?"

"I would take it there myself and set it up for her."

"That's even better. Thanks, Jack."

As Baker hurried out the door Jack thought about Joan. He decided to do the same for her.

Chapter 50

Harold Wills wasn't very bright, but he knew something was wrong with their information when the four women walked out of the fancy boutique. Wills had been told that Garrett's fiancée would be there and he waited, along with Josh Daniels and Bruce Stanley, for them to come out. When the women emerged, Josh Daniels scratched his head. "She must not be there, Harry. None of them are blonde."

"I can see that, stupid. She must have dyed her hair. My inside source is always right. She's supposed to be tall. Let's grab the one on the right."

He finished his instructions to three street kids and they ran off to a side street to await their signal.

When Wills signaled to the kids, they ran by the women and stole everyone's purse but Emma's. They didn't run very fast and the three women chased them, just as they had hoped. Emma was looking around for a policeman when Wills and Daniels approached her in their stolen Atlantis security uniforms. Instead of helping, they grabbed her and forced her in the front seat of a car where Bruce Stanley waited with a handkerchief soaked in chloroform.

They took her to an abandoned warehouse to wait for Tom Smith. Their information about the women, and even Jack's fiancée, was out of date. They thought Julie was still his fiancée.

Tom Smith had entered the old warehouse with high expectations. By grabbing Garrett's fiancée, he would be able to convince Jack to trade places with her and then he would have Jack all to himself. He would make Garrett pay for the death of his son, Steve.

He went to the warehouse to see the bait he would use to get Garrett. Emma was still unconscious, lying on a couch in the office portion of the warehouse. When he walked in and looked at her, he became furious with the kidnappers.

"What the hell is going on here, Wills? This can't be Julie Stevens--she isn't even a blonde!"

"We know that, boss, but none of them were blonde and our contact was certain Garrett's fiancée would be there. Stevens is supposed to be tall and this one was the tallest."

Tom Smith shook his head at their stupidity. He leaned over and noticed that her security badge was barely visible on her right side, clipped on her belt. He pulled it out where he could read it. "Emma Dawson".

He checked the Atlantis employee database his son had stolen. Emma Dawson was listed as the current Vice President of Corporate Communications. Well, even if they didn't have Julie Stevens, at least they had an officer of the Atlantis Corporation to trade for Garrett.

Emma regained consciousness slowly but she remembered what had happened. She kept her eyes closed and pretended to be asleep. Maybe she would hear something that would prove useful if they thought she were still unconscious. She had heard the exchange between Tom Smith and Harold Wills. She knew they were trying to get to Jack by kidnapping her, that they had mistaken her for Julie Stevens. She also heard them say they had an informant inside of Atlantis but their information was old and out of date. She listened carefully to everything.

Joan called Michael Baker and asked why a security team had taken Emma away. When he learned all of the details, he called Jack to let him know and then contacted Detective Rodriguez to request his assistance in getting Emma back. Baker didn't want the help of the local authorities but he was now sensitive to the corporate image.

He set up an Emergency Response Center in the Control Center and quickly developed a response plan should the kidnappers call. They also had the responsibility to come up with a plan of getting Emma back regardless of the kidnapper's demands.

Jack was waiting at the submarine docking station when the *Sea Merchant* arrived with Joan, Anna and Lucia. Joan ran to him and he hugged her with relief. They all headed for the Orion Building, where Baker and Detective Rodriguez were waiting to question them.

Jack, Bill, Detective Rodriguez, two uniformed policemen and Baker were present when the first phone call came. The kidnappers demanded to speak to Jack. Baker insisted he be allowed to play the role of Jack in all conversations, hoping the kidnappers hadn't seen or heard Jack speak before. If Jack were to be involved in their plans somehow, Baker would go in his place.

Baker pressed a button on a speakerphone and tried to imitate Jack's voice. "Hello, this is Jack Garrett."

"Let me speak to Jack Garrett."

"I just told you I'm Jack Garrett, you idiot."

"Stick it in your ear, Baker, and let me speak to Garrett."

Who knew them well enough to recognize Baker's voice? Rodriguez noted their surprised looks. Bill decided to take Jack's place.

Bill leaned closer to the speakerphone. "Okay, okay. You're right. This is Jack. What do you want?"

"You guys are too much. Who are you trying to fool, Howell? This is the last time I'm going to say this: let me speak to Garrett."

Jack was so surprised, his jaw dropped. "Garrett here. Who is this and what do you want?"

"Finally! I want you, Garrett. An even swap for Dawson."

Jack didn't answer immediately.

"Are you still there? Did you hear me? My patience with you clowns is starting to run out."

"What is it that you really want? Money?"

"No. Just you Garrett."

"I hope you don't mind if I ask why."

"You don't think I'm really going to answer that on this line, do you? I'm sure you're taping it, trying to trace it and--uh-oh, time to go. I'll be back soon."

"This guy is good," Detective Rodriguez observed. "He hung up before we could finish the trace. We did narrow it to somewhere in the southwest part of the city."

Bill fumed about the phone call. "Who knows us this well?"

"It would have to be someone in the city. Maybe someone who attends the monthly meetings," Baker offered.

Jack was lost in thought. "His voice was familiar."

They racked their brains to place the voice as they played the tape over and over.

Tom Smith had tried several times to get to Jack, only to fail when he changed his announced plans at the last minute. Putting the gel in the fuel system of the transport helicopter had seemed like an ideal way to get rid of one or more of the officers. When that failed, Alan Sands had come up with the kidnapping scheme and he had reluctantly gone along. Now that Alan was dead, only he and Marc Broussard were left of the old anti-takeover team at Future Plastics. He hadn't heard from Broussard in some months and his separation pay was running out. He had reluctantly agreed to this last desperate attempt to get Jack Garrett.

His son had taped a monthly meeting and played it back for his dad in case he ever needed to identify Jack's voice on the phone. Smith didn't even know that his son's voice had sounded exactly like his on the phone.

Chapter 51

Jack and Detective Rodriguez played cards to keep busy while they waited for the kidnappers to call back. Baker had nodded off and Bill nervously paced around the Control Center to work off his anxiety over Emma's kidnapping. He finally sat down at one of the consoles. It was late at night and only two operators were on duty.

Bill noticed a portable radio sitting on the console and played with the dial until he found a radio station he liked. He was idly looking at one of the computer screens when he noticed a small letter 'T' blinking on the bottom of the screen. It was so small and unobtrusive he wouldn't have noticed it if it hadn't been blinking. He wondered what the 'T' was for.

He looked around. The operators were out on inspection rounds, so he touched the screen. He jerked back as a full-screen display appeared. The screen was titled SECURITY BADGE TRACER PROGRAM. Tiny green dots appeared on a black background. He stared at it until he realized it was a plan view of Atlantis. When he looked closely, he saw faint blue lines defining each building in the city. Each green dot represented a security badge worn by someone; there were several numeric displays on the bottom of the screen.

Bill began playing with the display and found that when he touched the outline of a building on the screen, the display zoomed in to that building. If he touched the edge of the screen, the display rotated around that axis. He touched the Orion building and noticed a counter on the bottom indicating there were hundreds of people in the building. He touched the side of the screen and the display rotated to view the building from the side. He found that he could touch a single floor of the building and it filled the display, the counter indicating the number of active badges on that floor.

He touched the 75th floor and a graphical representation of the Control Center appeared. There were five green dots on the floor. He looked around and saw Jack, Detective Rodriguez and Michael but he couldn't see anyone else. When he looked more closely at the screen he saw that the fifth person was in the rack room.

Bill walked over to the rack room and swiped his card key in the door, and punched in the code. It opened with a hiss and he saw one of the programmers at work on one of the engineering computer stations. He smiled, closed the rack room door, and walked back to the computer console and sat down. Bill knew that they used a tracker program in case of emergencies to warn people and to ensure that a building was completely evacuated. He thought it was called 'Tracker' and not 'Tracer'.

He walked over to Jack, who looked up from his card game and smiled. "You all right, Bill?"

"I guess. Can I ask you something?"

Jack sat back in his chair. "Of course."

"Have you ever heard of a computer program called Tracker?" Bill was sure Jack knew about it. Jack knew everything about Atlantis.

"Sure. That's the security program that tells us where everyone is when there's an emergency. Why do you ask?"

"How about a computer program called Tracer?"

"Tracer? That sounds familiar." Jack thought a moment. "I don't think we ever implemented that. It was designed to log a badge's movement. We didn't see any advantage in that and some thought it would be an invasion of privacy. Where did you get that name?"

Bill motioned Jack to follow him and pointed to the computer display that showed the current occupants of the Control Center. Jack couldn't believe it at first. He hadn't authorized it and no one would spend the considerable amount of time it would take to build the displays if it were not an approved project. Unless--

Jack looked at Bill. "Stan Smith! So that's how he did it. He built the displays on his own time and utilized the Tracker program to get the data into a database he built. He then entered our badge numbers and tracked our movements until he saw a pattern. He probably could tell the other saboteurs exactly where we were and even where we probably would be."

"You know, Jack, there's probably still a few of them still in Atlantis."

"I know, but how can we ever find them?"

"Maybe we can log all entries into the Control Center for a few days," Bill said. "Only operators and programmers should be in here."

"That's an idea." Jack pressed a few buttons and then entered the Control Center coordinates into a logging function. When he was finished, he glanced up at Bill. "This should log anyone who enters the Control Center for the next few days."

Detective Rodriguez was bored and came over to them to

listen. Bill was staring at the display when he suddenly had an idea. "Jack, how are the coordinates of a person's badge determined?"

"Each badge emits a unique radio frequency. There are sensors at numerous positions in the city that pick up the signals put out by the badges. The direction of the signal is determined on the surface of the sensor and the computer performs a triangulation on the coordinates and puts it on the display."

"Jack, what if Emma still has her badge on?"

Jack's eyes got bigger. "We could track her!"

Bill got excited at the prospect of finding Emma. "What if we mounted the same kind of sensors on the bottom of the helicopters and fed the direction data back to one of these computers?"

"It might work, Bill. I think the sensors have a limited range, however; you'd have to fly pretty low over the city."

Bill turned to Rodriguez. "Can you help us get clearance for three helicopters to fly low over the southwest part of the city?"

Rodriguez smiled. "I think so. Let's give it a try!" He walked over to Baker and gently shook him.

Baker sat up quickly. "What happened?"

Rodriguez smiled. "We have a plan. I know you want to help so let's go to Cancun. I'll explain it on the way."

Chapter 52

Jack watched Bill secure the last spare sensor in Atlantis's warehouse on the bottom of his helicopter and give a thumbs-up sign to the other two pilots waiting for him. They climbed in, Bill completed his pre-flight checklist, and the airport tower at Cancun gave them permission to take off. Jack had a laptop, loaded with the Tracer program and watched a special display the programmer on duty had quickly hammered together to track Emma's badge. He smiled when they had first turned the sensors on and the laptop correctly identified Bill and him and the three pilots by their security badges. Jack pushed a few buttons so that the computer would ignore those badges.

The programmer had even found a graphical map of Cancun and managed to paste that into the display.

As the three helicopters approached the southwest part of the city, a small green dot appeared on the screen. Jack shouted the good news to Bill. "We've found her!"

As the other helicopters headed back to the port, Bill landed on the nearest spot he could find to the abandoned warehouse the computer had identified as the location of Emma's badge. She might not be there; the badge could have come off or they could be tracking the wrong badge, but they were determined to find out for sure.

Bill reached for a handgun and rifle he had taken from the security station at the port.

"What are you doing, Bill?"

"I'm going after her. They might try and get away before

Rodriguez gets here."

"That's pretty risky."

"I don't care."

Jack thought about trying to stop him, but Bill could be right. "All right. Let's do it together. Give me one."

Bill smiled, attached a powerful scope to the top of the rifle and handed it to Jack. He tucked the handgun into his waistband and headed for the warehouse. Crouching low as he neared the building, he tiptoed the last fifty yards to a door that was slightly open. He looked back at Jack, who had the rifle aimed at the warehouse door. He gave Bill the 'all-clear' sign.

As he stood next to the door, his back to the wall, Bill pulled the handgun out and listened for any signs of activity but didn't hear anything. He pushed on the door a little and it opened enough for him to squeeze through. Light filtered in through scores of broken windowpanes in dusty streaks. Old machinery and parts sat in clumps on the floor and he quietly moved from machine to machine. He looked back and saw Jack creep inside and sweep the interior with the scope. In the distance he saw a light in what appeared to be an office. He walked as quietly as he could until he was standing outside the office door and then peeked inside.

Emma sat on a moth-eaten sofa, her hands and feet tied with cloth strips. A strip of duct tape covered her mouth. She appeared to be asleep or nodding off to sleep.

Two men played cards at a table. Bill couldn't see anyone else. A light was on in another office in the back of the room, the door partly open. He couldn't see into the room from his position. He wondered if there were others he couldn't see.

He didn't hear Jack approach but he suddenly realized Jack was standing behind him, looking into the office. Bill looked at his watch. Baker and the others probably wouldn't arrive for another twenty minutes.

A door creaked open nearby and they quickly moved behind the nearest machine. Jack aimed the rifle and Bill took the safety off his pistol as a third man walked toward the office, carrying several sacks of food.

As the man neared the office, Jack saw his face. *I know him.* Suddenly it came to him: Hugh Bagly who supposedly died that night in Atlantis. A badly decomposed body was found a few days later, his badge still on. No one bothered to do an autopsy; they just shipped the body back to England for burial. If Bagly was here, then who died in Atlantis?

Jack and Bill nodded to each other. Jack moved with Bagly, keeping the machinery between them. Before Bagly got to the office, Jack jumped out and hit him on the head from behind with the rifle butt. He fell without making a noise. Bill picked up the bags and carried them into the office.

Bill pointed his gun at the two men playing cards. "Food's here." Jack walked in behind him.

The two men glanced up at them and pushed back in their chairs. One of the men went for his gun but he saw Jack's rifle and Bill's gun and thought better of it. Emma was awake, making grunting noises.

Bill saw her shaking her head. He knew she was trying to tell him not to shoot them. He looked back at the men. "Go on, try it," he egged a man who's hand inched toward the gun in his waistband. "You might be faster than me but I doubt it." The man put his hands up.

Jack gathered their guns. He unloaded them and tossed the guns behind the sofa Emma sat on. Bill took the tape off of her mouth while Jack watched the two men.

"Oh, Bill! I'm so glad to see you. Please don't hurt them. They've been nice to me but their leader is mean. He wants to kill Jack for some reason. He went somewhere but he should be back any moment. Please be careful."

Bill untied her as Jack told the men to lie on the floor. "Tie them up Emma. I'll watch for the leader." He went to the office door to keep guard while Bill and Emma tied up the men and taped their mouths.

Just as they finished, Jack motioned for them to be quiet. Emma walked quickly to a restroom in the back of the office. She heard a door close and approaching footsteps. Jack crouched behind the table as Bill stood waiting, his gun pointing at the door.

Tom Smith had just completed making reservations to fly to South America. Once he killed Jack Garrett he would go into hiding and pay off some local officials to protect him. He would let Bagly and the others pay for the crime. It was so simple he almost laughed out loud.

As he entered the warehouse he smelled food. Bagly must be back. As he neared the office, he heard a noise outside the warehouse. He pulled his gun out and crouched low, nearly panicking when he saw flashing lights outside. How did they find him so quickly? It didn't matter. He would use Emma Dawson as a human shield and get away, leaving Bagly to pay.

Still crouching, he made his way quickly to the office. In the doorway, he stared in disbelief at Harold Wills and Josh Daniels tied up on the floor. He looked up to see a gun barrel inches from his face, a wicked smile twisting Bill Howell's face.

"I don't know who in the hell you are, but if you make one wrong move you can say 'hi' to the devil for me." Bill wanted to shoot him so badly he had to use all the willpower he possessed to keep from pulling the trigger.

Smith knew there was no use in trying to out-shoot Howell. He dropped his gun.

Jack stood up as Emma came out of the restroom. She hugged Bill but he didn't lower his gun. "What are you doing, Bill? You can't shoot an unarmed man! He's given up."

Bill didn't look at her. He *wanted* to kill this man who had kidnapped Emma.

Smith was beginning to sweat. There was more than an even chance that Howell would still shoot him. "Listen to her, Howell. You don't want to go to jail for shooting scum like me, do you?"

"Don't shoot him, Bill!" Jack ordered.

Bill still didn't answer. Michael Baker and Detective Rodriguez came up behind Smith.

"Bill, what the hell are you doing? The man is unarmed," Baker yelled.

Bill's eyes never left Smith's face but he slowly lowered his gun. He glanced at the gun lying on the floor and then back at

Smith. "Pick it up," he ordered.

Smith breathed a lot easier now that Bill's gun was lowered. He was going to jail but that was still better than dying in this God-forsaken warehouse. "So you can kill me?" he snarled at Bill. "I don't think so. I know you were the Fast Draw champion of Texas. I wouldn't have a chance and you know it."

"It's the only chance you'll get." Bill's gun was still at his side.

Smith knew he would be dead in less than a second if Bill drew on him. His knees began to weaken. Howell might kill him if he didn't pick up his gun. If he did, Howell would kill him for sure. Either way, he didn't have a chance. Maybe the police would help. He yelled to them. "Hey, you guys can't let him kill me."

"Howell, put the gun down now!" Rodriguez ordered.

"Bill, do as he says--please!" Emma was afraid Bill would shoot the man in front of the police and go to jail for life.

Rodriguez' voice snapped Bill out of his desire to kill the man in front of him. He suddenly realized everyone was watching him. He looked at Emma and when he saw how scared she was, he dropped his gun and hugged her. "I'm sorry."

Baker and Rodriguez grabbed Smith, who was so relieved he almost fell down. Baker couldn't believe Bill had been the Fast Draw champion of Texas. How had his background checks missed that? "Were you really the Fast Draw champion of Texas?"

Bill smiled.

Chapter 53

Michael Baker was reading a report in his new office in Cancun when Bill Howell entered with an aluminum briefcase. He put it down on Baker's desk.

"What's that?"

Bill opened the briefcase and took out a gun and handed it to Baker, who began examining it.

"That's a Ruger Blackhawk, the most popular gun used in Fast Draw competitions." He then handed Baker an odd-looking holster. "This is the traditional Fast Draw holster." Bill began to recite the rules for Fast Draw, but Baker interrupted him.

"Wait a minute! We aren't going to have a Fast Draw match!"

"But I thought you wanted to see if you are faster than me."

"I do, but I wouldn't have a chance with this stuff. Here look at this." He opened the bottom drawer of his desk and took out a small mahogany case and handed it to Bill, who ran his hand over the case several times before opening it. The mahogany had been polished to a smooth surface. "This is exquisite."

"Open it."

Bill opened it and took a breath. The inside was lined with green velvet beneath a matching set of Colt .45 revolvers with pearl handles. The guns had been polished to a mirror finish. Bill had never seen anything like it. He looked at Baker. "These are incredible. Where did you get them?"

Baker smiled. "My army buddies went in together and gave it to me as a retirement gift."

Bill put the case on the desk and picked up one of the guns. It was lighter than he had expected.

Baker opened another small mahogany box and handed Bill a holster like those used in westerns. He then set a small blue box on the desk and unzipped the top. Bill recognized it as a thermoelectric cooler. Baker reached inside and took out two bullets and handed them to Bill, who looked at them for a minute. The head was made of wax like the normal bullets used in Fast Draw, but these were different. He looked at Baker expectantly.

"I have a friend who works for a special-effects company in Los Angeles. They furnish this stuff to movie companies all over the world. The tip is hollow and has a red dye in it. The powder charge is much smaller than normal."

"What are we going to do with these?"

"Have an old-style gunfight."

Bill was perplexed for a few seconds until it dawned on him what Baker meant. "You mean <u>face</u> <u>each</u> <u>other</u>?"

Baker nodded. "We stand back to back, each take twenty paces, and turn. When we're both ready, we draw. Simple."

"But that's dangerous. It's probably illegal, too."

"At forty paces, you'll barely feel the wax bullet. It's not dangerous unless you shoot me in the eye or something stupid like that. Even then it's just an irritant."

Bill had a lot of misgivings about the gunfight, but Baker

assured him there was no danger. They would do it behind the port warehouse, where no one would see them.

"You aren't chicken, are you Bill?" Baker taunted.

"Let's do it."

They walked outside, strapped on the holsters and loaded the wax bullets into the Colt revolvers. They stood back to back and then each counted twenty paces, turned and faced each other.

"Anytime you're ready, Michael." He would enjoy teaching Baker a lesson. He hadn't worn a regular holster in many years, but it somehow felt familiar. He waited for Baker to draw first.

Baker started to draw, heard a gunshot and felt a splat on his chest. He looked down at a red patch just below his heart. The dye pack hadn't hurt anything but his pride.

"That was a fluke, Bill. Let's do it again."

Bill laughed and waited.

Baker tried to draw the gun as fast as he could. He heard another gunshot and felt another splat on his chest before he could even point his gun at Bill. This time the red patch was over his heart.

"One last time!" he yelled, drawing his gun as fast as he could. There was another gunshot, another splat. This time the dye stained his crotch red. Bill was laughing so hard he was nearly bent over.

Enough was enough. "Damn! Where did you learn to do that, Bill?"

"Misspent youth," Bill laughed. "How about a drink? On me."

It was Baker's turn to laugh. "I bet I can drink you under the table!"

"Did I tell you about the straight shots of tequila contest I won in Cancun last year?"

Baker had certainly misjudged Bill. He put his hand on Bill's shoulder as they walked toward the security office. "No. Tell me about it."

The police interrogated Tom Smith and his accomplices for days without luck. Jack was relieved no one was hurt at the warehouse but he couldn't understand why Emma insisted they visit Smith in jail. He couldn't even figure out why Smith wanted to kill him.

He met Emma in Rodriguez' office and they all went to talk to Smith in his cell. Smith was surprised Jack had come to see him.

"Mr. Smith," Emma began, "I overheard you blame Jack for your son's death the night Atlantis was sabotaged and filled with water. I just wanted to let you know Jack had nothing to do with it. I killed your son."

Jack and Rodriguez stared at her in disbelief. Smith was surprised but skeptical. "I don't believe you."

Emma then explained how she had woke up after everyone had evacuated and happened on Steve Smith in the stairwell as he was running away from Baker. She told them how he tried to kill her near the Control Center and how she had fired into the darkness, apparently hitting him.

Jack stared at her. "Why haven't you told anyone this

before?”

“I didn’t remember it at first. I guess it was the trauma of nearly freezing to death. Later, when I did remember it, I just wanted to forget it.” She cried when Jack hugged her.

Rodriguez saw Smith back up and sit down on his cot. He took this news about his son pretty hard. Rodriguez almost felt sorry for him. “Now, Mr. Smith, would you like to tell us about Marc Broussard?”

Smith looked up and shook his head. “I’m afraid I can’t help you. I haven’t seen or heard from him in months. I don’t have a clue where he is. I swear.”

Jack was still holding Emma when Rodriguez walked up to them and whispered, “I believe him.”

Jack nodded. “Let’s go, Emma.”

She took a tissue out of her purse and wiped her eyes as they left the cell area. Jack looked back at Smith. His face was in his hands and, for a brief moment, Jack felt sorry for him.

Chapter 54

Joan and Emma spent the weekend in Mexico City looking at wedding dresses and talking with bridal consultants. They were both exhausted when they returned to Atlantis. They stopped for a drink at a bar on the 20th floor of the Ursa Minor building.

"Something just isn't right." Emma took a big swallow of her drink.

"I know what you mean. I was thinking the other day that someday I'll look at my wedding pictures and I won't be able to tell that I was married in the first city built on the bottom of the sea. You know... I remember Julie once saying she wanted to be the first woman married in Atlantis in ten thousand years. This is such a unique place, why don't we design the whole ceremony around that theme?"

"What do you mean, Joan?"

"We could make it appear as if we were getting married in the Atlantis described by Plato." Joan liked that idea even as she wondered how they would do it.

Emma was skeptical. "Even if the story of Atlantis were true, we don't have any idea how a wedding would have been held then."

"So, we make it up as we go. Who would know the difference?"

They looked at each other for a moment and laughed. "Why not?"

"Where can we start?"

Emma thought for a moment. "We have access to the Internet in the library, why don't we start there?"

Jack was preparing for another quarterly review when a phone call from Chicago revealed that a communications center was trying to establish a video conference call. The Atlantis operator patched it through to Jack's office.

Jack sat on the front of his desk as he waited for the video feed. When it came through, he was surprised to see Julie Stevens calling from her office at the Times.

"Hello, Jack. How are you doing?"

Jack thought she looked great. She looked prosperous. "I'm fine, Julie. How are you?"

"Great. I just wanted to congratulate you on your upcoming marriage. Joan is a great girl."

"Thanks, Julie. That means a lot to me."

"I also wanted to let you know that I really wanted to come, but I'm getting married the same week."

Jack flashed back to the time he left Julie in New Orleans. Some of the old feelings he thought were long gone came back to him.

"That's great, Julie. Do I know him?"

"Probably not. His name is Tom LaRosario. I took his place when he was promoted to vice president of the news division of New World Media."

When Jack didn't say anything, she continued, "We had several meetings to help me transition to the publisher position and a friendship turned into something more. He's a widower and a little older than you. His kids are grown and moved out, but I met them and they're really nice."

"Well, congratulations, Julie. I'm sure he's a very nice man."

"He's wonderful. Maybe not quite at your level, but I am in love with him. He thinks he can perform his job in Chicago so we're going to stay here." She paused. "I'll watch the weddings with the other billion or so who probably will tune in. I'm sure it will be spectacular."

"I don't know much about it yet. Emma and Joan are concocting something."

"Please say hello to everyone for me and tell them I really wanted to come but with all my preparations, I just couldn't make it."

"I will, Julie."

"Maybe sometime in the near future, Tom and I will vacation in Atlantis. I heard they finally approved the resort and land development project."

"Yeah. We're gearing up for it right now."

"Well, I have to go now, Jack. I wish you all the luck in the world. Say hi to Joan for me."

"I will. I wish I could be there for your wedding too. Maybe Joan and I will make it to Chicago one day and we can visit for a while. Give my best to Tom."

"I will. Good-bye, Jack."

"Good-bye, Julie."

Jack watched the screen go blank and let out a long sigh. Suddenly he was very tired. As he was about to get up and walk back to his chair, the screen lit up and a video feed from London appeared. Joan knocked on the doorframe and entered with Emma and Bill just as Spencer's face appeared on the TV.

"Hello, Jack. How are you?"

"Fine, Richard." He motioned Joan, Emma and Bill to come over, near him, so Spencer could see them.

"Ready for tomorrow's meeting?"

"Almost. I'm sure that's not why you called, though."

Spencer laughed. "You're right, of course." When he saw Joan, Emma and Bill, he was obviously pleased. "Well, just the people I wanted to see. How are you doing?"

"We're fine, Richard," Emma replied as Joan waved and Bill saluted.

"Ann and I were discussing what we might get the four of you for your weddings. We really couldn't come up with anything so Ann suggested we pay for the weddings. I liked that idea. What do you think?"

That seemed excessive to Jack. "That's very nice of you, Richard, but that's too much."

"You don't know what we have in mind, either. In fact, that's why we happened to be here. Joan and I came to show Jack the plan."

Spencer wasn't discouraged. "I don't care what you have planned, I would still like to pay for the weddings."

Emma and Joan looked at each other. "We agree--if you promise to play a role in the wedding," Joan said mysteriously.

"Of course. I would love to. What do you have in mind?"

"We'll email you the plan in a little while."

Spencer laughed. "What are the two of you up to?"

"You'll have to wait and see," Emma teased.

"All right. I'll wait. I'll see you tomorrow, Jack."

"Thanks for the generous offer, Richard."

"It's the least I can do. Good-bye Bill, Jack, Joan, Emma."

"Good-bye Poseidon," Joan chirped as Richard's image faded.

Jack frowned. "Poseidon?"

Emma handed Jack a copy of what they had developed. He sat down to read it. After a moment, he looked up at them. "Horses? Chariots?"

Lucia and Anna read over the wedding plan with Joan and Emma. They were having a great time imagining how it would appear if they could actually pull it off. Anna looked at Emma. "Where will you get the 'burly hunks' to carry the sedan chairs?"

"We'll advertise for them in the paper and conduct extensive interviews, of course," Emma explained.

They all laughed.

The basic plan involved blocking off the center of town and utilizing it as a gathering place for guests. As the time neared, each wedding guest would be handed a candle for a candlelight parade to the northeast park, which had the largest open area in Atlantis. The guests would then be seated as Jack and Bill arrived by a horse-drawn chariot. Emma and Joan would arrive on sedan chairs carried by the 'burly hunks'.

Then there was the dress code. Everyone had to wear a white tunic or toga or they wouldn't be admitted. Joan and Emma copied several images from ancient urns and they planned to send them with the wedding invitations. It would give the invitees an idea of the setting and background as well as women's hairstyles. Brightly colored sashes would distinguish friends of the groom from friends of the bride. Different colors were designated for representatives of the Atlantis Foundation and the news media.

Spencer would assume the role of Poseidon at the ceremony and Jack and Bill would be his 'sons'. Spencer would also escort Joan down the aisle, since her own father was dead. Following the exchange of vows, the wedding party would lead another candlelight parade to the Pegasus building downtown, where entertainment and a reception banquet awaited the guests.

That was the overall plan. Joan and Emma worked hard to fill in all the details and figuring out how many guests would fit into the Northeast Park of Atlantis. Developing the actual guest list would be one of the most difficult tasks because Spencer wanted to invite Foundation representatives and Emma wanted to invite a similar number of media reps. Emma would make sure the media would add 'of the decade' or 'of this century' when describing this event. After all, it was her job.

As soon as Spencer learned that Jack was on a plane

to London for the quarterly review, he sent an email to all Corporation employees inviting them to attend a video conference link of the meeting and hinting about an important announcement. The meeting would be held in the afternoon so it could be seen early in the morning in Atlantis.

Rumors about the announcement began to fly--from personnel cutbacks, to the sale of the company, to some new project involving Future Plastics.

The video conference room was packed. The signal was also broadcast on a local channel in Atlantis, should anyone else be interested. When the video link finally came through, the review meeting was well underway. The camera zoomed in on Spencer.

"I have one final announcement: the Board of Directors of Spencer Industries met last week and unanimously agreed upon a replacement for Charles Hawthorne, who is retiring at the end of this month. I am pleased to announce that Jack Garrett has been appointed Senior Vice President of the Chemical and Plastics Division of Spencer Industries, effective the first of next month."

Spencer smiled during the applause as the camera panned to Jack. Employees saw that he was as stunned as they were. He stood and thanked everyone, then sat back down, too overwhelmed to do anything else.

Everyone in the videoconference room applauded but silently wondered if Jack would continue as president of the Atlantis Corporation.

Joan was stunned. She had come to love living in Atlantis and would rather not return to London.

"Maybe he can fulfill the role from here," Emma suggested after the meeting.

"Yeah," Baker added. "With all the modern means of communications, it may not be necessary for him to be located in London."

"I'm sure Jack will stay here if he's given the chance." Bill tried to comfort her.

Joan smiled but there were tears in her eyes.

The conference room was crowded when Jack returned to Atlantis. He entered the room to a standing ovation. When he had their attention he tried to relieve their concerns. "Rest assured, I will still be the president of Atlantis Corporation. The role of senior vice president just bestowed upon me is largely ceremonial. I can perform whatever duties are associated with that job from Atlantis."

When Joan smiled this time, there were no tears in her eyes.

Chapter 55

It was late Friday evening and Joan was wrapping up loose ends before going home. The wedding was a week away and there were still a million things to do. It was nearly seven and Jack would be waiting to take her to dinner. She was putting file folders into her briefcase when the phone rang.

"Joan Mason speaking."

"Hello, Joan. This is Dr. Turner."

Jim Turner was her personal physician. He had examined her a few days before because she'd been feeling weak and tired. He'd done several blood and urine tests.

"Yes, Dr. Turner?"

"I have the results of the tests and I'd like to speak to you about them. Is this a good time?"

"Yes."

"Everything is normal. You don't appear to have an infection or a cold, but you do have a medical condition."

"What's wrong, Doctor Turner." Her heart pounded.

"You're pregnant, Joan."

A series of emotions washed over her. Pregnant? What would Jack say? She fell back into her chair. "How far along am I?"

"Very early, probably only three weeks or so. I'd like you to come in so we can talk about prenatal care, diets and so on. Make an appointment next week."

"Oh, yes. Certainly, Doctor Turner."

"I guess this must come as a surprise. I hope it works out well for you. Take care of yourself."

"Yes. Thank you, Doctor Turner."

Jack walked in as she hung up. She backed up in the chair, surprised.

"Hi, honey. What's wrong? You look like you've seen a ghost."

Maybe it was the timing, or a hormone change, but Joan cried loudly, surprising Jack. He went to her and held her against him. He could feel her trembling. "What's wrong, Joan? Why are you crying?"

She looked at him sheepishly. "I have a little surprise for you."

He laughed. "I have a surprise for you, too. That's why I'm here, in fact."

"What?"

"Mine can wait. What's your surprise?"

She couldn't get her mouth to move. He put his hand under her chin and lifted it. "Is there something wrong, Joan? You can tell me anything, you know that."

She put her head on his chest. "I'm pregnant!"

Jack's heart rate increased. "Are you sure?"

"After the last three months, it would be a miracle if I wasn't."

He laughed. He was finally going to be a father. He hugged

her tightly. "That's wonderful, Joan!"

"Do you mean that?"

"Of course I do! You'll make a terrific mother."

She hugged him tightly. "I'm a little scared, Jack. I've never had a baby before."

"You'll do fine. I'll be there with you."

"What was your surprise?"

"I want to show it to you. That's why I came here."

"You mean right now?" She was tired and didn't want to go anywhere.

"Yes. Actually, Bill and Emma are here and I invited them as well."

"To what?"

"To see the surprise!"

"What _is_ it?"

"I have to _show_ you."

"Why can't you just _tell_ me?"

"Because I want to show you."

She gave up. "All right. Show me."

"We have to walk a bit."

"Give me a minute." She closed her briefcase and started to take it with her, but put it on the floor by her desk instead. It can wait, she thought.

They took the elevator down to the first floor, where Bill and Emma waited. Emma saw Joan had been crying. She put her arm around her. "What's wrong Joan?"

"Doctor Turner just called. I'm pregnant."

"Pregnant? That's wonderful, isn't it?" Emma was thrilled for Joan. She glanced at Jack for his reaction.

"I think she'll make a wonderful mother."

"See there, Joan? I think you will, too."

Bill hugged Joan. "It's great, Joan! I'm happy for you." He looked at Emma as he spoke.

"Don't get any ideas, Bill. I'm not quite ready for that yet. And you know we need time to get to know each other better."

Bill let go of Joan. "Okay! Okay! I was just congratulating her."

Jack looked at his watch. "Can we go?"

"Of course. Lead on, fearless one," Emma quipped.

Jack took Joan's hand and headed toward the north end of the dome.

They stopped outside of Building 137 on the perimeter of the city. Even Bill didn't know the names of that many constellations. Jack held the entry doors open and they entered a richly decorated lobby that looked more like a hotel lobby than an office building. They followed Jack to a bank of elevators and entered one. Joan watched Jack put a key in the penthouse level.

"Where are we going, Jack?"

"We are almost there."

After a short ride to the top, the door opened on the 20th floor and they stood looking around for a moment. There wasn't anything particularly interesting about the floor except that there were very few walls in place. The air circulation system was on and the floor temperature was comfortable.

Bill looked puzzled. "So what is this, Jack? Are you going to re-locate your office here?"

"No." Jack went to the windows on the eastern side of the building and looked out. The others followed. The view was breathtaking. In the downtown area, the center buildings were almost completely occupied now and every floor was lit up. Most of the buildings in the 2nd tier had been rented and businesses were moving in. Even though it was 7:30 in the evening, there was a lot of activity in the center of town. If they looked the other way, they could see the lights of the submarine docking station and people jogging along the perimeter.

Jack motioned for them to follow him to the western side. Building 137 was next to the northwest park, where people strolled along sidewalks or played games. It was almost dark and people were beginning to go home. Except for the dome, it might have been any large metropolitan area.

Joan was impressed. "This is a beautiful view. What business is locating here?"

"Howard and I have been thinking we could get more rent in the downtown buildings if they were all occupied by businesses instead of apartments. We're going to offer great deals to get people to move to the edge of the dome to free up the downtown area. This building will be converted totally to condominiums."

"This building certainly has a great view with the park next door. How many condominiums will fit on this floor?" Emma tried to remember the square footage of each floor, but the number had slipped from memory.

"Only one." Jack stood next to Joan, who was looking out the window at the joggers and a group of people playing softball. She turned when he tapped her on the shoulder. "This floor is your wedding present."

"What?"

"This is going to be our home--if you agree, of course. Since this is a purchase instead of a lease, you will have to co-sign the paperwork."

Joan stared at him in disbelief.

To Bill and Emma he said, "I can get you a really good deal in this building if you want to move out of the downtown area. It's just an offer, if you want it."

Bill shook his head. "We couldn't afford something like this."

"Yes, you can. You can purchase as much of any floor as you want and make a condominium out of it."

"How big is this, Jack?" Joan still didn't believe him.

"All the buildings in Atlantis are two hundred feet wide and two hundred feet long, so this is about forty thousand square feet."

"A forty-thousand-square-foot condominium is ridiculous.

How would we ever furnish it?"

"Several CEOs of other companies signed over some of their stock options to me as wedding presents. I cashed them in and set up an account for you to use to decorate with. I think you'll be able to do it the way you want."

Joan hugged and kissed him, then walked to a corner of the floor. "I think I want the nursery here."

Bill looked lovingly at Emma but she avoided him and carefully picked her way over some debris to Joan to give her a hug. It was dark in the building now. Only a few work lights were scattered around the floor.

Jack looked at his watch. "Why don't we go eat? I'm hungry. It's on me."

As Bill was about to push the elevator button, a man wearing a hat and sports jacket walked out of the shadows and strode directly toward them. When he was close enough he shouted loudly, "Well, this is an unexpected surprise!"

They jumped at his words, not expecting anyone to be there. They turned to look at him but the darkness hid most of his face.

"I didn't expect to have this many officers in one place," the man said.

"Who are you?" Jack demanded. "This is a private floor. You'll have to leave right now." He made a move toward him until he saw light reflecting off the barrel of a gun. He stopped and backed up. He pulled Joan behind him. They all saw the gun now.

"I'm the last one."

Bill wished he had a gun at that moment. "The last one what?"

Emma moved next to him and put a hand on his arm.

"The last of the team that vowed to get revenge on Richard Spencer or his people for stealing Future Plastics."

Jack tried to remember the details, but the takeover had been completed by the time he went to work for Spencer Industries. "What are you talking about? That company was purchased from the shareholders in a public stock offer. Nothing was stolen. Spencer even paid a hefty premium above the current market value at the time."

"The market had taken a nose-dive right before Spencer made his offer. That made it look like it was a good offer," the man replied.

"Even so, the stockholders didn't have to take the offer."

"They were probably desperate after the nose-dive and would have taken anything."

"Spencer has put over a hundred million dollars into the company since he bought it."

The man seemed surprised. He lowered his gun a little.

"What does any of this have to do with us?" Bill didn't see a relationship.

"The team knew they couldn't get back at Spencer directly," the man explained. "He's too well guarded so they picked this project, or any officers of the company involved, to get revenge."

"What do you want? Money?" Jack demanded. "We'll give it to you, just don't hurt anyone here."

"No, I have plenty of money."

That surprised Bill. "Then what <u>do</u> you want?"

"I couldn't figure out an appropriate reprisal until I heard about your gunfight at the OK Corral. That was great. I loved that. No, I'm here for three things. The first is this." He tossed a weighted envelope at Jack's feet. "The second is this." He took a cell phone out of his jacket and snapped their picture, the flash blinding them for a few seconds. "And the last is this." He raised the revolver and emptied it. He quickly turned and ran to the nearest stairs. He was laughing so hard he had to stop near the bottom to catch his breath.

It took a moment for the building's air circulation system to clear away some of the gun smoke. Jack, Joan, Emma and Bill were frozen, uncertain what to do. Something had hit Jack's chest. He looked down to see a large red splotch on his shirt. There was another one on his right knee. He turned around to see Joan staring at him with a dazed expression. He hugged her, grateful she wasn't hurt.

Bill had also felt something strike him. There was a red splotch on his chest and another near his groin. He chuckled when he realized what had happened. Emma was still frozen in fear. He hugged her for a moment and then held her back a little to see if she had been hit with a dye pack. Her blouse had a large red splotch, but she'd also been hit on the forehead. Bill laughed as he watched tiny drops of red dye trickle down her face.

"What are you laughing at?"

"Nothing. I'm sorry," he said as he struggled to keep a smile off his face. He took out a tissue from his back pocket and wiped her face.

"Bill, what did he mean when he said 'your gunfight at the OK Corral'? What was he talking about?"

Bill's instinct told him to play it down as nothing, but they had promised to tell each other everything.

"When Michael Baker found out I had been a Fast Draw champion, he challenged me to a match. I thought he meant a Fast Draw match, but he meant an old-fashioned gunfight where you face each other."

"What?" she gasped.

"Michael has a friend who works for a special-effects movie company who sent him wax bullets filled with a red dye. We had a match and I won. That's all there is to it. That guy must have found the same type stuff."

He finished wiping her face and watched her expression. She was confused at first, then angry, then calm. Bill expected the worst but she smiled. "Why didn't you tell me about it? I would've watched."

Bill was visibly relieved "I guess I thought you might not like it and be mad at me for going along with it."

Bill had let his guard down and she kneed him in the groin, but not too hard.

Bill bent over, groaning. "Why did you do that?"

Emma smiled." Because you kept it a secret from me after we promised to tell each other everything."

Joan looked sweetly at Jack. "You didn't know anything about that gunfight, did you?"

He let go of her and took two steps back. "No! I swear I didn't."

Joan laughed and hugged him. "I believe you."

"Let's get out of here."

Bill straightened up. "Jack, don't you want to call security and arrest him?"

"We're just a few minutes from the tunnel. He's probably gone already."

"They can still stop him at the other end."

Jack shook his head. "Those bullets could have been real, but they weren't. I think in some strange way, he got what he came for."

Jack noticed the envelope on the floor and picked it up. It was a letter addressed to him. He went to a work light and started to read it but Joan tapped him on the shoulder.

"What does it say? Read it out loud."

He did.

Mr. Garrett:

You don't know me, but I'm the former CEO of Future Plastics. I authorized a team to stop the takeover attempt by Spencer Industries, but they went well beyond their authority by smearing Spencer Industries and Richard Spencer himself. I was in negotiation with another company that I hoped would come to our rescue and buy us at a higher price, a 'White Knight' so to speak, when this occurred. When the takeover was completed, Spencer fired the members of the team and me because I had authorized it.

I hold no personal grudge against Spencer Industries or Richard Spencer. I am a businessman and respect Spencer as such. In fact, I hope to purchase another small company soon with the golden parachute bonus Spencer was forced to pay to comply with company policy in affect at the time.

Several members of the team suffered from depression and one had a heart attack as a result of the takeover. The rest vowed to make Spencer Industries pay. When they began plotting physical attacks, and even spoke of killing members of the Atlantis Corporation, I distanced myself from them but I kept in touch, hoping to be able to warn you in advance.

I was in negotiations to buy the new company when the attack on Atlantis came and I didn't hear of it until it was too late. I'm sorry that several people died as a result. I promised Tom Smith I would help him get revenge for his son's death when Atlantis flooded. When he heard his son had been shot, he became convinced you were responsible somehow. This will be my only reprisal and I don't think anyone will be hurt.

To make up for this inconvenience, I have enclosed several hundred dollars to help clean the dye off and will provide the names of the last two conspirators: Jason Medley in the communications center in Cancun and Roger Jones in the construction crew. These are all that I know of.

I'm sorry we couldn't have met under better circumstances. I'm truly amazed at what has been done in the building of Atlantis and am proud that the plastic developed in Future Plastics' laboratory enabled such a marvelous place to be built.

-- Marc Broussard

When Jack finished reading the letter, he fished two one hundred-dollar bills out of the envelope. Emma grabbed them.

"This should cover the cleaning of my blouse."

Jack laughed, folded the letter and put it in his coat pocket.

"I hope this nightmare is finally over." Bill was visibly relieved at the news.

"Bill, why don't you and Michael pay a personal visit to these last two guys?"

Emma saw Bill grin. "Oh, no you don't. There's been enough of this horseplay."

"I thought you wanted to watch."

Emma thought about that. After a few seconds she laughed and Joan put her hand on Jack's arm. "You aren't going to let them do that, are you?"

Jack looked as innocent as he could. "Do what?"

Chapter 56

Bill Howell and Michael Baker read a printout of badges the Tracer Program had logged since Jack had activated the program. There was only one person who had no reason to visit the Control Center: Ben Kingsbury, an accountant in Howard Singleton's department.

"I think it's time to pay a little visit to Mr. Kingsbury."

Baker laughed, "Okay, but we're taking turns and I won the toss for the first one."

They found Roger Jones in a construction trailer near the edge of the dome. They hadn't bothered to knock and Roger looked up in surprise. His nervousness showed. He started to get up from his chair but Baker pushed him back down.

"A colleague of yours just paid Jack Garrett and me a little visit," Bill began. "Your name came up regarding the old anti-takeover team at Future Plastic."

Jones was really nervous now but he decided to play dumb. Maybe this was just a fishing expedition and they didn't have any hard evidence. "I don't know what you're talking about."

"I think you do." Baker pulled a revolver out of his waistband and pointing it at Jones. "And you're going to tell us everything you know, or get what's coming to you."

Jones almost fainted as he looked at the barrel of the Colt .45 a few inches from his face. His face twitched. "What are you doing with that thing?"

"You're a stupid man."

Bill motioned for Baker to back up. Baker was only a few feet from Jones but he backed up to the door of the trailer.

"So, what will it be, Jones?"

"I don't know anything about some crazy conspiracy."

Baker pulled the trigger. Jones closed his eyes when the gun went off. The noise was deafening in the little trailer. When Jones opened his eyes, Baker and Howell were watching him. "That was just a warning shot."

Bill pointed his Colt .45 at Jones, who was now shaking from fear. If they killed him here in Atlantis, who would know? Howell and Baker could probably hide anything they wanted.

"All right!" Jones squeaked. "There's only one other guy I know of. He works in the maintenance department. His name is Nathan Wilson. I swear, he's the only other one!"

Baker and Howell looked at each other as yet another name came out. Baker was so angry he raised his gun and emptied it.

Jones closed his eyes when Baker raised the gun. He felt something like tennis balls hitting his chest, but nothing that hurt. When he opened his eyes, he looked down and saw several red splotches on his shirt.

Baker chuckled. "Damn, that felt good!"

Bill laughed loudly and watched Baker reload the gun. "I feel like a doctor trying to cut a cancer out of a patient. Let's go find Nathan Wilson."

"Okay. You can do him and Jason Medley, but Ben Kingsbury is mine."

Two security personnel came in with a clean shirt and made Jones put it on. They then escorted him to the security station in Cancun to be handed over to Detective Rodriguez.

Chapter 57

Spencer and his wife, Ann, arrived in Cancun for the wedding. They were met by Joan and Emma who talked endlessly with Ann about the weddings as they traveled to Atlantis. The Spencers had not taken the scenic tour before and were impressed with the submarine ride through the reefs.

Their wedding apparel waited in their penthouse suite. Spencer had finished dressing and was putting a crown of laurels on his head in front of the mirror as Ann came out of the bathroom in her tunic. There were flowers in her hair and a belt of flowers around her waist. They both wore the gold sashes that distinguished them as part of the wedding party.

Ann noticed Richard staring at her. "Is something wrong, dear?"

Richard thought he'd never seen her look more lovely. He was reminded of the first time they had met. While it had almost been love at first site for him, it had taken a little longer for her. "You look lovely in that outfit, Ann."

Ann was pleased. Richard didn't tell her that very often. She knew he loved her, but he didn't often tell her that he did. Her first impulse when she saw him as she came out of the bathroom was to laugh, but as she looked at him, she was reminded of the first time she realized she loved him.

She kissed him lightly on the cheek. "It should be an interesting wedding."

They took the elevator to the ground floor. On the way down, the elevator stopped and a young couple dressed for the wedding entered. They all looked at each other as the elevator continued down and eventually giggles erupted into laughter. Spencer noticed their red sashes. He guessed they must be friends of the bride.

When the elevator doors opened, they walked to the main door where two torchbearers in togas were waiting for members of the wedding party. Oddly enough, no one laughed at the attire of the torchbearers. The Spencers followed them in silence to the center of town where a banquet table waited.

Servers dressed in togas passed out grapes, wine and water in brass goblets. By the time the wedding activities started, a considerable crowd had gathered. TV crews were also dressed appropriately and tried to be unobtrusive. The wedding would be carried live around the world to member countries of the Atlantis Foundation.

Spencer was the center of attention because virtually everyone there knew him or knew of him. Photographers were allowed to take pictures but could not use flash units so he really didn't mind all the attention. Even though the basic garments were white, the crowd was rather colorful in their different colored sashes and colorful flowers were entwined in the women's hair.

It was getting dark. The only light came from torches surrounding the banquet area. The tunics and togas and the celebration of a wedding by torchlight had a profound effect on the gathering.

At precisely 7:30 the person in charge of the wedding activities struck a huge gong to signal it was time to walk to the northeast park where the actual ceremony would be held. Dozens of torchbearers walked alongside guests as they made their way to the park, where they were directed to their seats to wait for the arrival of the wedding party.

As soon as all were seated, a trumpeter signaled the arrival of the grooms. Bill Howell drove a chariot pulled by two white horses at a stately walk and Jack held two torches.

When they arrived at the park, tenders held the horses as Jack and Bill walked into the park with their torches. Richard Spencer as Poseidon, was seated on a throne as the guest of honor. Jack and Bill walked to the throne, bowed and waited for Joan and Emma.

The trumpeter signaled the arrival of the brides. Joan and Emma were carried into the park on sedan chairs by 'burly hunks' in togas. Jack was impressed that Emma had found such handsome, well-built porters. Most of the women there thought the same thing. Spencer left the throne and went to meet them.

When the porters lowered the sedan chairs, Spencer escorted Joan and Emma's father escorted her to the raised platform where a minister waited with the grooms. None had seen the brides' outfits before this moment. They were in awe at how lovely the brides looked.

Both wore crowns and flowers in their hair and each had a belt of flowers around their waist. Large golden sashes with purple trim nearly covered their tunics. Clutching bouquets, they stood next to their future husbands. Several harpists played appropriate music as they entered and throughout the ceremony.

After the ceremonial kiss, the minister asked the crowd to greet the newlyweds. The attendees stood and applauded and Poseidon invited them to a post-wedding celebration on the first five floors of the Orion building.

He entered the chariot and with Michael Baker driving, began to lead the parade back to the downtown area. Joan and Jack sat on one sedan chair and Emma and Bill on the other. The porters lifted them and followed Spencer's chariot as the torchbearers led the remainder of the wedding party and an all-night party began.

The wedding ceremony had made a significant impression on Lucia. Michael Baker had been with her during the whole ceremony. She had been so happy for Joan and Emma she had cried on Baker's shoulder, much to his delight. He had wooed Lucia with a passion for months, often with limited results. His persistence, though, was finally beginning to pay off.

During the party after the wedding ceremony, he had asked Lucia if she would consider being his girlfriend. To his great surprise, she agreed. They left the party early to work on their new relationship.

Anna Mordid noticed George Atwell drinking by himself and invited him to a private tour of the museum. They each picked up a bottle of vodka and wished a good night to the nearest revelers who were still awake.

The next day, Jack and Joan flew to the Swiss Alps for a week of skiing. Bill and Emma flew to Egypt for a week-long tour of the pyramids and the temples at Luxor. They finished by sailing down the Nile to Cairo on a tour boat. The two couples met in Paris for a few days before returning to Atlantis.

Joan walked into their apartment and ran to the bed to lay

down. "It's wonderful to be home."

Jack entered with their suitcases. He smiled as he watched her kick off her shoes and pat the bed next to her. He lay down next to her and kissed her for a while. He put his hand on her stomach. "How are you feeling?"

"Wonderful!"

"I wonder if everything went all right while we were gone."

"Of course it did. Atlantis can run fine without us."

He sat up in bed. "Maybe I should check my email."

She pulled him back down. "Later. You're mine right now."

John Garrett was born on New Year's Eve and the proud parents held an extraordinary party to celebrate his birth. Spencer flew in for his baptism a month later and a party was held afterwards at the Garrett's new luxury condominium.

Spencer was impressed with Joan's efforts at decorating the huge condominium. The rooms didn't appear to have much furniture in them but what was there was done in extremely good taste. Jack's Picasso, which had been rescued from the flood in Atlantis, was on display in the entry foyer.

"I love your new condominium," Spencer told Joan.

"It doesn't look like it, but there's actually a lot of furniture in here. It's like trying to decorate ten houses at once."

Spencer laughed. He couldn't even remember buying furniture; Anne had done that while he was out buying and selling companies. He really liked their apartment, especially the views of the park and the downtown area. He liked it more than his own penthouse in the downtown area.

The newlyweds rented a small party room and invited a few friends over to help celebrate their first wedding anniversary. It didn't come as a big surprise when Lucia and Michael announced their engagement. Emma and Joan offered to help plan the wedding but Lucia planned a traditional Mexican wedding in her hometown, with close friends and family only.

It did come as a big surprise when Anna and George announced their engagement. Both came from small families and described a small private ceremony for a few friends until Lucia offered to share her wedding day and family celebration. Anna and George quickly accepted. Joan and Emma immediately began to help Lucia and Anna plan another double wedding.

Chapter 58

Two years after the Garretts' and Howells' weddings, the operation of Atlantis had become extremely routine. Research projects were underway in every available laboratory and the library had earned several awards from international library associations. The museum was also becoming well known for its vast displays of fish and sea life. Jack had recommended, and the Foundation had approved, the construction of several huge aquariums to be built out of the new plastic that would enable exotic fish from around the world to be put on display.

Jack held a small party for employees when construction on the last building in Atlantis was completed. Howard Singleton surprised everyone by announcing he had accepted an offer by Spencer to be the president of a new venture capital corporation.

Jack patted him on the back. "I'm happy for you, Howard, but I'll miss you."

Bill Howell and Michael Baker shook Howard's hand and invited him to a farewell dinner in his honor.

Jack also announced that the last permit had finally been obtained for the casino and that construction on the resort development was finally done. Work had already begun to convert Support Dome Four to the world-class casino. Two new Atlantis directors for the casino and resort were recommended to the Atlantis Foundation and approved.

Joan was happy to see construction begin on the casino since the resort was already completed. She thought Jack was beginning to miss the excitement of building. This would keep him busy for a while.

A regular police force was established. Most of the new officers had been members of Baker's security team. Baker campaigned for the role of Chief of Police and was approved by the Board of Directors. After his appointment was announced by Jack, Bill made his own announcement that Emma was expecting.

Joan whispered to Jack that she was pregnant again.

Andrea Garrett was the one hundredth baby born in Atlantis. A throng of well-wishers crowded around the viewing window in the hospital nursery. Jack passed out candy cigars to the males present and small heart-shaped boxes of candy to the women. By sheer coincidence, the ninety-ninth baby born was Mary Howell just one day before. Joan had been in the hospital to visit Emma and to see the new baby when she went into labor.

Chapter 59

The Garretts had just returned from John's fifth birthday party, when Jack got a call from Spencer asking him to come to London in a week. It wasn't time for the next quarterly meeting and he wouldn't tell Jack what the meeting was about.

"I wonder if he has a new assignment for me," he told Joan.

"I hope not. I don't want to move."

As soon as Jack was on his way to London, Spencer sent an email to the officers of the Atlantis Corporation inviting them to view part of the next Board of Directors Meeting at Spencer Industries. The video conference room was packed as Spencer announced his retirement as chairman of the board.

"Walter Pyne announced his intention to retire as Chairman of the Spencer Foundation and I've decided to take his place. It will become official on my sixty-fifth birthday next month. I've also recommended that Jack Garrett be my replacement and the Board agreed without dissent." He walked over to shake Jack's hand. "Congratulations, Jack. I can't think of a person more qualified for the job."

Jack was speechless. So was Joan, who watched five thousand miles away. She knew Jack couldn't resist an offer like that. She wanted to laugh and cry at the same time.

When Spencer's private jet landed in Cancun, Joan was waiting with the children. When Jack disembarked, she was surprised to see the Spencers were with him.

Richard hugged her. "We may have an offer for you too,

Joan, but right now we'd like to get back to Atlantis."

Joan gave Ann a 'nickel' tour of the condo. Ann was impressed with the furnishings and the view. She went to talk to Spencer while Joan put Andrea in her crib for an afternoon nap.

They were all in the kitchen drinking coffee when Joan returned. "She's asleep," she said, pouring herself a cup of coffee.

Spencer smiled at Jack. "Joan?"

"Yes, Richard." Joan sat down at the kitchen table with them.

"I know that Jack has somehow managed to perform his duties as head of the Chemicals and Plastics division from here, but I don't think he can do that as head of Spencer Industries."

Joan had expected this. They were probably going to talk about the need for Jack to re-locate to London. She faced the inevitable.

"Jack and I have a proposal for you."

Joan looked at Jack. "A proposal?"

Spencer smiled. "Ann and I have given some thought to the possibility of moving to Atlantis when I retired. At first we thought about purchasing a condominium in the new resort, but we really love living in Atlantis. We like our penthouse, but we really love your condominium. I asked Jack about the possibility of an even exchange of our house in northern London for this condominium. He's agreeable if you are."

Joan was in shock. *Richard's mansion? It's practically a*

landmark! She couldn't imagine living in such an enormous place.

Spencer guessed what Joan was thinking by the changing expressions on her face. "Our house in London is not as big as you would guess. The design leads you to think it's bigger than it is. It's actually quite smaller than this condominium." He looked at Jack. "Didn't you say this is forty thousand square feet?"

Jack nodded. "If you're curious, about thirty-seven hundred square meters."

"Thirty-seven hundred square meters!" Ann was incredulous. "I think our house is only twenty-five hundred square meters."

Joan looked to Jack for some direction but he was stone-faced on purpose, hoping she would decide in favor of Spencer's offer on her own.

Joan could hardly imagine living in Richard's enormous mansion. "Are you sure, Ann?"

"Yes. Atlantis is a new city with a lot of opportunities. Richard and I have talked at length about this. I would love to live here. It's only a five-minute walk to the Rodeo Concourse and it's a lot warmer than London, too."

Richard grimaced at the 'Rodeo' Concourse remark.

Joan got up and sat in Jack's lap. "Would this make you happy?"

"I would be happy living anywhere with you, but I think it's a great offer."

Joan kissed him. "Then I agree. I will miss everyone here,

though."

"You won't have to miss all of them. Bill will be offered the job of President of the Atlantis Corporation and Emma will be offered the job of General Manager of Communications of Spencer Industries. They can move to London or stay here, it's up to them. They don't know this yet, so please don't tell them."

Joan put her arms around Jack. The Spencers smiled at each other.

Bill Howell attended his first quarterly meeting as president of the Atlantis Corporation. His new executive assistant showed him his new office and he was certain it was the wrong one. At a few minutes before nine, his assistant came in to lead him to the meeting. When he entered the conference room, he was pleased to see Jack making a few last-minute preparations. He walked over and they shook hands.

"How are Emma and Mary?"

"Fine. How are Joan, John and Andrea?"

"They've adapted to London pretty well. Joan still gets lost in the mansion but she's really gotten into redecorating the place. Have you and Emma decided whether you'll relocate to London or stay in Cancun?"

"I can't seem to get her to commit to either location."

"How about Richard? I haven't heard from him in a while."

"When he isn't golfing, he's shopping with Ann or playing croquet with some friends in the Atlantis park next to his condo. He runs the Foundation from a video conference room in his condo."

They both laughed.

"Come and see me after the meeting."

"Sure thing, Jack."

Bill finally found Jack's office. It had been Spencer's office but Jack had refurbished it. Jack motioned him to a chair.

"What's going on, Jack?"

"Richard left a few ideas for uses of the new plastic. Some of these may interest you." He handed Bill a summary report from Future Plastics describing the feasibility of each project.

Bill scanned it and looked back at him. "I have a feeling you didn't ask me here to look at these proposals."

"You're right." He tossed a folder to Bill.

"What's this?"

"It's a request from NASA for information or, I should say, for a feasibility estimate for housing utilizing the new plastic."

Bill quickly read the request. He looked up at Jack. "On the moon?"

Jack smiled.

THE END